CW00386365

Chapter 1

Captain Mark Stewart rested his binoculars on top of the banking and ran a critical eye along the line of soldiers crouched in the dry creek bed below. Company Sergeant Major Niew Grbesa caught his eye, and Mark shrugged, lifting the glasses again to sweep the short cobbled street of the sleeping Slav village, on the other side of the open field.

Midway along, a door opened and a small white dog ran out. It halted, and sniffed the morning air, turning to bark impatiently at the old man in the doorway.

Mark watched the man and his dog disappear around the corner of the street.

"Nothing as yet," he told his CSM who had crawled to his side. "I hope we get it right."

"Would it make a difference if we don't, captain?" the squat sergeant asked, his voice gruff.

Mark adjusted the lens and focused on a woman standing on her doorstep, her hand resting on a broom handle. He understood what Niew meant by that comment. After three years of civil war where one side was as bad as the other, one more mission was not likely to make a difference. He would dearly have loved to play it safe and take his company back, for this was his last mission - Tomorrow home.

Of course he knew he could not do that. He could not leave these PFF, or Peoples Freedom Fighters, as they liked to call themselves, over there, and give them the chance to hit his own men sometime in the future.

He glanced at his watch. 0700 hours. It was already warm, even for this time of year close to the Adriatic. "Tell the men to get ready, sergeant," he told his CSM. "If they are in there, we will soon know."

Now the woman was brushing her doorstep. She could well be his own mother back home in Glasgow, yet he felt no guilt for what was about to happen. A movement to the woman's left caught his eye. He swung the glasses. Yes!

A man had come out of a house two doors away from where the woman worked. For a moment he stood there looking around him, yawning. Then, with a little shiver, stretched, and yawned again.

Mark gripped the glasses tighter as a second man appeared. He caught sight of the gun and slid down the banking. "Get your men ready, sergeant. They are over there all right. Two so far," he barked, levering himself back to his original position, the glasses now firmly focused on the open door.

Satisfied he'd seen enough, Mark rapped out an order to the men below. "Mortars! Range two hundred! Zero one five! Fire!"

A little way to his right a truck hurled around the corner of the road screaming towards the village as the first, clomp! clomp! of the mortars hurled towards their target.

Mark swung back, glasses riveted on the house harbouring the Reds as the first mortar hit the roof, throwing red pantillian tiles skywards, followed by a second shell quickly homing in on the neighbouring house.

Almost simultaneously both house doors flew open, spilling out a half dozen armed men, two instantly falling under Mark's Company's opening fire as the remainder bolted down the short cobbled street, savagely thrusting themselves in amongst hysterical villagers desperately fleeing from their homes. At the farther end of the village, the truck had swung to a halt, its lethal cargo of soldiers sealing off any line of escape from that direction.

A few minutes later Mark's company advanced upon the village, as men with hands above their heads appeared out of the smoke, prodded on by the force he had positioned at the rear of the village.

The mercenary felt in his tunic pocket and drew out a packet of cigarettes. Punching one out he lit it, his eyes travelling to an old man, a tiny dog at his heels, hobbling to where an old woman lay in the street. The old man looked up at him, anger in his eyes, hatred on his face. Unperturbed, Mark looked away.

Dunkirk to the concentration camps had left him almost devoid of all remorse. He had seen too many of his own killed and maimed to let one old man and his dead wife affect him. Besides, for him, this war was simply a question of money. It was his last day here, tomorrow he would be on his way home.

"Ten sir. We got them all."

Mark drew on his cigarette. "Well done. I can leave the rest to you?"

"I think so Captain, or we have learned bugger all from you these last years."

Mark smiled at the compliment and swept an eye over his men shepherding the prisoners towards the truck. He was proud of them all, though he would never tell them so.

Had this been a John Wayne movie, his men would now be lined up, while he shook their hands in a fond farewell. This, however, was the last thing he wanted of them, or they of him. There never had been any love lost between them. Respect, maybe? These same men had simply obeyed his orders to stay alive, for most of them had still been at school, while he had been enduring six years of total war.

"Keep your head down low CSM, and tell those 'apologies' for soldiers to do the same."

"Same goes for you captain," Niew Grbesa said in a voice devoid of all emotion. Then the squat Company Sergeant Major was gone, shouting out orders to the command Captain Mark Stewart had left behind.

It was dark by the time Mark reached Zaltx, the Capital. Before his driver had scarcely drawn to a halt in the barracks quadrangle, 'the Caserne', Mark had said his goodbyes and was on his way to check in his weapons before the jeep had time to accelerate away.

The chill in the Scot's flat, provided him with an excuse to pour himself a whisky. Flopping down on the couch he glanced at his watch, 2000 hours. He could still grab a bite to eat in the Mess. And should the Swede, the Frenchman, or any of the others also due to leave tomorrow, happen to be there, he might even force them to buy him a round or two. After all, he had a nationality for thrift to uphold.

Mark looked around his flat. There was not much to leave behind, only a few ornaments and a couple of cheap paintings. His eyes fell on his already packed suitcases standing in the corner. Somehow, the flat felt more empty than usual: hostile even.

He took another sip of his drink and laid his head back on the couch. It was over two years since he'd moved in here. "Beresford!" he said aloud, closing his eyes. "Poor old bastard!"

They had arrived in the country together, he from the 'luxury' of a Glasgow tenement, and 'Berry' from the 'opulence' of Tyneside. They had hit it off right away, and despite having had six years of war had still craved excitement, but now not only from a gun.

Cursing himself for remembering, Mark got up and tossed back the dregs of his drink.

Berry had hinted subtly to him on the way home, of how small the flat they shared together, somehow became crowded for three at night...that night. Laughing, he had wished his friend the best of amorous luck and stopped to wait for a taxi back into town.

It had been cold while he waited there for a taxi that never came, and he had just considered making his way down the street to the bus stop, when he heard the explosion. Somehow, it had never occurred to him that it was anything other than *their* flat. Why, he never did know. He had started to run, but while some distance away, knew that his worse fears had been realised.

Mark had found Berry just inside the door, where he lay grasping the stump of his right leg, a look of sheer disbelief on his friend's tortured face. He'd tried to stem the blood pumping through what was left of the leg, aware of the hot sticky fluid on his face, and as he bent to apply pressure to what was left of the leg, saw the detached arm for the first time. Then there were people all around pushing him aside... lifting Berry onto a stretcher ..someone wrapping the detached limbs in a cloth. Others guiding out Berry's unfortunate hysterical companion for the night. Then just as suddenly, the flat was quiet...empty.

They had not been the only ones bombed that night, or the only soldiers attacked. Thereafter, all foreign mercenaries had been ordered into the central barracks; the Caserne, all off-duty personnel, to remain armed.

Three days later his friend died.

A knock at the door stopped Mark from pouring himself another drink. As he crossed the room, his depression momentarily lifted at the prospect of a fellow officer inviting him to Mess, instead, a young lieutenant stood in the open doorway.

"Captain Stewart?" the young officer inquired nervously.

"Correct soldier," Mark answered, ushering him inside.

"I have orders to give you this, sir."

4

Mark took the envelope and tore it open and read the few lines. Why, he wondered, as he stared blankly into the face of the nervous young man, had the President of the Republic, chosen this particular time to order him to his office?

An hour later, dressed in his best uniform, the mercenary found himself in the presence of President Paule Kolybin, and despite his deductions- rational or otherwise- was still unable to comprehend why the 'great man' should wish to see him. Perhaps, he chuckled he had won a medal, or, more probably he was to be castigated for not paying some long forgotten mess bill. Comforted by his own humour, Mark took the proffered seat in front of the massive desk.

The President's room was dimly lit. The atmosphere reminiscent of an incident whilst working as a junior clerk with MacFadyen and Lyle in Glasgow, when he had been summoned to the head office, and ordered to explain why he had broken an number of elastic bands in one week. He had quickly found out that the management's sense of humour to his youthful explanation stretched even less than their elastic bands. He was told to leave the next day.

As Mark's thoughts returned to the room, the tall figure of Vice-President Molnar edged himself into a seat beside his President and acknowledged Mark with a brief nod, and for the first time the Scot was aware of a third person hidden in the dark recesses of the room; a bodyguard most likely, he thought.

Mark found it difficult to imagine that this dapper little man sitting back in his chair, blowing cigar smoke at the ceiling, was this country's greatest war hero.

When the Government of the day had fled before the Nazi invasion, it was Paule Kolybin, shoemaker, who had helped lead his countrymen in six years of guerrilla warfare. So it was natural to him, and others like him, that the people had turned, and not the returning exiled Government when Liberation had finally come.

"Can I offer you some refreshment, Captain Stewart?" For one who had witnessed the full brutalities of war the President's voice was surprisingly soft.

Mark could not remember having spoken to him more than a half dozen times before. However, he did remember one such occasion, when he and another hundred or so foreign mercenaries had been invited to a Presidential garden party, where he had briefly exchanged pleasantries with the 'great man'.

When Paule Kolybin, had moved on, Mark had been confronted by a woman of about his own age.

"Captain Stewart is it not?" the lady had asked, holding out her hand.

He had stammered that it was, surprised that she had spoken in English, until he remembered that this was Myra Kolybin, nee Myra Blakie, and the country's First Lady.

Myra Blakie, had met her husband to be, in the early years of the war whilst serving as an English nurse, when she and a few more of her countrymen, had found themselves cut off, after the fall of Greece, and it was as they tried to avoid capture that the Partisans had found them, and had taken them back to their camp high in the Black Orin mountains, where they had met their leader Paule Kolybin. It was after this, that she and a few others had decided to remain behind to help.

Myra Blakie had not gone home when the war had ended, and as far as Mark was aware, Paule and she had married less than a year later, by which time her husband had become President of the Republic.

"Perhaps a smoke instead?" the President was asking him, holding out a box of cigars.

Mark tore his unfocused eyes away from the President's left lapel. "Thank you...but no.sir," he stammered embarrassed.

Paule Kolybin nodded. Gently setting down the cigar box, he leaned forward, steepling his fingers. "No doubt you must be wondering why you find yourself here, at a time like this, captain, when tomorrow you will be winging your way home to your native England?"

Mark did not feel inclined to correct him in his reference to his homeland. To his irritation, he knew that to most foreigners Britain *was* England and vice versa.

"I shall be brief...well as any politician can be." The President gave a lopsided grin. Mark smiled back. "As you may know," Kolybin continued, "we have obtained a substantial loan...through the Marshal Plan...from the United States. This, we have achieved solely by the means of our current stability. No small thanks to you and your fellow officers, I might add." Beside him, his Vice-President grunted his agreement.

Unsteepling his fingers, Kolybin picked up his cigar from the ashtray. "So with the Communist terrorists now confined to the mountains of the far north, we find ourselves in the fortunate situation of now having to dispense with the services of our much beloved International Officers."

Mark waited while Kolybin drew on his cigar, silently amused by the man's phraseology. International Officers? It was the first time he had heard that one. 'Bloody foreign mercenaries was the usual term.'

Kolybin rose. Drawing deeply on his cigar, he balanced a hip on the corner of his desk, momentarily looking down at Mark without speaking. Then, as though a thought had just suddenly come to him, asked, "Tell me truthfully, young man, how long would it take my army with all you mercenaries gone, to oust out of the mountains, these self styled PFF?" Kolybin almost spat out the letters.

Mark studied Paule Kolybin's deeply lined face, his thoughts still in the midst of a diplomatic reply, as the Vice -President interceded. "This is in the strictest confidence, you will understand. Do not feel that anything you may say, would, or could be interpreted as being in any way disloyal to your superiors."

Mark's eyes left Kolybin to search the tall man's face, as the President hurried to assure him. "You may answer my Vice-President, Captain Stewart." Then as Mark's eyes drifted to the far corner of the room, went on, "Oh! Do not be concerned by our mutual acquaintance." He flourished his cigar in that direction.

Mark drifted back to the President. He cleared his throat. "Should they wish to stay -continue to be supplied from over the frontier, I should say indefinitely, Mister President."

Paule turned his head quickly to Molnar. "Just as I ...we had suspected." He swivelled back to Mark. "However, should they decide to leave the mountains -.do battle with us in the open -so to speak, what then?"

Mark shook his head. "The Reds have never been able to match our strength, even when things were at its worse-for us," he added with an apologetic gesture. "So why should they risk everything now? Even with most of us mer-International Officers," he corrected himself, and saw Kolybin smile, "gone, it would be nothing short of suicide."

"My feelings exactly. But should this stability we at present enjoy, suddenly disappear, would they then come down from their accursed mountains, do you think?"

"Stability?" Mark chuckled. "It would take nothing short of an avalanche to bring me down if I was their commanding officer."

Paule Kolybin took a final draw of his cigar. Stubbing it out in the ashtray, his lips seemed barely to move as he said, "That is why I had you brought here Captain Stewart - to help provide the avalanche. I am sincere when I say that I want you to assassinate me."

The cold hard look on Kolybin's face told Mark this was no joke, but he could not force himself to look away.

"I can assure you the President is quite sincere," Milan Molnar said softly, searching Mark for a reaction to his friend's statement.

"You will not actually kill me captain, merely make it appear so," Paule said with a glimmer of a smile.

Open mouthed, Mark looked from one to the other. He wanted to swallow, but was afraid of making himself appear more foolish.

"Our mutual friend here, who will remain nameless, will explain."

As if on cue the innominate man rose, and crossed the room to stand directly over the bemused Scot, while Kolybin returned to his seat behind his desk.

Without preamble, the man started sharply. "Every detail has been carefully worked out, all you need know, will be the time and place. At present I can tell you it will be done by shooting... blanks of course," he added, without humour.

"Hold on!" Mark jumped up. "I never said I had agreed to this!" His voice shook. He needed space...time to think. He moved behind his chair using it as a shield, eyeing the other three. What was he getting into? Or more precisely, what were they getting him into? Pretend to kill the President? Or so they said.

Naturally Kolybin would not want to die, so there was no question of it being real. But what else had these three in mind? He thought of the popular saying here, 'Never trust a politician, not even a dead one.' Was he to be used as a fall guy, with these three having something completely different in mind? Now all he wanted was to go home. He'd made his money for that pub he'd saved for. Besides, his folks would be expecting him. Hadn't he been through enough?

The War had come, and he had seized the opportunity to escape the humdrum life in a gents outfitters in Glasgow's Argyll Street by enlisting the same week as the recruiting office had opened.

His mother had sat down and wept, telling him that at twenty four he should be thinking more about getting married than going off to fight those accursed Germans in some daft war, as his father had done before him. He had countered by saying there was plenty of time to settle down. Anyway, he assured her, it would all be over by Christmas when he'd be home again, medals and all.

Many a time later, shitting himself in a trench at Mounte Casino, or Anzio, or another half dozen equally abhorrent places, he'd prayed to be back in that same shop. He had known every shelf, glass counter top, tie and shirt drawer, by memory. His main ambition, his only ambition in life had been to immerse himself in that mundane but especially safe life once again.

The war had ended and he had gone home. His job was still there. He had made it, back to Utopia. At first it had been all that he had imagined it to be. The manager, Mr Simpson was still there, and old Nancy, plus a new girl he did not know. The women had asked him about the War, but it was not something he had wanted to talk about. How could they ever understand? But he had made them laugh at some of the lighter side of things, while Mr Simpson had listened, folding up pullovers, saying nothing.

Six weeks he had stood it, then Utopia had disappeared. Every drawer and shelf, he'd prayed to God to see again had made him want to vomit- this for the rest of his life? The truth was, he could not adjust to civvy street.

One day Mark heard from Wee Hughie that they were 'looking fur sodgers' in some unpronounceable country in the Balkans-.or was it the Baltic? Or next door to it, he said. So he had made some inquiries, and had gone through channels, some official, some not so, and had eventually decided to take the chance to sign up.

His mother had cried when he had told her, remonstrating, on how her prayers had been answered when God had brought him safely home, only to find him up and away again.

Did he not think that he was tempting Providence that one wee bit too much? After all, he'd come through the War without so much as a scratch.

His father had sat by the black polished grate of the fireside, saying nothing. He'd seen enough of man's inhumanity to man without having to go looking for it a second time, as he had told his son at the outbreak of war.

Mark gripped the back of the chair tighter. He remembered how on that last day his mother had sat him down to a breakfast of ham and eggs, soda scones and jam. How she had hugged him as if mustering up all her strength to prevent his leaving, to keep him safe at home. He, breaking away from her embrace, her crying as he reached the door-he could still hear her now, in this the President's room.

As with all Scotsmen, his father had showed no outward emotion. All his father's feelings had been in the shake of his hand, as if telling him he would not see him again. Then he was on the stair, telling his folks he would send them money, and that they could get everything they had ever wanted. But he had known this was no consolation, it was him they wanted.

"I am going home," Mark said, looking Kolybin straight in the eye.

Letting out a gasp, the nameless man threw a quick look at his President for support, who gestured to Mark to sit down.

"As you will, Captain. I cannot prevent you. Unfortunately, all plans have been finalised. However, for this very great service and risk, I am prepared to offer you this," and as he spoke Kolybin slid a folded slip of paper across the desk.

Mark took it, and stared at the sum written on the cheque. This could buy him a dozen pubs: set his folks up in a house in Bearsden, they need never scrimp and scrape again. Yet, the voice inside him was telling him to walk away, his brain unable to absorb the pros and cons of it all. He needed time to be alone to think, but clearly these men would not afford him this privilege. Placing the cheque gently on the desk he slid it back across to the President. "I'm still going home," he reiterated firmly.

With a little shake of his head, the dapper little man reached into the top drawer of his desk and drew out a buff coloured folder. "Do you know what this is Captain? Of course you don't," he apologised, running a finger along an edge. "It is a report that came into my possession some time ago, which the upper echelon in the Caserne refer to, as the Meirra Incident."

Mark felt his throat suddenly constrict.   So that was it…
Blackmail. "That was…" Mark started to say. Cleared his throat. "
A long time ago. And as a soldier yourself, Mister President, you
should know in war, mistakes can be made." And for a moment was
certain he saw the little man blush.

Kolybin brought his head up slowly. "It would be in your best
interest, Captain Stewart if you were to do as I have proposed. You
will be well rewarded, as I have already shown. However, should
you decide otherwise..?" Kolybin drew his finger along the folder's
edge.

"And if I do?" Mark croaked. "Shall I be free afterwards to go
home?"

Kolybin sagged in his chair as if ashamed of his actions. "This
man will advise you of all the details concerning your involvement
in this affair," he gestured wearily.

The nameless man quickly took over, starting from where he had
so unexpectedly been interrupted. "The assassination will take place
exactly one month from today. The precise details of which will be
worked out with you closer to the time.   Naturally, you will be
unable to return home immediately following this, as this would
create too much suspicion.

To all intent and purpose, you have been summoned here this
evening, so we may attempt to persuade you to remain in our
country's service a little longer….with the added incentive of
promotion of course. We have also offered this latter consideration
to a few more of your fellow officers whose services we do not wish
to dispense with at this precise time," the nameless man explained.
"This way it also helps avoid suspicion."

Marks eyes followed the man slowly pacing back and forth in front
of him. This was a cold hard bastard, he decided, so cocksure of
himself. Probably, Kolybin's head man in his Department of Dirty
Tricks. "When you have carried out your duty," he was saying, "you
will return to your Regiment."

"With the rank of Major, I believe," Molnar said, as if feeling he
had to say something to justify his presence.

"As Major," the nameless man confirmed, a tinge of impatience in
his voice, as if he was unaccustomed at being interrupted, even by a
Vice-President.

"Are there any questions you would like to ask, Captain...excuse me Major Stewart?"

Molnar asked.

Mark swallowed hard, his voice was not his own as he asked, "How long must I remain with the Regiment?"

It was Kolybin who answered. "This will all depend upon the reaction to my.., death by the Reds," he said with a slight smile.

"With all due respect, Mister President, but how does your wife feel about all of this?"

It was the way Kolybin glared at him that Mark knew he had asked the wrong question.

"My wife knows nothing of this, and neither will Vice-President Molnar's wife, or anyone in Congress. Let me reiterate young man, outside of this room no one knows of this affair. Do I make myself clear?"

Although he had been taken aback by the President's outburst, Mark was too tired by the day's events to be overawed. True, he had arrived here believing that perhaps this man had invited him along with a few of his fellow mercenaries for a farewell drink. Now he knew differently. He was not going home...at least not tomorrow.

Somehow, the thought of going home was becoming more appealing by the minute. Three years here was enough. Yes, they had been financially rewarding; should he ever get to spend any of it.

Only a month after arriving here with the rank of sergeant from W.W.2 , he had gained a Lieutenat's commission, as had most other foreign NCOs'. Strangely, he had felt no affinity to those serving under him who had held his former rank, not even to Niew Grbesa, whom he had relied upon on many an awkward occasion. Perhaps it had been the language: though now he spoke it fairly well, at least well enough to have his commands understood, such as 'get your arse down, etc'. No, the real reason he was here, was money, and should the PFF have been in the same financial situation as Kolybin and his lot, those years back, he, and the rest of the mercenaries would most likely be 'working' for them.

Not prone to losing his temper; well not too often, Mark was seriously considering making this an exception by grabbing this wee man...President or not, by the scruff of the neck and informing him in no uncertain terms, that he could easily have his assassination brought forward a month or so, and he could make it real, so very real. Of course he would not, not with the Meirra Incident hanging over his head. Instead he said aloud, "I apologise Mister President."

Kolybin's hand still shook as he reached out for the cigar box. "Your apology is accepted, Major." Then a little less harshly. "Your concern is quite natural, and, I might add, commendable." He smiled thinly.

Chapter 2

Mark stood with his back to the lines of spectators who waited impatiently for the arrival of their president, and cast an eye down the almost deserted street to where a soldier stood posted at the entrance to each shop or office doorway.

A sudden cheer went up. Mark swung round. A black limousine had pulled up at the steps of the National Opera House, and Milan Molnar got out. For a moment, he stood there smiling, before turning to climb the steps to the House's lavish entrance, where he halted once again to stop and wave.

Mark stole a quick look at his watch. Exactly ten minutes from now, everything going according to plan, Kolybin should be the next to arrive.

He looked around him, unable to comprehend the magnitude of the intended deception. Only now was he beginning to realise just how many lives the upshot of these next few minutes would touch. Most of all, the reaction to the President's 'death' by the two dignitaries wives, who, by sheer 'coincidence' just happened to be on 'goodwill' visit to Paris. Moreover, should Kolybin bring off this coup, what would the International reaction be when they realised that their respective representatives had been deceived into mourning an empty grave? What of Congress? What of the ordinary people themselves? Kolybin was gambling on his 'death' throwing the country into such confusion that the PFF would seize the opportunity to rise en masse, and come out into the open where, he, Kolybin, could deal with them once and for all. But would they? Would they take the bait? Mark shook his head in disbelief at the enormity of the whole affair.

He remembered putting this same question to the little president when next they met. Kolybin had dismissed his concern with a glare. "How many countries do you think will trouble themselves to send a representative to my funeral? Eh?" He had sniffed contemptuously. "Perhaps the ones who do, may send a letter of protest when the subterfuge has been discovered. As to the Americans?" He sniffed again. "Their sole concern is to arrest the Russian sphere of influence from spreading in this direction, and should this mean their turning a blind eye to this little deception, then so be it."

Kolybin had taken a cigar out of its case, and waved it at him. "Our American friends have much more to lose than most, having invested quite considerably in our little country. Hell Major!" He had laughed. "I would not be in the least surprised, that in order to save face they did not suggest that it was they who had thought up the entire damned scheme in the first place!"

All at once Paule Kolybin's expression had changed, a small vein pulsating at his right temple as he leaned across the desk. "Even at the risk of offending the entire world, I'd not retreat from my plan, if by doing so it would bring this civil war…this killing, to an end. We have suffered too much at the hands of the Nazis to destroy each other now. Therefore, should it mean my own personal downfall, it is of little moment in comparison to what may be achieved should my plan succeed, which, after all is what we all yearn for: a lasting peace."

Now Mark understood by the passion in which Paule Kolybin had spoken, how easily those involved could have been persuaded into believing that his plan was feasible; even essential to the future of the country.

High above the hubbub of the waiting crowd, the thunderous roar of an explosion some distance away filled the air, the reverberations shaking the windows of the buildings all around. For a few seconds the crowd remained silent, and then turned to look at Mark and the nearest soldiers for an explanation, or a sign of reassurance that all was well, while others whispered to one another that though in all probability it was a PFF attack they would be safe enough, for it was well known that, however abhorrent the Reds might be, they at least confined their attacks to military targets.

"No need for alarm, it came from a few streets away," a soldier calmly assured them, spreading out his arms in an attempt to shepherd back to the barricade those with a mind to leave.

Further up the street an officer ran in Mark's direction, barking out orders to soldiers guarding the doorways, to 'follow him.'

"You, soldier, come with me!" he shouted out to the soldier guarding the doorway nearest to where Mark stood.

The young private hesitated, unsure whether or not to obey. "My orders are to remain here sir," he ventured nervously.

Mark cursed. Of all the soldiers, this had to be the one to question the order. He stepped forward. "I believe you should obey the lieutenant's orders, private."

The young soldier swung round. "With all due respect, sir," he stammered, recognising Mark's rank, "but my orders are, that on no account must I leave my post."

"You *will* follow *me*, private!" the lieutenant barked, stepping closer to the soldier, his eyes blazing.

Aware of those nearest in the crowd staring at them, Mark intervened. "Do as the lieutenant orders, soldier, I will remain here until your return. The explosion we heard might mean our president is in danger."

Now confronted by two senior officers, the young soldier gripped his weapon tighter. Then having decided he had no option but to obey, quickly trotted after the others. And as the lieutenant swung on his heel, he threw the Scot a look of appreciation.

Mark swore again. Clearly this lieutenant was also one of them, which put the lie to Kolybin's declaration that only those present in the room that first night were privy to his scheme. However, at this precise moment he had more important matters to attend to.

Behind Mark the curious bystanders had already turned their attention back to the Opera House, their interest in this little sideshow already forgotten, with only a few casting nervous glances in the direction of the explosion.

Mark looked furtively around him. Satisfied that no one was watching, he strode towards the nearest unguarded doorway. One quick glance around as he unlocked the door, and he was on his way up the steep stairs and on to the roof directly above.

The roof that Mark found himself on was flat, with a wall about eight feet high separating it from its neighbour. Running lightly to the front of the building, he snapped a quick look over the front parapet at the waiting crowd in front of the Opera House diagonally opposite. His hope was, that should anyone chance to look up they'd mistake him for a guard. Someone coughed on the other side of the wall and he was sharply reminded that this was the only unguarded roof.

A quick look at his watch told him he had only four minutes before Kolybin arrived. Crossing to an air duct in the middle of the roof, he removed the cowl, and for a few brief moments stared down at the gun case, knowing, that should he go through with this, there was no turning back.

Yet what options had he? He shivered. Could he face the consequences of the Meirra Incident? Knowing that he could not, he unzipped the leather case, and expertly assembled the rifle, checking the blank cartridges as he retraced his steps to the front parapet, almost dropping the telescopic sight on the way as a sudden burst of cheering reached him from the crowd below.

Kneeling down, Mark rested the weapon on the edge of the parapet, only too well aware of the guard on the other side of the wall humming softly to himself.

Mark swallowed hard. The President's car had drawn up at the foot of the Opera steps. The doors opened and Paule Kolybin stepped out. For a few brief minutes he stood there posing for the cameras and waving to the cheering people,-.his people -all crushing against the barricade- all struggling to get closer to their hero.

"Come on man," Mark breathed through his clenched teeth as he adjusted the sights. "Get on with it."

As if in answer to Mark's prayer, Kolybin turned and stepped briskly up the steps, halting once more to give a final wave. He looked up in Mark's direction, as if inviting him to fire, a broad smile on his face.

Mark squeezed the trigger. Kolybin staggered back clutching his chest, and slowly sagged down against the theatre wall.

Everywhere people screamed. Bodyguards ran to his aid. Startled dignitaries looked helplessly around. On either side of the roof, soldiers cried out.

With an effort, Mark tore his eyes away from the mayhem that he had created. Then, he was up and running across the roof, dropping the gun down the duct and hastily throwing the cowl back into place, before crashing through the open door and bounding down the stairs to reach the bottom, at the same time as the street door crashed open.

Mark swung round and threw himself flat on the stairs, his drawn revolver pointing upwards. "Careful men!" he shouted to the soldiers rushing through the door behind him. "He's still up there!"

As one, the soldiers drew to a halt as Mark got to his feet. "Keep your distance. Follow me," he ordered, cautiously starting to mount the stairs.

The guard from the neighbouring roof was in the act of clambering over the intervening wall when Mark emerged on to the roof. "Stop that man!" he barked. Instantly his order was obeyed by two soldiers rushing forward to pin the unfortunate guard against the wall.

Mark wheeled to the officer in charge. "Your name, soldier?" he commanded briskly.

"Rachwel, sir...Sergeant Rachwel, sir," the soldier snapped, coming to an attention.

"Well, sergeant, take your prisoner to your commanding officer. I must return to my duties by the President." Mark tried to inject anger as well as concern into his voice as he added, "God willing he is unharmed."

"Very good sir, I understand." The sergeant drew himself more stiffly to attention. "And thank you for your assistance…sir!"

Mark trotted back down the stairs with as much composure as he could muster. There were others on the stairs now, saluting and rushing passed, none bothering to halt or challenge him. His head swam. Had he succeeded in 'killing' Kolybin? Would that sergeant recognise him again when they realised they had apprehended an innocent man?

These thoughts and more rushed uncomfortably through his mind before the cold air had hit him and he realised he was in the street, and on his way to carry out his next part in this 'great deception'.

Everyone seemed to be running, shouting, screaming all around the President cradled in Milan Molnar's arms. Kos Dryak,-.the nameless man in the President's office, who had briefed Mark, rushed to his side. "I am a doctor!" he shouted out, pushing a security guard aside.

A young woman who had broken through the crowd, quickly kneeled down beside the 'doctor', and tore open the President's black Tuxedo jacket, then drew out her handkerchief to stem the blood pumping out of the white starched shirt.

"What are you doing?" Dryak roared at her.

The girl jerked back, shocked by the unexpected outburst from a fellow professional. "Doctor I can help! I am a nurse!" she exclaimed, once again attempting to arrest the blood flow.

Dryak quickly drew her hand away. "That will not be necessary. Guard!" he called out, desperately searching around for one of the

President's aides. Then as one emerged out of the chaos, added a little more gently, "Please be good enough to remove this young lady."

"But you need all the help you can get!" the girl cried almost hysterically as she struggled with the guard.

Ignoring the girl's angry protests, Dryak turned to Milan Molnar. "I think we should get him inside," he said quietly.

Milan gestured to two security guards. "Help lift the President." He rose, waving the distressed theatre manager to his side. "Can we use your office Mister Becko?" he asked anxiously.

"Of course Mister Vice-President," the dumpy little man's voice was a decibel higher than normal. "Oh dear, dear! The poor man. This way ...if you please!"

Molnar and Dryak exchanged looks. Was this silly old woman going to faint?

Becko quickly led the way, using his arms in a fair imitation of the breast stroke to part the crowded auditorium.

Reaching the office, Dryak cleared the manager's desk with one swoop of his arm, and quickly stood aside to let the bodyguards lay the wounded president gently on top.

"Lacko! Get your men to keep that crowd away," Molnar barked at the senior guard, referring to the jostling people filling the doorway. "Call an ambulance and have them bring it to the side entrance. Tell them we have a doctor here. Also Lacko, should anyone ask,-newspaper correspondents or such like, you will tell them only that the President has been shot. I do not wish that the President's wife or my own should know what has happened here, until I can inform them both personally. Do you understand?"

The man nodded, and licking his lips, nervously followed Molnar to the door where two guards were holding back the press of people clamouring to see inside the room.

"When you have done what I have asked of you, Lacko, you will need some assistance in keeping this mob at bay. Find out who is in charge, and have that officer brought to me," he snapped at the man over his shoulder.

"Yes sir." Lacko's eyes travelled back to where Dryak stood over Kolybin's prone body, wishing he knew more about his President's condition before he left. Then as he started down the corridor, he heard Molnar call out to him above the babble of the crowd jamming the doorway that he was not to be too far away.

Once inside the office, Molnar moved quickly away from the locked door. "We only have a few minutes, Paule, but, I think it is fairly safe at present."

Kolybin sat up and gingerly swung his legs over the edge of desk. "I thought I had given the game away. I was sure I was dripping with sweat," he croaked, mopping his brow with a handkerchief.

Molnar crossed to the desk. "It was nothing to have worried about; no one knew whether or not you were dead." Paule raised an eyebrow. "You know what I mean," Milan said irritably.

Kolybin knew his friend was feeling the strain. Milan had never been fullheartedly behind the scheme, for were it to fail, it would mean the end of both their political careers.

The President studied his blood soaked shirt. "Those satchels of yours, Dryak, are very convincing. Do you not think so, Milan?" he chuckled.

Dryak crossed to the room's only window, high above the street, and pulled down the shade. Next, he tugged at the velvet curtain until it came away from the rings that held it.

"I was quite surprised by the velocity of the shot. My chest still hurts." Paule rubbed his chest. A knock on the door stopped him. He threw Molnar a look and lay back down on the desk as Dryak quickly threw the curtain over him.

"First, making sure all was in order Molnar unlocked the office door, to find Lacko standing there. "I have called for an ambulance as you ordered, Mister Vice-President." The security guard edged into the room, half turning after a few steps to introduce Mark. "This is Major Stewart, sir, the officer in charge."

"Major Stewart." Molnar acknowledged the Scot, as if they had never met.

"Sir," Mark said, coming to attention, his eyes travelling from the covered figure on the desk to Dryak, in the hope that man would show him some sign of assurance that all had gone according to plan. There was none.

Behind Mark, Lacko asked, "Mister Vice-President, Senator Meloun and the Leader of the National Party, Senator Cibula, are anxiously waiting outside, they wish to know the President's condition. Also, may they please be allowed to come inside?"

Molnar held up his hand. "Regrettably no, Lacko. My apologies to both gentlemen. Ask them to be good enough to meet me at Admin." Molnar referred to the Government Offices. He snapped a quick look at his watch. "Say...in my office two hours from now?" He stepped closer to the guard, his tone confidential. "When the ambulance arrives, we shall take the President home." Milan Molnar turned to include Mark in the discourse. "Gentlemen, the President is dead."

Mark heard Lacko's sharp intake of breath, and felt the blood drain from his own face. Now, he wanted more than anything to know what was really going on here.

"My President is dead?" Lacko whispered.

Milan nodded. "So you see Mojir," he addressed the guard by his Christian name, as if at last he had some sympathy for the man's feelings. "Now more than ever I must rely on your assistance and discretion."

Ashen faced, Lacko made an attempt to pull himself together. "You can rely on me, sir," he said, looking his new leader straight in the face.

Mark looked on. Clearly the man was distraught by the death of his President. This was just the beginning, there were going to be hundreds, thousands similarly affected. He glanced across the room at Dryak who was deliberately obscuring Kolybin's body, then back to Molnar. "I am sorry to hear this Mister Vice - President," he said softly.

Molnar nodded his appreciation. "Mojir, find a funeral director." Lacko blanched. Molnar hurried on. " Any director. This must be done as quickly as possible. Tell no one of the President's death. Have this director come to the Presidential Residence, the Kasel. Word will seep out soon enough. See you are also there, Lacko." With the snapping of his orders, Molnar had returned to full formality with the senior guard. "Make sure there are no hiccups at the gate. No one is to be allowed past without my authority. Do you understand?" Then at Lacko's nod, Molnar continued hurriedly. "I will take, Major Stewart with me for security reasons. Now please be good enough to be on your way."

Once the door had closed behind the security guard, Kolybin sat up.

"Thank Christ for that!" Mark exploded, striding quickly to the desk. "I apologise for my language, Mister President, but I did not know whether I had injured you or not."

"Understandable, young man." Kolybin let the curtain drop around his ankles. "Have I time for a smoke do you think, Lieutenant Dryak?"

"I am sorry Mister President, we cannot take the risk. Your brand is too well known. It may arouse suspicion."

"Very well,"Kolybin conceded. "How long before my ambulance arrives do you think?" he asked, attempting to make light of the situation.

"Not too long, I should say sir"

Clasping his hands in his lap, Kolybin's next question was directed at Mark. "You know what is expected of you from this point on, Major Stewart?"

"Yes sir. My second in command will ensure that the theatre is cleared, which will leave me free to carry out my part." He did not feel inclined to use flowery language such as 'vacated' of onlookers."

Appearing to be satisfied, Kolybin nodded his approval.

Molnar ran a finger round the inside of his collar. Almost half an hour had passed since Lacko had left. Then, as if to alleviate his anxiety, there was a sudden sharp rap on the door. He shot his friend a quick look and Kolybin lay back down on the desk, the Scot stepping swiftly forward to cover him with the curtain as Molnar unlocked the door at a reassuring nod that all was ready from Dryak.

"It is the ambulance men, Mister Vice-President," Lacko announced, his voice little more than a whisper, as if afraid to awaken his 'sleeping' president, as he led the two white uniformed men into the room.

Dryak moved around Molnar towards them. He pointed to the desk, his voice cold and unfeeling, as he said. "Bring your stretcher over here please. I am a doctor, and I regret to inform you that President Kolybin is dead."

So much for bloody bedside manners, Mark thought, at the sheer look of incredulity on the faces of the two newcomers.

Dispassionately, Dryak continued. "Therefore, there is no necessity to have the President removed to hospital, it will serve no useful purpose. Instead, I believe Vice- President Molnar would appreciate that you convey the president's body to the Kasel. We shall of course, follow on. You will, until notified, tell no one of the death of your President. Do I make myself clear?"

For a moment, Mark thought one of the orderlies was about to protest, but presumably overawed by the situation and the rank of those present, decided to remain silent.

Lacko stepped in front of Molnar. "I have contacted a funeral director." He lowered his voice. "I have also informed him to make his way to the Kasel. I did not know what kind...type of...." the man swallowed, "coffin. I ordered the best, Mister Vice-President." Lacko's eyes came up to meet those of his leader, as a pupil would do to please his master.

"You did well, Lacko," Molnar said reassuringly.

"I have also informed Senators Meloun and Cibula of your wishes. They have both intimated to me that they will meet you at the Admin, as you suggested earlier."

While Lacko spoke, Molnar's eyes had followed every movement of the ambulance men lifting the shrouded figure on to the stretcher, and he was only vaguely aware of the man telling him, that the building was clear of all people, except that was, for the cast of the cancelled opera, who were all backstage, and therefore of no hindrance to their leaving. He also had Becko the manager standing by, to escort them to the side entrance.

Now that Paule was safely on the stretcher, Molnar turned his full attention back to the security guard. "Well done, Lacko. We can now leave." The relief in the tall man's voice only too plain.

Twenty minutes later they were all safely in Paule Kolybin's ground floor study in the Presidential Residence of the Kasel, the 'doctor' having suggested that it would be better to leave the president's body downstairs, rather than attempt to carry it to one of the upstairs bedrooms.

The ambulance had gone, the study door locked, and the staff informed of their master's death, together with the command that under no circumstances were they were to inform anyone of this at this time.

"It was thoughtful of old Kobik to bring us...or should I say you this," Kolybin said happily, reaching out for the whisky decanter. "I think the old boy could have done with one himself, he was simply shaking. I glimpsed as much while I lay under the blanket. Did you see him, Milan?"

Standing with his back to the blazing fire, Molnar jerked a hard look at his friend.

"There are many who will be similarly affected besides your butler by this day's work, Paule. I only hope and pray, we can justify all of this," he said caustically.

"You worry too much Milan, this has ever been your weakness." Kolybin gave a low laugh, and waved a hand at the decanter. "Help yourself gentlemen." He switched back to his friend. "Do you understand Milan what this will mean to our country, with the PFF defeated in one fell blow? Peace at last! An opportunity to rebuild!" Paule moved away from the small drinks table, his eyes bright at the prospect, and the fact that his plan so far, was succeeding.

Clearly disturbed by the many things he had not envisaged, Milan countered. "Do you still believe the act justifies the means?"

"Yes, were it to result in the future prosperity of our country...and," Kolybin was interrupted by a brief timid knock at the door.

Dryak took the President's drink and handed it to Mark, while Molnar helped his friend to lie back down on the stretcher on the floor.

Mark opened the door to face the old butler. "The undertakers are here, sir." The old man's eyes were red. Mark nodded, hating himself for his part in all this unnecessary grief. He should have refused to have had anything to do with it in the first place, and for a moment wondered what would happen if he were to blow the whistle on the whole sordid affair. He saw Dryak watching him as if having read his thoughts. Now, there was one cold bastard, who would not hesitate to prevent him from doing what he was thinking of doing.

"Have them come in, Major Stewart!" Molnar called out from behind.

Mark stood aside to let the two men enter. One, presumably the senior, offered a small bow to Molnar. "You have my sincerest condolences, Mister Vice -President. Our country has suffered a great loss."

"I thank you...Mister...?"

"Klubir, of Klubir and Son."

"Quite." Molnar said simply.

"Please also convey my deepest sympathy on behalf of my establishment to the First Lady." The man bowed again.

"This is precisely why I have asked you here at this hour." Molnar's voice had an edge to it, as he went on. "I know it must be quite awkward for you to be summoned here at such short notice. However, I can assure you of such a necessity. In a few short hours the entire country will know of this sad affair, in a few hours more, in all probability, the entire civilised world. You cannot imagine the volume of business I must transact within these same few hours. There is also the matter of trying to spare the late President's wife and son as much pain as possible, by ensuring that they first hear of the tragic circumstances from myself, and not from outside sources, you understand?"

"Quite. Your security guard intimated as much to me, Mister Vice-president." The undertaker fidgeted with his hard black hat.

Molnar gestured to a point behind the man. "This gentleman is the doctor, who, fortunately for us, was at the theatre when the president was shot." The undertaker did an almost pivotal turn to face Dryak. "However, despite doing what he could, I am afraid his efforts were in vain."

Molnar moved round Klubir, his voice suddenly authoritative. "All I wish from you at present Mr Klubir, is that you should leave the coffin, here." And at the look of amazement on the man's face, went on steely. "We must await a death certificate from a second doctor. Meanwhile, it is my wish that the president should lie in a more dignified manner."

"I understand, sir. But he should be laid out in a way befitting a great leader, a..." The agitated man began to object.

"Have I failed to explain myself adequently? Or should I seek the services of a more co-operative Establishment?" Molnar asked harshly.

Klubir twisted his hat savagely, his professional pride offended. "As you wish, Vice-President." He made a last desperate attempt to avert this sacrilege. "Is there any way I may be of assistance. A little make up here...a touch...?"

"No!" Molnar almost shouted. Then a little calmer. "Thank you. Simply have the coffin brought in here. The security guards will help you. And thank you again for your prompt co-operation, Mr Klubir. And I trust, your continued discretion."

"Well that's it done at last," Kolybin sighed, placing the last of the hardback books in the coffin. "We can now screw down the lid."

Mark moved forward to seal the lid, his head swimming with the feeling of unreality at what he was doing. He'd coped with more grotesque incidents throughout his six years of European war, but none ever quite so bizarre. Was he the only sane one here, in this room? Or had he too lost his marbles?

Locking the study door behind him, Molnar led Mark and Dryak into the corridor as the old manservant came round the corner.

"Just the man I was looking for, Kobik. I wonder if you will be good enough to assemble all the staff in the drawing room?" Molnar asked gently. "I should like a few words with them. The next few days will be a trying time for us all. First Lady Kolybin, will need all the assistance your staff can offer. You do understand?"

"I am sure we shall do our best sir," the old man's voice trembled. Then, as if remembering his duties, asked, "Can I offer you gentlemen some refreshment? Surely you cannot go on..."

Molnar gently touched the old man's shoulder. "Thank you for your consideration, Kobik, but we have much to attend to before this night is done."

If only you knew the half of it wee man, Mark thought, wishing there was a bus straight from here to Glasgow.

The front door opened. Molnar turned. "All is well, Lacko? You have dealt with the undertaker? You have emphasised again, that he is to inform no one that the president is not just injured, but dead?"

The security guard closed the door. "Yes sir. But there are so many at the gate. How they got to know he was here..."

"You do not think what happened tonight could be kept secret for long?" Dryak suggested sarcastically.

"Mojir! Take the good doctor here back to the city," Molnar intervened, scowling at the bogus doctor. "He has been most helpful. Major Stewart and I are about to leave for the Admin. We shall use the major's car. Please inform Admin. of our impending arrival." He held out his hand to Dryak. "I am most grateful for your assistance, doctor. I hope we may meet again under more pleasant circumstances."

Taking the outstretched hand, Dryak offered a slight bow. "I hope so, Mister Vice-President. However, I am sorry I could not have done more for our beloved President. Also, I hope who ever is responsible for such a dastardly deed will be quickly brought to justice."

"I am quite sure measures are already in hand to see this is so."

Although he knew this charade was for Lacko's benefit, Mark could not help but feel a cold shiver run down his spine.

After the security guard had escorted the 'doctor' out of the door, Molnar swung to Mark, his voice betraying his nervousness. "Now that Lacko has left with Dryak, and the remaining guards are by the main gate, the way should be clear for you to get the president through the house to your car. I will keep the staff busy with my little speech until I think you have had enough time to get him out. Then I shall join you as soon as possible.... Make sure the president is well hidden."

A splash of rain hit the windscreen, and Mark hoped it would not come to much. Then again, he had thought the same about the War. A flash of light cut across the gravel path, then darkness again. He sighed, thinking of what Lacko had said earlier about the number of arrests of suspected assassins; of a hysterical mob, who had chased and beaten to death some poor innocent sod, who had chosen to run after being seen coming out of an office near the Opera House, so he was at first unaware of Molnar sliding into the front seat beside him.

"Everything, all right?" Molnar asked, raising himself off the seat a little to glance into the back seat of the car.

"Yes sir. The President is on the floor covered by a rug and a few files and briefcases, as you arranged."

"Good. Then we can be on our way, Major Stewart."

By the time they had cleared the main gate and slid into the evening traffic, it was raining heavily. Mark switched on the wipers, recalling when passing through the house, how close they had been from bumping into a maid, who had been running late for Molnar's little lecture. And had she'd seen her dead president tip-toeing through the corridors, how much would that have altered the course of history?

"Turn here, major." Molnar pointed right. Mark swung the wheel and they entered the boulevard leading to the Administration Building. A few minutes later, they were through the gate and running up the drive to the front entrance, where only a few windows remained lit.

Molnar tugged Mark's sleeve. "Don't drive too close to the entrance major, let's keep the car in the dark." Mark nodded and drew up the car just outside the pool of light.

"I will send the guards to search my office for security reasons, which, after what has just happened they will not find at all suspicious." Molnar put his hand on the door handle as he spoke. "Once they have left the foyer, you will bring the President to the elevator." Molnar swung himself out of the car. "Wait for my signal." He stretched back into the car to lift a briefcase from out of the back. "Did you hear that Paule?" And in turn was rewarded by a slight shake of the rug confirming that his instruction had been understood.

Molnar closed the car door and strode confidently to the entrance. Pushing the glass door open, he stepped into the vestibule, where he stood for a moment conversing with the two guards.

Mark gripped the wheel tighter as one of the men turned to look in his direction, before hurrying off to meet up with his companion, who had already left to carry out his Vice-President's instructions. He saw Molnar stand by the elevator door, then turn, and gesture to him that all was ready.

"It's time Mister President." Mark got hurriedly out of the car, and opened the back door. There was a flurry of rugs and briefcases being thrown aside and the figure of Paule Kolybin emerged. The wiry little man got hurriedly out of the car and trotted after his mercenary through the glass door to where Molnar stood by the open elevator door.

"We must hurry. We have not much time," Molnar said, ushering them inside.

Molnar took a key out of his pocket and closed the door by inserting it in a lock under the service panel. The lift gave a slight jerk and began to move. Instinctively Mark looked up at the indicator, and was surprised to see that it had not moved. A few seconds later, they stopped. Molnar gave the key a half turn to the left and the doors opened to reveal a full length wooden panel. He leaned forward and put his hand down the space between the wall and the lift, and a panel slid back at his touch. "So far so good," Molnar breathed, stepping out of the lift and switching on a light.

"Welcome to my new home." Kolybin ushered Mark out of the lift with a flourish of his hand. "Courtesy of the late Third Reich," he added at Mark's amazement. "We are at present two floors beneath the basement. Bomb proof! Sound proof! Waterproof! What more proof do you need?" he bellowed, clearly relieved by his plan so far having succeeded.

Mark took a tentative step forward and stared around him in disbelief. The room was large; large enough to accommodate three armchairs and a settee, luxurious as to afford a thick piled carpet, a drinks cabinet, and a quite large mahogany table. One corner, which was clearly reserved for business, boasted a desk and a row of filing cabinets.

Kolybin seized Mark by the arm. "Master planners, master builders, the Germans, don't you think, Major?"

"Master race," Mark answered caustically.

Kolybin tilted back his head. Laughing, he marched Mark to the opposite end of the room. "Here is my adequate kitchen and supplies." He threw out a hand to encompass the small alcove. "And over there," he nodded to a separate room, "is my bedroom! What do you think of it, Major Stewart?"

Mark would have liked to have said he had never seen anyone so excited over a room and kitchen since his Aunt Nellie had moved into one up a wally close in Maryhill, but, somehow he didn't think this little man would understand or appreciate his sense of humour. Instead he said, "quite ingenious, Mister President...quite ingenious."

Molnar did not share his president's enthusiasm. Pouring himself a drink, he sat himself down on the arm of a chair. "I have only a few minutes before the guards start looking for me, Paule." He flicked a glance at his watch. "The senators are also due to arrive within the next few minutes. Is there anything we may have overlooked that is likely to come up for discussion, do you think?"

"No, Milan. Conduct the meeting as planned. I am sure as acting president, you will cope quite adequently." Kolybin smiled across at his friend.

Molnar downed his drink. "In that case, there is nothing more to discuss." He rose, setting down his empty glass on the edge of the polished table. "except to say, besides thank you for your assistance, Major Stewart. Also I regret to say, you will have to remain within the building until I have concluded my business, for, we must not forget, that you are here in the capacity of my personal bodyguard, and, I have a feeling Major, that this is going to be a very long night."

Chapter 3

The guns boomed out from the old citadel in the city, the reverberations echoing around the hills as people took their last farewell of their leader.

Clutching a single rose, Myra Kolybin, accompanied by her stepson, moved slowly to the graveside. She halted, her lips moving in final farewell, letting the tiny flower fall into the open grave.

As the grieving woman and the boy moved slowly back, the Honour Guard stepped smartly forward. On command they raised their rifles to the sky. A single volley rang out and at a second command, the Guard withdrew.

Impassively, Mark watched the line of mourners file passed the late president's wife and her stepson; first, the American and British Ambassadors, next, the French Attaché, and so on, each shaking the hand of Kolybin's son, dressed in the uniform of a naval cadet, then, that of the woman, all expressing their condolences in subdued tones, before shuffling on.

Mark caught Molnar's eye, and gave himself no prizes for guessing what was going through that man's mind. He looked around for Dryak, the fourth conspirator, but failed to see him amongst the crowd. Then it was his turn to stand in line.

The lawn of the Kasel, still wet from a morning shower, sparkled in a weak sun; a sun which somehow had managed to poke out from behind a leaden sky.

Mark needed a drink after that morning's ordeal. He looked up to where Myra Kolybin stood a little distance away on the patio talking to a group of people, and felt nauseated by the whole sick affair, all around him, a hundred or so people enunciated their grief in as many different ways. Cynically, he wondered to himself, what their reaction would have been had they known that it was an old pile of books they'd been grieving over. It was something he could tell the folks back home in Govan all about...worth a free pint or two. Maybe even raise a smile or a laugh, and he himself not taking it as serious as he was doing right now.

He caught sight of Molnar talking to General Jakofcic, their respective wives by their side. Since his appointment as Commander in Chief of all the armed forces by Kolybin, Jakofcic had gone after the PFF it as if by doing so, he was unleashing six years of pent up energy he had stored when he was a Prisoner of War by the Germans. The General had also continually harassed those brave enough to have attacked his men in open combat. Others, not quite so openly brave and who had been found guilty of assassination, he had imprisoned or executed. At the same time, he had built up an intelligence service which had effectively put an end to all street bombings in the city.

Mark reached the marquee, found himself a drink and wandered back out onto the lawn. General Scurk had now joined the party, though by now, the First Lady was absent. No one could fault the elderly general for his meticulous planning and overt caution. Although, by the time his plans were finally implemented the net was usually empty. Thus earning him the nickname of 'The Tortoise'.

Scurk moved around the small gathering to speak to Jakofcic's wife, who Mark guessed would be around thirty, some fifteen years her husband's junior, her mourning clothes doing little to hide her voluptuous figure. Apparently, the hierarchy had a penchant for younger women.

"I do appreciate your coming...Major Stewart?" Mark had not heard Myra Kolybin, come up behind him. She pointed to his insignia. "Congratulations on your promotion. I must confess I was unaware of it when we spoke this morning."

Mark saw the red puffed eyes, and the wan smile that did little to hide her grief. "I would hazard a guess and say that you had far more important things on your mind, but thanks anyway." Mark did not know what else to say, except he would have liked to have taken her aside and told her the truth.

She saw his frown. "You were listed to return home were you not, Major?"

Mark pulled a face. "Let's just say I was persuaded to remain a little while longer. Besides, the pay is good."

Myra Kolybin eyed him coldly, and the brave wan smile had rapidly disappeared. "Is that why you came in the first place?"

Mark realized his attempt to lighten the conversation had fallen flat. "How about you dropping the Major for a start...at least for today. My mammy named me Mark," he said, hoping this time his humour would succeed, and in so doing, perhaps discourage her from asking the question again.

"Very well...Mark." The faint smile reappeared, this time a little warmer. "Oh no!" She drew closer to him. "There are some people I do my utmost to avoid, even in the most gay of occasions, but today of all days."

Glancing over her shoulder, Mark saw the reason for her distress; three elderly women converging on them.

"It was so nice to speak to someone in one's own language for a change," Myra said conspiratorially. Then as if in afterthought, asked, "Are you on duty this evening, Maj...Mark?" She read his thoughts. "Have no fears Major Stewart, we shall not be alone....Ah ladies!" she announced, and walked to meet the three old matrons.

Close on an hour passed, it was time Mark decided to make his way up to the house.

Pushing open the French windows he stepped inside, and was surprised to find that except for a few oil paintings, a long mahogany table and a few high backed chairs lining the wall, the large room was bare. He heard voices and made for an open door at the end of the room, his steps intrusively loud on the polished wooden floor.

This room, in contrast, was large and brightly lit, where tiny groups of people clutching drinks stood talking in subdued tones, his unexpected entrance turning a few heads in his direction. He stood there feeling as conspicuous as a referee wearing green at an Old Firm football match, and was on the verge of beating a less than discreet retreat when, against all reasoning, he decided to take a step or two further into the room.

Through a partially open door to his right, he caught sight of a lighted fire. He stepped closer. At that moment, Stefan Kolybin chose to step aside, and he saw the First Lady seated by the hearth. She looked up and gestured him to join them.

Poor kid Mark thought, as he stepped towards the Ante-room. By now, he must be completely exhausted, compelled to listen to some old farts extolling his late father's virtues. Late father! He almost choked.

"This is Major Mark Stewart, a countryman of mine, Stefan," Myra said by way of introduction, at Mark's entrance.

"I am pleased to make your acquaintance, sir." The boy snapped smartly to attention, inclining his head, his face colouring.

"Likewise, Naval Cadet Kolybin, or perhaps for today we could dispense with formalities?"

For a moment, the boy's features softened. He turned back to his stepmother. "If you think that is all, Myra, then I will leave you to speak to the Major," he said politely, excusing himself with a slight bow.

The room emptied, leaving them alone. "You looked surprised that Stefan should address me by my Christian name, major."

"It showed?" He sat down on a chair across from her, and thought how tired she looked. Evidently the journey back from Paris and the recent drastic events had taken there toll.

"Stefan was seven years old when the war broke out." Mark listened, unsure whether this was some kind of an explanation for her stepson's manner, or rather that she just felt like talking to someone. Myra went on. "After the Army had capitulated, Paule, with many more, took to the mountains to continue the fight. Stefan rarely saw his father from then to the Liberation." Myra paused while a servant wheeled in a tea trolley. When he had left, she took up the story. "Stefan's mother was taken by the Nazis. Stefan himself was only just saved by his uncle."

"What happened to his mother?"

"She died in a concentration camp...so I believe," she said softly, pouring out two cups of tea. She held one out to him, a little spilling into the saucer. "You can imagine the boy's feelings when his father brought me home to meet him when the war ended."

Mark declined her offer of cakes from a plate with a wave of his hand.

"The poor boy had spent five years hiding from the Nazis, not knowing whether his mother was alive or dead, or that his father had not been killed or captured." Myra put her cup and saucer down on the trolley. "Stefan's only hope..., his sole reason for living was, that some day he'd be reunited with his family."

Mark thought he should leave. The woman looked exhausted, but he felt she wanted to go on..let it all out...especially today. He stirred his tea. "How did you two meet...you and your husband?" He had heard stories, but now was his chance to hear it from her.

"We ...that is to say, a few of us nurses...I think there were four of us, and two doctors, somehow managed to get ourselves separated from the others." Myra sat back in her chair, her eyes half closed, reliving those days. "Partisans found us wandering in the foothills, just before a Nazi patrol did. They took us to Jan Tetek." She opened her eyes to gauge his reaction. "Ironic isn't it," she smiled wryly.

"The same Jan Tetek that has given us so much trouble these last years?" Mark asked.

Myra nodded. "Jan was leader of the local Communist partisans. We remained with his group for almost three months, attending to the sick and wounded. Sometimes we would go down into the villages to do what we could for them...many were close to starvation." The recollection brought back a shudder.

"Anyhow, one day a man came to our camp, he told us that his group had been badly mauled by a large body of Nazis and had suffered a great many casualties, and as they had heard that we had doctors and nurses in our camp, would Tetek allow us to help them?"

Myra sat staring into the open fire. "That is how I came to meet Paule, his group had been practically destroyed. They had lost their leader, and many of their senior officers. There were wounded everywhere." She shook her head sadly. "We did what we could for them, but without medical supplies..." she shrugged, at the futility of it all.

"We stayed on for a couple of weeks. Tetek wanted us back. We told him we were still needed where we were. He insisted. Paule confronted him...he had been elected the new group leader. There were a few heated words. I thought it might even end up with the groups fighting each other, which would inevitably end with more casualties." She gave a little grunt at the irony. "Eventually a compromise was reached, I and a doctor stayed behind."

"I fell in love with Paule. Perhaps being young, it was easy to see him as a knight in shining armour." Myra laughed to hide her embarrassment. "He was a kind man, Mark. ...Oh, I know many see him...saw him" she corrected herself, "as nothing other than a cold ruthless man, but they did not know him as I knew him."

For a time the young widow stared into the fire without speaking, reliving the past, so much so, that Mark thought she had forgotten he was still there. "I remember the day he learned the Nazis had taken away his wife. The look on his face. He knew deep down that he would not see her again. That was the day Paule Kolybin, changed."

Myra rose and walked slowly to the window. She stared out, her voice cold. "I have never seen a man driven by so much hatred, he was relentless in the pursuit of the invaders; no quarter asked, no quarter given. I think the only thing that kept him going was the thought of seeing Stefan again.

"By the time Liberation came, Paule was a national hero," Myra went on, her back to Mark. "I was still in the forces, so I had to return home. I missed him so much. When he wrote that his wife was dead, I did not know what to feel." She turned to face him. "Can you understand that? I wanted so much to be with him again, but I knew this could never be, not while his wife was still alive. Then suddenly there were no more barriers."

The woman walked back to the fire. "I came back here when I was demobbed. Paule was so pleased to see me. I believe he thought a young woman of my age would soon forget all about him and return to a safe and normal life. Now all Paule wanted was to become a shoemaker again."

Wrapped in the past, she laughed, the warmth reaching her eyes. "A shoemaker? In my wildest dreams I could never image Paule as that, not him, the daring partisan. However, the people trusted him...wanted him. Almost everyone preferred him to those government cowards who had run away at the very first shot of the War."

Myra let out a long sigh and sat down, as if suddenly tired of her narrative. "The rest...or almost all the rest you know. We were married one year later."

"And Stefan?" Mark asked quietly. "How did he take it?"

She looked at him as if just remembering how all this had started. "We came to a mutual understanding, him and me. I agreed never to attempt to take his mother's place; which was preferable in the circumstances considering my age, or that I come between him and his father."

"Has it worked?" Mark wanted to know. Then hurried to apologise. "I mean..."

Myra brushed his apology gently aside. "I should like to think it has...Speaking of Stefan...I should be attending to my guests, instead of leaving it all to him."

She rose. Walking slowly passed Mark between the settee and a small table, she stood for a moment toying with one of the miniatures. "Can you call on me again sometime, Major...Mark? It's nice to talk to someone from home."

"Do you miss it?" Mark edged round in his chair to face her.

"I wanted to go back to see my folks in York, but Paule seemed to think it would be awkward to arrange, security and all that. I don't think I'd ever thought too much about my position here until then. It's all changed of course. Now I'm just plain Mistress Myra Kolybin," she added ruefully. "I wonder when they will ask me to leave here?"

"Do you think they will?"

"I suppose so. It is the Residence of the President after all. I won't be too sorry to leave it," she shuddered. "Paule loved it. He once told me, how one day he'd come here as a boy with his father. Seemingly, this house had been the home of some prince or other, and Paule's father had made him a pair of riding boots. Apparently it was quite something to own this type of boot. The better the craftsmanship, the more pride the owner had in wearing them. When Paule told me how pleased the prince had been with the boots his father had made, his face lit up with pride. He stood there by the window," Myra nodded to where she herself had stood a short time ago. Paule said, *This* was *his* house!" She gave a little chuckle. "How his eyes shone when he said it. He said, never in his wildest dreams had he ever believed that some day he would come to live here." She put the miniature down and walked back to Mark. "He loved this place, though he could never bring himself to believe he actually lived here, he a simple shoemaker and now President of the Republic."

Myra halted in front of him look round the room, at the huge oil paintings of stern moustached men in military attire, adorning the walls. "To me it is nothing more than a colossal museum." She shuddered again.

Mark heard Stefan's voice grow nearer. He got up. "I'll try and see you again. However, I expect to be leaving shortly...to where I cannot say. You understand"?

Myra nodded. "I quite understand, Mark. Please do not leave it too long, I may decide to just up and leave, for home."

Mark tried to hide his astonishment. Here, he thought, was a situation, Paule Kolybin had not counted on. That he should come out of hiding to find his wife, believing him dead, had returned to England, to be a plain housewife. Mark smiled to himself at the thought that Myra Kolybin..nee Blackie could ever be plain, or ordinary. He looked around him at the splendour of the surroundings. No not ever again.

The temperature in the room was hot, as much from the heat of the argument as from the Samovar in the corner. For the third time that evening, the guard at the door of the flat had left his post to request them to lower their voices.

At the head of the table, Petr tucked his thumbs into his braces, and sat back in his chair, giving each of the three men an impatient glare. "Well comrades, are we anywhere near reaching a decision?"

The only one in the room not already in his shirt sleeves stood up to discard his jacket. "I am in agreement with Petr," Vaclaw said, hanging the garment over the back of his chair. "We shall never have a better opportunity than this."

"We do not have the strength to launch a city campaign, far less one out in the country. I believe it would be nothing short of suicide to attempt it," Pavel, his host, said next to him.

"Listen to the old woman," Vaclaw retorted, now more comfortable without his jacket. "It makes me wonder if you really did fight the Nazis, old man."

"No Vaclaw! You cannot say that of Pavel," Miro said angrily, coming to the rescue.

By far the youngest in the room, and here purely because Kimmo, his Section Leader, was ill, he was in awe of these men who had so gloriously fought the Nazi occupation of his country.

Here in the capital, four Sections made up one Group, of whom Petr was Group Leader, and who was also on the National Group Council of the Peoples Freedom Fighters, or PFF, so to Miro, when Petr spoke, he listened.

"If we do decide on a show of strength, what will we attack, hero, Pavel?" Vaclaw asked sarcastically as he lifed the vodka glass to his lips.

Miro's understanding of Pavel was, that prior to the war, he had left the coal mines to enlist in the International Brigade in Spain, where he had learned something about artillery and explosives, an asset that the wiry little man had put to good use during the Nazi occupation and since.

"We are so weak here in the capital, we could not organise one good snow ball fight, far less a street bombing," Vaclaw went on. Miro nodded in agreement.

Vaclaw, Miro believed, worked in a lawyer's office somewhere on the other side of the city. Petr, he guessed to be a public servant ...Always neat and tidy...hands that had not known manual work since the occupation.

Although all four had conspired together for some time, they had never met one another during the Occupation but had only come together to fight for the Communist cause after the war was over. Also, it was an unwritten law that they should not learn too much about one another for security reasons, therefore referred to one other as they did this evening by their code name.

"As yet, the northern goverment garrisons remain practically empty, as the regiments that came here to help control the crowds, and take part in Kolybin's funeral procession, have not so far returned," Pavel was saying. "When they start to do so, then will be our chance to ambush them as we did in the old days," he ended with conviction.

"You fantasise you old fool, Pavel," Vaclaw teased.

Petr crashed his fist down on the table. "Enough! Comrades enough! We must make up our minds. It is getting late and we cannot jeopardise Comrade Pavel's safety, whose hospitality we enjoy."

"I cannot be sure of anyone in this building anymore," Pavel grunted sadly.

"I think Pavel's idea, of ambushing the soldiers on their way back up north, is a good one. We must take advantage of the confusion in the Senate. Molnar is no Paule Kolybin."

"I am glad you think so, Vaclaw." Pavel half turned to look at the taller man, switching his look to the head of the table. "However, I should like to hear your opinion, Petr."

Petr took his time to answer. "The way I see it," he said, slowly measuring his words. "The Senate was totally unprepared for

Kolybin's death, and, as they believe the only remaining resistance will come from the northern mountains...a fact substantiated by sending home the foreign mercenaries; after earning their blood money." He spat out the words, "they will most probably turn their attention to the politics of appointing a new president, with all the dirt and corruption that entails," he sneered. "Therefore, I would suggest while the attention of those honourable gentlemen are elsewhere, we give them something else to think about."

Halting for effect, Petr looked at each one individually. "They think we are finished, comrades," he began, "incapable of even capturing a street! Let us prove them wrong. Shake them all the way to the very roots of their corrupt foundations. Let us not capture a street, but a city, comrades! A town!" Petr beamed at the looks of disbelief written on each face. "Yes comrades, a town! The coastal city of Pienera! Think of it comrades! If we capture that city, we also hold a fine port. Can you imagine the effect that would have on the entire country? Besides sending the Senate into a panic! I believe Tetek could do it for us. By the time the Government forces here in the Capital are organised, Tetek could be down off the mountains."

"Yes! Yes!" Pavel cried. Then realising how loudly he had shouted, put a hand across his mouth. "Sorry," he apologised, his eyes sparkling. "The garrison closest to Pienera will still be undermanned, as will the city itself!" he enthused.

"Is it settled? Do we have an agreement?" Petr asked, casting a look around, daring anyone to disagree. "Shall we recommend to National Council, that Comrade Tetek, attack, capture and hold Pienera?" Three heads nodded in agreement.

Satisfied he had achieved what he had originally hoped for prior to the meeting, Petr sat back. And when we have it, he though to himself, where will we go from there?

They left Pavel's flat at discreet intervals, until only Petr and Pavel were left. Pavel pushed a glass of Vodka across the table. "What worries you old friend?" he quietly asked. "You have been preoccupied since you first got here, and I do not think it is about our attacking Pienera."

Petr ran a finger around the rim of his glass. "You are correct, Pavel. You heard each one deny having sanctioned, or being in any way involved in Kolybin's assassination."

Pavel remained silent, waiting for his friend to go on, unburden himself of his fears.

Petr stared across the table into the Samovar. "Should it have been any of the young people in one of our Sections, I am sure we would have known by now, they could not have kept their pleasure, or their pride at what they had done, hidden for long."

"They, Petr? You say they."

Petr sipped his drink. "It could not have been the work of one man alone. I have discovered through our people in the Caserne, that the bombing of a car immediately prior to Kolybin's arrival at the Opera House, was merely a diversion, in order to leave that particular street unguarded. The ruse worked. Therefore, it stands to reason that more than one man was involved."

Pavel rubbed his nose. "And the weapon?"

Petr pushed his glass towards the vodka bottle. Pavel poured him another drink. "Russian. The same type as most of our own people use."

"Then we are no closer to finding out."

"No. And if it is any of our people...A cell within one of our Sections, what is their next objective? Perhaps next time it will not be one of them, perhaps one of us."

Shocked, Pavel silently watched his old friend down his drink.

Chapter 4

Stefan Kolybin was almost outside the Opera House before he realised why so many people were gathered around its entrance. An old woman stepped awkwardly between the rows of flowers that covered the steps on her way down to the pavement. He put out his hand to help her, and she thanked him without looking up.

Glad that he had not been recognised, he stepped on to the bottom step where a tiny wreath lay at his feet. It read 'Paule Kolybin, always one of the people. You will be sadly missed'. On the next row of steps, the sentiments were the same. He felt a lump in his throat and looked away from the wreaths to give himself time to regain his composure, as it would never do for the son of this country's greatest hero to be caught crying. Moved by the extent of the floral tribute to his father, he walked up a few more steps.

He could never hope to emulate him. Just when he was beginning to understand the passion his father had had for his country, he had been gunned down, ironically by one of his own people.

As a child he had cried when his uncle had told him what had happened to his mother, and had consoled himself in the childish belief that his father would find her and bring her home again. Instead? He had found a woman ...a foreign woman, to take her place.

In the first year of Liberation, between politics and his new bride, his father had very little time for him, just when he needed him most. To be fair, now that he was a little older, he had come to realise in retrospect the magnitude of the task that had befallen his father. The man was no politician, only a simple shoemaker. Yet, despite the seemingly insurmountable difficulties that had confronted him, he had succeeded in uniting the country... at least partially.

His father had loved him, this he knew by the deep concern he had for his safety, which, is why he had suggested he enlist in the Navy, instead of the Army. A suggestion which he had at first rejected, then, not wishing to cause his father additional worries, had accepted. Now, he was glad he had.

Stefan was almost on the concourse before he was aware of colliding with a young girl dressed in a nurse's uniform on her way down.

"I am sorry. It was entirely my fault," he apologized, knowing as he helped her regain her balance that she had recognised him. He shot a quick look around in the hope no one else had noticed, then back at the girl.

"It was up there that it happened. Did you know?"

Stefan looked up to where the girl had pointed. He climbed the last step to the concourse, the girl by his side to where a half dozen or so wreaths lay where his father had been struck down.

"It was there," the girl said.

Stefan looked down at the spot. What final thoughts had run through his father's mind as he lay there dying? Were they thoughts of him? Or of his stepmother? Or of his country, at having left so much undone? This he would never know.

"There was a doctor. I tried to help, but he just pushed me away, even when I told him I was a nurse."

Stefan turned to look at the girl, as if seeing her for the first time. He cleared his throat, not knowing how to ask the question of someone he did not know. "Was my father still alive?"

"I believe so. But as I said, this doctor had them pull me away. I thought he would have been grateful for any assistance at all."

"Thank you for telling me. I wanted to come here...to see for myself," he said, softly.

"I understand."

She was lovely, he thought, and the nurse's uniform suited her. He saw her study him and hoped she approved, and while part of his mind was still full of rushing thoughts of his father, another part was seeking refuge to be with someone his own age. On an impulse, he asked, "Perhaps you could find more time to tell me about..." He indicated the concourse. "Are you off duty? I should like to take you for a cup of coffee, or something, if there is a cafe around here?"

"Would it make matters simpler if I said yes to all three of your questions?" she suggested, feeling drawn to this shy, awkward young man, despite a small voice from within, reminding her that this was the son of their country's late president.

Stefan wrinkled his brows, thinking upon the girl's answer. "Oh good! Except...."

She took his arm, guiding him down the steps. "Not to worry, just follow me."

"I will gladly, if I knew who I was following."

She squeezed his arm, as if she had known him all her young life. "My name is Indra Staron, and you, I know, are, Stefan Kolybin."

He looked puzzled. "How did you know that?"

Indra shrugged giving him a tiny smile. "There was a photograph in a newspaper of you and..." She hesitated not knowing whether to say father or president.

"...my father?" he ventured. She nodded.

Four streets on, the fashionable area of the Opera House left behind, Indra guided him passed the shells of several bombed out buildings and on to a narrow cobbled street. She saw him look curiously at the few quaint shops on the opposite side of the street, and guessed he had never been in this part of the city before.

"The cafe is down there." She indicated the direction with a slight movement of her hand. "You have never been here before, have you?"

"No," he said, looking around him.

"Then you are in for a special treat, this cafe makes the best strudel in town."

There were six tables in the cafe, two of which were occupied: one, by two students deep in heated debate over some obscure political policy, the other by an elderly couple seated near the window.

"How are you today, Mister and Mistress Hafner?" Indra asked politely of the old couple, leading Stefan passed them to a table in a corner.

"Very well, thank you, Indra," the woman answered warmly, her eyes on Indra's young man as he sat down.

Stefan bent across the table. "She knows my face, but does not know where she has seen me before," he whispered, shrinking into his greatcoat.

"Do not worry; Mistress Hafner sometimes has trouble remembering where she has seen Mister Hafner before," she whispered back.

Stefan drew back laughing. Indra joined in, happy that she had made him forget his grief, even for a little while.

They had coffee and ate the cafe's famous strudel. Stefan spoke to Indra about his father, and in so doing, the telling of it helped to ease the pain. Somehow he had the feeling that she knew it too.

He poured out more coffee and saw her look up at the clock on the wall. "I am sorry, I must be boring you," he apologised.

Indra shook her head, her cup at her lips. "No. Not at all," she assured him. "But mother will be wondering where I have got to. You know what mother's are like. How they worry over practically nothing at all." She placed her cup carefully in the saucer.

Stefan would have liked to have said that he wished that he did, but said nothing. Instead, he got up, helped her on with her coat and paid the bill.

They walked backed to the corner. "Do you think you can find your way back from here?" she asked.

"Oh, I think so. Should I get lost I can always navigate by the stars...if and when they come out," he chuckled. "After all I am a navel cadet. However, should I flounder, Indra Staron, will you come to my rescue?" he asked, amused.

Indra thought how much he looked like his father, with his jet black hair and hazel brown eyes. Eyes that now held a sparkle that had not been there when first they met. "If you want me to?"

"Spendid! I will try to get away tomorrow. It is easier now." His voice faded as he realised he had been about to say, now that I am no longer the son of a president. Aloud he asked, "Will you meet me tomorrow, same time, same place?" His voice rose in hope.

"Yes I will." The young nurse smiled broadly.

It was more than he dared have expected. "Then I must certainly pay attention to my navigation for the return voyage." He took a few paces away, then turned as if in afterthought. "Please give my regards to you mother. Tell her not to worry should you be a trifle late tomorrow."

"That I shall, Stefan," she answered, unable to keep the gaiety out of her voice.

They both waved their farewells. She, unable to believe she had spent the afternoon with the son of Paule Kolybin, who lived up in the Kasel. He, that he was in love with a beautiful young nurse from a part of the city he did not know, and who, for a short while had helped make the pain more bearable.

Miro left Pavel's flat elated by the thought that not all was lost, and that years of self denial had not altogether been wasted. They were going to take a *town*! Take a town and hold it in the name of the

PFF just when the entire country believed them to be totally defeated.

Miro nodded cheerfully to a passer by, who gave him a look, suggesting he was mad, and he returning a look suggesting he was not. He was that happy.

Light spilled out from the delicatessen on the corner. He would buy a bottle of that red wine, Kirsty, his wife, liked so much. It would go down well with his news at supper.

Dear Kirsty, he thought, remembering when he, Gerd Brovwers, code name Miro, had first met Krystyna Kaarels.

Gerd took the cog out of the vice, and examined it, then flashed a quick look at the clock on the factory wall. Eleven fifty it read, ten minutes to go, on this Saturday morning.

His friend Fiebo came up behind him, and slapped him on the back. "Well old buddy, old friend, how many goals do you think we will win by today?" he asked, happily.

Gerd puffed out his cheeks in mock disdain, replacing the cog in the vice. "Who is to say we will win? Especially with the centre forward we've got!"

"Would you care to venture a small wager on it pal of mine?" Fiebo inquired, ignoring the inference to himself as centre forward.

"I should not like to take your hard earned money, Mister Cocksure."

"Enough of this banter!" The exclamation came from a tall, slim, young man, crossing the floor to join them. "This is no way to ginger yourself up before a match, especially this match!" Laughing, the two swilled round to face their friend.

Karl Tanttu, threw his hands in the air. "Five more minutes and we are out of this palace of charm until Monday!" He grew serious. "Oh how I will miss it 'til then."

"You could stay on, if it means so much to you, Karl. You wouldn't miss much," Gerd suggested, deadpan.

"Watch it pal," Fiebo warned, as the sound of the factory horn terminated further raillery.

"See you both at the match!" Gerd gave Fiebo a quick slap on the back, and hurried off to collect his bicycle from the yard.

On the way home, Gerd narrowly missed a car as he turned the corner, both driver and rider leaving their respective rude pejoratives hanging in the air as they continued on their separate ways.

Passing the bombed out buildings, Gerd crossed the derelict wasteland to his own street: a single row of two storeyed houses, mercifully or miraculously missed, courtesy of the late Luftwaffe.

His mother looked up from where she was stirring a pot on the fire as her son entered the scullery. "Going to the match today, I expect?" The inference in the woman's voice implying she should have known better than to have asked.

Gerd turned on the water tap, shivering a little as the cold water hit his hands. "Yip. Should be a good game. If we win today, we're through to the semi-finals," he answered, referring to his factory team.

"I expect you'll be going to the Villamy after the game as usual?" his mother said, resignedly.

"I suppose so. Celebrate if we win; drown our sorrows if we lose."

Gerd splashed icy water on his face, rinsing himself with his eyes shut tight against the soap suds, and groped for the towel that hung beneath the sink. In the background the muffled voice of his mother muttering something about there only being potatoes and cabbage for dinner and that meat had gone up in price again. The only thing, she said, that ever did come down in the country was rain.

Gerd put the towel back on its nail, and leaned forward to look out of the window at the sound of the excited shouts from the small boys on the nearby wasteland who were completely engrossed in their own important football game. Suddenly, the ball took a deflection off one of the young defenders and smashed against the window.

"What was that?" his mother cried, hurrying back to the scullery. "Those damned boys and their football games!"

"No harm done, mother," Gerd grinned, giving a friendly wave to the little boy delegated to retrieve the ball.

Kids! he thought. He knew them all. The little sandy haired one, who'd come for the ball, was the son of Matti Marfelt, a local policeman, who lived four doors away. The War had been over for almost four years, and still there was not much for them to look forward to, Gerd thought sadly. There never would be any prospects for them with this lot of corrupt capitalists' politicians in power. With an abject shake of his head, he turned for the kitchen.

Gerd halted at the corner of the street to look back at his house. It was a ritual he'd adopted every time he left on a 'mission'. His thoughts that it could very well be for the last time. Should he be caught or killed, it would be his mother who would suffer. He tried to put the inconceivable thought from his mind. What would she do? She would have to leave the neighbourhood. But to where? And how would she live?

He had always given her a little something extra from his wages when leaving on a mission. A Penitence, a sort of talisman against his being caught.

His mother, he knew, usually went over to her sister's on a Saturday night to listen to the radio, and have a game or two of cards. It was something she had done since his father's premature death from the after effects of five years in a concentration camp. Gerd sighed. Poor mother, if only she knew that it was a different sort of ball game *he* was going to, on this chilly March Saturday afternoon.

A half hour later Gerd jumped off the tram, crossed the road and walked briskly up the overgrown lane to the derelict church beyond. This was an important mission Petr had given him, as Kimmo, his Section Leader was to lead the remainder of his Section on another mission out of town that same afternoon. Although, he quietly suspected that Petr had some misgivings as regards Kimmo having the ability to carry out such a mission.

He was late. Kimmo threw him a stare as cold as the crypt around which the three men and the girl now stood.

"Your train leaves in twenty minutes, so I'll be brief." Kimmo looked at each in turn. "As you can see, we have a new member present." He halted to let them acknowledge the auburn haired girl.

Gerd took in the neat figure dressed in a brown skirt and jacket, and guessed she would be in her mid twenties, looking lovely but scared. And who could blame her? "And who, for obvious reasons," Kimmo went on, "has been code named Henna." The encouraging smile he gave her rapidly disappeared as he turned his attention back to the men. "She has been fully briefed in today's mission, so there will be no need to add anything further. The sooner we disperse the better, as I must look to my own section."

"Miro," Kimmo referred to Gerd by his code name, "take two pistols and ammunition from the usual place, one for you and Hainz. You will take Henna with you. She knows what to do. The three of you will travel on the two twenty seven, outbound; the usual precautions, single tickets only. Any questions?"

"Who's my ringer?" Gerd, now Miro asked, referring to his stand - in at the football match, who would report to him later of any incidents he should be expected to know and comment about when he, Gerd, and most of the team met in the Villamy Bistro after the game. The rest of the company found something else to do with their eyes while he asked the question. Only Kimmo understood what he meant. "I'm afraid we have not got anyone left to take your place," he said abruptly.

"Chri...!" Miro thought. He had a bad feeling about this mission. A new operative, who looked as if she had already peed herself, and that shit head, Hainz, who had still not made up his mind if he was George Raft,from the American movies, or Al Capone. And now, no ringer! And he fully expected that there would be no lack of incidents at this football match...both on and off the field. Miro bit his lip. He would have to come up with some excuse for not being there to wish the players well as he usually did before the match. Also, it was to be hoped the crowd would be big enough that he would not be missed during the match.

"You'll carry it off, Miro," Kimmo assured him. "Just improvise. I'm told you know the ropes."

"As the priest said to the bellringer," Miro muttered under his breath.

Miro stared out of the compartment window. The passing countryside was nothing more than a blur as he went over the mission step by step for the hundredth time.

A decision had been taken, that the elderly judge who had sentenced to death three of their comrades should himself pay the price. This, it was hoped would not only act as a warning to others, but also to demonstrate that no one was out with the reach and vengeance of the PFF.

God only knew why they had not yet been caught, when he had to associate with 'Tram Ticket' soldiers like Hainz.

'Tram Ticket soldiers', Miro reflected was the term applied to those who had fought the Nazi occupation from the comfort of their own homes, who unlike himself had given up his, to fight in the mountains.

Hainz winked across at Henna sitting opposite him. "Won't be long now. You'll be all right, just do as we say. The first one's always the worst." He looked across at Miro who threw him a look of contempt which he deliberately ignored with a laugh, and winked once more at the girl.

They alighted at a countryside station about thirty kilometres from the capital. The dark clouds scudding across the sky matched Miro's mood of foreboding. It would rain soon, he told himself.

Hainz linked their arms, and together they trotted down the station steps, the symbol of three happy young people returning home for the weekend. Only Hainz's laughter, was genuine.

Miro did not feel like laughing. Everything depended on the girl playing her part well. And to compound it all, this was her first time in the field. Why had Kimmo insisted on her going? After all, it was an important mission.

At the bottom of the steps they let go of one another. "The car should be about half a kilometre down the road," Miro said to the girl, trying to sound cheerful, as if he did this every day of his life. "You know what to do? Don't you?"

"Yes," she nodded. It was only the second time she had spoken since boarding the train.

"The old judge comes home every Friday night," Miro explained, "there should only be him and his wife in the house, plus a butler-manservant, whatever they call him, and a cook."

"Yes I know, I was briefed, too, you know."

"Sorry," he apologised, and saw her relax a little.

They rounded a bend on the quiet country road, to where a black car was parked in front of a farmer's gate. The driver, a stocky little man of indeterminate age got out as they drew near. "I judge it could rain," he greeted them, running an eye over all three.

"Hanged if it will," Miro responded, feeling foolish over the choice of passwords.

The driver's face softened. "Jump in. I'll take you up a side track 'till it's time."

Hainz took the girl's arm, and with a mock bow opened the back door of the car.

Shit, Miro seethed, it's time I put this arse hole in his place and remind him, who is in charge of this mission.

They drove down the deserted road for about a kilometre before stopping. The adept driver reversed onto what was little more than a track, before finally bumping to halt about a hundred metres from the road.

Miro turned in the front seat to face the two occupants in the back, but addressed himself mainly to the driver. "The house should be a little way down the main road from here, if I have been briefed correctly."

The driver nodded, pulling at the fingers of his glove. "Around half a kilometre on the left, I should say. It stands on its own grounds about fifty metres back from the road."

"Our train leaves at five eleven," Miro continued. "We shall give ourselves ten minutes to do the job and get back to the car."

"I'll have the car waiting this side of the house." The driver draped a glove over the steering wheel, and sat back in his seat.

Hainz bent forward. "Have the engine revved up, driver," he snorted, "'cause, when we come out of there, we won't want to hang around. Okay?"

"I think the man already knows that," Miro replied angrily, at the look of annoyance on the stocky man's face. "As I was saying, that should give us twenty minutes to where you will drop us off about…"

"Just this side of the bend before the station," the driver suggested. "Hopefully, that way, no one should associate you with the car, should you be seen entering the station."

"Sounds all right to me," Miro went on. "Should everything go according to plan, we'll reach the station about five minutes before the train arrives. This will give us just about enough time to collect our tickets without having to wait around too long. That's just about it." He turned round in his seat to the face the window. "We'll allow ourselves another half hour, before we start getting ourselves ready."

Miro looked at his watch. "It's time." His voice broke the silence. Beside him, the driver pushed open the door and walked to the back of the car, and opened the boot as the rest got out.

Wordlessly, he handed Henna a pair of torn stockings, who, taking them, put a foot on the running board, and pulled up her skirt. Hainz gave a low whistle and pushed back his Fedora. "Enjoying the scenery, are you?" The girl swung sharply to face him.

"Don't you have something better to do?" Miro hurled at him angrily, embarrassed for the girl.

"Nope," Hainz replied, grinning broadly.

"Then have the decency to turn your back."

"Or the stupidity," Hainz grinned, turning round.

Miro glared at Hainz's back. Why, he thought, did he let this cocky bastard standing there dressed like some American gangster, so easily rile him? Why didn't Kimmo demand that he dress less conspicuously? Why had he himself not demanded it as mission leader? Could it be that he was jealous of Hainz and his good looks? Or was it his ability to afford clothes that he himself could not? Self consciously, Miro took in his own sombre well worn attire of black jacket and trousers. At least he wouldn't stand out in a crowd. The thought led him to think of the football match. Why was he here at all? When, at this very moment most of his countrymen - and women, were no doubt enjoying a weekend doing, what most decent people should be doing. He sighed. God help us, if this is all for nothing.

"Put this on dearie." The driver's voice interrupted Miro's thoughts. The girl stepped into the long brown coat he had handed her. "Is this your first time?" he asked sympathetically, noticing how her hands had shaken when fastening the coat.

"Not with a figure like that!" Hainz guffawed.

"In that case you'll still be a virgin!" Henna flashed back at him.

Taken aback by the girl's quick retort, Miro and the driver let out a laugh.

"Well said, dearie," the driver chortled. "However," his voice grew serious, "now for the hard part. And no wisecracks from you," he warned Hainz.

Sitting the girl down on the running board of the car, the driver took a handkerchief and a medium sized bottle from his pocket. Opening the bottle, he poured a little of the red liquid onto the cloth.

"Whew!" Hainz drew back, holding his nose. "What foul smelling shit is that?"

"Fowl's the right word, smart arse." The driver dabbed the girl's cheek. "Considering it came from a chicken." He bent over the girl, and poured some of the obnoxious red liquid down her leg where the flesh showed through her torn stocking. Henna gave a little shiver.

"You all right?" Miro asked, concern in his voice. The entire mission rested on her.

She gave a nod. "It's just the smell."

"Shall I get Hainz to move away?" The driver laughed.

"Very funny," Hainz retorted, moving away from the car. Humiliated, he took out his pistol and made an elaborate show of checking it for the girl's benefit.

Miro stepped to the car. "Enough! Lets go." He had let the banter go on long enough, though, it was as good a way as any to block out what they were about to do.

Once in the car, the driver drove them to within a hundred metres of where the big house stood back from the road.

Miro snapped a look at his watch in the gathering darkness. "We're bang on time. Once you've done your job, Henna, get yourself back down here as quick as you can. Start changing straight away. The driver will help you clean the blood. But should anything go wrong with us," he jerked his head in the direction of the house, "get the hell out of here."

Although no one spoke, Miro knew they understood what he meant. He let out a deep breath. "Then let's do what we came to do."

They kept to the bushes all the way up the drive, ducking under the windows, where upon reaching the house, Henna made for the front door. She took a quick frightened look at the two men flattened against the wall, each with a pistol in his hand, and took a grip of the door knocker.

Miro nodded his encouragement from behind his mask and Henna tapped on the door.

"You're supposed to be hurt. Bang the bloody thing," he snarled at her, now fully convinced his misgiving had been right all along. She was no good for the job. How had Section the audacity to choose her?

Henna bit her lip. Grasping the brass knocker tighter, she started rattling, screaming and kicking at the door, her sudden unexpected performance drawing surprised looks from both her accomplices.

"Well I never!" Miro whistled softly. The girl was putting on a good act. Though by the look of sheer terror on her face, how much was acting?

At last the door opened fractionally and the face of an elderly woman appeared at the slit.

"Please help me! Oh please help me!" Henna pleaded, taking a step closer to the chained door. "I ....we've been in a car accident..." She threw a hand in the direction of the road. "My husband's still in the car...he needs a doctor!"

Undecided as what to do, the woman stared back at her.

"Have you a phone I can use? Please! Please help!" Henna begged, collapsing against the door jamb. "If you don't want me to come inside, please phone for a doctor or an ambulance. I'll wait out here."

"Oh you poor child!" the woman cried , unlatching the door.

Even as the chain fell away, both men had rushed passed the girl, Hainz, pushing the elderly screaming woman towards a door at the end of the long hallway.

Miro smelled floor polish and varnish, and almost knocked over a plant that stood in a corner in his haste to reach the door on his left, which according to his information was where the old judge and his wife should be dining.

Savagely twisting at the handle, he flung the door wide and rushed inside, drawing up in horror, for, instead of only the predicted old couple, the room was full of people seated round the dinner table.

His eyes a mixture of horror and surprise a small boy looked up at him. Next to him, a woman, who Miro took to be his mother, leaped up, a hand held over her mouth to stifle a scream.

Miro swung to the judge, pointing his pistol at the grey head, unable to bring himself to fire for fear of hitting the gurgling infant bouncing on the old man's knee, its tiny hands pumping up and down with excitement at this unexpected intrusion. Miro gulped, he had only a few seconds to decide what to do before they were out of here.

Beside the judge, the old woman dropped her knife and fork with a clang. the child's mother rounding the table to rescue her offspring.

Miro felt a push at his shoulder and suddenly the room reverberated with the sound of gunshots. The old judge's head disintegrated in a mass of flesh and bone, blood spilling over the tiny child and the old woman.

Hainz took a step closer, emptying his pistol before Miro could stop him.

"Enough! Enough you moron!" Miro screamed, savagely hauling Hainz from the room. The cold hard stare in the old judge's eyes before he died imbedded in his mind.

Together they bolted out of the house, the gravel driveway crunching beneath their feet as they ran. "You're a f...' mad man Hainz!" Miro gasped at him, and in return heard the younger man's shrill insane laughter fill the night air.

They reached the car and threw themselves into the back, slamming the doors behind them. "Did you get him?" The driver threw at them, accelerating away.

"Get *him*?" Hainz roared with delight. "We got the whole f' lot of them!"

"Shut up, idiot! And don't exaggerate!" Miro snapped. "The less they know, the better."

Sitting between the two men, Henna curled up the torn stockings into a ball until her knuckles were white, unwilling to ask what had happened back at the house.

"Too late for the show, are we?" Hainz sniggered, pointing at the stockings.

"Give me a break you obnoxious little man!" Henna spat at him, unable to believe what this madman used for a brain. Clearly not all had gone to plan back there. Yet here was this moron, who was evidently enjoying himself, trying to act the great lover.

"Language, language," Hainz scolded her.

"That's enough, Hainz!" Miro stormed. "Did you get the phone?"

"Sure. But you didn't tell me there two phones. The old girl who answered the door ...Wasn't it suppose to be the butler who did that?" Hainz broke off to ask sarcastically. "She gave me some strife. Wouldn't stop howling about how it was her fault she had let us in. Anyhow, I pulled out the phone and I was on my way back when I heard someone on another one."

The car skidded round a corner, Hainz gripped the seat in front of him. "It was the old butler. I knew I was too late to stop him, so I hurried to tell you." Hainz sat back as the car righted itself. "Only to find you standing pointing that thing in your hand like some virgin who didn't know what to do with it," he sniggered.

Miro ignored the intentional sarcasm. "So they've probably got through to the police by now."

"You want me to drive to the next town?" The driver broke in, revving up another gear.

"No I don't think that's a good idea." Miro stared out of the side window. He needed time to think and put Hainz's actions out of his mind: force himself to focus on the present situation. "My guess is, they'll be on the lookout for at least two men and a girl." He leaned forward and touched the driver gently on the shoulder. "You'll be safer on your own."

Out of the darkness, a car travelled towards them, and for a moment everyone tensed, waiting for it to draw closer. Their sighs of relief were clearly audible when it rushed past.

Miro started again. "Drop us off at the spot you had decided earlier. We've got about...." He held up the watch to his eyes, peering at it in the semi darkness of the car.

"Fifteen minutes," Henna informed him.

"Thanks Henna. You had better get rid of the bottle, stockings and coat just in case you are stopped."

"I've already thrown away the bottle," the driver acknowledged.

"Good. We'll dump the rest."

"We're almost there." The driver turned his head slightly. "You all set back there?" He pulled up a little way beyond the bend. "Best of luck to you all. I won't hang about if you don't mind."

They got out of the car and the driver gave them a brief wave as he drove off.

"Now we are on our own," Hainz winked at the girl, and threw the shoes and tattered stockings over a hedge.

"Hainz," Miro said sternly, growing more impatient by the minute and vowing never to let this braggadocio come on a mission with him again. "You go into the station first. Just buy a ticket for yourself. Henna will come in later." The girl nodded that she understood as she pulled on her own coat and threw the long brown one over the hedge. "We'll all keep clear of one another. Okay?"

Five minutes later, Miro stood on the dimly lit platform, cursing the unpunctuality of their appointed train. A little way down the platform, Hainz stood casually smoking a cigarette. Somewhere between them Henna sat hidden behind her evening newspaper.

Miro glanced impatiently at his watch. Was this it? Was this to be their undoing? Caught because of a late train?

Out of the growing darkness came the distant sound of a police siren. Miro saw Henna look in his direction, awaiting his reaction. He turned away at the same time as the train came chugging round the bend, engulfing them all in smoke as it drew to a halt. Then above the clatter of carriage doors as people rushed past, the distinct sound of the siren drawing closer.

Miro stepped up into the corridor ignoring Hainz and Henna squeezing past him. He stood there, his eyes on the station entrance, waiting inevitably for the blue uniforms to appear. He was not disappointed. As the train jolted to a start, the first of the three policemen appeared on the platform. Involuntarily Miro drew back from the window, and strode quickly down the corridor.

Hainz and Henna sat opposite one another in an empty compartment, Miro slid back the door and sat down. "I think the police know we are on this train. Hainz! You get off at the next halt. Henna and I will do the same at the next station, and make our way back to the capital from there." Hainz nodded. "And Hainz, I should stuff that hat in your pocket, if I were you."

For a moment Miro thought the man was about to refuse, then Hainz gave a smile and an exaggerated shrug. "Okay." He stood up. "See you both back in town." He stepped out into the corridor, turned and leaned back into the compartment. "...And Miro," he winked, "don't do anything I wouldn't do. Okay?"

"That should give me plenty of scope," Miro retorted. "Now bugger off."

It was fully twenty minutes before they reached the next station. Miro took Henna's hand and led her to the ticket barrier, his eyes darting everywhere for any sign of a uniform.

They reached the barrier and Miro held out both tickets to the old ticket collector, who punched them and was about to let them pass when he glanced at the tickets again.

"Why are you getting off here? These tickets are to Zaltx" he asked suspiciously, holding up the offending items in front of Miro as if they were obscene. Henna moved on a step.

Miro hoped she was not about to run. "Women! I was all ready to see that Yankee movie, Gone With the Wind. I had looked forward to seeing it all week. . Then *she* .

"Miro gestured angrily at Henna," decided she wanted to visit her mother."

"That's women for you son," the old man commiserated with a shake of his head, and stood aside to let Miro pass.

"Must you tell everyone?" Henna stormed at him in mock anger, swinging on her heel to hurry off. Shouting his apologies, Miro hurried after her.

"That was good thinking back there."

"You didn't do too badly yourself." Miro returned the compliment, setting down his glass of beer. It would be twenty minutes before the next bus to the Capital.

"What now?" Henna looked across the bistro table at him. "I mean when we get home."

Behind them a group of rowdy students were challenging one another to a beer swilling competition. Miro swung round, holding up his own glass in pretence of enjoying the fun. He turned back to face the girl. "We have to go to the Villamy. You know the Villamy, don't you?"

Henna nodded. "What do you mean we?"

"I need you as an alibi, and to show you off as my girl friend. I should have been there by now, getting drunk and making a fool of myself with another dozen or so drunken football bums. Now I don't even know the score."

Henna ran a finger round the rim of her glass. "I see."

"Of course you'll have to tell me your real name, or something other than just Henna."

The girl smiled.

"What's so funny?" Miro asked, a little annoyed that she should find the situation so amusing, when at any moment they could be arrested. He dared not think of what would happen to them after this night's work, if they were.

"It's only how romantic you are as a boy friend, that's all." She gave a little laugh.

Miro scratched his head. "Sorry."

God! This girl was too nice, too innocent for this sort of work. "How did you come to get yourself involved in this?" he asked, and was suddenly afraid of her answer.

"Don't you mean what is a nice girl like me doing in a place like this as they say in the movies? Or something to that effect."

Now she seemed more relaxed, and it was he who was feeling decidedly jumpy. "Something like that." He took a sip of his beer. "But if you'll take my advice, you'll quit while you're ahead." He saw a flash of anger reach her eyes, and twin spots of red, colour her cheeks.

"You mean you didn't think I could get you into the house?" Then sharply before he had time to answer. "What did happen back there?"

"You don't want to know."

"I'd rather hear the real story from you than the newspaper version."

Miro shrugged. She was right of course. But did it have to be now?

He told her briefly what had happened, or what he thought had happened, although he was still not quite sure himself.

"So it was really that fool Hainz's fault?" All her anger seemed to have left her as she digested the ramifications of her fellow conspirator.

Miro shook his head. "Section...in fact Group won't see it that way. I was in charge of the mission, and therefore responsible for what took place."

"But that's unfair!"

"Perhaps, but that's the way it is," Miro sighed, though he could not help wondering what the papers would make of it. Neither could he get the little baby out of his mind. Had Hainz hit the child? Good God he hoped not, and not only for the child's sake.

The bus came. They talked all the way to the city, exchanging names as a matter of necessity. Both man and woman were more at ease with one another now that it was all over, or almost so.

Miro replaced the gun in its hiding place. Then they made their way along the crowded street, mingling with the Saturday night revellers and cinema goers, until they reached the Villamy.

The place thronged. Miro took the girl by the hand and fought a way through the smoke and crush of shouting people to where Fiebo stood on a table, a giant jug of beer clasped in his hand. All around him his fellow work mates, shouting and singing and looking up at him in drunken admiration.

Through his drunken haze Fiebo saw Miro, and then the girl, and let out a whoop of joy. "Were we not terrific, Gerd?" he bawled down at him. "Two, one!"

"Well at least I know the score," Miro said, out of the corner of his mouth to the girl. "At least it's a start."

"What did you think of my goal, Gerd?" Karl shouted through Fiebo's legs.

"I must remember to call you, Gerd," Henna whispered.

"That's why I insisted we tell one another our real names on the bus." He switched again to his friend, and gave him the thumbs up. "Not as good a goal as Fiebo's!" he shouted back.

"I didn't score you ignoramus!" Fiebo hurled down at him.

Henna's hand tightened on his. "You didn't?" Miro hurled back. "Then who scored for the other side?" All around, his friends whooped with laughter at his joke.

Fiebo jumped down off the table. "Great game. Great game. The second was the best. What about that tackle I-."

"All right, Fiebo, you were magic as usual. But I want you to meet my girl!" Gerd gripped his friend by the shoulder. "Krystyna, meet my very good friend but not so good footballer, Fiebo."

"Jealousy will get you no where, pal of mine," Fiebo grinned, his eyes roaming over Krystyna. "Well it's about time too. I thought you were seriously thinking about becoming a monk, pal." He leaned towards the girl. "You have my condolences," he whispered in her ear, loud enough for Gerd to hear.

"Thank you kind sir," Krystyna laughed.

Fiebo tried hard to focus on the girl, and failing, he took a swig of his beer. "However, sweet damsel, should you at any time wish to call on me personally..." He made an attempt to offer a deep bow but his friend had to help to steady him.

"He's been reading the three musketeers again," Gerd winced. "Come on Krystyna, let's get out of here before he wants to sword fight as well." He took the girl's hand and drew her in the direction of the door.

"See you tomorrow, you lucky sod!" Fiebo shouted after him, above the din.

"Sorry about that," Gerd apologised, holding the door open to let another couple enter.

"Sorry for what?" The girl smiled at him. "I think your friend's quite nice. Pity we couldn't wait for a drink."

Gerd looked startled. "I didn't… I mean.." He gestured back at the tavern.

"It's all right, I must get home anyway."

"At least let me thank you for coming in with me. It saved me trying to piece together what happened at the game today. Hopefully, by Monday, they will have forgotten half of it themselves."

"You are not going back to join your friends?" Krystyna asked, wrinkling her brows.

"Now, what sort of a boyfriend would I be to do a think like that? No. Besides, I'd rather see you home."

Krystyna blushed. "Thank you. But is that not against the rules?"

"I suppose so, should you mean to carry on with this lark. Somehow I don't think you should."

The girl's eyes narrowed angrily. "You mean I'm no good as an operative. It's people like Hainz you prefer? Killers!"

Here we go again, Gerd thought. How quick this girl was to change. He had not meant to insult her, only to save her ever having to go through this kind of thing again. He waved a hand in explanation. "No. I didn't mean that. Hainz is a shi.. a brainless idiot:much too ready with a gun."

He took her gently by the arm, and steered her away from the door of the Villamy. "Make this your last mission. Take the chance to lead a normal life. Don't live in fear of every knock on the door. Or always having to wonder, if you have given yourself away by what you may have said, or what someone else may have said."

"But I believe in the cause," Krystyna interrupted him, her voice pleading. She stepped away from him turning to stare up into his face. "I must do something to help!" she said in desperation.

Gerd took her hand, and they started in the direction of the tram stop. "You can. There are other ways; every way as vital." He saw her give him a sideways glance. Was she about to turn and berate him for being so patronising? To his relief, she slowly nodded her head. "That way," he said, "I could call on you... at home."

"Be your alibi ...my boyfriend?" she asked cheekily.

"I asked for that, didn't I ?" Gerd blushed. "No. Leaving all things aside, I would like to see you again."

"Well in that case, I think I should like that too."

And that is how it had all started, Gerd alias Miro thought.

Chapter 5

Gerd went into the delicatessen, chose the wine, exchanged a few words with the old man behind the counter and left.

The evening had grown cold; he turned up his coat collar. It would be nice to be home, and sit by the fire. The house was much better than the one they had moved into after their marriage, neither of them having wanted to live with their respective parents.

Krysty, as he called his wife, had known he had been worried about how his mother would survive financially without his wage, and had suggested he still help her, as they were both working and could afford to give her a little 'something' every week. Dear Krysty, she deserved better. How had she ever put up with him, always there to support him, especially after the mission to kill the old judge?

To think about the aftermath of that night those few years back, still chilled him to the bone. The newspapers had crucified the PFF *'P.F.F. Massacre women and children'* the headlines had read....... Photos of the judge's house.- Photos of the family.- Children at play ut most condemning, had been a close up of the child that had sat on the old judge's knee, taken lying in hospital, with its left arm missing. He still had nightmares of how the baby had looked up at him, as he flew into the room, its tiny eyes sparkling, squealing in delight at this new game. He clutched the wine bottle tighter wishing he had not remembered.

Shortly after the disastrous mission, he and Hainz had been summoned to the cellar headquarters to appear before their respective Section and Group Leaders. Both had sympathised with his reluctance to fire at the judge under such circumstances, but had condemned him as mission leader for failing to restrain his fellow comrade whose irresponsible actions had resulted in the death of the old couple, with serious injury to the woman, little baby, elderly cook and butler, with only the small boy having escaped unscathed.

Petr had scared Miro the most. Even now he could still not believe he had not faced a firing squad. His Group Leader had sat there calmly relating the irreparable damage inflicted on the Party by this one mission...which he, Miro, had led!

Already, many members throughout the nation had secretly renounced their membership, which had been a grave concern to all

Section and Group Leaders, considering the security involved, for, should any one of those defectors turn their disenchantment or revulsion into anger, what damage could they not do? Through necessity, more stringent security measures had to be instantly imposed. Code names and meeting places changed. Then, at last, Petr had lost his temper.

The court-martial decision had been that Hainz and he would take no further part in any future missions until ratified by National Council. All PFF activities in towns and cities postponed until further notice. Only guerilla engagements emanating from General Tetek, and his forces in the mountains, would continue.

Miro had left the cellar, his intended resignation hot on his tongue. He had carried his anger back to Krysty, who to his surprise had not encouraged him to do what at that moment his anger decreed he should do. Instead, she had pointed out to him his years of dedication to what he thought was right. Right for him, right for his country, and all the risks he had taken. Quietly but sternly, advising that, he should not to let one injustice deprive him of what would eventually be his...his own Section Group, then ultimately, a place on the National Council.

He had courted Krysty for seven months after the fateful mission before proposing to her. Much to his surprise and delight, she had agreed, with Fiebo ecstatic at being asked as Best Man.

Then one day two weeks before the appointed day-

"So you believe, do you Ruiz, that after you die you return as a lesser being?" Fiebo asked incredulously, holding the workshop door open for his friends as they returned from the canteen, one lunch time.

"In that case, Fiebo, this will be your last trip!" Gerd laughed, his pals joining in, as they walked across the floor to their workbenches.

"Very funny pal of mine." Fiebo shot two fingers up at him. "Seriously, what do you think, soon to be hanged by the neck, Gerd?"

Gerd shrugged. "Once you're dead, you're dead."

"You do not believe you die and go to another life, Purgatory, Heaven or Hell? You do not believe in our Church?" Dietmar, the youngest of the group challenged with a despairing shake of his head.

Gerd thought it time to be careful. The last thing he wanted to do was spout Communist Ideology here. "All living things die. You die, and feed the worms, hens feed on the worms, we feed on the hens, and so on and so on. Just like me and my bike, everything goes around on cycles." He laughed, hoping his pun would steer him clear of any further awkward questions as to his personal beliefs.

"But...." Dietmar had started to ask, when the door crashed open behind them, spinning them all round.

Oh no! God not now! Gerd bit his lip as the soldiers burst through the door, machine - pistols at the ready. What had given him away? A word? A gesture? Had he been recognised on the night of the 'judge's' mission'? Bile rose in his throat. Had Krysty also been caught?

The soldiers fanned out in a semi circle heading past him to the workbench opposite. Gerd groped behind him for his own workbench to steady himself, unwilling to trust himself to stand, relief and trepidation simultaneously running through his body.

The man the soldiers were after stood stock still. There was nowhere he could run. They seized him, pinning his arms behind his back, frog marching him to the door. In a few seconds it was all over.

Recovering from their shock, the work mates slowly converged in the centre of the workshop floor.

"Well I never! Who would have believed it! Frederick, a dirty Commie?" Ruiz let out a low whistle.

Gerd bit his lip, suddenly afraid of his friends.

Frederick was a man, whom he'd never particularly liked. A father of three, who kept himself to himself. The last man he would have ever suspected of being one of them.

"What makes you think he's a commie?" Young Dietmar asked, clearly shaken.

"What else? It was soldiers who came to arrest him, wasn't it? It would have been police had it only been a civil matter," Ruiz said expressively.

Gerd caught Fiebo's eye, and felt he had to say something. "He's been here longer than any of us."

"Let's get back to work." Fiebo swung away from his friend.

Gerd watched him cross the floor to his bench, surprised by his reaction, for he'd never known Fiebo to be the first to start work, especially when there was the possibility of the makings of a good natter. *Good God,* he thought, he's really shook up as well. Could it be that Fiebo, his friend, was also, PFF? He found himself strangely disturbed by the thought that it could be so. But how would he ever know? Or more to the point, did he really want to know?

That same evening there was a note in his 'letterbox'; the secret place where messages were left by their fellow conspirators, that he was to meet in the cellar.

Kimmo, his Section Leader, and Petr sat waiting for him.

"How are the wedding arrangements coming along, Miro?" Petr asked as he took his seat. Gerd, now once again Miro, felt that the man was genuinely interested.

"Very well thank you," he answered trying to match the Group Leader's mood. "I was supposed to be helping K...Henna tonight" he swiftly corrected himself.

Petr laughed. In this case. the use of the code name was superfluous. His smile quickly vanished. "I apologise, Miro. Indeed if this meeting was not of the utmost importance, I would not ask it of you at this inappropriate time."

Miro tensed. What was Petr up to, to be apologising to him...a lowly Section member...and a disgraced one at that?

To compound his suspicion, Petr pushed a packet of cigarettes across the rough table. Miro reached out, aware that his hands were shaking as he slid one out of the packet.

"Miro, I...we, have need of your help." Petr waited patiently until Miro had lit up. "As you undoubtedly know, your work mate, Frederick was arrested today."

So that was it. This was the reason for the contrite tone, the flowery language, his Group Leader needed him. He sat back in his chair while his leader went on. "It will do no harm to tell you that Frederick was a member of our Group here in the city. Which Section I will refrain from saying...you understand?" Petr halted to draw on his cigarette. "Normally in a similar situation, we would enlist the help of a member from another Group, so that in the event of his arrest, he would not be in a situation to disclose any information concerning his adopted Group. However, in this case, we have no alternative but to use one of our own. One close enough...one intimate enough with those concerned, to find out what we need to know."

Petr blew out smoke, flicking ash into a bottle top on the table. "You...Miro. We need someone who can find out what gave Frederick away, and how much of his Section has been compromised. This we need to know while we try to get to him in the Caserne."

Miro leaned forward and stubbed out his cigarette in the makeshift ashtray, twisting the shreds of tobacco and paper between his thumb and forefinger in an attempt to keep his hand from shaking. He knew very well what Petr meant. Block 3 in the Caserne was where the Nazis had held their captors during the occupation. Nothing had changed since then, except the jailors. Tortured by Government soldiers, or assassinated by his own, one way or another, the poor sod was already dead.

"How can I be of more help than an outsider? I did not know the man at all outside of the factory. I never had any idea he was one of us! Who can I ask without inviting suspicion upon myself? Jeopardising my own Section"

"Why don't you start with your best friend?" Kimmo suggested angrily.

Miro jerked round to face the man, who had sat silent until now. Was Fiebo, after all, PFF? He riveted his eyes on his Section Leader. "You mean Fiebo?"

"Yes! I mean it was your very best friend, who denounced our comrade!" Kimmo seethed.

Miro felt the blood drain from his face. It was not the answer he had expected. Fiebo was not one of them, on the contrary, it was he who had denounced one of them! "Fiebo?" he said weakly.

Petr toyed with the bottle top on the table. "I'm afraid so, Miro," he confirmed with a slight outake of breath. "Now you can see why you have the best chance, of finding out just what did give Frederick away."

Miro rubbed agitatedly at an old wound on the side of his leg. "You want me to betray my friend.... worm out of him..." His voice faded at the ramifications of what these men were asking him to do.

Petr threw the bottle top across the makeshift table, while Kimmo's eyes blazed hatred at him, blaming him for Fiebo's actions.

"It's the only way." Petr looked up and there was the slightest hint of apology in his voice, as he drove home his point. "You must think of your comrades... and their families, should Frederick be forced to tell what he knows."

"And Fiebo? What happens to him, Petr?" Miro asked bitterly, wishing he was anywhere on earth but here, and not having to ask this question.

"He dies!" Kimmo barked at him across the table. "This has always been our policy!"

Choosing to ignore his Section Leader, Petr snuffed out his cigarette. "Were I to guarantee your friend's immunity, what then? Would you do it?"

"You cannot!" Kimmo cried, starting to his feet. "It has never been done before. Whoever is responsible for the arrest, or death of one of ours, pays with his life. It has been ...it is the only way to drive fear into our enemies! Besides, it is for the National Council to decide, not you, Petr!"

His eyes still on Miro, Petr silenced the outburst with a chop of his hand. "National Council have already approved," he snapped. Then a little more calmly to Miro "What do you say? Will you do it?"

Miro passed a hand across his brow. "If you give me your word, Fiebo will not be harmed."

Clearly relieved, Petr's face broke into a smile. "You have my word, comrade Miro. You can count on your friend being your Best Man at your wedding."

On the pretence of wanting to discuss formalities for the forthcoming wedding, Fiebo did not need a lot of persuading to go for a drink with Gerd after work. To his surprise, Fiebo appeared morose. "What's up Fiebo.? Is the thought of having to buy the next round too much for you?" Gerd joked.

His friend made a moue. "No. It's that bas...Olavi." He ran a finger round the rim of his glass.

Gerd took a sip of his beer. He knew Oli to be a pretty decent guy. But then again, how much tolerance could there be to Fiebo's almost continual absence from work every Monday, after a weekend on the binge? "What's he been saying?" he inquired sympathetically.

"Want another one?" Fiebo stood up waiting for Gerd to empty his own glass.

Gerd's eyes followed his friend to the bar. He would have to find a way of bringing up the subject of Frederick without arousing his friend's suspicions. God! How he hated doing this. They had been friends since their school days.

"Got your speech all ready for next week?" Gerd asked, when Fiebo had returned. Fiebo nodded, tilting his glass to his mouth. "I hope it's clean. Krytsty's parents and my mother will be there," he laughed.

Fiebo's eyes roamed over Gerd's shoulder to the door, inspecting everyone who entered the beer hall. Gerd tried again, changing tact. "Mother has bought herself a new dress. Thinks she's really something, which she is, God bless her. It's the first new dress she's had since the War," he chuckled.

"Mmm? Fiebo's eyes returned to Gerd. He downed the Schnapps he'd bought with his beer, and stood up. "Another one, pal of mine?"

"Steady on Fiebo, at this rate you'll not be fit for work tomorrow, and it's only Tuesday. You don't want old Oli at you again. Do you?"

"Bug...old Oli." Fiebo turned unsteadily on his heel and headed for the bar.

The clock on the wall read ten twenty. Gerd returned from the bar clutching the drinks, setting another glass of Schnapps down in front of his friend.

"I think you should make that the last one, Fiebo, youv'e work tomorrow."

Fiebo sat back heavily in his chair. He had trouble focusing on this stranger with two heads. Slowly the heads converged into one. "'Suppose you're right." He lifted his drink, and belched. "You know what's worrying me, pal of mine?" He fell forward leaning heavily on the table. "Frederick."

Gerd felt his heart skip a beat. Could it be Fiebo was about to tell him what he wanted to know? He shook his head. "Yes, a sad business. You work beside someone and think you know them." He sighed and took a moment to look around the beer hall, as if pondering over the subject. Then, as if he had already dismissed it from his mind, said suddenly, "Now I think I should get you home, Fiebo." For he wanted Fiebo to remember ; if at all possible in his inebriated state, it was he himself who had brought up the subject.

Fiebo waved a hand for Gerd to sit back down. "Do you know how it happened?" He lifted his drink pointing the glass at Gerd. "Well I'll tell you. It was last Saturday night... I remember leaving the Villamy, then not much more. The next thing I knew, I was lying in the park looking up at the stars. Then there was this voice I thought I recognized, but I must have passed out. I came to, sitting on a park bench, and Frederick was cleaning vomit off my jacket. I reckon I must have blurted out my anger about Oli..." Fiebo straightened up, sitting back in his chair. "I only vaguely remember Frederick going on about all management being the same. How they did not give a toss about the working class.... Spouting on about this being the trouble with our country. How it was only people like me that could change it.

"I don't know how long he talked. I wasn't sure how much I took in. Anyhow, I probably passed out again, for the next thing I knew was, coming round, and seeing Frederick bending down at the foot of an old statue across the path. At first I thought he was having a leak, until I saw him put some papers into his pocket." Fiebo put out a shaky hand for his drink.

Ch...! Gerd thought, 'his letterbox!'

Fiebo went on. "I thought no more about it at the time. Frederick helped me onto a bus for home." He let out a deep sigh. "Next day, Something -don't ask me what- made me suddenly remember Frederick standing by the statue." Fiebo stopped, his eyes staring over Gerd's shoulder.

Suddenly, Gerd realised his friend was afraid. Afraid that h*is* friends the PFF, would find out it was he who had denounced Frederick.

Fiebo returned to his friend and his story. "Curiosity got the better of me, I went back to the park, found the statue...wasn't easy," Fiebo grunted, "considering the state I had been in."

"I'll bet!" Gerd forced a laugh.

"Do you know what I found, Gerd?" His friend shook his head. "More papers!" Fiebo set his glass down with a thump.

Oh God no! Gerd thought. He took a sip of his beer. "What did you do, Fiebo, hero of our country?" He tried to sound flippant, as if the whole damned thing didn't really matter.

"I took them to the police station. You will never believe who was on duty, pal of mine? None other than your old neighbour, Matti Marfelt!"

"From our street?" Gerd affected a laugh. "Well, what do you know?"

"The very same," Fiebo chuckled, now feeling much better that he had gotten the burden of having a man captured and most probably put to death off his conscience... well at least shared, and who better than with his best friend. "Boy was I glad to see someone I knew. Matti suggested I take the papers to the military, which I did. Then they came to the factory for old Frederick."

"So you're a hero, pal. But if I were you, I'd not mention it to anyone...for your own sake that is," Gerd suggested.

And that is how, Gerd, alias Miro, left it, to report back to his other friends, the PFF.

The wedding reception was going well. Gerd followed Fiebo into the toilet, holding the door ajar for Dietmar, following a step behind.

"Your speech went down well, Fiebo," Dietmar said happily, crossing to the wall mirror and taking out a comb, while his work mates made for the adjacent urinals.

"Yes you did all right, Fiebo. Kept it clean. Even my mother was impressed," the groom said, adding his approval.

"Oh, it was nothing, any genius could have done it," Fiebo shrugged.

An insect buzzed in through the open window from out of the late August sun, and landed on the corner of the mirror.

"And so modest," Dietmar guffawed, flicking the insect away with his comb.

"What time have you ordered our taxi for, Fiebo?" Gerd asked, referring to Krysty and himself.

"Seven fifteen. Your train leaves at eight, which leaves you time for a few more drinks."

Fiebo did up his trouser buttons and stepped back.

"You've done very well, pal of mine." Gerd mimicked his friend's favourite saying, staring straight at the urinal wall.

There was a crack and Fiebo' s head hit the wall, blood and brains smearing the dull green paint work as he slid to the floor, in the background a strange strangled cry from Dietmar at the wash basin.

Even before he threw himself on the floor beside his friend, Gerd knew Fiebo was dead. Sobbing, he cradled his best friend in his arms, silently cursing Petr for his treachery.

The door swung open, music and laughter invaded the toilet.

"CH...!" Ruiz exclaimed transfixed.

"Close the door, for Ch..sake, Ruiz!" Gerd cried up at him. The sound of jocundity from his own wedding now an obscenity to him.

"What has happened?" Ruiz gasped, leaning against the closed door, and feeling he wanted to be sick. Fiebo's shattered head told him this had been no drunken squabble or accident between friends.

"Never mind!" Gerd snapped, then quickly apologised with a wave of his hand. It would never do to loose control. "You know Matti Marfelt?" he asked, trying to keep the anger at Petr out of his voice.

"The policeman?" Ruiz, tore his eyes away from the inert body of his work mate.

"Get him, Ruiz, he has a table near the band." And as the shaken young man made to open the door, added as quietly as his anger would allow. "And Ruiz, do it without anyone knowing. You understand?"

At the police station, the senior police officer questioned Dietmar, and Ruiz separately. And when it was his turn, Gerd answered that he did not know anyone who should want to kill his best friend, although, Matti Marfelt could have cleared it up in seconds had he mentioned Fiebo's, involvement in denouncing a member of the PFF But there was no way he Gerd, was going to admit to Fiebo having told him. Clearly Matti was scared, dead scared, perhaps, even too scared to inform his senior officer that it was on his suggestion that Fiebo inform the military, regarding Frederick.

At last, they asked him to wait out in the corridor, and he had time to let his anger simmer. He would have no more to do with the PFF His trust in Petr had led to his friend's death. Today of all days! Once again, Gerd cursed his own stupidity.

The door opened and Matti stepped into the corridor. "Come on Gerd, you and your friends back to the reception," he said quickly. "You have just enough time to pick up your bride and catch your train, if I drive fast enough."

Gerd rose. "I'm free to go?"

"Unless you know more about your friend's death than you're telling us?" Matti suggested, taking him by the elbow and ushering him down the corridor. "We've got your honeymoon address, so if we need to get in touch, we can."

"Honeymoon!" Gerd cried increduously, trying to free himself of the policeman's grasp. "How can I go on a honeymoon with my best friend dead!"

"You now have a wife to think about. We can handle things here," Matti insisted, taking a firmer grip of Gerd's arm.

Gerd bunched his fists until the nails bit in to the palms of his hands. Disjointed thoughts hurled through his brain. He had known all Fiebo's family since childhood: father, brother and sisters. Funeral.?..Where was Krysty? How was she taking this? His mother? The wedding reception?. Did they know what had happened? Had they any idea who had been responsible?

They reached the door. "Take your wife away from all of this for a day or two Gerd. We'll contact you when all the arrangements have been made," Matti was saying.

Arrangements had been made! Gerd shuddered at the meaning. *And when they have, and I do come back*, he decided, *then I know what I am going to do.*

Gerd slid out of his side of the bed. Taking a cigarette from a packet on the bedside table he lit it. He did not want to waken Krysty. Poor girl, what a way to spend a honeymoon. Soon it would be light.

"How long have you been awake?"

Gerd jerked round looking down at his bride. He shrugged. "Not long. Thought I'd catch the first day of the rest of our lives, Mrs Brovwers." He bent forward and kissed her on the cheek.

"Mrs Brovwers," Krysty let the words roll around her tongue, savouring the flavour. "Yes I think I like the sound of that" She smiled up at him, trying to break his evident despondency.

Gerd squeezed her hand. "It's not the honeymoon I had planned, Krysty. You deserve better."

She drew herself towards him, putting an arm around his shoulder. "I know, but it's not your fault. But as you said, Gerd, we have the rest of our lives to look forward to."

"And without the bloody, PFF," he said angrily.

Krysty rested her cheek on his shoulder. "Don't be too hasty. Wait until we're back home, then find out exactly what has happened, then..."

"If I find out Petr was behind this, after all his fine talk about Fiebo not being harmed," he interrupted her, his eyes gleaming vengeance. "I'll shoot the bastard myself!" he seethed.

Rain trickled down the side of the open grave, seeping into the yellow clay below.

The priest's words were nugatory and comfortless to Gerd's ear, as the young man's eyes bored through the polished wood, asking, pleading forgiveness, for what his friends had done. For what he, Gerd had done to Fiebo, his best friend, and promising him, there would be no more killing. He was finished with the PFF..after he had finished with Petr.

Gerd forced himself to think of happier times they shared together. Perhaps Fiebo's death had not been in vain, and this was fate's way of giving him another chance to live a normal life.

He let the cord drop into the grave, stooping to throw a handful of earth onto the coffin, and uttering the words that only he could hear. "Good bye pal of mine."

Gerd walked towards the grieving family to offer his condolences, and heard from them as he stood there, how much his friendship had meant to Fiebo. His bent head and averted eyes, taken by them as a sign of his own personal grief, not as he knew, out of guilt and shame. Or that it had been his own kind that had done such an evil thing.

Along with his work mates, Gerd shuffled to the graveyard gates, their silence broken only by the occasional muffled cough or whispered word. None were able to comprehend that Fiebo would not be with them again. Or that he would not be playing next Saturday in his favourite game, nor laughing and joking in the Villamy afterwards, as he had done only a few short days ago.

Gerd looked up, biting back a gasp of surprise at his mother standing just inside the gates, her hands playing nervously with her scarf at her throat. He drew closer, about to ask the obvious question when, her eyes, red rimmed, she stammered, "They have murdered Matti Marfelt, he died a short while ago."

They carried their policeman, neighbour and friend to the graveyard as was their custom, as Gerd had done with Fiebo a few days before, then returned to the house of the widow.

Gerd looked round the small parlour, at his mother sitting beside Mrs Marfelt, comforting her. Neighbours flitting around with plates of food trying to be helpful, pretending to be cheerful. He caught sight of Shev, Matti's eight year old son and jerked his face into some of comfort. Damn the whole PFF Movement. The time dragged. It seemed an eternity before he felt it prudent for him and Krysty to leave.

Gerd tore savagely at his tie, draping it over a chair in their bedroom. "I'll drop a message in my 'letterbox' that I want a meeting with Petr. I'll tell him where to stick his precious PFF"

"You'd give up everything you have believed in?" Krysty neatly folded up her blouse. In his anger she knew Gerd might do something he could regret later. It was up to her to remain calm.

"That's the point," she heard him say. "I no longer know what I believe."

Suddenly, Gerd wanted to lash out at something...someone. He clenched his fists, his face contorted with rage, hurling his anger and frustration across the bedroom at his wife. It was all very well for her to appear calm, show no emotion, she had not grown up in the movement as he had. "What good has come out of it at all? Eh! It was bad enough ambushing soldiers: no different from what I had done in the War, but to murder an old man and his wife! Maim a child! Lose my best friend!" He threw himself down in a chair, his anger spent.

"You are a soldier in the Cause, Gerd. In any war...rebellion, there must be casualties. If you think you have been betrayed, then find out by whom. Force a hearing, prove them wrong work to become their superiors. Don't just run away, so that they can do the same again, to some one else."

Gerd stared at the floor. Krysty was right, that's what hurt; he, who had always prided himself on his own composure. A composure which in the past had got him out of some tricky situations. "So that's your advice? That's what you think I should do?" His sarcasm was intended to hurt her. "Well, I'll tell you, wife, I don't give that," he snapped his fingers "for all of them. I would trade the lives of any one of them to have Fiebo back, or not to have to look at Matti Marfelt's little boy in the face, and say sorry lad, but I helped kill your father."

He sat slumped forward in his chair, cupping his head in his hands. "I'm afraid Krysty. Afraid for you, for my mother, afraid of what these same neighbours would do, were they to find out the truth. No Krysty, no good has ever come out of anyone I have ever had the misfortune to have met in the PFF And tomorrow I will tell them, just that."

"No one, Gerd?" Krysty asked, her resolve to remain calm rapidly dissolving in tears.

Suddenly realizing what he'd had said, Gerd jumped up and crossed the room to take his wife in his arms. "Oh, no Krysty love, I did not mean you. You are the best thing that ever happened to me... in or out of the movement."

Krysty looked up into his face. "You had better mean that, Gerd Bovwers," she said, attempting to smile through her tearstained cheeks. "Or I'll find another way to make you pay."

"Cut off my conjugal rights?" he asked, squeezing her tight.

"No, I was thinking of something a little closer to hand," she answered with a mocking laugh.

Gerd nursed his anger throughout the following weekend. Then on that Sunday morning started off for his 'letterbox', the coded note in his pocket, determined to arrange a meeting and confront Petr with his treachery. He drew near the graveyard. What could be more natural than a son visiting his father's grave? Perhaps, also take a few extra minutes to pay his respect to his former neighbour and best pal.

There was little Sunday traffic about. He crossed the road, and turned right towards the graveyard. A woman hurrying passed, brushed against him, knocking her handbag out of her hand. Uttering an apology, he bent to pick it up, his mind still on Petr and his treachery.

"Tomorrow night in Freigberg Square, seven thirty, Miro,"she muttered, bending down beside him. Then, as they straightened, she made an elaborate show of thanking him for his courtesy and was gone.

It had been a rush to reach the square by the appointed time. After finishing work, he only had time to grab a bite to eat, and into the change of clothes Krysty had laid out for him, before he was out, and running for the seven ten tram.

In the square, he stared at his watch, giving it another encouraging shake to make certain it still worked, before sticking it back into his coat pocket. It was already turning cold. The recent warm spell that had blessed their wedding had vanished. The clock face of the church across the cobbled square light up as it boomed out the half hour. It would soon be dark.

He walked a step or two away from the corner, more out of impatience than to keep himself warm. Something important must have come up that they were not meeting in the cellar?

They would come. The message must be genuine, for after all, the woman had used his code name. Yet what else may have happened since Fiebo and Matti's deaths? Could others also have been apprehended? Was this a trap?

As if to allay his fears, a black car slid alongside the kerb, and the face of his Section Leader peered out at him from the front seat. The back door quickly opened and he climbed inside.

No one asked him about the wedding, or the honeymoon, and he was grateful for the silence. He was in no mood for casual conversation, all he wanted was to get the journey over and face Petr.

Soon they were out of the city and heading for the country. Twenty minutes later, the car swung off the road and through an open gate, bumping across a fallow field to where a black sedan stood outside a dilapidated hut.

"Good to see you, Miro." Petr indicated that he should take a seat at the rough table as the others arranged themselves around the walls. Kimmo, Miro noticed had not come in.

Is it? Miro thought, at the same time determined to refrain from saying what was in his mind until the right opportunity presented itself.

"Although I...we all wish to congratulate you on your marriage," Petr began, stopped, cleared his throat and began again. "I know it would be insensitive to dwell on the subject, considering what took place later."

Expecting Miro to comment, Petr hesitated, slightly disturbed that the man's only reaction was to fold his arms and stare at him across the table. "Your friend's death was not sanctioned by me, of this, I can assure you," Petr emphasized, regaining his composure. "The assassination was carried out by Hainz."

Miro bunched his fists under his armpits, determined to match his Group Leaders equability, though he wanted to jump up, grab him by the throat and squeeze out of him where the sneaky little bastard was. Instead, he asked as calmly as possible, "And Matti Marfelt ?"

"Now that is a different matter." Petr held up his hands in front of him, as if using them as a buffer. "He, after all was an informer, and partly responsible for Frederick's capture...and subsequent execution."

Miro felt the colour leave his face. So Frederick was dead. He found himself feeling more sorry for the man's wife and children, than for the poor sod himself.

Petr rose. "This is why you are here. It is now time to deal with this matter."

Miro followed Petr and the other four men out of the hut, across the field and into a coppice. As Petr stood aside, Miro caught his first glimpse of Hainz. Now all he wanted to do was rush across the short distance between them and crush the life out of the man. Kimmo, a black blindfold in his hand moved to the assassin's side.

"We all know why we are here," Petr began. Hainz pushed back his Ferado, as if in an act of indifference, his lip curled in a smile at Miro. "It is because standard procedures have been broken, and in so doing have put at risk the lives of the entire Group. Why?" Petr's voice rose angrily. "All because of a personal vendetta against two men. Oh, I know!" Petr waved a hand, "they deserved to die. After all, they had denounced one of our own. But the assassinations were carried out without my authority as Group Leader. This cannot be tolerated."

Now that the time had come for Hainz to die, Miro felt strangely devoid of feeling. All he wanted was to have it over and done with. Perhaps, when it was all over, he'd feel better. He might even begin to believe in the Cause again in the knowledge justice had been done, and that Hainz had paid for the death of his friends.

For a moment, Miro took his eyes off Hainz to study the men standing in a semi circle around him, each looking at the ground in front of him, each understanding that this was no game that they were playing, that as an army, orders were to be obeyed, that no one could act on his own without due authority from above: in this case Petr as Group Leader.

Miro sensed, rather than saw the gun suddenly appear in Petr's hand. He switched to Hainz, whose attention appeared to be centred on a bird chirping on the branch of a tree, seemingly envious of this small creature that would still be here when he lay lifeless on the ground.

Miro had been through this many times before during the Occupation. He had seen the last look on the face of the doomed, and had long ceased to wonder how he himself would react should he find himself in a similar situation. What last thoughts would flee through *his* mind? However, for this condemned man, he could feel no pity, for Hainz had not been his friend.

Miro heard Petr cock the pistol, heard him say, "I sentence you to die, for you knowingly went against my explicit orders." Heard the explosion, saw the blindfold in Kimmo's hand leap in the air as he fell.

Shocked, Miro did not know where to look first, whether at Petr, Hainz who stood mystified, or at the men standing there. Then, as if in way of explanation, Petr calmly turned to him. "Kimmo was there the night we agreed your friend was not to be harmed, yet he took it upon himself to order Hainz to do the killing. Hainz did so in the mistaken belief the order came from me. I cannot execute a man for carrying out the order of his superior." Petr had swung to encompass Hainz in his last remarks.

Blowing out his cheeks Hainz arranged his hat squarely on his head, and despite himself, Miro wanted to smile at the action.

"Why did Kimmo want Fiebo dead so much, Petr?" Miro asked hoarsely. "I know how set he was against anyone getting away with killing one of our own, but after you had given strict orders...."

"A coincidence, Miro. For years Kimmo had lived in the same street as Frederick, neither were aware of the other being PFF Also, both families socialised together, and in fact had become good friends. So, when Frederick was arrested, Kimmo was determined that his friend should be avenged."

As he put the pistol back in his pocket, Petr knew by Miro's eyes that confidence in the Cause had been restored and, while all may not necessary be forgiven, it was at least understood.

Impassively, Petr watched as they dragged Kimmo's body away to the ready dug grave, acutely aware, that had Miro continued to condemn the Cause he had so unceasingly worked for all of those years, there would have been two graves here this night.

Two weeks later, Miro, formerly, Gerd, replaced Kimmo as Section Leader.

Chapter 6

Mark replaced the map in its folder and strode down the hillside to meet the convoy of trucks. It was now two weeks since the President's 'death' and the nation was still in shock. Each newspaper had expounded their own particular theory as to who was to blame, and had surprised no one by their accusations.

The first to alight from the trucks was his old CSM, who signaled to the column to halt, while he walked on alone to meet Mark. "Company Sergeant Major Grbesa, reporting for duty. **S***ir"* The soldier barked, drawing himself smartly to attention.

"At ease Sergeant Major," Mark replied, his face expressionless.

"May I, on behalf of the company, congratulate you on your promotion, **M***ajor, Sir.*"

"Thank you Company Sergeant Major Grbesa." Mark addressed the soldier by his full title.

There was no outward expression on Grbesa'a face as he quietly inquired. "Did you think you would miss our wonderful country so much, that you have decided to stay, major?"

The wee nyaff's having a shot at me, Mark thought to himself. *This must be the only way he knows of saying he is pleased to see me back. Well, he would teach* him!

"No Sergeant, I did not miss your wonderful country. However, I was concerned by what you might do to a perfectly good company of men." By the grins on the faces of those closest to them in the column, he was sure that they had heard his remarks. Chuckling, Grbesa studied his feet.

"Seriously though, Sergeant," Mark drew a little closer to the soldier. " Dismiss the men if you please. I want a word with you."

A little later, standing under a tree; neither man having touched upon the subject of the president's demise, the mercenary offered his CSM. a cigarette.

"My orders are to take three companies North East of here." Mark held out his lighter. "According to our information the PFF should be on their way down the mountain to attack the town of Pienara." He stopped. Grbesa's only reaction was to blow smoke into the air. *Ever the cool wee bugger,* Mark thought. And not for the first time admired his sergeant's composure. "We'll have to wait in a ravine, here...." He stabbed a finger at the map in his hand. "We cannot get too close for fear of being seen, or those sons of bitches would know for sure it is a trap. 'B' and 'C' Company have already left. Your 'A' Company is now the last to leave."

Mark drew on his cigarette. "Colonel Ziotkowski, will work around behind the PFF from the east, putting himself between them and their bases in the mountains, should any of them succeed in breaking through our lines. This is all I can tell you at the moment, Sergeant."

Nipping out his cigarette between his thumb and forefinger, Grbesa dropped the stub into the top pocket of his tunic. "When do we start, Major?"

Mark studied his watch. "Exactly twenty five minutes from now. We shall have to march through these hills for most of the day. Okay?"

Grbesa slung his rifle over his shoulder, and had started to move away, when Mark stopped him. "You will tell nothing of these orders to any of the men, including your NCO's, Sergeant. I have told you only out of necessity, for as yet no officer has replaced me in 'A' Company. Therefore, technically you are in command until one can be appointed. Do I make myself clear?"

"Yes Major!" Grbesa snapped to attention. "With your permission sir, I shall prepare the men for departure."

Mark's former company had been short of officers since the mercenaries had been dismissed for home. To compound the situation, Grbesa had refused an officer's commission which would have effectively put him in command. *Well the wee bugger would have to get on with it*, Mark thought somewhat harshly. For, now that he was commanding officer of this little expedition, he was responsible for all three companies involved. Therefore, he had no time to wet nurse Grbesa, though if the truth be known, this he never need do. Or he did not know Niew Grbesa very well.

It had been a cold night spent in the ravine. Mark's officers stood in a semi circle around him, rubbing their hands and stamping their feet to keep warm while he addressed them.

"I shall command 'A' Company' in the centre. 'B' Company will be on my right flank, 'C' on the left. We shall not move out until we are certain the PFF have attacked Pienera. Is that clear?" There was a murmur of affirmation, above which, Mark asked, "Any questions?"

"One sir," a young lieutenant ventured. "'A' Company, excepting yourself, are without officers, do you think this is fair on yourself sir, considering you are in overall command?" Blushing, now that he had asked the question, he awaited his commanding officer's reaction.

"Thank you for your concern, Lieutenant, but I have previously commanded 'A' Company quite adequately, in exactly the same circumstances...as a humble captain, I might add." He broke into a smile. "However, Company Sergeant Grbesa will in effect be in command in my absence. Any other questions...daft or otherwise?"

Embarrassed, the young lieutenant joined in the stilted laughter. "No sir."

"Good. Then let's get on with the job in hand."

Mark shone his torch on his watch. "One hour to dawn," he said aloud to himself, "then we'll know if our information is reliable or not."

At the same time as Mark looked at his watch, two trucks swung into a cobbled square in Pienera, drawing up on the opposite side of the road from the garrison gates.

Dropping down from the back of one, a workman handed down a wooden barrier to a work mate, while from the second truck a squad of workmen set about unloading an assortment of tools, amongst them an iron brazier, which they promptly set about lighting. This latter action invited a burst of laughter from the two sentries on duty at the garrison gates. The time was 7.a.m.

At exactly 7.10.am., the morning train carrying employees to the gasworks and power station in the town passed the workers bus on the road running parallel to that of the railway line. This morning both modes of transport carried a few extra passengers.

In the cabin of his crane high above the roofs of the dockside warehouse, Savell Posavec poured himself a cup of coffee from his thermos flask.

Below the coffee drinker, a cargo ship they had just finished unloading had weighed anchor and was heading out to sea. Out in the bay, a second ship, which had arrived overnight, prepared to move into the empty berth.

Savell took a bite of his sandwich. *It would be a good four hours before they could start unloading that ship*, he thought. They still had to move the crates off the wharf from the last one. Meanwhile, he had time to finish his breakfast, and perhaps have a little nap before the stevedores started shouting up at him, that unlike him, they had a bonus to earn. Yawning, Savell took another sip of coffee. The time was now 7.15a.m.

Wooden barriers now completely enclosed the hole gradually growing in depth in the cobbled square, from the bottom of which a squad of workers threw up shovelfuls of earth over the dug up cobbles that now surrounded the perimeter. Nearby, a second squad stood round the lighted brazier warming their hands and drinking coffee, waiting their turn to take over.

From the barrack gates, a sentry, unable to contain his curiosity, walked across the square and halted at the barrier. "What civil servant has sent you lot out at this time in the morning?" he wanted to know, staring into the hole. "Usually you lot don't start making a nuisance of yourselves until eight or nine. Must be urgent," he said stepping onto the mound of earth surrounding the excavation.

"It is, soldier." A man, carrying a clip board, appeared from behind a truck. "A gas leak was reported a little while ago, that's why we're here so early. Got me out of bed it did, bugger it."

The soldier muttered his understanding. "Well keep up the good work. As for me, I'll be off duty in an hour."

"Lucky you," the foreman muttered enviously, as the soldier turned away laughing."Tell the rest of your mates, not to come too close, especially if they're smoking, or we're all likely to arrive home early!" he called after him. Around him, his men chuckled at the joke. The time was 7.45a.m.

In a flat directly above the sedulous workmen, a fourteen year old boy stood at the window, his eyes firmly focused on the garrison across the square. Lifting an imaginary rifle to his shoulder he fired it in that direction. "One day...when I'm old enough," he vowed.

Pouring boiling water into the coffee pot, his mother rounded on him angrily. "That sort of talk will get you into trouble some day, my lad. Come. Your breakfast is ready. You will have ample time to be a revolutionary after you leave school."

At 7.50.am., a young woman pushing a pram towards the convergence of Meisa and Raiff Street , had her progress idly watched by two weary soldiers manning their machine guns post from behind a row of sandbags. Waving them a cheery good morning, she turned up Raiff Street, and halted at a bakers shop.

At 7.55.am., the first group of workmen heading up Meisa Street to the gasworks called out their usual ribaldry to the soldiers behind their sandbags as they passed. Across the street, the woman came out of the bakers, putting a loaf of bread she had bought into her pram.

Two minutes later, the last of the workers hurrying passed the machine gun post were startled by the distant sound of gunfire. Hesitating, the stragglers looked anxiously across at the soldiers for an explanation.

The woman outside the bakers shop, also hearing the shots, hurriedly pushed her pram across the street towards the barricade, the soldiers waving and shouting at her angrily to get out of the way. Ignoring them, she quickened her stride, reaching down inside her pram to comfort her child. And as the soldiers shouted again that she was in their line of fire, she drew away, hurling the grenade she had extracted from the pram with deadly accuracy at the two astounded men. The barricade disintegrated, and the last of the passing workmen took to their heels as fast as they could.

In conjunction with the explosion the first of the PFF, trucks roared into sight, alternately sweeping up Meisa and Raiff Streets, the woman with the pram waving to them as they passed. By 8.20a.m. all of the town's major installations were in PFF hands. Ten minutes later the garrison siren sounded. In response, the quadrangle immediately in front of the tall garrison block, so recently deserted, sprang to life, as the first column of trucks sped towards the gate.

Across the square the tailgate of the workmens trucks crashed down, the machine guns inside catching the leading truck broadside as it swung onto the cobbles, scything down the rows of packed soldiers standing in the back. The truck behind crashing into the gatehouse from a burst from a second machine gun, as the remaining trucks screeched to a halt spilling out their human cargoes desperately fleeing from the decimating fire.

With a 'crump', two mortars winged their way over the nearest trucks from the man made trench across the square, exploding on the hard bitumen surface of the quadrangle, scattering fragments of red hot shrapnel in all directions.

Above the screams of wounded men, the garrison began to open up from the upper floors of the building, their fire increasing as they recovered from their initial shock, supported a few minutes later by their comrades from behind the barricade of trucks, the sheer intensity of the returning fire shaking the tarpaulins of the 'workmens' trucks as if blown by an invisible wind.

Clutching his bleeding arm, the 'foreman' slid to the bottom of the trench. "I hope they get here on time, or we will have dug this blasted hole for ourselves," he said caustically, to one of his squad tying a tourniquet on his arm.

At the furthest end of the quadrangle, the long barrel gun of a tank poked round the corner of the garrison building, rumbling passed the soldiers crouched behind their immobilised trucks. From deep inside the metal monster a motor whined, transversing and depressing its gun. The first shell blew the nearest workmen's truck apart, and exploding ammunition from the truck shattered windows and penetrated the homes of all around the square. The flat immediately above the disintegrated truck took the full blast, killing the woman, and a boy who wanted so much to become PFF. While below the burning flat the foreman crawled through the hot jagged shrapnel littering the foot of the trench to help his wounded squad.

From around the gable-end of a tall five-storey building at the end of the square, three men of the PFF ran towards the perimeter fence. Though the garrison succeeded in hitting one, they failed to stop the other two carrying the anti-tank gun from reaching the fence, firing and hitting the tank before it could reload.

All around the burning square, more PFF were arriving.

Meanwhile at the rear of the building, troops rushing across the training ground heading for the gate in the perimeter fence with the intention of taking the enemy in the flank, were themselves caught in a hail of fire from the tall grass beyond the fence. The foremost through the gate and fortunate enough to have survived, retreated back to the perimeter gate to be met by those following on behind. Taking advantage of the confusion, a machine gun opened up on the mass of men jammed in the gateway, wounded and dying, screaming as they fell. The garrison was now completely surrounded. The time was 9.25a.m.

In the mountains a few kilometres north of the town, Mark was dismissing the last of his patrols. He swung quickly to his wireless operator. "Inform 'B' and 'C' Company to proceed to their allotted positions. Immediately!"

"So this is it." Grbesa prosaic voice muttered at his side.

"Yes Sergeant, Tetek has taken the bait, so let's get it over with." He moved down the slope, thinking austerely, "then I can get on home, and away from your wonderful country."

From his jeep twenty five kilometres south of the town, General Predrag Scurk placidly watched his columns emerge from their hiding place in the disused quarry, concluding, as he glanced at his watch, that all being well, the column to east and west of him should also be on the move. As usual, he had been meticulous in his planning. It was now up to his subordinates not let him down, and if they did not, he'd show that braggadocio, Jakofcic, strutting about in the Capital as a decoy, how it should be done.

Jan Tetek perused the map spread out on the desk, completely ignoring the plump little man standing before him. He did not offer the man a seat, although this man was the Mayor, this was his office, and this was his desk, which he now sat behind.

The middle aged, slightly balding General had deliberately kept the man waiting, treating him as a schoolmaster would his pupil. Eventually, his perusal over, he looked up.

"Your town is now entirely under the control of the Peoples Freedom Fighters," he began rigidly. "The Government garrison is completely surrounded, and all major installations are in our hands. Therefore I suggest," Tetek emphasised the last word, "that in order to save lives, you make just such an announcement over the radio." These last words dispelling the glint of hope in the perspiring little plump man's eye, "By doing so," Tetek went on to explain, "not only will you be informing this town, but many other such towns throughout the country..." Tetek's voice rose sharply, "that contrary to popular belief the army of the PFF are far from beaten! That, we are still capable of taking a town; in this case *your* town, Mister Mayor!" The general allowed himself a dry laugh.

The plump little man swallowed hard. "May I ask you what your intentions are, General? I mean..." he swallowed again, "after I have done as you ask," he added shakily.

Tetek knew he had taken an enormous gamble by agreeing with National Council's recommendation that he attack the town. Not, that he was so compelled, for as Commanding Officer in the field, he was permitted to make his own decisions. However, he knew he could not hope to hold the town for long. But, if the man he knew as Petr, and his Group carried out their part by ambushing reinforcements on their way here from the Capital, then it might just be possible to hold out that little bit longer...if for no other reason than propagation. To the obese little man still perspiring under his eye, Tetek replied, "my intentions, Mister Mayor are no concern of yours. When they are, I shall let you know. Guard!" he shouted. "Escort this man to the radio station, immediately."

General Scurk, never the most cavalier of soldiers, halted his men five kilometres short of the town. Now drawn up in full battle order, Scurk awaited the return of his forward patrols, plus confirmation that Major Stewart's three Companies were in position. At last, satisfied by all reports, but still cautious, Scurk ordered his men forward.

For the past hour, the sound of gunfire had grown louder. Savell's first thought was that it was the garrison soldiers out on their practice range, but now, that it seemed to be coming from several different direction, he was not so sure.

The crane driver leaned on the outside rail of his crane and looked down at the stevedores gathered together in little groups on the quay, their gang leaders having scurried off to find out what was going on in the town. For a moment, he let his eyes stray to the cargo ship coming into port. There was no chance of her being unloaded today. Hadn't her captain heard the firing, or seen the other ships making out to sea?

"Can you see what's going on, Savell?" a stevedore called up to him.

"No!" he shouted back, spreading out his arms in an exaggerated shrug. "I cannot see anything over the top of the sheds, but there is smoke coming from the direction of the tyre factory."

It was time Savell thought, of going home. His wife would be anxious, as he was for her. Yet, there was his job to think of, and at his age they were not easily come by. Therefore, should he decide to leave, what then? If only he knew for sure what was going on.

Those sons of bitches in their offices should be out here telling them what to do.

Angry now, Savell turned his attention to the men below, each waiting for someone to take the lead. Then, as if in silent agreement, they began to trickle slowly towards the gate. Some of the younger ones began to run to find out for themselves what was going on, others, less anxious, took their time.

Savell swung his leg over the rail. It was time to follow. Whatever was happening, transport would be the first affected, just as it had been the day those accursed Nazis had rolled in. Everywhere, abandoned buses, trams, cars, you name it, he had seen it.

"It's the PFF! They've taken the town!" someone cried. "They won't let us out of the docks!"

A leg on the first rung, Savell halted. The men whom he had seen heading for the gate were returning. So that was it he thought, that is what all that shooting was about. He should have known. Cursing, he swung back over the rail. It was precisely 11 a.m.

By 11.30 a.m, all gunfire had ceased.

An hour later, all along the dockside men cautiously emerged from the shelter of the warehouses, as they would after a shower of rain. The silence was more unnerving than the recent tumult.

The cargo ship Savell had watched all morning had now settled down in the berth opposite his crane. On her bridge, an officer called down to some stevedores to help tie her up. With nothing else to do, they complied.

Suddenly, there were soldiers swarming all over her deck, making for the hastily lowered gangplanks. Stunned, Savell watched the Government soldiers hurriedly disembark. An officer waved up to him calling out something and pointing to the ship's open hold. Savell let out a long sigh. It looked as if he was about to unload this ship after all, except, this cargo was nothing like he had expected.

Jan Tetek closed his office door against the brouhaha in the outer office. He had received reports of PFF sympathisers making their way up town looting and settling old scores on the way. And, having issued orders as to how this latest crisis should be dealt with, he now sat back exhausted in his chair.

After a few minutes, aware that his second command was still in the room, Tetek asked of him, "Should we...." He began again.

"When we find it necessary to withdraw, what supplies can we take? I don't want all this to have been for nothing."

"A great deal, Jan," the man answered. He made to rise, and at the sharp knock at the door, changed his mind.

"Enter!" Tetek commanded.

A teenager, wearing the distinctive red armband of the PFF, rushed into the room. Then, as if suddenly realising where he was, drew to an abrupt, if not very dignified halt, snapping a salute at the man behind the desk.

"Sir! Government troops are on the outskirts of the town. They are *everywhere* sir!" The youth cried, his eyes wide.

Tetek lifted a hand to calm the frightened young man. "Precisely where are these Government troops, soldier?"

"Everywhere!...sir!" the boy blurted out. "South and East of the town! It has also been reported that they have landed by boat and are in control of the dock area!"

Displaying composure even his seasoned second command found hard to believe under such circumstances, Tetek carried out his interrogation of the youngster for a few more minutes before dismissing him.

When he had gone, Tetek rose to look out of the window. "This has been nothing short of a trap, Anton." He addressed his fellow officer without turning round. "Government troops could not possibly have arrived so quickly, especially by sea, unless they were already on their way before we attacked, or were hidden close by, for exactly the same reason."

His friend rose quickly. "Then we must evacuate immediately, before we are completely surrounded!"

Tetek turned to face him. "Yes, I agree. But I also wonder what other little surprises they may have in store for us."

Mark's 'A' Company, was positioned between the two main roads running out of Pienera.. He knew the west road, which led through open farm land, offered little protection for an army in full retreat. Therefore, it was to the mountainous north road, he expected Tetek to retreat.

Mark put his field glasses to his eyes and scanned the landscape beneath, raising them a little now and again until they were firmly focused on the outskirts of the town.

There had been an explosion just after midday, which his scouts had informed him had been the radio station. It was now 1600 hours and the PFF still resisted.

He hoped that laggard Scurk was not his usual over cautious self, and let Tetek escape south or west. If he had, they would all look more than a little stupid. An explosion interrupted his thoughts. He swung his glasses in that direction. A second explosion followed, this time louder than the first, and a ball of fire shot high into the sky.

"I'd say that was the power station, and the gasworks," Grbesa said at his side, his voice nondescript.

"Tell the men to stand to, CSM." Mark refocused his glasses on the dirty grey cloud slowly rising into the air, which reminded him of a giant barrage balloon similar to those he'd seen floating above the cities back home during the War. "I don't think we will have much longer to wait," he muttered, as much to himself as to his sergeant.

By 1800 hours, there was still no news of Tetek having made an escape to the mountains via the north road. And, knowing the Commie General's reputation for craftiness, Mark was getting decidedly jumpy, and to compounded matters, it would soon be dark.

Unable to see the north road from where he was positioned, Mark was relying on 'B' Company on his flank for information.

"Sir!" Grbesa pointed to the west road.

Mark lifted his glasses again, this time focusing on the town's outskirts, picking up a solitary car speeding in their direction, This was followed a few second later by another, which in turn was followed by a few more; the trickle of departing vehicles rapidly becoming a stream, a stream a torrent, a torrent a flood.

Major and Sergeant looked at one another, both having the same thought, Tetek was evacuating the town by the west road! He was coming through, mixed in amongst civilian refugees!

Mark lowered his glasses. He should have relied upon the wily wee man to do the unexpected. "Sergeant, send a message to 'B' Company immediately. One third of their strength to reinforce our position here! We shall take half our company down to the west road." Mark scanned the road lying about two kilometres away. "We cannot hold back a flood of refugees on the straight road leading out of town. Even if we could, Tetek's men would see what we are up to. Therefore, we shall set up our road block, there!" Mark pointed into the distance. "At that spot, about a kilometre beyond the bend, where that low stone wall stands on one side, and those woods on the other. Advise 'C' Company of our intentions, also to support our left flank."

A half our later, two felled trees blocked the road from either side at a distance of fifty metres apart, forcing all vehicles to stop and zig zag their way through. His mind still on how many of Tetek's men had escaped before the barricade had been constructed, Mark was only vaguely aware of the first of the vehicles slowly approaching.

It was a bus. It came on a little, drawing to a halt to let a private soldier and his corporal climb aboard to search. A little distance behind which, came a steady stream of buses, cars and horse drawn carts, each loaded down with every conceivable type of bric-a-brac imaginable.

The soldiers their search done climbed down off the bus, and disappeared in amongst the crowd of refugees who had reached this far on foot, and who were pushing forward around the timber barricade. Each male stopped and searched by a soldier as they filed passed. Somewhere in the press, a child cried, a dog barked, a horse whinnied. Ever in the background, the incessant chatter of gunfire from the town.

Mark bit his lip. What if he was wrong? What if this was simply a diversion and in fact Tetek did intend to break out via the north road to his beloved mountains?

It was as he fumbled in his pocket for a cigarette, his attention momentarily drawn to a woman struggling with two small children that at first he was unaware of an old ramshackle bus creeping towards the roadblock. Until with a sudden surge of acceleration, its rusty bodywork shaking, it leaped towards them, taking his men and himself completely by surprise. The frightened face of the driver staring out at them from behind the windscreen, a gun held to his temple.

Mark choked. How many PFF. were on board? How many innocent women and children were there? How many would die if he gave the order to fire?

The decision was made for him as the gunman let loose on the private and corporal standing by the side of the road, waiting to search the next vehicle through, hitting refugees in his line of fire as the bus hurled passed.

Instinctively Mark's Company opened up, raking the bus in an explosion of shattered glass and hissing steam, as it careered into the first of the felled trees.

Stampeded by the firing, a hysterical mass of men and screaming women and children surged towards the roadblock, where a few succeeded in scrambling over the wall to get passed by way of the open field on one side, or to the woods on the other, only to have their panic accentuated by Mark's, 'C' Company emerging out of the semi darkness from amongst the trees.

Still they came on, yelling and screaming. Behind the column, shots rang out. More people fell wounded, or were pushed to the ground by fellow refugees in their panic to get passed; away from it all. A gunman ran out, spraying refugees and military alike until he himself was cut down by a hail of bullets.

It was useless. Mark choked, he could not hope to stop such a mass of people. Yet, if he did not do so, how many PFF would escape to fight another day? Nor could he afford another incident.. Suddenly, the Meirra scene flashed before him.

Five of his Company had already died that day when they chased the PFF through the tiny mountain village. Grbesa had spotted them going to ground in a barn, which they had quickly surrounded.

They had all been angry at their losses, he remembered, which was why, when they saw someone at the barn door they had opened fire and had not halted until the barn was reduced to ashes from their grenades and mortars. It was not until later, that they learned, there had been women and children in the barn, held hostage by the Reds, one of whom had been the woman sent out with the white flag to negotiate.

Although Mark had seen many atrocities in France, and later in Germany, he had never knowingly been party to the killing of women and children...not until that day. Though he and his Company had not intentionally set out to kill those innocent, the fact remained they had done so, and he, Mark Stewart, had been in command.

He had always believed that for political reasons the incident had been hushed up and conveniently forgotten. After all, such atrocities were strictly reserved for the PFF And all this time he had been wrong.

Mark returned to the present. He was damned which ever decision he made.

Still the people crushed forward through the roadblock, or ran across the field. Behind which, adding to the panic of this seething mass, angry and frustrated drivers revved their engines and blew their horns. Somewhere further back, shots rang out.

By the side of the road, Niew Grbesa awaited his senior officer's command. When none was forthcoming, and certain that none would, or when it did, it would be too late, he strode to meet the onrush, spraying a burst from his sub machine gun erratically over their heads as he did so.

Screaming hysterically, the foremost threw themselves to the ground, and were instantly trampled upon by those still rushing on behind. Niew fired again, this time not alone, as other soldiers on either side of him joined in. Drawing his own pistol, Mark moved to support his NCO.

Most of the refugees were on the ground now, burying themselves into the earth, hands clutched behind their heads. Grbesa and his soldiers in amongst them, roughly hauling aside and searching anyone attempting to rise. Gradually order was restored.

"Order them to go back to their homes, Sergeant." Mark heard the weakness in his voice as he sought to regain control of himself. Bugger all politicians, he thought.

"Yes Major," Grbesa answered, as if his action was what was expected of a humble CSM.

Mark holstered his weapon. He had stopped Tetek escape, or rather his sergeant had. Now it was up to Scurk, to keep the wee man in Pienera until he surrendered.

Chapter 7

Paule Kolybin heard the whirr of the elevator's descent. A few second later, Milan Molnar strode quickly into his office.

Although it was not yet three o'clock in the afternoon, and not much of a drinker, Milan made for the drinks cabinet, tossing the newspaper on to his President's desk as he passed.

Paule picked it up *'civilians killed and maimed in Piernera debacle'* read the headlines.

"They almost crucified me in the House!" Milan threw himself down in his usual chair across from Paule's desk.

Paule tilted the paper towards him, taking in photographs of women and children lying in postures of death or injury in what looked to be a muddy field. "I wonder how they got those? Staged do you think?"

Milan shrugged, taking a sip of his drink. "You know newspaper men, they can sniff out a story before it happens; effective in this case."

Paule looked up from the damnatory column. "All our planning gone for nothing," he seethed, clenching his fists.

Tetek had out thought them all. He had never intended to break out by way of the west road. The shooting at the roadblock had simply been a diversion. Instead, he had set fire to the buildings and warehouses around the dock land area and, under cover of darkness had in fact escaped by the very cargo ship, which earlier had brought in the Government troops. By the time, this had been discovered he was several kilometres up the coast, back in the safety of the mountains.

"Who was in charge of the roadblock?" Paule tapped the newspaper.

"Stewart."

"Ch…not him again!"

Milan rubbed his glass between his hands. "Perhaps it's about time we sent the mercenary home. Should the papers find out he was to blame, he may let out the whole story of your assassination to save himself."

Reaching for the cigar box, Paule took his time to light one before settling back in his chair. "It would be the wrong time to let him go. There may be questions asked as to why, when he had just accepted an extension of service and a promotion. Inquires could lead all the way back to you, Milan. After all, he helped you the night I died!"

Milan shuddered at his friend's choice of words. "Perhaps you are right. What do you suggest?"

Paule blew smoke up at the ceiling. "Stewart is part of the 4th Regiment, is he not?"

Milan nodded. Paule flicked ash into a tray. "I should think that as they have been in action for quite some time...culminating in distinguishing themselves so well at Pienera, a spot of leave would now be in order. Do you not think so Mister Vice-president?" he smiled affably.

"I suppose so," Milan replied without much conviction, his mind still on the Senate. "What do you suggest I do about all these questions being asked about the Pienera affair?

"Some senators are asking why Jakokcic was left here in the Capital and not in overall command. I cannot very well tell them we hoped the PFF *would* attack in strength after your ass..." He had trouble with the word. "And that it was you who had drawn up the initial plans for just such an occurrence. Even though, we did not know until our sources told us the Reds had chosen Pienera as their objective."

Paule rose. Rounding his desk to the drinks cabinet, he poured himself a drink, and studied the bottom of the glass. "You have been in politics as long as I...forced in," he added with a wry smile. "However, this much I have learned Milan, when in a political crisis, as in war, create a diversion....Make much of how well our soldiers did at Pienera.... The number of PFF killed and captured." Paule waved his hand. "Emphasise that Tetek held the town for less than a day before we ran him off. Understand?"

Milan put down his empty glass. "Perhaps I could turn it to our advantage. Although the truth be known, our loses were heavier than Tetek's."

"Who is to know? Certainly Scurk will not admit as much."

Returning to his desk Paule sat back in his chair, his head tilted towards the ceiling. "Announce in the House..." he halted, a finger poised in the air revising his thoughts and began again. "Announce.

we shall shortly start a building project." He drew slowly on his cigar. "We shall clear away the bombed sites in the Capital, start rebuilding there."

Infected by what had started as a vague idea, Paule swivelled round, his eyes gleaming across the desk at his friend. "What! With greedy Senators chasing contracts, and the unemployed thinking of the work this will create, Pienera will soon be forgotten." He sat back grinning at the simplicity of the solution to the whole problem.

Milan shook his head admiringly. Rising he looked down into Paule's smiling face, the little man's cheeks puffed with pride. "And I suppose all this will be done with the American loan?" he suggested tongue in cheek.

"Of course, Milan," Paule chuckled. "How else could we reconstruct our poor little country?"

Milan turned for the elevator. "Should this succeed, you will be a very popular man, Paule," he said sliding back the panel.

"There you are wrong, Milan. Should this, and everything else succeed, *you* will be a very popular man. But do not forget, when this is all over, whose brain it was that lay behind it all."

Milan turned the key in the elevator panel. Yes he thought, it was something he had had in his mind for quite some time. Or from the day the president had been successfully 'assassinated' to be precise.

It was not until he had gone that Paule realised that Milan had not left him the necessary papers for tomorrow's questions in the Senate. Damn! They were important. It was not that Milan was any less astute than he, the only difference was, that the planning was all his, and without those papers his friend might leave himself vulnerable to any unforeseen inventualities which may arise. It was almost noon. He had hoped to have started work on them. They were probably in his own, now Milan's office on the top floor. If so, there was no way of reaching them until the office staff had left. Therefore, his only hope lay in Milan realising he had forgotten to give him them, and return after the Senate had risen for the day.

Despairingly, Paule took in his surroundings. "I hope to God I don't have to spend too much longer down here." He already missed his wife and son. He did not want to ask Milan too much about how they were taking his 'death'. He was trying desperately to erase this aspect of his planning from his mind, although it was not easy.

He recalled what Milan had said about being the only man he knew who was privy to his own eulogy, after his 'death'.

Heads of State of the Western powers, in particular, had said so many glowing things about him. Therefore, he trusted they would forgive his subterfuge when, with the PFF beaten, the killings ended, the country once again united, they would remember that it was he, Paule Kolybin who had achieved all of this. And that there could have been no other way than the way he had chosen. Perhaps then he could return to a grateful nation and continue to serve his country for the rest of his life.

Lost in his vision for a fraction of a second, Paule's eyes gleamed. Then, as if suddenly awakening from a dream, cast a look around him at his present surroundings. *Oh, how different it could have been, and so swiftly, had all gone according to plan.* "Tetek!" he said aloud. "Tetek, if not for you, all this..." He encompassed the room with a swing of his hand. "would already be consigned to the past."

It was close on 7.30 before Paule decided on an attempt to reach his old office. The indicator above the elevator door told him which floor the car was on. At present, it was descending from the fourth, informing him that there were some people still inside this side of the building. Should he wait, take a chance, knowing what the inevitable repercussions would be, should he be discovered? The papers were important. He must try and reach them, having now given up any hope of Milan returning. He would try a little later.

Paule sat, his eyes fixed on the indicator panel as if was a clock. The elevator had not moved from the ground floor for over a quarter of an hour. Now was his chance! The indicator on the main floors of the building would continue to show the ground floor as long as he operated the key. Anyone pushing a button to summon the lift would merely think the panel light on their floor inoperative, and wait. This had been the general reaction when they had made their test runs. He turned the key, heard the whirr of the motor and waited. The usual 'clunk' told him it had arrived without him having to look up. He turned the key again, and stepped through the open doors into the lift. Another turn of the key, a button pressed for the top floor, and he was on his way. *No turning back now*, he breathed. *Let's hope everyone working late are on the opposite side of the building.*

The journey took forever, his only reaction, a slight quickening of his heart. At length, he was on the top floor, and as his sinewy hands turned the key to open the lift doors, he felt the reassuring feel of his pistol in his pocket; not that he wanted to use it. God! he knew every guard in the building...had fought along side most of them. Ironic if they should die by his hand, after all they'd been through together.

The doors opened, Paule stood back, listening, waiting; no one. He stepped out of the elevator, glancing left and right, his office keys already in his hand. He took off, running for his office at the end of the corridor, the sound of footsteps behind him. He ran faster; undignified for a president, he puffed, but not for what he really was, a shoemaker turned guerrilla fighter, come president.

He reached his office and thrusted the key into the lock. It did not turn. He tried again, twisting savagely. He heard the unmistakable sound of a guard's footsteps just around the bend in the corridor. "Sweet J....the lock's been changed !" he swore, wrenching at the key once more. Should he stop? Turn upon the guard, shoot before he was recognised? If so, would the shot be heard? Suddenly the door yielded and he was in the room, and using all his restraint from slamming the door shut behind him.

Paule locked the door and leaned weakly against the wall. Footsteps stopped outside, the handle turned, first one way then another. Then as he held his breath, his relief as the footsteps receded down the hallway.

Blowing out a long breath, Paule took stock of the darkened room. Nothing had changed. Pocketing his pistol, he gently negotiated his way across the room to where the cabinet stood by the window, whispering, "third drawer down."

By force of habit, Paule stood to one side of the drawer as he pulled it open, his left hand on top, which he had always done to avoid dropping ash from his cigar in amongst the files. Grunting with satisfaction that he had found what he wanted, he quickly closed and locked the drawer, and in a matter of seconds was back poking his head cautiously out of the door, and running down the empty corridor for the elevator once more.

"Do not forget to lock up when you leave, Jana!" the office supervisor warned the young typist.

"No. I won't forget, Mrs Dobok," Jana answered politely, glancing up from her typing. Locking her own desk, the supervisor swung for the door. "Goodnight, Jana, try not to stay too late."

When her supervisor had gone, seventeen year old Jana Hafner rose quickly from her desk. Crossing the room to a row of filing cabinets, she threw a furtive glance in the direction of the door before opening the first drawer. It was not that the drawer held any top secrets, not even important ones, at least not to her, though Miro seemed to think so. "Do not write anything down, commit everything to memory," her Section Leader had warned her. "Every so often you will be searched. They must not find anything that would connect you with our organisation."

Jana had done as she had been ordered, memorising mundane details, such as stores, munitions, food supplies, machine and engine parts, anything in fact requisitioned by the Army from private contractors. As Miro had explained, this information would help determine troop movements. Or such things as strengthening garrisons throughout the country, which had made her happy to help. Proud, even, when Miro had told her how the information she had already passed on had greatly benefited the Section.

It was what had happened to her father that had decided her on joining the PFF During the War, her father had fought in the mountains as a guerrilla, but, while people such as Paule Kolybin had been treated like heroes upon their return, many more like her father had been conveniently forgotten.

Hindered by the loss of a leg and unable to find work, her father had been forced to live on a meagre pension. This, and the fact he had to rely on what his wife could earn from any odd job that came her way, and Jana's own earnings as a typist in the Administration Building, had made him rapidly lose his self respect

"The country has no need of a one legged man now that the Nazis have gone. But they are happy to forget who it was that sent them on their way," Jana's father had told her bitterly.

Each evening he had sat by the fire, his anger festering at the senators who had meekly capitulated to the Nazis, now grew richer every day, whilst he and his family practically starved. This, he had said, was not what he had fought for. Kolybin had betrayed his country. More importantly, he had betrayed those who had fought by his side.

Jana found what she was searching for. Studying the sheet of paper in her hand, she memorised it over and over again to herself then, at last satisfied that she had omitted nothing, returned to her typing.

Jana's mother did not know she had joined the PFF. Her poor mother would be terrified if she knew what other work she was carrying out. She had thought of telling her father, if for no other reason than, to give him something to live for…to be proud of. Then she had thought it over again and had decided against it.

The young girl turned the knob on her typewriter and took out the last sheet of her typing, placing it neatly in a folder before locking it away in her desk. Then, satisfied that her desk was also neat and tidy, she covered her machine. It was already dark outside, she must hurry or she would miss the 8.10.p.m. tram to Odera Street.

She stood up and crossed to the door, stopping to take a last quick glance around the big empty office to ensure everything was all right before switching off the lights. All seemed to be in order, if not, she thought, doubtless the security guards would notice.

Jana closed the door and stepped into the hallway just as the elevator dropped quickly passed her floor. Annoyed that she could miss her tram, she quickly headed for the stairs.

By the time, she had reached the reception area on the ground floor she was out of breath and gasping out her personnel number to the old guard behind the desk.

Slowly, too slowly for the girl, the old man reached under the counter and brought out a large black book. Jana quickly turned it round, scribbled down her name and gave him the keys, noticing with further annoyance that it was raining outside. Lucky she had brought her umbrella. "Oh no!!" she cried out, remembering she had left it, and her father's pills in a bag by her desk.

"What's wrong, young miss?" the old guard asked, wrinkling his brows.

"I've forgotten my father's pills! They are painkillers. He needs them for his leg!"

Jana was annoyed with herself. Had she only forgotten her umbrella she would not have minded getting soaked, but her father had become reliant on those pills, too reliant she thought. Nor did she wish to face him without them.

"Where did you leave them miss?" the old guard was asking her.

"In my desk...in my office," she stammered.

"Sorry miss," the old man apologized, "but security will have locked up by now. It is more than my job's worth to let you back up there."

"But he *needs* them !"

The man saw her agitation. The girl, he knew, lived close to his own home. The last tram to Odera Street was just after 8 o'clock and to miss it would mean a walk of over two kilometres, and it was raining heavily. "All right miss" he said, making up his mind. "But I will have to call a guard. He will have to go back up with you."

"Yes! Yes! That will be all right," she stammered, eagerly.

It was a further five minutes before Jana and the guard reached her office, and while he unlocked the door, she stole an impatient glance at her watch. Ten minutes to the tram. She would have to hurry. Less, if that old guard asked her to sign out again. The guard stood aside as he opened the door and Jana brushed passed him and groped for the light switch, missing the correct switch and only flooding half of the room.

Jana did not wait to rectify her mistake but instead ran to her desk at the darkened end of the room, snatching up her bag by the leg of her desk and, as she turned again for the door, glimpsed a shadowy figure at the top floor window of the opposite wing.

The young girl came to an abrupt halt, frozen by what she saw, or what she thought she saw. She pressed a hand to her mouth. It could not be! It was not at all possible!

Her heart throbbing, all else forgotten, Jana moved hesitantly to the window. Behind her, the distant voice of the guard at the door was asking if she was all right and had she found what she was looking for? For a brief moment, she saw the familiar outline against the window: the unmistakable stance of President Kolybin as he stood beside the cabinet.

The guard called out again and she answered him in a choking voice. Dazed, she started for the door, more than ever convinced by what she had seen. It *was* him! It *was* the president!

At the door the security guard stood aside to let her pass, mistaking the flush on her cheeks as the sign of her haste to catch her tram. "Better hurry if you want to catch that last tram! I'll lock up miss."

Speechless, her mind in a whirl, Jana nodded. Still unable to believe her eyes, she looked at the guard as if to speak, to ask him if he knew the president was in his office. Then thought how stupid the question would sound. However, if she was right, and it was him, then she must get word to Miro right away!

Jana caught the tram with seconds to spare. Eyes staring, her heart pounding, she knew nothing of the journey. Four tram halts later, she had made up her mind to contact Miro at his home.

She did not know where her Section Leader lived, or what was his real name, but she had his telephone number, which she was allowed to use only in the event of an emergency: and this, she decided was an emergency. Of course, she could have found out more about Miro, but that would have gone against security. He was married, this she did know, having had her previous calls to his home answered by a female voice, which she naturally assumed to be his wife. Secretly, she hoped he was not. She liked Miro...he was handsome. A bit old for her...possibily in his early thirties?

Jana dragged her mind back to the present problem. What would her Section Leader think when she told him of what she had seen? What if she was wrong? Agitatedly she crumpled the tram ticket in her hand. Perhaps it would be better if she were to forget about the whole affair. Kolybin was dead. And, as her father had said, good riddance to the traitor. But if she was not wrong? Jana squeezed her hands together, wishing she had not forgotten those damned pills, then she could have avoided this dilemma.

In her mind, she heard Miro's voice. "Report everything no matter however trivial you may think it may be, it is not for you to decide how important or unimportant it is, this is for the Section or Group Leader to determine."

Jana looked up. The tram had almost reached Zacia Street. There was a phone box on the corner she remembered, she would call Miro from there.

Staff Sergeant Juri Trybala was in a hurry to get home, as he' d forgotten to get little Max his son, a cough bottle at the chemist. By the time he'd reached the shop it was closed, forcing him to detour to a chemist well out of his way. Now he *was* late. This was the worse part of all, deceiving his wife and child.

Juri moved his car out from behind a lorry, its spray flooding his windscreen. He turned the knob for the wipers. They did not move. "Ch...!" he swore, "one more job to do when I get home!"

He peered through the rain splattered windscreen. It was time to put an end to it all. But how? Lomova Jakofcic was not a woman to take no for an answer.

He'd tried to sound her out once about what would happen to her...them, if her husband, the General, was ever to find out about their little affair. Would it not be better, he had told her, to end it before he did find out? He remembered how she had laughed, had answered coyly, in a way only Lomova could, that they must ensure her husband never did. Then decisively, that she had him, and was going to hold on to him.

"Silvo is at least twenty years older than me, for heavens sake!" she had exclaimed, sitting half naked on the bed of the flat she had 'acquired,' in a rather dingy part of the city. "All he ever wants are medals. Glory! As for me? I want to be conquered more than every other calendar month!" Lomova had crossed to where he sat by the fire sipping vodka. "Now you, Juri? There are less years between us, and much more in other ways."

Juri grasped the wheel until his knuckles were white. That was his trouble, he could not resist her. That skin! God! What a beautiful body! He closed his eyes for a brief second, to rid himself of the vision.

How many people was he deceiving, including those most dear to him? To go home, as he was now doing, kiss his wife, mutter how hard a day he had had at the Caserne, take little Max on his knee, and ask him what he had been up to.....Ask questions concerning the daily running of the house, of his wife...Act the ideal husband and father, while all the time deceit. Climbing into another woman's bed. But what a woman! What love making.

In his anger, Juri stepped too hard on the accelerator and touched the brake to check his speed.

What of the General? Juri ran a hand down the outside of his right leg as if it still hurt. General Jakofcic had been good to him after the accident. It had not really been an accident. He'd been a lance corporal at the time, driving the General back to Field H.Q. in his jeep one night, when they were attacked by PFF He'd swerved off the road and fired on the attackers with his sub machine gun while the General lay unconscious. There was an explosion and that is all he remembered, until he came to, in a hospital bed, his right leg shattered and thinking his career in the army had come to an end.

He'd lain there staring up at the white ceiling, wondering how to provide for his wife and unborn child, when the General had called in to see him.

Juri swung the car round the corner to Zacia Street.

Jakofcic, had shown his gratitude by promoting him to staff sergeant, to be permanently stationed in the Caserne. That is how he had come to make the acquaintance of Mistress Jakofcic.

When the General was away, usually up north, known as 'the front', Juri worked out of his own office in the Caserne and not from the General's office in his own home across the barracks square, as it would have been deemed improper to have done so. However, there was always some little detail the General had missed whilst absent, which had resulted in him having to visit the General's house and offer his wife his most sincere apologies for disturbing her. After a while, Lomova's door, plus everything else, was always open to him.

Jana pushed back a wet strand of hair as she struggled to put the three coins in the phone box. After a pause, she heard the familiar female voice at the other end.

"Can I speak to Miro, please?" she asked hurriedly, giving her code name. There was a slight pause, whereby she was asked to hold on. "Hurry! Hurry!" she fumed at the mouthpiece, leaning impatiently on one leg then another.

Now that she had made the decision to tell Miro, she was anxious to be quit of the information. Let someone else sort out the rationale of it all, she thought.

There was a car at the end of the street, its headlights flooding the box. "Hello?" she heard Miro say at the other end. She forgot the car and drew closer to the mouthpiece.

"Hello, Miro. It is me Savi!" she cried, giving him her code name, and barely able to control her excitement. "I saw him, Miro! I saw him! It was ......" There was a blinding light, she stopped for a moment; Miro's voice in the distance, asking if she was all right. The box splintering and cracking at one side; the coin box flying up to meet her; a sliver of glass hitting her with the velocity of a bullet.

Seventeen year old, Jana Hafner was dead before she hit the floor.

Juri Trybala knew he had hit the side of the phone box. There was a sickening crunch of torn metal and shattering wood as he fought to straighten the car. He'd taken the corner much too fast, thought he'd gotten away with it until he saw the box and the frightened face of the young girl inside, as he flew passed.

Screeching to a halt, Juri sat there for a moment his hand on the door handle staring at what was left of the phone box through his rear view mirror. Was the girl dead? Injured? Most assuredly. The box was shattered. Either way, how could he explain his reason for being away out here in this part of the city? Yet, if she was hurt, he could not just leave the poor girl lying there.

Juri got out and ran back to what was left of the box, and even as he knelt down beside the girl knew she was dead. In the background, he heard the sound of windows and doors opening. He looked around him, panicking. There was nothing he could do. *Get out of here! Get out of here*! the voice inside him cried.

Taking a last look down at the dead girl, offering her a silent prayer of apology, Juri Trybala, took to his heels.

Chapter 8

Although it was Section and not Group business, Petr had agreed to meet Miro at their headquarters in the underground cellar instead of at Pavel's flat. The Group Leader scrambled through the rubble of broken bricks and mortar of the bombed out building, squeezing passed the huge lump of concrete and stone fused together by the heat of a Luffwaffe air raid, that concealed the cellar door.

Miro was there first. He greeted the older man with a wave of his hip flask. "Doesn't matter how warm it is outside, this place is always bloody freezing," he shivered.

"Perhaps you would like the organisation to move to the Ritz? I am sure the Senate will be only too happy to oblige!" Petr softened his cursory sarcasm with a brief smile. He had had a bad day, and this grouse of Miro's was the last straw.

"What do you find so important that we should meet, Miro?" Petr asked, the usual soft timbre of his voice returning.

Miro poured a vodka into the cup of his hip flask. "Young Savi telephoned me last night. Around 8.p.m. I'd say it was." Miro pushed the cup across the makeshift table. "All she got out to me was, 'I saw him'." He halted while Petr swallowed his drink.

"And...?" Petr handed back the empty cup.

"Savi was killed in that phone box while she was making that call. Knocked down by a car. I do not think it was an accident."

"I see..." Petr said slowly, digesting what Miro had said. "Any trace of the car, or the driver?"

Miro shook his head. "Not yet, but I'm working on it. I've got my men on the look out for any civilian cars going in to the Caserne or any garage throughout the city, that look as though they may have been involved in an accident. A pretty big job," Miro added, as if to impress his leader. Petr said nothing. He waited for Miro to go on. "The car that did this must be pretty badly damaged, if the condition of the phone box is anything to go by."

"No witnesses I take it?" Petr asked quietly.

For all the years he'd had known Miro, he had never really liked him. Too ambitious, Petr thought. Perhaps it had been a mistake to have asked for his help after Frederick's capture. Since then, he had grown in self-confidence, as though his censure over the 'judge's mission ' had never existed, and that he, Petr had forgotten it all.

This man, he thought wearily, would never be content with just being a Section Leader, he wanted his own Group, and would do anything to impress him as Group Leader and member of the National Council to get it.

Miro pushed the half full cup across the rough table. It caught slightly and he corrected it. "Plenty,..but all giving different descriptions. When it comes right down to it, none, just a lot of people saying they ran to their windows when they heard the crash."

"Well keep trying. But who do you think this...Savi?" Petr stopped to ascertain whether or not he had the correct code name. Miro confirmed with a nod. "Who do you think she had in mind when she said 'I saw him?"

The younger man shrugged. "It had to be someone important. I've spoken to her father. He's a bitter old sod. I pretended to be from Admin. He told me she had been working late. Didn't come home with some sort of pills he needed for his leg-or lack of it," Miro added sarcastically. "The girl's mother was distraught. I could get nothing out of her. I'm sure neither of them knew she was working for us. So, whatever Savi thought was so important she had to phone me at home, I'm sure she could only have found out last night."

"You are quite certain in your own mind it was not an accident?" Petr asked, tapping his pocket for his cigarette case.

Miro furrowed his brows. "Why do you ask that, Petr?"

"Just that I do not think it likely that Security would have mown down Savi before they found out what she knew."

Miro felt the blood drain from his face. He had wanted so much to impress his senior, but instead had only succeeded in making a fool of himself.

Petr's searching for his cigarette case gave Miro time to offer an alternative theory. Rubbing his right ear to give himself time to think it through, he started slowly. "...Perhaps, what Savi found out, was important, perhaps too important, that Security had to kill her before she told anyone what she knew?" Miro's bland expression concealed his feeling of triumph at his own deduction.

Petr focused his eyes firmly on his drink. "Then, if it is as you say, Miro, we are all indebted to Security, for had they first arrested her, we might not now be sitting here discussing your theory."

Again, Miro felt deflated by his Group Leader's reasoning. However, Petr appeared not to have noticed, and had gone on. "Jakofcic would be my guess. If he is the reason, he must be doing something extraordinary to have Security go to the length of having your agent killed almost immediately upon leaving her office." The Group Leader gave a tired sigh. "Now it is up to me to find out what our beloved enemy is up to."

"Don't you think you were taking a hell of a risk?" Milan attempted to keep the anger out of his voice as he watched Paule break an egg into the pan.

"Yes. But it was a chance I had to take if you wanted that motion to go through." Paule jabbed at the rashers of bacon with his fork.

Milan stood back to let the little president slide the eggs on to a plate. "Want some?" Paule asked, showing him the pan. "There's plenty here. I have two plates."

"No thank you. I have to get back soon. I've an appointment with Meloun at two."

"In that case, we had better discuss the artillery situation, eh?" Paule squeezed passed his friend.

Milan followed him out of the tiny kitchen, and sat down in his usual chair by the desk. "I arranged to have the export payment made in the usual way. The guns are now at our Silia factory, having been assembled at various factories throughout the country as you suggested." He snapped a look at his watch, then at Paule eating his breakfast, thinking that the aftermath of Paule's 'death' had not at all gone according to plan as his old friend had suspected. There had been no general PFF uprising against the Government as a result of his assassination. Then again, perhaps Paule did not hold this country together as he so firmly believed.

After attacking Pienera, Tetek had not, as hoped, swooped down towards the Capital where Government troops could engage him on the open plains with their heavier armament of tanks, and their latest acquisition of heavy artillery. On the contrary ,Tetek had held Pienera with only a token force, and had proceeded to win a moral victory by extraditing his troops from the very trap set for him. Leaving Milan to ponder, which side had the better Intelligence.

"Good! When I have arranged the next little surprise for our friend Tetek, those guns will play an important part." Paule dabbed his lips with his napkin. "You are certain no one knows where the guns are at present?"

"Positive, Paule."

Paule pushed back his empty plate, got up from his desk, and accompanied Milan to the elevator. "Thank you again for calling on Myra,I appreciate it, Milan. I am glad she is taking it so well,... Stefan too. The boy makes me proud. In fact I am proud of them both."

Milan slid back the panel. Myra was not taking it well, and for a moment considered telling Paule the truth, in the hope that his friend might change his mind and tell his wife he was still alive. Yet, should Paule refuse, after he had told him, he would only have succeeded in adding to his friend's worries. "Myra and Stefan miss you very much Paule...could you not...."

Paule shook his head. "I miss them too, Milan, much more than I can say. But our country comes first, as it did during the occupation. We all had to make personal sacrifices then too, you know. If we had not, our children would be speaking our language with a different accent!" Paule laughed to hide his pain.

Milan squeezed Paule's shoulder. "Very well, old friend, as you wish. But let us hope this magnificent deception will not be for too long."

Paule stepped away from the open elevator. "I will drink to that...but not too much," he smiled ruefully.

Miro could hardly contain his excitement. He' d wanted to meet Petr in the cellar or at Pavel's flat - break the news to the entire Group, but Petr would not hear of it, and had reminded him angrily, that he should know the rules by now. The less they met, and in particular, the fewer there were of them, the better and safer it would be. So Petr had suggested they meet at the Canal Bistro on Saturday afternoon.

Miro jumped off the tram, leaving it clanking and swaying up Biesa Street. Edging through jostling shoppers heading for the town centre, he saw Petr sitting at one of the pavement tables and crossed to meet him.

"Afternoon, Petr," he said cheerfully, pulling back one of the iron chairs.

Petr looked up quickly. "Miro" he said simply.

Miro looked around him at the bustling street, then at the narrow canal flowing in quiet contrast. "I found out the name of our accident driver," he said with a conspiratorial smile.

Petr sipped his coffee, as if he had not heard. Miro leaned forward, eager to repeat the question.

"I heard what you said, Miro." Petr put down his cup.

Miro glanced around him apprehensively. "Are you sure this is the best place?"

Petr remained impassive. "It was during the war." He made a slight sweeping gesture with his hand. "These people are all too wrapped up in their own affairs to be bothered with ours. So, tell me what excites you so much, before you burst. Eh!"

Miro blushed, feeling that once again he'd made a fool of himself. Annoyed too, by the way the older man had, of cutting a person down to size. He drew his chair closer to the table. "The driver's name is Trybala.....Sergeant Juri Trybala,"he said, his voice little more than a whisper. Then as Petr made no comment went on. "He is Jakofcic's Staff Sergeant."

Petr raised his cup to his lips. "You think because of this, that the man your agent referred to, was the General?" he asked, sipping his coffee.

"Can I get you anything sir?" A waiter hovered over Miro, a round silver tray in his hand.

"A coffee, I should think, for my friend." Petr's features softened as he looked up at the waiter. "Also, if you would be so kind, two pieces of that most delicious looking cake." Petr pointed to the table opposite, where an enormous fat woman sat devouring a large cream sponge.

"Very good, sir." The waiter bowed politely.

Petr turned back to Miro. "You still do not think it was an accident?"

The other shook his head. "There was no reason for Trybala to be in that part of the city at that time of evening."

"Then I take it you know where this Sergeant lives?"

"Much more than that." Miro's eyes shone.

The waiter returned with the coffee and cakes, giving Petr time to sum up the situation, especially in reference to his Section Leader, who obviously had found out a great deal more, and intended feeding him little bits of information at a time, like a fisherman slowly reeling in his catch.

Petr cut a slice of cake with the edge of his fork. "The cake looks delicious Miro, and when you are digesting it, also digest this," Petr growled, his eyes boring into the younger man. "I have no time to play games. Therefore, you will impress me only by divulging all there is to divulge. Do I make myself clear?" he hissed. The fat lady eating the cake at the next table turned her head slightly in his direction as he spoke.

Miro gripped his fork tighter. With the information he possessed, he had wanted to feel superior to his Group Leader just this once, instead, he had made a mess of it, Petr would probably have him demoted after this.

Petr drew his eyes to the canal. He must not allow himself to be angered by this parvenu. Two swans swam passed, a third, hovering in the background. The brother, Petr thought,... or the lover. And was calmed by his own humour.

A few people with tables closer to the edge of the canal were throwing crumbs at the passing swans.

"Just as it used to be before the War," Petr said, loud enough for the lady eating her second piece of cake to hear. She smiled at him, her mouth full.

His composure returned, Petr signalled with his eyes for Miro to continue, as the lady resumed her oral demolition.

"I found out the General's wife and Trybala are lovers." For once Miro was sure he saw a flicker of surprise in his Group Leader's eyes. Encouraged, he plunged on. "They have a flat on the opposite side of the city where they meet whenever Jakofcic is not at home. This Staff Sergeant has a disability which keeps him at the barracks. Something to do with his leg, I believe. Seems this is his only disability," he chuckled. Petr did not appear to have noticed the joke, but kept on eating. Frowning at this, Miro went on. "Zacia Street was not on Trybala's way home from their lovers nest. Therefore, if he was not on his way home from there, then his sole purpose for being on Zacia Street was to stop Savi from passing on what she knew. Something important enough for the staff sergeant to go after her, as soon as she had left her office. Also, he has had his car repaired on the other side of town, which in itself is suspicious."

Petr pushed his empty plate away. "Your coffee is getting cold, Miro," his voice devoid of its former harshness. "You have done well."

Surprised, though gratified by Petr's unexpected praise, Miro ventured to suggest. "We can have the General's wife picked up anytime...or them both, if you wish, Petr. Or at least threaten to let their partners know what is going on should the lovers fail to supply us with a little information now and then. Eh?"

Petr's face had darkened long before Miro had finished. "You know we do not make war on civilians...especially, when they are women," he seethed. "This is a mistake we learned from early in our campaign. It was found to be counter-productive. It served only to turn the public against us. As for our staff sergeant? Have him watched. Your suggestion of having him questioned will come all in good time."

Miro gulped down his stone cold coffee, relieved that the meeting he had so eargerly looked forward to was at an end. His one and only consolation over his Group Leader, being a tiny jot of cream sticking to the corner of Petr's mouth.

"Where are those papers, Sergeant?" Jakofcic moved out from behind the desk in his study.

Juri came out of the small room where his own desk was situated, "I have them here sir."

Jakofcic took them and walked into the lounge of his house. "I'll also need those reports before you go off duty, Sergeant," he called out over his shoulder.

"Coffee, Sergeant Trybala?" Lomova asked pleasantly, coming into the room carrying a coffee tray.

Taken by surprise by Lomova's unexpected appearance, Juri reached out automatically for the cup she had offered him. "The girl's dead," he whispered, annoyed by Lomova'a beguiling smile. He had waited an eternity to tell her, and here she was tantalising him with her husband only a few metres away in the next room.

Juri leaned forward to help himself to the sugar, gently placing his free hand on her's to prevent her from moving away. "Should they find out it was my car that was involved in the accident, I'm history." He heard the despair in his voice, felt the sweat on his brow as he always did when thinking of that night.

He'd taken the car to a rundown garage on the far side of the city, telling the owners that he could not afford to have it repaired in any of the big city garages. He'd also told them he had lied to his insurance company about the cost of repairs, which was also untrue, because there was no way in which he could make a claim without there being an investigation. He knew the owners were suspicious, but was certain they needed the business, so he was fairly sure they'd keep quiet. If not?

"Cream?" Lomova was asking him in a voice intended for her husband to hear. She bent closer, her voice low. "When will your car be ready?"

"Tomorrow ,if I can find the money."

"I'll help," Lomova said softly.

"Is that you dear?" the General called out.

Juri stood aside as the tall good-looking man with the shock of grey hair strode back into his office.

"Yes darling!" Lomova called back. "I was just offering the sergeant a cup of coffee."

"Only for the sergeant?" the General teased. "Officers and husbands excluded, eh?" Juri and Lomova laughed together.

"I only saw the sergeant when I was in the garden, Silvo. He looked as if he needed a drink. Shall I fetch you one?"

"No, my love, I have a lot to get through before this evening's meeting."

Juri saw the adoration in the old man's eyes as his wife crossed to the French doors that led out into the garden.

The General treated him almost like one of the family, which is why he was allowed when in private to hear them address one another so intimately. He lifted his coffee cup from the General's desk with the intention of returning to his own office.

Damn! How had he allowed himself to get involved? Did he not have a loving wife and a little son to be proud of? Even before the accident with the girl, he'd been planning a way of ending it. Convincing himself, the only way was for Lomova to grow tired of him: make her become less satisfied with his lovemaking. So far, he had failed. Should she ever suspect? Ch...It was all a nightmare."

"When you have finished those reports, Sergeant" he heard the General say, "Take twenty four hours off, that, should give you some time to spend with that lovely wife and little boy of yours."

"Thank you sir. I appreciate it. And so will my wife"

"Good. I hope *my* wife appreciates *my* company as much. What do you say dear? Perhaps, I can afford a few hours off too, some time?"

Lomova toyed with arranging flowers in a vase by the window. "That would be sweet, darling," she said lovingly, her eyes on Juri.

"You know, Sergeant, we four must get together some time. Forget about rank for once. Hell! We never know what is in front of us. Do we?" The general chuckled.

"No sir," Juri answered, furtively glancing at Lomova.

"You can say that again darling," Lomova said. "You can say that again."

"How is Myra?" Paule asked, climbing down off the chair where he had been putting in a new light bulb.

Milan thought his friend looked tired, as well he might after almost two months in this rat hole. "She's coping well, Paule." He made himself comfortable in his usual chair. "Stefan has a young lady friend – a nurse, so Eilzbieta tells me." He forced himself to sound cheerful in an attempt to lighten the atmosphere for what he was about to say.

"That's nice. Perhaps my son means to keep it a family tradition," Paule joked sitting down behind his desk. "What does Myra think of her?"

"I don't think they have met as yet. The girl comes from the Biesa side of the city." Paule's face twitched.

"Don't say you disapprove?" Milan teased. "Become a snob, have we?"

Paule drew a plate of sandwiches towards him. "No. Do not be so damned stupid, Milan. I was only thinking of what type of person has come out of there; Commies mostly." He lifted a sandwich and began to eat.

Milan did not want Paule annoyed, not with what he was about to discuss with him, as he was not sure how the little man would take it. "Fine guerilla fighters too," he said quietly.

Paule nodded. "Forgive me, Milan, living down here longer than I had anticipated is becoming a trifle wearing. Besides, I worry about Myra and the boy," he said chewing.

"I understand." Milan edged forward in his seat. "Paule!" he began. "I do not wish to add to your worries, but something quite important has come up."

Paule studied the map in front of him. "Go on," he said without looking up.

Milan cleared his throat. "Our Party believes it is now time I was elected President." He halted to see what effect this statement would have on the man so assiduously wrapped up in his map.

Paule looked up, and put down what remained of his sandwich. "Why? I thought you and I agreed that you should stall any election until next year. Or until we had dealt with these Commie PFF bastards, when I had returned out of hiding?"

"Yes I know. But the Party has stated they will nominate Meloun if I do not stand now and put some stability back into the Party. You know what that will mean."

Paule continued to study his map, as if he had not heard one word his friend had said.

Milan drew himself to the edge of his chair, beginning to feel annoyed by Paule's obvious apathy. He would have to do something drastic to shake up the man. He began. "Unless, in the event of Meloun being elected you were to take him into your confidence. Otherwise, he is likely to go his own way and pursue his own policies. Then where will you be? You could never achieve what you hoped to achieve. And if not, how could you justify your own assassination, or your reappearance?"

Paule brushed aside the crumbs from his sandwich as he did Milan's deductions.

"Then become President and guarantee my policies are pursued."

Milan drew a hand through his hair, agitated by the little man's absorption in his map. Paule did not seem to understand, so firmly did he believe that the final defeat of the PFF would justify everything he had done, and would do in the future. "How can I take an oath to my country as President, Paule, knowing you are still alive? I'd…we would be crucified!"

"We *shall* be, if we were to loose this country of ours to the Commies. Even worse to a fool like Meloun, who only seeks appeasement! Compromise! Has he forgotten a certain little Austrian Corporal?"

"Then you think I should stand?"

Paule sat back in his chair his study of the map momentarily forgotten. "We must see this through to the end, Milan. No one else can do this except you. Do you understand?"

"Yes Paule," Milan said wearily. "But, how I wish it was the end."

Lomova Jakofcic liked the tennis club, it was in a less depressing area of the city. And from where she sat on the balcony, the skeletal bombed out buildings on the outer suburbs were hardly visible.

Gathering the white cardigan, casually draped around her shoulders more closely about her, she absently watched the singles match on the nearest court being fought out by two ageing opulent women, her mind on what she would make Juri for supper at the flat. She smoothed out her tennis frock and glanced at her watch: another hour.

Red ash rattled against the wire door of the court. One of the participants bent to retrieve the ball, her breath loud and labored.

"I think Vasi will burst if she plays another set."

Lomova swivelled round at the sound of the voice. Zofia Wysocki beamed down at her while making herself comfortable in the chair opposite.

Lomova said something quite unladylike under her breath. She detested Zofia Wysocki, as she was sure most people did in the club.

A woman, of whom Silvo had said, if her reputation about knowing everyone's business was true, should be in the Secret Service. But then again, he had added with a wry smile, it would not be a Secret Service for long.

"Zofia!" Lomova tried to pretend she was glad to see the woman.

"How is your delightful husband, the General, Lomova?"

"Very well thank you," Lomova answered, toying with the straw in her lemonade glass.

"Is he very much away from home these days, my dear?" Zofia jabbed, quietly satisfied by the younger woman's scowl. "Oh I don't mean to pry, my dear, I know all about security and all that. What I really mean is...well... with all the mercenaries gone, and this beastly war of ours as good as over, you might be seeing a bit more of him: he might not be away so much."

Lomova pretended to be engrossed in the overweight tennis match. "Oh, I do see quite a bit of him now," she said lightly, sipping her drink.

"It must have been simply awful, his being away so much during the 'Emergency'." Zofia referred to the official term used for what had been – still was nothing short of civil war. "What, with you being so young! A woman of your age would have felt it more than an old crone like me," Zofia tittered. "I am surprised you were never tempted, with all those good looking soldiers in the Caserne all around. Or were you, my dear?" Zofia tittered again, delving into her handbag, as if what she had just said was of the merest flippancy.

You know you old cow, Lomova thought. You know about Juri and me.

Zofia rummaged through her handbag. "Oh, I seem to have forgotten it," she said despondently, her head still in her bag. "My nephew so idolises your husband, Lomova. He asked me…well not in so many words, if I could put in a word for him. He wants so much to be attached to your husband's staff. As I said, with the Emergency almost over, there will soon be little opportunity for promotion. Ive says, 'where there is action, there is the General'!" Zofia tittered again. "Also, it is not easy to support a wife and two small children on a Second Lieutenants pay. Oh! Here's what I was looking for, Ive , my nephew's details, just in case you can do something for him." Zofia lifted her head to push a slip of paper across the table.

"I cannot influence my husband on military matters, Zofia, you should know that. Silvo appoints and promotes whom he wants." Lomova tried to keep the hostility out of her voice, though her every instinct was leap across the table and scratch the old viper's eyes out.

"Oh! I know, my dear! However, I am sure you have some influence on some military affairs?"

"Perhaps , Zofia. I will see what can be done, but it will take time, you know."

"Of course. I quite understand. But not too long I hope?"

Suddenly Zofia pointed over Lomova'a shoulder. "I just knew it! I do believe Vasi, has fainted! Overindulging has its penalties! Don't you agree, my dear?"

"I met that old cow, Zofia Wysocki at the tennis club today, Juri. I'm certain she knows about us." Lomova sat at the shabby dressing table, brushing her hair.

Juri pulled on his trousers, and felt himself tingle at the swell of her breasts. Perhaps this was the opportunity he had been waiting for.

Lomova's auburn hair fell down her naked back. She opened up a hairgrip with her teeth, sliding it over a shock of hair.

Juri cleared his throat. "Perhaps it would be safer if we were to stop seeing one another for a little while. If this Zofia...whatever her name, knows how many more do? How long before the General gets to hear of it?"

Lomova edged round a little in her seat until she was facing him, sitting on the edge of the bed. She knew he wanted to end it, she could sense it, see it in his eyes. Of course, he wouldn't, not when he saw her as she was now. He loved his wife, but he wanted *her* more, just as she wanted him, and not Silvo. No Juri, I will not end it unless I choose to, she thought bitterly. "She won't tell Silvo. At least, not until she knows whether I can have her little lieutenant of a nephew appointed to his staff."

"So that's her game. If you can get her nephew on to the General's staff, do you think it will stop her? Will it end there?"

"I suppose so. At least, until she thinks of something else to help her up the social ladder. I hope she falls and breaks her neck in the process," Lomova exclaimed bitterly, standing up.

Juri's heart beat faster. He wanted to make love to her again, but knew there was no time. It would be dark soon, and even the trusting General would become suspicious of his wife coming home from a tennis match in the dark. *Unless*, he thought, *she played with luminous balls...certainly his weren't.* Despite the potential seriousness of what Lomova had just told him, he had to smile at the thought.

"Have I said something funny, Juri?" Lomova asked, her face lighting up.

Juri thought quickly. "Yes, what you just said about that old cow falling off a social ladder. Is it harder than a window cleaners or a..."

Lomova reached out and pulled him to her naked breasts. "Harder than what?" she asked, reaching down.

"No Lomova!" Juri laughed, trying to extricate himself from her embrace. "We haven't time, my love!"

"Love?" Lomova queried. "Were you at the tennis club, too?" she mocked, grabbing him tighter. "Perhaps, it was you who put that old cow up to it? Eh?"

"You're hurting me!" Juri yelled, unable to stop himself from laughing.

"Then one volley from you and it will be game, set, and match!" Lomova giggled in his ear.

"I'm game for one more match, but it must be quick." Juri straddled his way back on to the bed, Lomova still in his arms. "But it's you that has the advantage," he laughed.

Silvo sat on the edge of his bed winding up his watch. Lomova put down the pearl-handed hairbrush and rose from the dressing table, discreetly pulling down the shoulder straps of her nightgown a little more. "I met Zofia Wysocki at the tennis club to day" she said with a feeling of deja vu.

"Is that the old busy body you told me about before?" Silvo asked, without looking up.

Lomova moved around the bedroom, putting odds and ends into various drawers as she went on. "Yes, except this time she had a favour to ask. She told me you are her nephew's hero. All he wants out of the army is to be assigned to your staff."

"Not a very ambitious young man, is he dear?" the General chuckled, carefully laying his wristwatch on the bedside table.

"On the contrary dear, he believes you are always in the thick of things, always near the action. Were he to be there also..."

"He'd get a medal, or promotion. Eh, dear?" Silvo pulled back the bedcovers. "You know that is not how the army operates, not how I operate. If I were to start doing favours, helping someone who is the such and such of someone else, I'd soon be surrounded by yes men, and not a soldier amongst them."

Lomova knew it would be difficult, that is why she had judged this the right time to begin her subterfuge. "No, he is not like that Silvo. Zofia says his father was killed by the Nazis. He never knew what happened to his mother. He just wants to make a better life for his wife and children. He thinks being in the front line would help. Also, Zofia says, he believes that's what his father would have wanted of him."

Lomova came and stood over her husband. "I know it was wrong to have brought up the subject. I told Zofia that it was not right that

I should ask you." Her voice low, purring, and at the same time a little pleading. She drew Slivo's head between her breasts, thinking, now, it is up to you my dear husband.

Silvo drew away. He always had a soft spot for those who had lost members of their families to the Nazis. In wars, soldiers were expected to die, but not innocent women and children. This last war had changed all of that. Besides, he wanted to make love to this irresistible young wife of his. "Leave his name and regiment with me, and I'll see what can be done. I'm making no promises, mind you," Silvo said, finding his mouth covered in kisses.

It was going to be a good night for love making, Silvo thought. It was going to be a long night, thought his wife, thanking him in the only way she knew how.

The Regiment had not had their leave after Pienera as promised. Instead, they were up here in these mountains, outnumbered and outfought by that bastard, Tetek.

Mark slid his field glasses over the rim of the slit trench, inch by inch at a time. They'd have to wait for darkness, and that would be a long time coming. Cries of their wounded, they'd been forced to leave behind, reached him from the defile where they had been caught earlier that day.

Adjusting the sights, Mark focused them on the opposite mountainside. "Do you know where the rest of Corps is Sergeant?" he whispered, edging round to scan the rocks above.

"Those who made it back through the defile, are probably half way to the Capital by now," Grbesa said caustically.

Mark slid down into the hastily made foxhole. "How bad are we hit?"

"Not too bad, Major, we were lucky to head up here instead of trying to get back through that crack in the rock down there." The N.C.O. slid down beside his senior.

Mark gave an almost imperceptible nod. "I think they are above us on this side as well."

Niew leaned his back against the narrow trench wall. "You could well be right, sir. I think, Colonel Ziotkowski is still somewhere on our left."

"Good. See if you can make contact. Tell him I believe we should try getting ourselves over this side of the mountain, before we are completely surrounded."

"Okay sir, I'll try sending a runner. The wireless is R.S. although we couldn't use it even if we wanted to." The sergeant was up and over the side, before he had scarcely finished speaking, leaving Mark to sit and speculate on whether his suggestion would find favour with his Commanding Officer.

The Scot cursed. He had hoped Kolybin would have found some way of having him sent home by this time. He still felt uneasy, mistrustful of the little President. What if he had decided that it was safer not to have him around anymore? Perhaps, he'd already got rid of the bogus doctor and the unknown man. The one who had created the diversion so that he, Mark, could get on to the roof. Or was Kolybin hoping he might 'header' a bullet, if sent on one mission too many? Was this the reason why Company leave had not come through? Steady Mark he told himself, you are getting a wee bit paranoid here. Let's just concentrate on the matter in hand, or there will be no need to worry at all.

For a fraction of a second, a shadow loomed over the trench. Mark raised his Thompson as Grbesa tumbled in to the foxhole.

"Colonel Ziotkowski sends his compliments," Niew gasped. "I ran into a corporal heading this way with the same message. Seems as though our Colonel has had the same idea," Niew smirked. "Great minds and all that, Major!" Mark glared at him knowing the remainder of the quotation.

Niew hunched himself at the opposite end of the trench. "Colonel's orders are, we try and get up to the crest from this side of the mountain. He will cover us while we do. Then we cover him from the top when it's his turn. He gave zero as 2100 hours."

Mark checked his watch. "Good. How many wounded do we have? And how many do you think can make it up there?" Mark nodded to the cliffs above.

"At the last count, our Company had twelve wounded. I don't think five of them can make the climb." Grbesa attempted to ease the burden a fraction, aware of what was in his major's mind. "They'll be all right, it's Tetek over there, not some shit of a fanatical Commie."

Mark gave a sigh. It was comforting to know Tetek had a reputation for compassion. A man, so he understood, who treated his prisoners humanely, in the belief they might be converted to the Cause . A sentiment in direct contrast to most of his subordinates. "I hope you're right Sergeant, I'd hate to leave any of my men to the mercies of some of those bastards."

Niew felt strangely disturbed by the remark. He had never counted on any mercenary having any feelings towards his command. After all, weren't they here just to sell their trade? To make themselves rich and get the hell out of it, no matter what the cost – to others that was. Then he remembered the odd occasion when the Scot had done something contrary to his theory, not often, but enough to show he was human. Such as the roadblock at Pienera, when he had shown a little compassion for the women and children involved, and had not wanted to open fire. Niew looked at his major sitting huddled there, toying with the straps of his field glasses. Perhaps, this soldier should just satisfy himself with the fact that it wasn't him that was wounded. PFF did not take mercenaries prisoner – at least not for long.

Niew nodded in the direction of the cliffs above. "I think I should take a couple of men, and start to find a way up there."

Mark peered at his watch. "You have the best part of an hour to find one, and be back here by 2100 hours. Also, it will be almost dark by then, that's when the Reds will expect us to make our move."

Ten minutes after Niew's Grbesa's departure, heavy guns unexpectedly opened up from the defile below. Mark snapped a look over the top of his trench. It was what was left of their own heavy guns from further down the valley. Well! Well! Well! Would you believe it, Mark thought, Corps had regrouped and were now fighting their way back through the defile to relieve Ziotkowski, and what was left of them on this side of the mountain.

Grbesa was back in forty minutes he, and a young pale faced private vaulted headlong into the trench.

"I've found a way out," Niew gasped at Mark. "Some sort of chimney that will take us up almost to the crest. If we use it, not only could we get up this mountain, but with luck get above those sons of whores who are firing down on us."

"A chimney, Sergeant? Who do you think you are, Santa Claus and his reindeer?"

Gbesa's face remained deadpan. "It doesn't go all the way to the top, but it will help. The Reds can't hit us from where they are at present because of the rock overhang, but I saw them starting to come down the mountainside on our right flank. Once they are low enough, they can pitch grenades right into our lap."

The enemy barrage from the opposite hillside, aimed at the defile, intensified. Grbesa rested his sub machine gun against the wall. "Corps, doesn't expect us to fight our way through that, do they?" he asked, searching his tunic pocket for a cigarette.

Mark shook his head. "The best we can expect from our lot down there is, to use their fire as a decoy while we get ourselves up our chimney" Or go up in smoke, Mark thought sardonically.

He turned to the young soldier, hunched in a corner of the tiny trench, whose face was the colour no soap powder could ever hope to achieve. He'd seen this 'sprog' before with other new recruits, all laughing and joking about what they'd do to the Reds. This was before they had seen one of their own killed. Then the laughing had stopped. After a while, to mask their relief that they themselves had survived, the wisecracking had started again. It would only be when they were alone that the fear would return, and with it the knowledge that it could happen to them, either tomorrow, or the next day, and the wisecracking would start all over again, perhaps this time without them.

"Private, I have work for you. Get back to Colonel Ziotkowski and tell him about the chimney." He struck a match for Grbesa's cigarette, cupping it in his hands. "We'll leave men to show him the way to the chimney. Give him my compliments and my suggestion, that we let the firing from our Corp, coming through the defile, act as a diversion. We'll leave now, instead of at 2100 hours, so, with any luck, we can cover him from the crest when he moves out. Do you understand, Private?"

Clutching his rifle, the youngster ran his tongue over his lips, and muttered something unintelligible. He tried again. "Yes Sir." He made to scramble to his feet, and his major caught him by the arm. "Wait with the Colonel. Lead him out. Okay?"

"He's a bit scared sir." Grebesa said, when the young soldier had gone.

"Aren't we all Sergeant?" Mark gripped the Tommy gun. "Well, Father Christmas, let's get started."

The enemy artillery opened up from the opposite hillside, as Mark and his men made their way up the mountainside. Mark knew he was acting without his Colonel's direct approval. What if Ziotkowski, now that Corps were trying to fight their way back through the defile, had changed his mind and had decided instead to try and link up with them? If he had, to put it bluntly he was now in the shit. Oh well, he had never wanted to be a Major in the first place, he chuckled.

Mark raised his glasses to the opposite side of the valley. In the half light, he could just make out the enemy guns being manhandled down the mountainside. In another few minutes, they'd be within range of his men. Mark cursed and hauled himself over a chunk of rock.

On that first day up there, Tetek had let them through the defile, drawing them deeper into the mountains. He had even let them get their heavier guns through as well, before counter attacking and driving them back, blasting them to pieces as they retreated back through the defile.

Mark slipped on the loose shale. A stream of bullets stitched an arc above his head and he scrambled for the shelter of a rock. A shell burst a few yards down the mountainside, and he cursed the irony of these being their own guns, captured by Tetek in their haste to get back through the defile. His Company, along with two more, had not made it. Hence, their being stuck up here.

He scanned the valley again. It was almost dark. The enemy gun flashes were now further down the mountainside, any time now they'd be within range. If he and his men did make the chimney, Ziotkowski, should he still have a mind to stick to his original plan and follow him up the mountainside, might still be caught between the enemy shellfire from across the valley, and those Reds already above them.

A little further up the slope, Gbesa and half a dozen men were firing at targets a little to their left. He moved towards them at the same time as a figure came at him out of the darkness. Mark brought up his gun, his finger on the trigger.

"Don't shoot, Sir! This way," the soldier gestured. "The CSM is distracting them a little, while we climb the chimney."

"Almost got your stupid effen head blown off, soldier." Mark moved after the shadowy figure, muttering to himself about how close he had come to firing. A few more of his men joined him, all climbing towards the elusive chimney.

A shell landed close by. Loose shale flew up cutting Mark's cheek. He scrambled for the shelter of the rocks above, commanding his weary legs to move faster, while somewhere below someone screamed.

"'We're here, Major." Their guide's voice cut through the darkness.

Mark grunted, edging closer to the small opening. How Grbesa had ever found such a small crack in the rock, he would never know.

Wriggling under the rock, he came out into a small open space, the shape of a boot above him. The boot disappeared, and he guessed he had to follow. A long ten minute climb later, Mark emerged at the top, where his men waited patiently for him to appear.

The relieved major crawled to the edge of the ridge and took a timorous look over. The gun flashes below told him his Colonel was on his way. He crawled back a little. The enemy on the opposite mountainside, anxious not to let them escape from this side of the mountain, had made the mistake of bringing their guns within range of the government troops in the defile below. He stood up, barking at his men to fan out and cover Ziotkowski and his men scrambling across the mountain to the chimney below.

Now caught by surprise by Mark's men on the ridge from above, the Reds began to gradually give way back down the mountain, carefully keeping out of range of the Corps in the defile, and what remained of Ziotkowski's men still making for the chimney.

"Well done, Major!" Mark swung at the sound of the voice. Colonel Ziotkowski, stood a little way back from the ridge's edge.

Mark strode smartly to meet him, snapping to attention. "When I knew we had a means of escape, I thought it best to use it, and also to cover you from here while you crossed the slope to the chimney. I also took the liberty of leaving before the appointed time, Colonel."

The buoyancy in Mark's voice made him feel like a schoolboy, who, having known he had done correctly, stood in expectation of praise from his schoolmaster. It annoyed him, and he was glad there was no one to hear him from his old Glasgow Regiment, or he would never, as 'a wee crawler' ever be able to live it down. In fact, it was due to his CSM, that he was standing here at all.

"You took the correct action, Major. If you had not found a way to the top here, we'd have had a devil of a fight on our hands to get away, and would also have to leave most of our wounded behind."

"The credit should go to CSM Grebesa, Sir." Now, Mark thought, he sounded more like himself, "as it was he who found the escape route."

The Colonel did not seem to notice his major's change of demeanor. "Very well, Major, put that in your report when we get back."

"Well I'll be a effing monkey's uncle!" A little way back, Niew Grbesa stifled a gasp. "I did not think that bloody foreigner held any surprises for me at all," he said, turning to a soldier standing in the darkness by his side. "Not after all this time. Then would you believe it? Two in one day!"

Chapter 9

"Now that you have been elected President, Milan, shouldn't you be thinking of moving into the Kasel?" His wife Elizbieta drew back in order that the maid could clear away the dishes from the table.

At the other end of the table, Milan drew a deep sigh from behind his newspaper. He did not really want to think of this, of how he must go about putting Myra out of her house, especially under the circumstances. How could he put that to Paule?

"You know you will have to eventually," his wife was saying. "You know this place is too small to accommodate all those foreign ambassadors Paule used to entertain…Miche! Bring the President more coffee," Elizbieta threw over her shoulder at the maid.

Milan knew how much his wife enjoyed using the term 'President', for by doing so it reminded everyone, that she was the First Lady. Sometimes, he thought, by the way his wife had of speaking to the staff, she had forgotten who she was. What she had been. What he had been before the war. How, he as a lawyer, and a mediocre one at that, had risen to the Vice Presidency, simply by the beneficence of Paule Kolybin. True, he was not a stupid man, or his Party would never have allowed him to have risen to the heights he now enjoyed, but it was to Paule he owed his success.

The maid set the coffee pot down beside him. She was a pretty young thing, so too had been her mother at her age. Milan's eyes wandered to a picture on the wall, staring through it to the past beyond. That had been so long ago, now both the young girl's parents were dead. One killed in the war, the other knocked down by a car, of all things…after having survived the atrocities of the occupation.

"Will you speak to Myra about us moving in, Milan?" Elizbieta had risen from the table and was supervising the clearing up.

"Mn?" Milan buried his head in his paper. She was not going to give up, he thought. "I'll probably not have a chance to see Myra until next week," he mumbled.

"Do you want me to speak to her?"

"No!" Milan's reply was harsher than intended, which had the affect of his wife and maid halt in what they were doing to stare at him.

Milan extricated himself from the folds of his newspaper. "No, Elizbieta, that would not be diplomatic. Some things are best left to the President."

Milan drew back the elevator panel. The air was rancid; he wanted to cover his mouth and nose. Paule stormed to meet him.

"The bloody drains are choked! The smell is almost knocking me out!" he yelled. "Where the hell have you been? There's no food left either! What do you expect me to live on? And don't dare say fresh air! Not in this effen place!"

Milan recoiled before the tirade. He'd never seen his friend so tired and dishevelled. Neither, had he ever heard him lose his temper so badly. "I was in the House until three this morning. I finally got approval for that dam you suggested should be built to help the unemployment around Gravst." Milan fought to control his own temper. Now was not the time to mention his own triumphs in the House.

Two months previously, through diplomatic channels with their country's neighbour, he'd hinted that a contract for heavy machinery, engineering goods, vehicles, in fact everything that was necessary to help build the Gravst dam; equipment they themselves could not provide, could be negotiated, were they to find a means, diplomatic or otherwise of preventing Tetek's. PFF from escaping across to their side of the frontier, each time the Government troops had them on the run. It was nothing short of a bribe, Milan knew, but, considering the value of the contracts involved, their neighbour had agreed.

Milan saw, rather than heard, his old friend rant on about this rat hole of a place he'd been cooped up in for the best part of three months, and decided to keep his coup to himself for the time being.

Perhaps it would be best to play out all the angles. If Paule's plan to attack the Reds in their own mountain stronghold did materialise, and Government troops did get behind them sealing off the frontier: a frontier that, thanks to him, the Reds could no longer cross with impunity, they'd be forced down the mountains. Perhaps onto the plains itself, where Paule's long awaited heavy artillery, which was so neatly hidden away at present, could be brought to bear against them.

Then there was the other angle he was playing. By building the dam, power station and reservoirs, they'd help raise the standard of living, which in turn would give the people something to live for, give their lives some meaning. God they deserved it, after all they'd been through, and hopefully in the end, deter them from joining the PFF.

As for the Americans? To them his government's policy was as always, to destroy Commies. So when he'd produced his treaty as a means of defeating the Reds, they'd agreed to resume the balance of the initial payment of Marshall Aid.

"We must attack now, Milan, when the weather is on our side and there is sufficient daylight to prevent those bastards escaping over the frontier." Exhausted by his outburst, Paule threw himself down behind his desk. "I have prepared a plan. We'll have our heavy guns moved secretly to their designated areas in the north. Therefore, to everyone concerned, this will be your plan Milan. Since you are the President, no one will oppose you."

Milan sat himself down in his usual chair across from Paule, noticing as he did so, the twitch at the side of his friend's mouth for the first time. Paule needed a doctor. He was certain the man was not very far from having a stroke. And he wondered again, if he should try and persuade him to let Myra know he was still alive.

Paule's hand trembled as he lifted a sheet of paper. "These are the number of troops involved in the east pincer movement."

Milan reached out for the paper. He read the figures. Chr... He went over the figures again. "Paule are these figures correct?" Then wished he had not asked by the look on the man's face.

"What!" Paule's faced twitched badly. "You find something wrong with my figures?" he choked, a vein throbbing at his temple.

"No! No!" Milan quickly countered. "I was just amazed by how you have produced such a precise number of troops. You...well being down here as you are," Milan lied to pacify his friend, for the numbers shown were far in excess of their total strength.

His expression relaxing, Paule beamed. "I know, Milan, old friend. When this," he nodded at the sheet of paper Milan held in his hand, "is all over, people will see the genius and fortitude of what I have done."

The little man's eyes shone. "Now while I try and free these damned drains, how about bringing me some food? Or do you want me, either to suffocate or starve to death?"

Milan gave a little smile, thinking it might not be such a bad idea.

Lomova pulled her wide straw brimmed hat down a little more. It was a lovely sunny Saturday afternoon in the market. She put on her sunglasses again, absently taking in the rows of stalls filling the square and canal side.

Close by, a man was haggling over the price of a radio set. At the next stall, an old woman scrupulously inspected a large iron kettle. Losing interest, Lomova looked away, picking up Juri winding through the crowd towards her, two ice cream cones clutched in his hands.

"Quick, Lomova before they melt!" the soldier laughed, thrusting the cone at her.

She took it from him, licking the cream already running down the side. "It's so pleasant here," she said with an exaggerated sigh. "If only it could be like this all the time." Lomova leaned back on the rail staring up at the cloudless sky. "Me, with no husband...You..?" She stopped herself in time, not wishing to spoil the mood.

"No point wishing for what you cannot have, Lomova." Juri bit into his ice cream.

A slight breeze caught at the woman's hat, and she put a hand up to hold it down. "It surprises me how long Silvo has gone without so much as a scratch, considering the risks he takes. Must have a charmed life. What do you think Juri?"

"I thought he did have, with you around?"

"You are sweet, Juri," Lomova pouted. "Have I told you that before?"

"Not in public." The soldier threw his last piece of cone into the canal, having it snapped up by a passing duck. "Well done Donald!" He threw the duck a mocking salute.

"That was corny." Lomova made a face, happier than she had been in a long time.

She took her hand away from her hat. "Silvo has found a position on his staff for the nephew of that horrible Wysocki woman. I think things will be all right again. I don't believe, Zofia the mouth, will say anything, now she's got what she wants."

"At least for the present," Juri answered sourly, his hands on the rail and looking down the length of the canal at the rows of stalls, where anything could be purchased from hardware to knitwear. Anything could be purchased, he thought bitterly.

It was then, Juri saw his wife and little Max walking in his direction. For a moment he stood transfixed, comparing the quiet serenity of his wife, to the ostentatiousness of Lomova. His wife knew nothing of his affair, never having as much as suspected he had another woman, trusting him explicitly, as she had done, before and since their marriage. She was smiling down at their son, who was walking by her side, clutching the toy yacht he'd bought him especially for today.

Juri had never felt so guilty, so unclean. "They're early," he choked at the woman by his side, flashing her a look. Hating her, hating himself for his weakness, and for allowing it to have gone this far. He never should have agreed to have come here with Lomova after their lovemaking at the flat: not in broad daylight. What if they were recognised! It had been stupid.

Unemotionally, Lomova stared passed him. "The boy is your image, Juri. You must be proud of him?"

Suddenly, Juri wanted to lash out at her, hurt her, inflict a wound as deep as he was feeling right now. "I'll have to go before we're seen together." His words harsh. Bitter.

"I understand, Juri. Same time at the flat tomorrow?"

Juri knew it was not really a question. "If I can get away."

"Oh, you always can," Lomova smirked. "I'll have something special on the boil for you. Do not disappoint me, Juri."

Juri walked quickly to meet his wife and child, as if by doing so he could negate these last few moments, and with it, all of the past.

His son saw him and ran to him calling out, and proudly holding up his toy. Juri caught him and lifted him high into his arms, kissing his cheeks and hugging him tight. Karina laughed, both surprised and embarrassed by her husband's unusual show of affection to their son in public.

"It is a beautiful day, is it not?" Juri beamed at his wife. "Now for the lake...eh?" he suggested, gently putting the child down.

And for the first time since his affair with Lomova had began, he knew what he was going to do.

At a stall no so very far away from where Juri stood embracing his son, Miro examined an iron kettle. Putting it down, he followed the happy trio at a discreet distance, sliding inconspicuously into a doorway, as the Volkswagen with the newly repaired wing, accelerated passed. "Some day, Sergeant Juri Trybala," he swore. "Some day."

Ignoring the many appealing attractions to be found in that part of the city on that sunny Saturday afternoon, Miro headed for the damp dark interior of their cellar headquarters. He had something on his mind. Something, which if proved correct, could help chasten his egoistic pharisaical Group Leader.

Despite the heat of the day, the cellar was colder than Miro had expected. Once inside, he pulled back some timber slats leaning against the far wall and inserted a key into the metal door behind. With a hand that shook slightly, Miro entered the inner sanctum.

The room was about three metres square, built of red brick, now in an advanced state of disrepair. Miro lit an oil lamp and set it down on a small wooden table, from which he lifted a narrow metal tray.

Carrying this to the far wall, he jammed it against a brick, carefully sweeping the powdery cement from its pointing into the tray. This done, he pulled out the loose brick from the wall, reaching in to extract a small bundle of papers from the cavity beyond.

Spreading out the papers on the table, Miro poured over them assiduously, repeatedly arranging and, rearranging in some sort of sequence the information, Savi had found out while working in the Administration Building for the short time before her death. It wasn't much, he conceded, for as a junior typist Savi had no access to any important documentation. Everything she had given him had been by word of mouth, which in turn he had meticulously set down to peruse, as and when necessary.

Miro moved the sheets of notepaper together, his attention drawn to the dates. His curiosity aroused, he sifted through another sheet. "Troop movements.....troop movements," he repeated quietly to himself, tapping his teeth with his pencil, knowing that military information such as this, would be held in the Caserne and not Admin. and only Petr would have official access to it here in the cellar. Yet, if his theory was correct? Miro sweated despite the chill in the small room. If he should do what his instinct told him to do,..

but should his instincts prove to be wrong ? He felt weak kneed at the thought.

Miro decided to take the risk. A few minutes later, he sat disappointed that Petr's private papers had not divulged the information he had hoped for. And should his Group Leader ever find out? Miro shuddered, quickly gathering the papers together. It was as he lifted the last sheet from the table that a date and a place caught his attention. Scarcely able to contain his excitement he set about studying the papers again.

The new Section Leader shivered, he was cold and hungry, it was time for dinner.

Peering at his watch in the shimmering light of the lantern, he stifled a cry. It was almost midnight! He had lost all track of time and shook his head in disbelief at what he had stumbled upon. It defied all imagination! Now all he needed was the proof, followed by a full Group meeting. "Then we shall see, my supercilious Group Leader," Miro chuckled.

Miro's steps sounded hollow on the stone stairs to Pavel's flat. It had taken three weeks to gather all the necessary documentation to present to a full Group meeting, Petr having at first refused him on safety grounds, until he had insisted.

A door opened fractionally on the floor above, and the outline of a face appeared at the crack. Pretending not to have noticed, Miro made an unobstusive show of his box of chessmen tucked under his arm. The inquisitive face disappearing as he reached the top step.

The guard let Miro into the flat. Pavel acknowledged him with no more than a muttered greeting, while Petr at the head of the table gave him the briefest of nods. Vaclaw, reluctantly drew out a chair for him to sit down.

Miro sat, his self confidence already beginning to evaporate at this less than warm welcome. Clearly, he was about as popular as a boil on a jockey's arse.

Without ceremony, Petr brought the meeting to order. "As you well know, in the interest of safety and out of concern for our host, I am in favour of the fewer meetings we hold here the better. However, Section Leader Miro believes that due to information now in his possession, it is essential that we meet." Petr stared coldly at his youngest Section Leader. "Let us hope this is so. Now Miro, perhaps you would like to further elaborate?"

Miro cleared his throat, his much practised speech flying from his mind. "Thank you comrade." Sweat gathered on his brow as he thought back to the meeting on the canal side, and how Petr had humiliated him. Perhaps he had been a bit too cocksure of himself; after all, he had worked hard for that information. Aware of three pairs of eyes on him, he brought himself back to the present.

"Three weeks ago," he began, "I followed up a hunch I had concerning the murder of a member of my Section, by a certain Juri Trybala, a staff sergeant to General Jakofcic. After spending some time at the cellar, I came to certain conclusions." Miro saw the look of impatience cross Petr's face and hurriedly changed tact. " May... I ask, comrades..." He paused for affect, and a little flattery, for it was essential he gain their attention if not confidence, especially for what he was about to lay before them. "As you are all more experienced than I...in shall we say, matters of war, and subterfuge... though I have had a little myself..., a question? Or even several?"

"Do not shit about, Miro," Vaclaw grunted, impatiently. "If you have something to say, then damned well say it!"

"What is your question, Miro?" Petr asked quietly, at the same time pacifying Vaclaw by pouring out a measure of Vodka and sliding it across the table to him.

Miro's eyes followed Pavel pushing the other two drinks in front of him and Petr, waiting while their host motioned to the guard to pick up a third. "The questions are...." He looked at each in turn. "Was it Kloybin's death which presented us with the opportunity to attack Pienera? Or was it the absence of the mercenaries?"

After a few moments of silence, Petr responded first. "When I met with our National Council, it was agreed that despite the absence of the mercenaries, we still did not have the strength to launch a general uprising. However, Kolybin's death changed all that. With the Senate in seeming disarray, we did hope, wrongly as it turned out, to raise the country against them. But what is the point of this, Miro?"

The Group Leader's quiet tone took Miro off guard. He would have much preferred an all out confrontation. At least that way, he would have known where he stood, but with this quiet silky approach, Petr was at his most lethal.

Miro took his courage in both hands. It was time to put his cards on the table, and blow the consequences. "As you have confirmed Petr, the Council agreed to our plan of having Tetek attack, Pienera, simply because of Kolybin's death and the general situation in the country. Therefore, when I sifted through all the pieces of information my Section had gathered, it soon became evident that the preparation for the Government counter offensive to our expected uprising had been made several weeks *prior* to Kolybin's death."

Miro spread out a sheet of paper in front of him, as if expecting his statement to be rudely challenged, continuing at the ensuing silence, "for example.... the supplies for the cargo ship which so innocently docked in Pienera harbour, were ordered in February. The ship itself sailed for Pienera only two days after the late president's funeral...with Government troops on board, I might add." Their continued silence encouraged him to go on. "Various importation of heavy machinery..." He took his time, enjoying having gained their attention, "which turned out to be artillery pieces, ...November of last year."

"Perhaps Kolybin drew up these plans hoping the absence of the mercenaries would provoke an attack from us," Vaclaw said flatly. "The fact that he was killed, although unfortunate for him," he chuckled, "was the spark we needed to launch our offensive."

"I agree with Vaclaw," Pavel said, refusing to be dictated to by someone as junior as the likes of Miro. "It is the only logical explanation."

Miro's eyes strayed to the head of the table, where his Group Leader sat toying with his vodka glass. Petr looked up. "You do not think this is so? Do you Miro?" His lip curled in a smile. "You have already dismissed this from your mind. Am I correct?"

"Yes Petr," Miro conceded. He had come too far to stop now. He must go on, get it over with. "I hope what I am about to admit to, will not anger, or upset you, comrades." He steeled himself. "I spent a great deal of time finding out more about the military situation prior to Kolybin's death. I could only obtain this from your Section within the Caserne, Petr."

"You what!" Pavel and Vaclaw echoed.

"You went over Petr's head?" You went into *his* Section?" Vaclaw stormed, his eyes blazing in anger and disbelief. "Petr!" he choked.

Miro prepared himself for the onslaught. To his surprise, the only reaction from his Group Leader was to slide his empty glass across the table for Pavel to refill.

"I have had men shot for less, Miro," Petr said softly, his eyes fixed on his glass. "You have breached security at every level: broken every rule. These rules were not enforced to prevent you from seeking out the truth, rather, that in the event of your capture the less you know, the less you can divulge."

It was the quiet menace in his voice that scared Miro. He knew, Petr was not above personally carrying out his threat. He swallowed and tried to keep his voice from shaking as he said, "I searched through your papers in the cellar, Petr, I wanted to make sure of my facts before presenting them here."

"...And they are?" Petr asked.

Miro felt the hammering of his heart. He had reached the point of no return. He had to go on. "The decision to make Pienera our target came from this room. From your suggestion, Petr, which I expect you then presented to National Council?"

"Enough!" Vaclaw stammered, leaping to his feet. "You are not suggesting...."

The guard came as far as the inside door, putting his fingers to his lips. Signalling an apology, Vaclaw sat back down.

"No." Miro took the courage to stare Vaclaw straight in the eye . "If you will bear with me. The decision to attack Pienera was made here, by us. Petr suggested it. We supported it. No one knew of this decision before that night, not unless Petr had already decided on it beforehand and had discussed it with someone else."

"Petr would not do that!" Pavel shot a look at his leader for confirmation. "You only decided it here Petr, did you not?" His tone asking his friend to deny Miro's insinuation.

Petr swore under his breath. Now he knew Miro's game. The man had never been the same since he'd put him in his place that day by the canal. It was these petty umbrages that had almost ruined their united front against the Nazis. "Naturally I had given it some thought before I came to the meeting." He ran a finger round the edge of his glass. "But no one knew of my idea prior to my discussing it here, or presenting it to National Council, who took it upon themselves to approve it."

"I know, Petr," Miro said softly. "It was never my intention to suggest that you had. I merely brought up the point that Government troops could not possibly have been in position to trap Tetek at Pienera from plans drawn up *after* Kolybin's death." Miro felt himself relax a little. "Now that I knew what to look for Petr, your Section provided me with the answer.

"We now know Government troops were aware of the town we intended taking in the north, to be Pienera...this was due to a breach somewhere in our security. Also, I have discovered Government troops commenced to slip out of this city the night after Kolybin's funeral, and subsequent nights after that. Hence the reason they were in position to entrap Tetek so effectively. That Tetek had decided to attack Pienera, with only a token force, is the only reason that our entire army was saved from annihilation."

"So... they kept, Silvo Jakofcic, here in Capital City as a decoy." Pavel spaced out the words, pondering the possibility.

Miro felt a small surge of triumph at Pavel's support, however minute. Was it conceivable he had succeeded in convincing one of those present?

"I believe so. However, the point of my argument is this. Bearing in mind the political and civil climate here in the city, as a result of the president's demise, who could have masterminded the plan to surround Pienera after the assassination?" Now in full flow, Miro went on to answer his own question. "Jakofcic was in the north the day of the assassination. He would have had to be a genius to have ordered troop movements of such a large force in so short a time after his president's death, And if so, would he have returned to the capital to act merely as a decoy? Therefore, if not the illustrious General, Who? Certainly not Scurk, it would be the first anniversary of the president's death before that old woman had the plans drawn up." Miro ventured a grin, intending to relieve the tension in the room as well as making his point.

"Miro you are not saying anything more than was said at the beginning of the meeting." Vaclaw thumped the table with his fist. "Kolybin drew up the plans, hoping that with the mercenaries gone, we would attack one of three towns in the north, which was logical, as they were near the mountains and Tetek's power base. When he died, Molnar as Vice-president simply continued with the plan."

Miro knew he was taking too long with his argument, but if he could not make these men of experience understand what he was aiming at, he would be unable to convince them of his final deduction, something of which he had difficulty in believing himself.

"On the evening Kolybin was killed, there was one mercenary on hand to help, a soldier by the name of Stewart. He helped Molnar and a doctor to take Kolybin's body back to the Kasel. Remember, Kolybin was not taken to a hospital, but directly to his residence."

"The explanation is simple enough, Miro. If Kolybin was already dead there would have been little point in doing so. All that would have achieved would have been to draw newspaper men there like flies to shit."

Having said his piece Pavel stood up to stretch himself, angry at having had this young upstart almost convince him there was something sinister, something deeper threatening their organisation. But now where was he heading?

Across the table, Vaclaw gave Petr a look implying it was now time he shut up this young fool.

Miro caught the look. He knew he was losing them again and quickly rammed home his point. "When I knew what I was looking for in your Section in the cellar, Petr, and other information I had found, and by putting it all together, I came up with this." He pushed a small piece of paper across the table to him. Picking it up, Petr studied it while Miro went on. "The sum written there is a sum paid into a bank in Scotland, in the name of Major Mark Stewart! Quite a lot of back pay, would you not say?"

Taking a final look at it, Petr passed it to Vaclaw, who letting out a low whistle, held it up in turn for Pavel to read.

"I think you should tell us what you have discovered, Miro, and what it is you have on your mind." Petr sat back in his chair, grudgingly conceding that perhaps he had misjudged his Section Leader's motives.

Miro felt a surge of triumph at winning Petr's approval. He started. "At first I believed, in order to gain political power, Milan Molnar had his old friend assassinated. With the vacuum this would create, coupled with the mercenaries gone, Molnar was certain we would stage an uprising, which once out in the open would lead to our ultimate defeat, which would make him, Milan Molnar, a greater man than Paule Kolybin. This would also account for the plans being made long beforehand.

"Makes sense," Pavel nodded, pushing a cake tray into the centre of the table.

"Except." Miro's hand shook as he lifted his glass of vodka. "Kolybin was not dead!"

"*Not dead*!" Vaclaw guffawed. Then realising how loud he had spoken, added a little quieter, and caustically. "Come Miro, we've listened to your ravings long enough. You had me almost convinced. But Kolybin, not dead!" he sneered.

"Why not, Vaclaw?" Miro asked, one eye on Petr for his reaction. "Have you forgotten my poor murdered operative Savi? What were her last words to me? I have seen *him*. We all took this to be Jakofcic, simply because it was the General's man who crashed into that telephone box. But, I believe the real reason Savi had to be stopped that night, was because she did see the President, Paule Kolybin...!" Finished, Miro sat back exhausted, his hand shaking as he lifted his glass.

Absently Vaclaw sliced a piece of cake, then cut it again. Pavel clicked his teeth and looked across the table at Petr for guidance. The only sound in the room the faint hum of music from the flat above.

At last, Petr broke the silence. "Do you think a president....any president of a country, would be prepared to go to such lengths to fool his enemies? And by doing so, also fool those dignitaries, especially, of those countries aligned to him who attended his funeral, Miro? How could such a man justify his deceit to the world, do you think?"

It was a question Miro had asked himself over and over again. "I do not know, Petr. Perhaps he thought to rise from the dead, as did Our Lord, in three days or...as close as damn to it." To his surprise and relief, Petr laughed, the others joining in.

"You have worked well, if not correctly, Miro. It is an interesting theory you have presented."

"Yes Petr, I agree," Vaclaw nodded. "But too far fetched."

"I do not know about that my friend," Pavel mused, toying with his glass. He had listened to this young man, and had been just as ready to dismiss his ravings as that of a lunatic...worse , an ambitious upstart, but the more he thought about it, and knowing the diminutive shoemaker as he did? "I would not put it past that bastard Kolybin to think up such a diabolical plan. He did during the war."

"We can always put it to the test." Vaclaw pushed away his empty plate, as if the thought had suddenly occurred to him. "Tell the papers: anonymously of course, let them do the investigating, do our work for us. That would set the cat amongst the pigeons. Can you imagine what the Senate would make of that? Which is supposing none of them were party to the conspiracy."

"This is what I fail to understand," Pavel broke in. "Kolybin's wife must be a pretty good actress, for I'd swear she is genuinely grief stricken."

"Perhaps no one knows except those closest to him, such as Molnar and this mercenary Stewart. I'd like to know exactly what that soldier's part is, in all of this."Vaclaw made a face.

Petr held up his hands. "We can theories all night, it is proof we need. This can only be obtained in two ways. First, we can have Stewart and Trybala brought in for questioning. Or, secondly we can dig up the martyr's grave."

"Sound thinking, Petr." Pavel's eyes glowed with admiration, happy that the meeting was at an end, and some positive action could now be taken. Also in the light of what had been discussed, he could now stop looking for the late President's would be assassins in his own Section.

"Let's start with the staff sergeant," Petr suggested. "Vaclaw, I will leave that to you, as. Miro has already done his share."

And with this, Miro knew he had been forgiven, at least for the time being, or until his theory had been disproved.

Chapter 10

The sound of Lomova humming contentedly from the bedroom reached Juri as he switched on the bathroom light. God! How, he almost choked, loved that body. In truth, he meant desired it. The thrill when stroking her skin, fondling her breasts! He looked away from the bathroom mirror, not wanting to see his face, his resolve having once more melted away at the tingle of her touch. His wife and child thrust to the back of his mind, as was the young girl he'd *killed-.killed* because of Lomova! Because he had been here! God help him, would it never end?

"Must you go, Juri?" he heard Lomova call out to him. Splashing water on his face, he answered that he must.

When Juri returned to the bedroom, Lomova was sitting up in bed, her head propped up by a pillow. He looked at her naked body, never tiring at what he saw, his guilt suddenly returning at the thought that when he left here it would be straight home to his trusting wife and little son.

"Same time tomorrow, Juri? I don't know when Silvo gets back? Do you?" she purred. Juri grunted. "What did you say darling? Don't you know how long we will have before he returns? It would help you know, Silvo would not confide anything military with me. After all, I'm only his wife," she mocked.

Lomova's tone made Juri unaccountably angry. "He did not confide in me either. Why should he? I'm *hors de combat* as they say."

"Who says so?" Lomova teased, sliding on to her knees. "You tell me who they are. I bet they're not women. No woman could ever say that about you darling." She reached out for him.

Annoyed, Juri drew away. "I must go Lomova," a tinge of anger in his voice. "I'll try and find out when the General is likely to return." He was aware as always, of referring to Jakofcic as the 'General' and never 'your husband.'

"Then we'll make provision for tomorrow."

As Juri reached out for his tunic, Lomova put her arms around him, kissing him full on the mouth, using her tongue as only she knew how. Juri felt himself stir, but this time controlled himself. Gently but firmly, he pushed her back. "I must go, Lomova."

"'Til tomorrow then?"

When he reached the door, he did not look back. So many times he had steeled himself to say, 'that was the last time Lomova, it was fun while it lasted. I will not be back.' Although he knew it would sound corny, it was what he intended to say, but each time had reneged on his self promise. He closed the door softly behind him.

Juri rounded the corner of the building. It would be dark in an hour. His car was parked in a cul-de-sac three blocks away from the flat. On the way, he searched his pocket for his keys, smelling the rain in the air.

It never failed. Each time he saw the new wing of the car it reminded him of the young girl he had killed, and found himself trembling at the thought of what would happen to him should he ever be found out.

There was a noise behind him as he turned the key in the door and a voice telling him not to look round. He felt the cold muzzle of a pistol pressed against his temple, and cursed his own stupidity for allowing himself to be taken so easily.

In a few brief seconds, Juri found himself blindfolded and ordered to lie down on the floor in the back of his own car.

The soldier sweated. This was it. They were going to take him into the country and murder him, as they had done to so many of his comrades. He tried to listen, to discover which way they were taking him, on the off chance he would survive.

Twenty minutes later, he knew by the sound of traffic he was still in the city. A church clock chimed the hour, the same one he'd heard a quarter of an hour before. Obviously they were trying to confuse him, prevent him from knowing where they were taking him. His hopes rose, they would not go to such lengths if they meant to kill him. After a time, the sound of the traffic receded. They were heading out of town.

Almost an hour later, the car hit a bump. Juri's head banged off the bottom of the door, and the vibration under him suddenly shifted from hard bitumen road to the soft yielding bounce of grass. A few minutes later, the car drew to a halt.

Juri was still dazed from the bump on his head when they dragged him from the car, and was only vaguely aware of the smell of wet grass; the sting of the rain on his face;the unexpected feel of a wooden floor, before rough hands were thrusting him into a chair,

143

tying his hands behind his back, and a voice inches away asking in a tone that only added to his fear.

"Staff Sergeant Juri Trybala, why did you kill that young girl?"

Juri's head spun as he tried to assemble his thoughts and make some sense out of what the voice had asked. His mouth felt dry. He had been asked about the girl he had knocked down in the telephone box! But how did they know? Now, he hated Lomova even more, even more than he hated himself for allowing this to happen.

The voice repeated the question, giving him no time to answer before he felt the numbing blow on the nape of his neck. The question came again. He felt sick. The rubber truncheon hit him again. "It was an accident!" he shouted, surprised by the sound of fear in his own voice.

"An accident?" the voice asked. "Then why did you drive away? Why did you not call for assistance? Trybala you left her there to die.

Juri's head jerked forward as the truncheon hit him again, smashing his head into the table. "I told you it was an accident," he moaned.

"What was it the girl saw that she had to be silenced, Trybala?"

Juri tensed in anticipation of another blow: none came. He tried to clear his head and make sense of the question. He screwed up his eyes under the blindfold, awaiting the inevitable blow. "I don't know what you mean."

The blow finally came, harder this time. Someone behind grabbed his hair, jerking his head back.

"Do not play games with me, soldier!"

The voice had changed. Juri felt cold fear. "I am telling you the truth!" he cried in desperation. "I was on my way home. I skidded on the corner, and hit the phone box -.I stopped-went back- she was already dead. I took off."

"Why? If it was an accident as you say?"

Juri shrugged helplessly. "I knew I was in the wrong. If I was found out, my career would be at an end. I've a wife...."

"*Career* at an end!" The blow was particularly savage this time. "*Career at an end!*" The voice howled. "That young girl's life was at an end!"

An ominous silence followed, more terrifying to Juri than the blows, or the shouting. At last the voice came again, this time a little calmer, softer. "Your route home from the Caserne would not bring you anywhere near Zacia Street. So why did you happen to be on that side of the city, if not with the express intention of preventing the girl from relaying what she knew to us?

There were several little people inside Juri's head banging away with hammers. He must force himself to think. This girl, whoever she was, must have been some sort of spy for 'them'...them being PFF Evidently, he had knocked her down before she had time to pass on whatever she knew. Now they wanted to know what that was. *God help him*. Aloud, he said. "I was on my way home."

They hit him until he lost consciousness, soaking his face with water to revive him. He tried to remember where he was. How many there were of them?

"Why did you take your car to a run down garage for repair? I suggest you did this by order of your superiors, to allay any suspicions of what you had done."

There was that voice again. He smelled cigarette smoke. He ran his tongue over his lips. "Had I taken it to my regular garage, they would have asked questions... maybe have put two and two together. I could not take the risk, so I took it to a garage I thought would be grateful for the business, and not ask too many awkward questions."

Juri waited for a resumption of the blows. Instead the voice came at him again with exaggerated tiredness. "If you tell us the truth as to why you were there on that side of the city, we will spare your life. If not..."

Juri felt a lump in his throat. He thought of his wife, of little Max, the fun they had had together, particularly that day by the lake playing with the toy yacht. If ever he were to get out of this alive, he swore, he'd finish with Lomova, and spend all his spare time with them both. He swallowed saliva. If he was to tell them of his affair with his General's wife, they'd blackmail him for every piece of information he could lay his hands on, then some more.

"I am waiting Juri Trybala!" the voice said impatiently. "Confirm what we already know, and we will spare your life. Lie, and we shall have no hesitation in killing you."

The pain in Juri's head intensified as he tried to concentrate on what they'd asked him. What did they already know, or think they knew? They knew he'd knocked down the girl. Also, that he was on the staff of General Jakofcic. What else? Maybe the whole thing was nothing more than elaborate bluff to have him disclose something they wanted to know, or thought he knew, and was using his knocking down of the girl simply as blackmail.

"I am running out of patience, soldier."

Juri decided to risk telling the truth, at least partially the truth. " I was on my way home. I left a flat in Wasela Street." He swallowed. "I have a mistress there. I did not want my wife to find out." He stopped, hoping this would be enough.

"A mistress?" the voice repeated. "Would this mistress be a certain General's wife, Juri Trybala?"

It was what Juri had feared all along, to hear someone utter those fatal words. He felt himself crumple. He nodded. His desolation was complete.

No more blows came. He was aware of bodies conversing in whispered tones behind him and steeled himself for the shot. How long he remained, waiting his fate, he did not know. Afraid to move, he listened for the slightest sound that might tell him his captors were still present. All he heard was the rain on the roof. Taking a chance, he struggled to his feet. No one pushed him back. He was alone.

Indra's trim figure was accentuated by her smart nurse's uniform as she strode eagerly to meet the handsome young naval cadet. To hide her embarrassment at the way he was looking at her, she made a face.

Stefan leaned forward and kissed her on the cheek, his eyes sparkling with delight. "So you managed to get away all right."

A passer-by smiled at this young love. Indra blushed. "Yes. I changed shifts. I am not due back on duty until tomorrow night."

"Good!" Stefan beamed, linking her arm in his, and leading her back the way she had come. "I know the very place we can dine," he whispered conspiratorially in her ear. "Dance the night away if you so wish, and anything else your heart may desire."

Caught up in her young man's cheery mood, Indra whispered back, "And where would this astonishing place be young sir, may I ask?"

"My home of course!"

Indra pulled up sharply. "The Kasel!"

"Not good enough for you?" He faced her, chuckling. "Then young miss, where else may a young navel cadet entertain you?" His gleaming eyes searched her worried face.

"I cannot go *there*, Stefan. It would not be right. I mean..."

Stefan wrinkled his brows. "What do you mean?"

"That is the President's Residence; it is not for the likes of me. It could be very embarrassing for you and your career, Stefan."

"It is my home, Indra.... at least, for a little while longer." Suddenly serious the young man asked, "Would you not like to see the inside of my home, or our president's residence? It may be your one and only chance." He squeezed her hand.

Indra gazed into the eyes of the young cadet with whom she was rapidly falling in love. "Yes, I think I would like very much to see your home," she said softly.

Stefan's smile was one of relief. "Then let us not keep our chauffeur waiting." He bowed with a flourish, waving her towards the kerb. "Your coach awaits your highness."

"It is beautiful, Stefan!" Indra's face gleamed with pride and astonishment. "I had no idea!"

Tapestries and oil paintings lined the walls of the large room in which they stood.

She left him to slide her hand down the length of the long polished table, set with silver plates.

Stefan met her at the foot, and he took her hand. "Now I shall show you my favourite room."

Happily, he led her out of the door and down a statue lined corridor, letting go of her hand at the entrance to an elaborate furnished room.

"This is *my* room!" he proudly announced. "Is this not magnificent?"

Indra took a timorous step into the large room, where a fire burned brightly in an enormous stone fireplace, flanked on either side by a chaise-longue. Above the mantelpiece, the portrait of a hussar charged his mount, sabre thrust out before him at some unseen foe. Chandeliers glittered and sparkled from the ceiling the entire length of the room.

"This is my country's history!" Stefan cried, in a voice charged with emotion.

Spellbound, Indra gazed around her, not wishing to miss the smallest item, so much wanting to remember this for the rest of her life.

"Of course," Though a little less excited, Stefan's voice had not lost its pride. "Most of these portraits were hidden during the occupation." He encompassed the room with a wave. "However they did belong to the Counts and Dukes of the Hapsburg Empire, prior to us becoming a Republic," he offered in a way of an explanation and apology.

Taking her eyes away from the portrait, Indra moved to the window, and for a moment stood there looking down the long sweep of the hill to the twinkling lights of the city below, and the twin beams from the cars making their way along the rain soaked streets.

"As a child I used to look up here and believe this where the beautiful Princess and the handsome Prince lived." She rested her cheek on the soft velvet curtain, feeling the richness of the texture. "Then the Nazis came." She gave a little shudder. "And there was no more fairy Prince or Princess."

"There could be again." Stefan was by her side. "At least for tonight, if you wish."

Indra turned slowly to face him. "I should like that very much, Stefan. But perhaps we should wait."

Disappointed, yet not unprepared for her answer, he nodded. "We could at least dance?"

The girl gave a little laugh at the sobriety of his expression. She touched him on the tip of the nose. "At least *that* we could do." she teased.

The last of the servants had retired for the night. A low fire threw giant shadows on the unlit room.

Indra lay curled up on a chaise-longue, her head of Stefan's chest. "It's been a wonderful evening, Stefan," she sighed.

"Will your mother not be anxious to know where you are?" Stefan reached over her for his glass of wine on the side table.

"No. She will think I am still on duty at the hospital. I did not tell her I had changed my schedule." She turned her head to look up into his face. "What of your mother...I mean step-mother, where is she Stefan? Won't she be home tonight?"

"Myra? No. I believe she is somewhere on the coast, taking a last look round so to speak, before returning home to England."

It was the way Stefan had used his step-mother's Christian name that made Indra ask, "You dislike her Stefan?"

"Dislike Myra?" He thought for a moment. "Myra is all right. She does...did love my father," he corrected himself. "No, not dislike, resent is more the word I would use."

He stretched out his arm to replace his empty glass on the table. "She is a foreigner after all. Does not appreciate or understand all of this." He jerked a hand at the room. "To my stepmother, this place is no more than a mausoleum."

Indra drew away to lift her own glass from the table. She took a sip waiting for him to go on as he stared into the blazing log fire in the great stone fireplace. His deep tan accentuated by his white open necked shirt. At length, he began. "My father was a shoemaker before the occupation.... Of course, everyone knows that. 'Shoemaker to peacemaker' I believe was the general quotation." Stefan grunted. "He was a good shoemaker, Indra."

Stefan refilled his glass. "My job was to polish all the shoes after they'd been repaired. Many a tingling ear I got for not having done the job to his satisfaction," he chuckled, putting a hand to his ear as if he could still feel the pain. "We were happy there, the three of us."

A shower of sparks cascaded into the hearth, momentarily lighting up the room. In a voice tinged with sadness, Stefan continued. "I suppose while I was going to school, running errands and playing games as all children do, you were riding past in a tramcar, staring up here for your fairy prince and princess? We might even have passed one another in the street." He gave her a teasing little squeeze.

"I think I should have remembered you, Stefan Kolybin. Though, I was not often on this side of town. Besides, your much, much older than I," Indra added tongue in cheek.

"Now you have broken the spell," he chided her good humourdly. "As a child I never could comprehend Nazis goose stepping down Alcia Street, passed Burda the baker: old man Coen the jeweller, who like my mother later 'had to go away' as they told me at the time. It all seemed out of place...unreal.

"I remember the day my father closed his shop for the last time. He saw me watching him, and kneeled down. He put his hands on my shoulders and said, 'I must go away now, Stefan. Fight for our country.' Knowing I did not fully understand he tried to explain, 'I am going away to keep bad men from coming here to hurt you and your mother, and people like old Mr Coen. You like Mr Coen, don't you son?' I nodded. 'Then I shall come back and you will polish shoes for me again, and everything will be as it was before.' He hugged me. 'So be a good boy, Stefan. Do everything your mother asks of you, and in turn you must look after her for me until I return. You are the man of the house now. I cried, I did not want my father to leave, but he did, that night." Indra squeezed his hand.

The memory of those days deep in the embers of the dying fire, Stefan went on. "One night...I don't know when, I was awakened by the sound of breaking glass and the pounding on the door downstairs. I was still half asleep when my mother rushed into the room and bundled me into her arms. She was crying, her lips trembling as she pushed the bedroom window open and told me to stand on the ledge around the side of the house, and hang on to the drainpipe. She kissed me, telling me whatever happened, or whatever I heard, I was not to make a sound, and that I must stay there until someone came for me. Then she closed the window. I was terrified, afraid to look down into the backyard below. I heard my mother scream. Sounds I didn't understand, then all was silent."

Stefan reached for his glass, his hands trembling. "How long I stood on that ledge I do not know, but it seemed forever. I remembered what my mother had said about someone coming for me. I was old enough to know it would not be her, so I cried. My feet hurt on the narrow ledge and my arms ached grasping the overhead guttering. At length, I was forced to move. I edged my way back to the window, but at six years of age I had not the strength to lift it open and hold on at the same time."

"How did you get down Stefan? You must have been out of your mind with fear," Indra gasped, aware of her own heart pounding as she envisaged the scene of that little boy.

Stefan shrugged. "Oh I was terrified all right, more from the thought of the bad men who had come to our house, than from the fear of falling. You will understand that Indra. You have lived through this as well."

Indra shuddered, drawing closer.

"Someone did come for me: a neighbour, if I recall correctly. He took me to his house further down the street. I asked him about my mother...when would she be coming back? And he just kept saying,' sometime Stefan, sometime.'

A few days later my uncle came for me. I wanted to go home, for I was sure my mother would be waiting for me, but he wouldn't let me. He took me away in his old truck. It seemed as though we travelled for days." Stefan made a bitter sound.

"Uncle Karl had a farm in the north. It was a big farm...at least it seemed to me at the time.... Everything seems big when you're still growing up. He told me I must not let anyone know I was there. But if anyone did speak to me, or ask my name, I should tell them that it was Stefan Biez...That was my uncle's name," Stefan explained, pouring out some wine into two glasses.

"I remember him telling me so very sternly, that no one should ever know I was the son of Paule Kolybin. He gripped me by the arm so hard Indra, that it hurt. 'You don't want the bad men who took your mother away, to catch your father, do you Stefan?' He was kneeling down and staring into my face, terrifying me, as he said it." Stefan handed Indra her glass. "Now I understand why he was so severe."

"Did your father ever come to the farm?" Indra asked, enthralled by the story, and understanding Stefan's fear, and what he must have gone through.

"No. This is what I did not understand at the time. Some nights, Partisans would come to the farm, and Uncle Karl would let them in, give them food, and in the winter let them sleep by the fire. He thought I was always asleep and did not know, until I asked him when would my father come. He told me the mountains where my father was, were too far away. I did not understand this, as I thought all the Partisans who came to the farm were all those who fought for our country, and this being so, why was my father not amongst them." Stefan gave a little laugh at his own stupidity. "I lived with my uncle and Aunt Zofia until the end of the occupation."

"Did anyone discover you?.. Neighbouring farmers, I mean?" Indra asked, surprised, that the question should give her the same indescribable feeling of fear experienced all those years ago, when a truck full of Nazis would whiz passed in the street, and her mother would pull her into the nearest shop out of the way.

Gently freeing himself, Stefan walked to the fire. One hand on the mantle shelf, he stared down into the fire. "Yes."

Indra sat up on the couch, wishing by his tone she had not broached the subject.

"It was one day ...in the Spring, I think. My uncle had left me to fish by the bank of a river, telling me he'd be back shortly. As the day grew warmer I fell asleep. The next thing I knew, a man was hauling me to my feet and asking who I was, and how I came to be there. I was terrified. He shook me like a rat, asking me my name over and over again. Eventually, when I continued to say nothing, he gave up, saying he would take me to the village.

It was then my uncle returned. The man was a neighbouring farmer, who collaborated with the Germans, who, my uncle knew would betray us all, should the Nazis learn of my existence, especially, if they were to find out I was the son of Paule Kolybin...a terrorist."

Stefan left the fire to sit by Indra, who took his hand, patiently waiting for him to go on. "There was a fight. They both landed in the river. The man went down, and my uncle pushed his head under the water."

The boy's voice rose as he relived the scene, his free hand gesturing helplessly. "The man kept thrashing about! His hands came up out of the water, again! and again!, trying to grab my uncle, who would push him back under. It seemed to go on and on for ever!" Stefan shuddered.

Taking a sip of his wine, he stared into the fire for a few seconds before going on. "At last there was no more fighting, the water became still again. I stood up from where I had been watching from the banking. I saw the neighbour's body float away. My uncle looked up, saw me, and I will never forget the look on his face as stood there, his eyes saying it had been all my fault, and wishing I was not his sister's child and that he had left me back in the city. I will never forget that look, Indra."

Indra's fingers curled round Stefan's. She bent forward kissing him on the lips. "Poor boy," she whispered, wishing she had never asked the question.

Stefan gave her a wan smile, grateful for the sympathy. Although angry at himself, for this is not what he had planned for to night. He looked into his glass. " I don't know why I am telling you all this. It was a long time ago. This was supposed to a happy evening, before I return to duty."

"A long time ago is only yesterday when you are young, Stefan. Please tell me what happened after that."

Stefan made a moue. "It was my fault, I should not have fallen asleep. I always knew my uncle was afraid someone would find out about me. In fact, a few weeks later the Germans did come. They pushed my uncle around a bit. Then they came into the barn where I was hiding and stole some chickens, and hit my uncle when he tried to stop them. For his pains they took away one of his best pigs.

"Later, my uncle told me, the neighbour's body had been found floating in the river a few miles downstream, and he could only surmise its decomposition had hidden the marks of the struggle. He never let me out of his sight again.

"He was a good man, Indra. He would teach me my schooling each night before I went to bed. One night having forgotten something, I crept downstairs. I heard my aunt quarrelling with him over the danger my being there put them in. Also, as a growing boy, how much I ate and the clothes I needed." Stefan choked a little. "I decided to run away, and find my father. Then I thought, what would happen to me, to them if I was caught, so I stayed.

"Then one day, just as the winter was nearing its end, news came that the Nazis were on the retreat. We all jumped up and down for joy, until we heard they were burning and destroying everything in their wake. Uncle made me help him drive what little stock he had left to a tiny island in the middle of a marsh, a good four kilometres away from the farm. We toiled all day taking what foodstuffs valuables and clothing we could, for my uncle was sure the Germans would pass by that way. He was right; they came one morning, truck after truck load of them. We ran from the farm, hiding in a nearby wood while watching our home go up in flames.

"I do not know how long we stayed on that island, but it was horrible. We could only light a small fire at night for fear of being seen. Thanks to Uncle Karl's foresight, we had enough food for days. "However, the partisans found us. I had always believed them to be our friends .. our countrymen, but they stole everything. When

I asked my uncle why they had done this to us, he answered simply, 'communists'."

Indra sat staring into the fire. Suddenly Stefan jumped up. "No more unhappy stories, Indra! Let's dance!" He forced the sorrow out of his voice.

A gramophone stood in the corner of he room by the window, Stefan wound it up and set the arm. Indra smiled shyly as he took her in his arms, and he smelled her perfume as she rested her head on his shoulder, still mystified by what he had told her, she, whom he scarcely knew, about a time in his life he'd never really discussed with anyone, including his own father.

The record finished, he left her to switch it off.

Quite unexpected the girl heard him say from across the room. "With the War over I expected to go home and find my parents waiting for me. It was wishful thinking of a twelve year old." The laugh was at himself. "Instead there was my father and this strange foreign woman. Oh! My father was overjoyed to see I was safe." Stefan turned to look out of the window. It had stopped raining and there was less traffic in the streets at this late hour. "I know my father loved me." His voice was little more than a whisper. "He knew how much I loved and missed my mother." Stefan took hold of the velvet curtain, bunching it in his hand. "But did he have to take that woman into my mother's bedroom every night?" He swung angrily to face the girl. "I was old enough to understand, Indra! My father had forgotten all about my mother. He had given up on finding her! But I had not!

A little while later, Myra left for home. I was glad! Oh how glad I was! I had my father all to myself again. I thought he would search for my mother. Instead he told me she was dead. I argued, how did he know for sure? I accused him of wanting her dead, of not caring." Stefan drew a finger down the curtain. "I thought my father was going to really hit me. Now, I know he was only trying to spare me the pain of how she had died."

Stefan crossed the floor and took Indra in his arms again. "This is not the kind of night I had planned." he apologised with a kiss.

"I would not have missed it for the world, Stefan Kolybin. You have been through so much." She returned his kiss, holding him to her.

Stefan drew away, tickling her nose, making her giggle. "And now you must be tired. I can offer you the choice of several bedrooms," he said light-heartedly, hoping to erase the melodrama of the evening. "There is the blue room, as used by visiting dignitaries; the green room, for high society...snobs in other words." He pulled a face. "Then there are also several rooms on the upper floors. Which one would madam care for?" He gave an exaggerated bow.

Indra gazed up into his eyes, loving him more, now that she knew more about him. "How about your room, Stefan Kolybin? I think I should like to spend the night there."

Stefan took her face gently in both his hands. "If you are sure, Indra. Only if you are sure."

"I am sure Stefan, as sure as I know that I love you."

Chapter11

The water felt good on his skin. Mark turned lazily onto his back and closed his eyes against the glare of the hot afternoon sun. The weather was hot, unlike Troon or Largs, where sharks came up the Clyde Coast wearing wet suits.

Mark's joke brought back otherwise forgotten days of his childhood. Such as his mother pushing him at a sea, coming directly from the Arctic complete with icicles, and he with less meat sticking to him than on a butcher's pencil. In contrast to here, where the beach was deserted, with no weans screaming for ice cream cones, deck chairs to wrestle with, or half buried daddies to circumnavigate or your way to the toilet. Yet it was his home. Mark closed his eyes for a moment, willing himself to stop himself thinking about his home and how he should have been there by now. He must not become too morbid, and let it spoil the remainder of his 'leave'.

It had been good to get away from it all on this deserted part of the coast, Even though his so called 'beach house' was little more than a shack. He flipped over again and swam the last few strokes to shore.

He had changed since coming here. Now he was no longer from a Glasgow tenement, who like so may more had made the best of it after being demobbed, and getting through life with the usual sense of humour. Now …perhaps because of the language that sense of humour was almost gone …gone with old Berry, the only one who he could have had a real good laugh with. And now that he was a Major…he sounded the word out loud still unable to believe that he was one, and was expected to act as such. Quite a contrast from a foul mouthed private from WW2. and as common as dirt.

His self appraisal done treading water, Mark trudged across the beach to where he'd left his towel, and threw himself down, resting his back against a sand dune. *Another four days and this would all be over* he thought, draping the towel around his shoulders and swiping at a fly attracted to the glistening sweat on his brow.

It had now been five months since Kolybin's assassination. It was now time for him to go home. But how to get word to the wee man, or Molnar, this was the problem.

Army procedure demanded that he go through the proper channels, which was not quite so simple as it may appear, at least not in his situation, not without it raising a few suspicious eyebrows.

Mark yawned at the ebb tide, the flotsam and jetsam left behind, a reminder of the similarity to his own life.

At least his money was in the bank back home, which had been confirmed by his mother's last letter.

The wee soul had written that she was worried. Mark smiled, he had never known his mother not to have been. She was worried she had said, about the amount of money he had deposited in her name, and hoped he had come by it honestly.

He'd memorised the letter. When was he coming home? He'd been away far too long. It was time for him to settle down.... That nice girl in the Co-op had been asking for him again. Mark tried to think of the lassie's name. Home had been a long time ago.... Father wished him well...The Jags had managed to win a game.

Mark shivered, he did not know why, and remembered the old saying of' someone walking over his grave. Would he ever get home? How deeply was he involved in this country's politics without his knowing it? Did he know too much to be allowed to leave? How often had he had these same thoughts? Surely Kolybin or Molnar would honour their agreement, for after all, they had paid over the agreed amount.

He twisted round at the alien sound of a car door closing. A woman walked towards the beach house. Grabbing his shirt he stood up. The woman was almost at the veranda when she saw him. She waved, turning to walk back to meet him.

She was all in white from her cotton blouse and skirt to her light toeless shoes, a cardigan draped over her shoulders.

"I was told I'd find you here, Major Stewart." Myra Kolybin's voice floated cheerfully out over the intervening sand dunes.

"I thought my security was first class," he called back.

Myra halted, letting him cover the short distance between them. "It is, but I still have a little influence," she smiled.

Mark thought of the contrast from when they had last met. "To what do I owe this unexpected pleasure?" he asked, drawing closer.

The smile faded. "I'm going back home to England."

God, Mark thought, this was not on the cards when her husband had made his plans, but neither had the time element of five months.

"Does Molnar know?" Mark inquired, then wished he had not. "I mean... you were good friends, were you not? He'll be sorry to see you leave." He took a few steps closer. "What about young Stefan, what does he think of it all?" Mark attempted to cover his original faux pas in a flurry of questions.

"Milan and Elizbieta are both sorry. Milan was especially surprised by my decision."

I bet his was Mark thought. "As for Stefan, he has a girlfriend now. Besides, he has his career to think about."

"Has he any relatives?" Mark asked, taking her by the arm and guiding her back to the beach house.

"Some uncles and aunts, I believe. The only time I ever saw them was when they called on Paule for money." She gave an amused little laugh. "As for my step- son, he will be all right. He is a very resourceful young man, he has that of his father in him."

Mark had enough in store to offer his unexpected guest a meal. When they had finished they sat on the veranda, looking out over the blue green ocean.

"Just like the Clyde on a good day," Mark chuckled, swatting a fly.

"Oh, I don't know, Mark Stewart, I've been up that way, and it can be exceedingly beautiful, besides being a whole lot safer, so don't down your own country," Myra scolded.

"You're right," he sighed. "Sometimes you forget how lucky you are at home. Although you would not think so, the way we grumble all the time."

"That's what makes home so endearing, the fact that we can grumble."

"We are philosophical today are we not?" Mark chided good humourdly.

Myra waved her hand apologetically. "Sorry. A bit too heavy?"

"On a day like this? Yes." He stood up. "Let's enjoy the sunshine while we can."

They strolled down the beach talking about everything and nothing in particular, both neatly avoiding the obvious question of the moment.

Mark knew why she had come, he had seen it in her eyes when she told him of her intention of returning home. She was lovely, and he could easily understand why Kolybin had been attracted to her. And he hoped she would not spoil the day by making it awkward for him. 'Hell hath no fury' etc.

But what would she think of him, of herself, should they make love, and she was to find out later her husband was still alive and he had known it all along?

They left the beach, heading inland over the dunes, and when Myra stopped to empty sand from her shoes, she had held on to his shoulder for support, taking his hand in hers when they resumed their walk.

Mark looked up into the cloudless sky, wondering if Myra's intentions were to stay the night. "Don't you have bodyguards anymore First Lady, to get away on your own? Or did you cunningly give them the slip?" He asked in a way that suggested the thought had just come to him.

"Oh, I'm no longer a state asset...or should that be, liability?" She squeezed his hand good naturedly. "I was only of some importance while Paule was still alive." Myra kicked out at a turf of grass. "Stefan and I have to vacate the Kasel in a month's time to make way for President Molnar, and First Lady, Elizbieta."

"Do I detect a hint of resentment there, former First Lady, Myra,?" Mark joked, knowing he could not return to the formality of First Lady, having let things get this far, and already regretted it.

If only Kolybin was not still alive. He looked up at the sky again. It would serve the egotistical wee bugger right, if he was to take his wife. Lord knew she wanted him to. Even as the thoughts passed through his mind, he was aware of doing the wee man an injustice. Kolybin was taking an enormous gamble doing what he thought was best to end almost five years of civil war. It was not as if the man had not already suffered enough for his country.

"I think we should head on back now, Myra. You'll want to be on your way before it gets too dark."

The hand in his stiffened.

"Oh I'm not in too much of a hurry to get back, after all to what, to very little now that Paule has gone."

The mercenary felt sorry for her. It had been more out of love for Paule than that of his country that had brought her back here from England after the war. Therefore, now that her sole reason for remaining in this foreign country had gone, it was only natural that she should turn to someone her own age and background. Despite her attempts to be cheerful, her eyes still betrayed her loss. She would never forget this man. Silently, he cursed. It could prove fatal were he to show any weakness now, or give her any hint he wanted her to stay.

It was as they topped the sand dune on their way back that he saw two men running in a half crouch towards the beach house. *"Get down"* Mark jerked her hand, pulling her quickly down behind the dune. "Not yours, I take it?"

Myra shook her head. "No. I'm really only required to let Security know my intentions."

"Did you tell them, here?" Mark raised his head to take another look. When she didn't answer, he asked her again.

"Not quite. I mean...ethically."

He grunted his understanding. "Well, at least we know who they are not. Let's surmise, PFF I would say you are a bigger fish than me to catch."

"PFF don't usually attack civilians, Mark. You should know that."

Suddenly, he didn't feel sure anymore. "Well, which ever one they are after, let's make sure they fail."

They watched the men converge on the beach house from opposite directions, then disappear round the front, to re-emerge a short time later to stand scanning the sand dunes for a few seconds.

Mark tapped Myra on the shoulder. They slid out of sight.

"What do we do now?" Myra's asked calmly. She had been through a lot worse than this in six years of war.

"Do you have your car keys?" Mark asked, chancing another quick look over the dune.

"No. I left my handbag in the shack."

"Shack!" Mark uttered in mock horror. "Beach House if you don't mind, lady."

Myra felt a lot better that she had someone with her who could find time to joke. She knew the Scots were like that; an odd people the Scots. "Sorry. Beach house."

"I should think so too. I'd hate to be paying so much rent for a shack."

Inwardly, Mark was not feeling as jovial as he made out. If those men down there had searched Myra's handbag and found her keys, they'd know she had no way of escaping. As for himself, his keys were on the table. He'd also violated security by not carrying his weapon at all times.

"What do you think we should do now, Mark?" Myra crawled up beside him.

"Wait. See what they do. If I were them, I'd be thinking we'd gone for a stroll and wait for our return."

"Which we did."

Mark nodded. "It would appear that I'm right. One has gone up the track to where our cars are parked, probably to put them out of action. I can't quite see him from here. Now all they have to do is wait for us to show up. Perhaps we can make a move, now that we know they are not coming to look for us." He took her hand. "Come on, let's get out of here."

Mark headed further inland, carefully keeping the dunes between themselves and the beach.

"Keep heading in that direction." Mark pointed to scrubland. "I'm going back a little way to make sure they haven't found our trail."

"Please be careful, Mark." Myra gave him a worried look.

"I have been 'till now," he winked. "You too."

She winked back. "What? This is child's play after what I've been through."

An hour later, Mark caught up with the woman as she fought her way through waist high scrubland, running a kilometre or so from the road.

"I thought you'd got lost. Or worse, went looking for a rebate on your 'shack', knowing how mean you Scots are," she wisecracked, feeling the relief flood through her at having him back again.

"Very funny, previous first lady," he retorted, not unkindly.

"The track that meets the main road to the town is not too far from here," she announced, swiping at an insect. "I remember seeing it on the way here."

"I know, I've just been on it."

Myra swung on him. "You've been *what!*"

"I went looking for those guys' car. They had to have one. They could not have walked all the way."

"Did you find it?" Suddenly Myra felt tired. Her dress was crushed and stained, her feet cut and bruised. Had she known this was going to happen, she thought, she would have come prepared.

"Yes. It's back there about a kilometre or so. It was locked. I couldn't get it started at all, so I did what they had done to ours."

"Well at least that's something."

They came upon the main road leading to town, about an hour later.

Hopping on one foot to shake out a stone from her shoe, Myra looked up the empty road. "I hope we get a lift soon."

"I hope so too. It will be dark in an hour or so. Though, I don't know whether that will be in our favour or not."

Wearily the travelers trudged on, and had just reached a bend on the road when they heard a car. Hastily, Myra threw off her white cardigan ready to wave the vehicle down as soon as it appeared.

"Careful Myra, I think you're a wee bit too far out on the road," Mark called out from the verge.

"I'm going to make sure they see me. This is the first car we've seen on this godforsaken road," she shouted out determinedly.

Suddenly the car was upon them, Myra frantically waving her cardigan in the air. The driver swerved at the last minute.

"Myra!" Mark bellowed at her. "Run! It's one of them!"

For a moment, the woman stood mystified. Then, suddenly recognising her own car, took to her heels.

"This way!" Mark grabbed her hand pulling her after him into the wood skirting the road. "What a fool I am. I should have known they wouldn't knobble both our cars," he gasped.

"Where's the other baddie?" Myra 's breathing was laboured, as she asked the question.

"Probably back at the beach, in the off chance we return."

They ran through the trees. Myra hopping until she had both shoes in her hands. Running barefoot would not be easy.

Behind them a branch sprang back and Mark realised whoever was following was not so far behind.

"You go that way," Mark threw out a hand pointing to his right. "I'll draw this bugger off. Make your way back to the car if you can. I'll meet you there." Mark veered away from the gasping woman, before she had time to protest.

Now separated, Mark followed a narrow path until it petered out, leaving him little option but to fight his way through shoulder high scrub. A shot rang out and a bullet whistled in to the undergrowth close by. He spun round as his assailant aimed again and threw himself into the wet vegetation. Another shot quickly followed. Mark sprang up, bolting for the protection of a clump of bushes, his speed helped on by a bullet thudding into a tree inches above his head. Lungs bursting, he swerved to his right, hoping to draw the would-be killer away from Myra.

Ahead of him lay a glade, a huge rock at its centre. He had an idea. Running at right angles to the clearing, he dodged back in amongst the trees and stopped.

Mark had not long to wait. A few seconds later, his pursuer emerged from the woods at almost the exact point as he had done. For a moment or two, he stood there catching his breath, undecided as to what to do. Mark ventured a look from behind his tree. Now the man was scanning the glade, turning in his direction. Mark drew back.

When he looked again his antagonist, was in the act of circling the outcrop, until eventually satisfied that no one was hiding behind it, took off across the glade and disappeared into the trees beyond.

The watcher heaved a sigh of relief. It was time to head back to the car, which, with any luck may still have its ignition key...if not 'the ba' was burst' as they would say at home.

Mark had almost reached the road when Myra suddenly stepped out from behind a tree swinging the tree stump she was using as a club. Mark ducked quickly. "Ch...! You almost frightened the shi..." and stopped himself just in time.

"Sorry," Myra apologised, grinning at Mark's expression, both verbal and facial.

They ran to the car, its door wide open. Mark snatched a look inside. "Great! The keys are still here. Shall I drive? Or do you want to drive your own car?" he asked hurriedly.

Myra's answer was to get into the passenger's seat. "You drive. I think I could do with a bit of a rest."

Mark did not halt in the neighbouring town, but instead drove to where Myra had said she had set out from that morning.

He let out the clutch, changing gear. "When we reach the town, I'll get out a few streets away, and leave you to drive back to your hotel on your own. We don't want any scandal do we?"

"Don't we?" Myra said coolly. "Doesn't make much difference, I'm no longer of any importance or interest to anyone, now that Paule is gone."

"Perhaps you should consider his memory, and what he meant to the people of this country." Mark hated himself for saying it, but it was his only way out. This, and the fact he could not believe what he was doing, refusing the advances of a beautiful woman.

Taking a sudden interest in the approaching town, and without turning her head, his passenger asked coldly, "What about your car and belongings?"

"The car is hired. As for my belongings?" Mark shrugged. Just a few things. However, there will be some awkward questions to answer about me being unarmed." He swung the wheel, letting it spin back through his hands as the car came out of the bend.

"What will happen to you?" Myra shifted in her seat to face him.

Mark shrugged again, surprised by the sudden note of concern in her voice. "With any luck, they will drum me out of the service. Rip my buttons off, and all that," he said deadpan.

Myra drew closer to him. "I hope not. Won't your trousers fall down?" she returned, equally serious.

Mark laughed. "I hope not. Not with my legs. Perhaps with luck, they'll send me home. Then we can meet over there. What do you say?"

Myra rested her head on his shoulder. "Yes I think I would like that. Yes I would like that very much."

They were all together again in the cellar. Petr called the meeting to order. "We have some very important issues to discuss. I thought it safer to meet here rather than at Pavels flat."

The others nodded in agreement so Petr continued. "Firstly, there is the matter of Juri Trybala. I shall leave Miro to present this issue to you." He gestured that the Section Leader take over.

Miro cleared his throat. "Carrying out Group instructions, we captured Sergeant Juri Trybala, we then proceeded to..."

"Spare us the formalities, Miro, if you don't mind," Vaclaw sighed impatiently. "I'm freezing my balls off here."

The younger man glanced nervously at his Group Leader for support. Petr nodded, secretly pleased that the other two men had a way of keeping this ambitious young man in his place. "Tell us in your own words Miro."

Miro decided to comply. Obviously, they wanted it neat and concise. It did not matter that he and his Section had done the dirty work, all these three wanted right now was the result, and to get the hell out of here, denying him yet again the opportunity of displaying his efficiency. This way, he'd never command a Group of his own.

When Miro had concluded, all three leaders sat back, each mulling over his report.

"What do you think, Petr?" Pavel asked. "Do you believe this Trybala fellow, when he swears it was an accident?"

"He told us the truth about his love affair with Jakofcic's wife," Miro emphasised.

"Only when he was forced to do so," Pavel reminded him.

"Would you not have done the same, you old fool?" Vaclaw rose, reaching for the vodka bottle.

Pavel ignored him. "What do we do now, Petr? Should we start to put pressure on him? What a source of information we have found! A direct source to Jakofcic no less, and hell knows what more! And he cannot say a word. Beautiful! Beautiful!"

Miro hid his anger, throwing a furtive glance at Petr in the hope he would acknowledge that it was to him the credit should go for finding the source in the first place.

Instead, Petr took a glass of vodka from Vaclaw. "No, Pavel." He took a sip. "Much as I am tempted to milk the golden goose...if you will excuse the mixed metaphor," he grinned. "I think we have much more important work for Staff Sergeant Trybala."

"Then you believe this soldier?" Vaclaw sat back down, pushing a glass of vodka across the table to Miro, who in turn pushed it back with a shake of his head, in no humour to drink with comrades who had chosen to ignore his worth.

"I think I do, Pavel." Petr stood up to stretch his legs. "However, the course I intend to use is to let the man sweat. Each day let him sweat a little more. Have him wonder when we are going to make contact."

Eager to hear more and scarcely able to control his excitement, Pavel gulped down his drink. Petr obliged. "He cannot inform his superiors without disclosing his affair with his Commanding Officer's wife. Plus, as yet, he does not know what information we are likely to ask. So, until then, I believe he will do nothing. The longer we remain out of contact, the more relieved he will become. Then, when he thinks he's safe, we will finally pounce!" Petr punched his fist into his open palm.

And Pavel laughed with the sheer joy at the thought of his squirming victim.

"Now to our second piece of business." Petr sat down.

"How about a piece of Pavel's sister's cake before we start, Petr?" Vaclaw suggested. "After the frail old man has carried it all the way here," he chuckled.

"I thought your balls were freezing?" Miro sneered.

Vaclaw glared hatred across the table. "At least I have some to freeze."

It was the opportunity for which Miro had been waiting. "Meaning!" he yelled, springing to his feet. "Who the hell was it that brought Trybala in? Got you this information!"

"Lost Stewart..." Vaclaw smirked, casually pouring himself another drink.

Rocked, Miro sat down. He had not known Vaclaw already knew about his failure to bring in the Scot. He'd reached the beach house where he'd been reliably informed the soldier was holidaying, only to find it deserted; and by the look of the place, had been for several days.

Sensing trouble, Petr butted in, gesturing with a dismissive wave of his hand. "Calm yourselves, both of you. No blame can be attached to Miro. What is done is done."

Having chosen to ignore the confrontation, Pavel calmly sliced a piece of cake. "We lost Stewart, so he can't tell us whether Kolybin is alive or dead. What now, Petr?"

"The only thing we can do to prove our theory, or should I say...Miro's theory is,"

And the way Petr said it, Miro knew he was to be held responsible, left to shoulder the entire blame should he be proved wrong.

It was cold and dark. Miro waited until Vaclaw's Section had melted into the trees skirting the graveyard. Now, it was up to his own Section.

As expected, they found the graveyard gate locked. Miro motioned to the big man nicknamed 'The Bear' to use the bolt cutters and moved back to give him room. At the same time, glimpsing the deathly white face of the boy who stood beside Jan, whose reassuring grin, made him feel that bit more at ease.

"Should be thunder and lightning for what we are up to," Miro said cheerfully, attempting to put the boy at ease.

The boy continued to stare passed him into the night. Why had Petr insisted on the youngster accompanying them tonight, Miro pondered? He supposed the Group Leader was right, the boy had to start somewhere. And with any luck, there should be very little danger of them having to fight their way out.

There was a snap, a click and the heavy chain fell to the ground, and Bear pushed the gate open with a squeak.

Fifty metres away in the midst of the night, a light spilled over the graves from the caretakers cottage. Somewhere a dog barked. Miro signaled to veer away from the light.

"Where is it?" he whispered to the boy, whose job it had been earlier, to locate the exact position of the late President's grave.

The boy pointed a trembling finger into the darkness. Miro led the men forward. The dog barked again. Bear stumbled, swearing obscenely. At last, the boy halted. "There," he pointed nervously.

Switching on his torch, Miro played it on the headstone simply inscribed 'Paul Kolybin, beloved President of our Republic' and the date. Beside which the earth had not yet settled nor the turf knitted, motioning to Jan and the boy to start digging.

One eye on the caretaker's cottage, Miro's thoughts were on what they would find. After all, it was his theory that had brought them here. If Kolybin did not lie here, what propaganda would Petr choose to use? If he was? Miro shuddered.

Miro swapped his torch for Jan's shovel. He worked fast, piling earth on the opposite side of the grave from the earth. It should not take them long to reach the coffin, for Kolybin's father and mother were also buried here. He felt more composed now that he had something to do and the caretaker's dog had stopped barking. His shovel hit something solid, and he knew instinctively it was the coffin.

"Steady." He put his hand on the boy's arm, at the same time as the caretaker's door opened and a shaft of light cut across the graveyard about sixty metres away. The dog started barking again, this time more urgently.

Miro stopped digging. "What's happening up there, Bear?"

"I think the caretaker's let his mongrel out for a piss," the big man said gruffly.

"Can we be seen?"

Jan answered first. "I don't think so Miro, but I can't see where that damned dog has got to."

Suddenly, the dog flew at them out of the darkness, growling, teeth bared, ignoring its Master 's command from somewhere behind to come to heel.

Miro let the shovel fall, and had one foot on the side of the grave to leaver himself up when he heard a slight whimper. Jan stretched out his hand to help him up. "What's happened?" Miro asked, searching the darkness for the dog.

Bear wiped his knife clean. "No worries."

In the background the caretaker's voice grew nearer, calling out to his dog. This was not going according to plan, Miro thought.

"Shouldn't we get out of here?" Jan asked in the same calm reassuring manner Miro had grown accustomed to, the boy having already got himself out of the grave, ready to run.

"We'll wait, Jan," Miro answered quietly.

The caretaker was now close enough for Miro to see by his stooped figure that he was an old man. Miro hesitated, the feeling of deja vu, of that night in the old judge's house.

Suddenly the old man lurched back, an arm around his neck. A glint of steel, a spurt of blood and he slid to the ground.

The boy swung away. "Sweet Jesus! Mary Mother...!"

Jan's hand lashed out catching the whimpering boy in the mouth. "Shut up. Are you a man or not?"

Miro quickly crossed the ground to where the old man lay. Bear straightened up from cleaning his knife on the grass.

"Was that strictly necessary?" Miro hissed. The big man twisted his lip, and gave an indifferent shrug of his massive shoulders.

"What now, Miro?" Jan asked with his usual cadence.

"Let's finish what we came here to do, and fast."

"What if there is a Mrs. Caretaker?" Jan asked, gesturing in the direction of the cottage.

Miro threw Bear a shovel staring angrily at him. "If there is, I will deal with her myself."

For the next few anxious minutes while Bear and the boy dug, Miro kept his eyes trained on the open cottage door.

Jan tapped his leader on the shoulder, as bear and the boy climbed out of the grave. "We're ready. We can open the coffin now."

The cottage door closed, now Miro knew, there was someone else inside. Whether they were aware of them and had bolted the door he did not know. "Does the cottage have a telephone?" he flung at the boy beside him. The youngster shook his head mumbling something incoherent.

"Well, we'll have to chance it. Let's get on with it. Jan! You better go back. Let Vaclaw know what's happened." He could well surmise what that maniac would think of him and his Section when told.

Miro turned to face Bear, ignoring the boy's angry stare at not being sent instead of the older man. "Open it up, Bear," he said grimly.

The big man knelt down and slid back the coffin lid, jerking back with an oath, at the smell of decomposition. Reluctantly Miro knelt down beside him, and was surprised by how well preserved the figure to be, considering the number of corpses he had seen during the war, who had been in a far worse state than this for a much lesser period of time. Then again he thought, those had been lying out in the open.

Taking the torch, Miro bent closer. Holding his hand across his mouth, he inhaled slowly, concentrating on the smell of nicotine on his fingers to help negate the smell from the coffin. Somewhere in the background, a woman called out anxiously for her husband. He inhaled again playing the torch over the face.. the face that *was* Kolybin. He had been wrong, their country's president was dead after all.

"Careful with that crystal Anna!"

Elizbieta rounded on her husband, sitting behind his desk. "If these servants of ours are not more careful, we'll have nothing left of value to take to the Kasel."

"Why do you want to take so much, Elizbieta? There's all we will ever need over there."

"We shall be obliged to entertain, you know, Milan. I shall want to show off something of my own," she firmly rebuked him.

"How about your warm personality, my dear?"

Aware that the three maids had overheard her husband's jaundiced comment, and were vainly trying to hide their amusement, Elizbieta fixed her husband an icy stare, which said, that he would pay for those remarks later...and how. Angrily, she spun on her domestics. "Come on! Come on! We only have a week, not a month, you know!"

The maids gone, Elizbieta busied herself by the bookshelves. "You will have to get yourself new clothes, Milan, those you have, will never do to entertain dignities. I do not want to be embarrassed by you looking like a tramp." The anger at her husband was still in her voice.

Milan marked the passage of text he'd been reading, with a finger. "Yes dear," he sighed, now regretting his inexcusable outburst. "But remember, this is still our home, so there is no necessity to take quite so much. After all, were I to lose the election next year, it will be all the less to carry back."

"There is very little likelihood of that happening," his wife snorted, taking a book from a shelf and studying the title. "You have done splendidly since Paule died. Just look at what you have achieved by yourself? That massive dam construction...or whatever, at Gravst for instance." She waved a hand. "Not to mention how popular you are with all the newspapers...well, almost all of them," she amended, replacing the book.

Elizbieta wagged a finger at her husband. "Just keep on doing what you are doing. Keep all those argumentative senators in their place."

"Yes dear." Milan shook his head, amused by the way his wife had likened him to an old schoolmaster toiling to keep an unruly class in order.

The magisterial lady's voice softened fractionally as she changed the subject. "It was good of Myra to let us take up residence in the Kasel so quickly. Although, I cannot say I am surprised by her decision to return to England." She walked back to the bookshelves, picking up a flower vase on the way. "After all, she is a foreigner. It was the man she loved, not his country."

Milan took his finger off the page. Not his country, he thought, only the man? Well if that were so, she had an undying love for him which saw her remain in those mountains for the best part of six years of the occupation. During which time, what were you doing my beloved wife? No, that was unfair of him. He watched his wife for a time, amused by her transformation of persona since his becoming President. Oh dear wife, what would you say to my achievements if you were to find out, that all of them were of Paule's making?

"Are you going directly to the House this morning, Milan?" Elizbieta set down the vase on a small table, standing back to admire it as if having never seen it before.

"No. I'm going directly to my office. I hope to be in the Senate sometime this afternoon."

"Good. So remember what I told you. You *are* the President. Be firm with them Milan. Be firm."

Milan returned to his book, staring blankly at the page before him, and casting his mind back almost a month. It had been no easy task to contact Lieutenant Dryak without having the source traced back to him.

Milan's secretary knocked on his office door announcing the presence of a Mr Josef Kalas. Milan never would have recognised the overweight man with the protruding belly, receding hairline and short thick beard streaked with grey, as the man who had played the doctor the night of Kolybin's assassination, unless he had been expecting him. Therefore, it was little to be wondered at, that the man entering his office was generally accepted as one of the country's best undercover agents, and had been during the occupation. A fact Kolybin had not been slow to exploit in his own administration.

Thanking his secretary, Milan rose to meet his visitor. "Mr Kalas, I presume. Please have a seat. Can I offer you some coffee? Tea perhaps?" He shook hands, indicating a chair in front of his desk.

Playing his part before the waiting secretary, Dryak responded. "A good day to you Mr President. No, to coffee, or tea." He eased his bulk into the chair.

"That will be all Anna," Milan addressed his secretary, waiting until the door had closed behind her before continuing. "To allay suspicion, I can only allow you fifteen minutes, as I would any other person with similar, business," Milan apologised, facing the soldier across the desk. Dryak nodded his understanding.

Milan reached for a box of cigars, offering one to his visitor.

Dryak declined with a shake of his head. "But with your permission, Mr President, I shall shed a few kilos," he grinned.

Milan smiled sympathetically while the man opened his coat to loosen his padding.

Anxious to put an end to this distasteful business as quickly as possible, Milan began.

"At first when the president...by that I mean Paule." Dryak gave him a twisted smile. "When Paule first disclosed his plan to me to have himself assassinated, I must confess I found myself totally opposed to the whole idea." Milan leaned forward steepling his fingers. "The concept of deceiving the people...and in some ways the world, I found completely abhorrent. However, Paule defended this by saying, that by doing so he could bring this civil war...civil discontent?" he corrected himself, "to a swift and successful conclusion."

Milan reached slowly for a pen. Toying with it, he went on. "I tried to argue...reason with him of the repercussions should his plan fail. I suggested, instead of assassination, he pretend an incapacitating illness, or even kidnapping. In fact, anything which would render him unable to govern for the short period of time he'd calculated necessary for the coup-de-grace, to the PFF Paule was adamant however, that nothing short of his death would entice the Reds and their supporters to come out into the open...hence the assassination." Milan threw down the pen. "How wrong I was to go along with it" he snapped bitterly.

Dryak turned his head slightly towards the window. "In hindsight we can all see our mistakes. I also was party to the deceit. What I did, I did out of loyalty to my President and my country."

"You, sir, had very little option but to do what you did out of duty." Milan pushed at the pen with a finger. "It was much easier for me to refuse than you."

"That is most generous of you, Mr President. But as your predecessor...if I may use the term...also convinced me of his plan's infallibility...which you yourself said was based on a swift conclusion to the fighting, I had no hesitation in playing my part in its implementation."

Milan sat silent for a time staring out of the window, as if totally unaware of the others presence. His eyes still on the window, he said at length, "It is as hard for me to say, as it undoubtedly for you to hear, but Paule Kolybin is not the man either of us knew those few short months ago.

"When Paule returned from the mountains at the end of the war, he was a national hero, one with whom the people could readily identify. So it was, with the exiled government rejected, that he became the natural choice."

Milan stood up, hesitated, then crossed to a cabinet, where he opened the glass door and took out a glass of whisky and two glasses. "What I am endeavouring to say, is this...Paule was an excellent guerilla leader and by living and fighting in the mountains for almost six years he had time to learn his trade, something which was denied him in politics." The recalcitrant President handed Dryak a measure of whisky and returned to his desk. "He has made mistakes. Haven't we all?...But he is the only man who could successfully have brought so many factions together. Only the communists refuse to co-operate; hence the present situation."

Dryak looked puzzled. "Then what is your point? How has Paule Kolybin, altered?

Milan took a sip of his drink, and waved the glass in front of him. "Paule gambled everything on his death enticing Tetek to come down from the mountains where the weight of Government forces could defeat him, and as you know, the old soldier did not take the bait."

It was still early in the day, but for what he had to say, imply, Milan felt he needed this drink. Taking another quick sip, he slid his glass across his blotting pad, carefully measuring his words. "Paule did not expect to live in that cellar all of this time. As you are well aware, it was originally built by the Nazis to protect their maps and secret papers from air raids, not for anyone to live in for any length of time. It is cold down there, and it is now autumn. However, I have managed to smuggle in an electric fire, but it is not easy...Should I be discovered." He trailed off.

"Quite." Dryak rolled the spirit around his mouth.

"Paule is in continual need of food, also a change of clothing. The toilet too can barely cope. That is only the start, the list is endless."

"I take your point, Mr President. Do you want me to explore the possibility of having him moved? Or is there a totally different reason that has you summoning me here?"

Milan emptied his glass. "As each day passes, Paule becomes more unstable, more depressed: at times, even unrealistic. The entire episode has affected him mentally. He has drawn up plans for a mountain offensive." Milan's voice rose sharply, splaying his hands in desperation. "I do not know what to do." He stopped for a moment, staring at the man sitting across from him. "Paule's plans involve army Divisions that don't *exist*!"

"Shades of a certain Austrian corporal, I should say," Dryak smirked.

Milan threw him a look of hostility. "Paule Kolybin is, the greatest patriot this county has ever known," he rebuked.

"Sorry. So what are you telling me is, that our former president has lost his marbles and you think you should take over? Am I correct? This is the real reason you have asked me here?"

Milan was about to repudiate the allegations when there was a sharp knock at the door. Annoyed by what he knew to be the prearranged signal informing him that fifteen minutes had elapsed, Milan shouted his acknowledgement a little louder than intended.

Dryak rose but instead of heading for the door, walked to the drinks cabinet and carefully poured himself another drink. "What do you want me to do, Mr President?"

Milan's anger at his visitors complacency, gradually gave way to resignation. He shrugged helplessly. "What can I do?" His question was little more than a whisper.

Dryak took a sip of his drink. "Besides ourselves, there is only a certain army Major who knows of this little subterfuge."

"Perhaps it is time we gave him back his passport?" Milan suggested, clearing his throat.

Dryak shook his head. "With Stewart alive, you would never be absolutely sure of your position should he for some reason or other decide to talk."

Suddenly weak at the knees Milan sat down heavily. "You mean?"

"Is this not what you also intend for your friend?"

It was the arrogance of the man that angered Milan. Suddenly he hated him and all he stood for, almost as much as he hated himself, for now he had to face the question he had been at so much pains to avoid. Had it come to this? Had he started something which might never end? Would there perhaps come a day when it was his turn, and have Dryak or someone like him deal with the problem, as if it were an every day occurrence?

"Do what you must" he heard himself choke. "But there is also another man. You know, the one who helped you create the diversion the night of the assassination."

Dryak laughed out loud. "Oh! You need have no fear there, Mr President, one does not have to fear one's own brother!"

"Milan! Will you be taking any of these books with you to the Kasel?" Elizbieta's voice shook Milan out of his reverie and his recent meeting with Dryak.

"I'll have a look later," he muttered, watching his wife hustle the maids again.

To Elizbieta, his being President meant nothing more than that she was the country's First Lady, having no more affection for her native land than the person she had so recently vilified.

Milan closed his book and walked out of the room by the French doors into the garden where a tiny bird took off at his coming. He sank down on a bench, watching it fly effortlessly over the trees by the high red brick wall, recalling his last meeting with the erstwhile President.

Paule was in jubilant mood, greeting Milan like a long lost friend. "My plans are complete, Milan. By the time all the mercenaries have returned, all will be ready for an autumn offensive. Tetek will not get out of this, not this time!" he cried enthusiastically.

Attempting to match Paule's mood, Milan smiled and held out the bottle of wine to him. "Then it's fitting we toast our intended success with your favourite wine."

The little man studied the label, his eyes glowing. "Maros Dry Red!" he grunted happily. "Do you remember the first time we tasted such a wine, Milan?" He inserted the corkscrew, his face lighting up at the memory.

"Yes Paule. We had been hit bad. We thought we'd never survive."

"You remember, old friend! How could we ever forget such times! Then the last of our patrols came in." There was a 'pop' as he extricated the corkscrew. "And they had half a dozen bottles of this same wine with them.!" He held up the bottle, his voice loud and cheerful.

Paule filled a glass, handing it to his friend. "I was going to say they were good old days, but they were not. Funny, how the mind tends to remember only the good times while conveniently choosing to forget the bad."

"Perhaps that is how we survive, Paule. Perhaps that is how the whole damned world survives," Milan sighed.

Paule poured himself a drink, rounded his desk and sat down. "Now that I have negotiated an agreement with our neighbours, preventing Tetek from crossing the frontier, when things get too hot for them this side...." Paule pointed his glass at Milan, "which they will. We can be assured of a very swift and decisive victory." He laid down his glass. "Then I can get out of this stinking hell hole and be with my wife and son again."

The diminutive president stood up, his voice rising. "Can you just see the people, Milan, lined all the way from the Caserne to the Kasel...cheering and cheering? You and I in an open top car. Rank after rank of victorious solders marching behind!"

Paule's face was flushed with excitement as he visualised the scene, his fists opening and closing, staring well beyond the confines of the cellar to the glory he was sure would come...to him the greatest of this country's heroes.

Embarrassed, Milan looked away. *Poor old friend*, he thought. He looked back, willing to forgive him his belief that the frontier negotiations were all his doing. It was too late now for incriminations.

Drawing himself to his full height, Paule held out his glass. "A toast Milan, old friend, to this great little country of ours," he proudly proposed, as Milan raised his own glass in salute. Paule drank deeply. "How quickly can we begin this offensive of mine do you think, Milan?" he asked eagerly, his eyes gleaming at the prospect that it would soon be all over.

Milan's heart hammered in his chest as Paule sat back down. He tried to make his brain work. It was no use. What was the point? He cursed himself for not saying something to his oldest friend. *Friend,* he thought despising himself.

Why of all days had Paule chosen to be so cheerful and so full of life for the first time in weeks? Why could he not have been in an argumentative mood: shout at him; insult him, something to leave him hating the man? But not like this.

Paule put down his empty glass, staring. Perhaps something in Milan's eyes betrayed him. He put a hand to his throat. His eyes, as much as the voice, asking, "why ? Why Milan?"

Unable to meet those accusing eyes, Milan Molnar quickly looked away . And when he did bring himself to look again, Paule was slowly sliding to the floor. Milan did not move. He knew his friend was dead.

Now it was up to Dryak and the unknown man he called his brother.

Juri put the papers Jakofcic had requested on his desk. He heard Lomova in the next room and quickly made for the study door.

"Oh, I didn't know you were in here, Juri."

Too late he found himself trapped. For the past two weeks he had successfully avoided Lomova with one excuse or another. He had not told her of his apprehension by the PFF, explaining the bruises on his face as the result of having hit his head on the steering wheel of his car while braking suddenly to avoid hitting the vehicle in front. Thankfully, Lomova had accepted this, and the resulting headaches which had prevented him from seeing her at her flat.

The soldier had already made up his mind not to see Lomova again, but how to tell her was another problem. His capture, detention - call it what you will - by the PFF had made him realise how much his wife and son meant to him. At first, he had thought of telling her about the incident, hoping it might scare her into distancing herself from him. But should it not?

He jumped every time the phone rang, certain it was them asking, or more likely ordering him to betray everything in which he believed. The cold sweat he felt when he thought of what information they might ask, and how many lives it might cost.

Finally, he had come to a decision, he would ask the General to take him with him to the 'front'; the term used for their search for Tetek in the northern mountains. Though in truth, there was no 'front' as such, no lines of troops drawn up facing one another.

Of course, he knew, Jakofcic would refuse him on the grounds of his physical incapacity, most likely fob him off by telling him he was more important to him here at home. Or, that he must put his request for a transfer to combat duties through the usual channels, knowing very well how long this would take.

Yet should the General agree? Despite the sadness of not being with his family, at least he would be out of the reach of both Lomova and the PFF here in the city.

Lomova came close to him, her eyes flashing angrily. "We have not seen one another for the best part of two weeks. If I did not know better, I'd say you are trying to avoid me, Juri. Those frightful headaches are usually a woman's excuse, you know," she seethed.

Conscious of how much he missed her body, and the self control it had taken not to have picked up the phone and arrange a meeting, he blushed, carefully avoiding her eyes. "How could we have met, with the General at home all of last week?" he pleaded, hoping his voice carried enough conviction.

Lomova's features softened. She wanted him badly. As much, as she was sure he wanted her.

"Love will find a way, Juri, my darling," she pouted, drawing closer.

Juri felt himself stifled. "Be careful, Lomova...the General," he stammered, afraid of the man making a sudden appearance.

She raised an eyebrow. "You are afraid of something, and it's not of being discovered by Silvo." Teasingly, she pushed a strand of his hair back into place. "I know you only too well, Juri Trybala," she mocked, pursing her lips close to his. Then, as if tired of the game she was playing, and with a brisk flick of her head, pushed him away, and crossed the room to rearrange a vase of flowers on her husband's desk.

"I have a few problems. You will have to give me time to sort them out, Lomova," Juri's voice trailed after her.

"Good morning, Staff Sergeant," Jakofcic's voice boomed out cheerfully from the doorway.

Startled by the General's sudden appearance, Juri stammered, "Good morning sir." Blushing, he searched his senior's face for any hint that the man might have overheard their conversation. Though he was sure if he had, he would have known by now, and in no uncertain terms.

"The papers you requested are on your desk sir." His statement was hurried. Perhaps a little too hurried, he thought guiltily.

"Thank you Sergeant." Jakofcic crossed his study to his desk, raising an eyebrow at his wife's presence. "I did not expect to find you in here, Lomova?" he said pleasantly.

"Can't I at least pick some flowers for my husband," she replied, kissing her husband lovingly on the cheek as he dropped into his chair.

Embarrassed by this unexpected show of affection, Jakofcic shuffled the papers around on his desk, clearing his throat to ask of his aide, "What time are you off duty, Sergeant?"

"Fifteen hundred, sir."

"Good. We have a great deal of work to get through before then. I am treating my lovely wife to a first class meal. She deserves it the way she contends with my irregular trips to and from home. Don't you darling?" He beamed at her.

You don't know how well she copes, General, Juri thought, feeling a sickening in his stomach. Forcing him to ask in a pretence of good humour, "You are not thinking of engaging Company cooks, sir?"

Jakofcic laughed, pulling a face. "Obviously you have not eaten in the mess lately, Sergeant!"

"No sir, never," Juri lied, grinning, and feeling more guilty than ever at deceiving this honest, decent man.

"Some day" the General was saying, "hopefully very soon, when there will be no more need for security, I shall take my wife to the most expensive restaurant in the city." He pretended to sigh, "Alas until that day arrives, we shall have to make do with dining at home." Jakofcic looked up at his wife. "However, these security restrictions do have their advantages. Do they not, my dear?" he winked.

Lomova gave her husband a smile devoid of all warmth. And as Silvo turned his attention to his work, Juri caught the utter look of contempt on her face.

Shocked, Juri Trybala wondered how he had ever let himself become involved with such a woman. Now, more than ever, he hoped the General would agree to transferring him to 'the front'.

"I think my mother really likes you, Stefan." Indra squeezed the boy's hand.

In the growing darkness intermittent squares of light flooded into life from the grey stone buildings they passed on their way to the tram stop.

"Of course! Why would she not?" Stefan replied in mock surprise.

"Perhaps she is attracted by your modesty." Indra squeezed even tighter.

"Could be."

They crossed the road, dodging an oncoming car on the way.

"When will I see you again, Stefan?" The girl now suddenly serious.

"You know I can't tell you that, Indra."

"Sorry."

Stefan had not meant to hurt her by the sharp way he had spoken, but there was a 'push' on, and when he reported for duty this evening, he'd be confined to base until they sailed; which he had a peculiar feeling was imminent. "Can I phone you at the hospital? Tell you when I can see you again?"

Indra appeared not to have noticed his rebuff. "Yes, but you will have no way of knowing when I'm on duty."

"Then I shall have to keep on trying."

"Matron will give you a hard time if *she* answers the phone," Indra moaned.

"As long as she does not take it out on you, if she does let me know, and I will personally operate on her beard."

"Oh, Stefan, you are nasty!"

"Yes I know. This is why I never had a girlfriend before."

They reached the tram stop. Indra laid her head on his shoulder. "You will be careful," she pleaded, in little more than a whisper.

Stefan put his arm around her, drawing her closer. It was no use pretending he did not know what she meant. Even if the ordinary person in the street did not know, when, they at least knew there was another offensive on the way against the PFF.

"Oh, it will not be too dangerous, if I keep my fingers out of the way."

Quizzically, Indra looked up into his face, furrowing her brows. "How will keeping your fingers out of the way, prevent what you are doing from being dangerous?"

"Operating on the matron's beard," he said deadpan.

"Oh, Stefan! as I said before, you are nasty." She hugged him hard.

He brushed her lips with his. "You should see me to the tram stop more often. Though it is most ungentlemanly of me, for it is I who should be seeing *you* home."

"You can if you like, it is just around the corner," she laughed.

"Speaking of home, that reminds me, Myra is going back to England, so I will be out of a home shortly. The Molnars move in next week."

Thinking of the lovely house he had shared with his father for so short a time, Indra felt sorry for the boy, and not a little angry that his step-mother should just up and leave him, especially at a time like this. Surely, she had a little affection for the son of the man she had loved. "I'm so sorry, Stefan." She would not let him know what she thought of the heartless English woman. "What will you do?"

"Probably live on the base. At least until things are safer in the city. Then when they are, and hopefully, soon, I can find my own place ashore. Who knows, someday I may even want to share it with someone that can cook."

Indra drew away, to look at him. "I can cook."

"Mm. I'll keep that in mind when I advertise." Stefan stared into the distance as if mulling over the proposition. "Of course it could be some time yet before I aspire to anything. A junior officer is not the most highly paid person in the Service. Although, no doubt it would be on a permanent basis, if I do find someone suitable."

"I can wait!" Indra cried out enthusiastically, rushing forward to hug him. "Do I take it, that was some sort of a proposal?"

"Some sort!" Stefan answered indignantly. "Some sort! I thought it was a bloody good proposal!"

They were strolling along in the almost empty park, Petr sheltering Miro from the smir of rain with his umbrella. "I've had my eye on you for some time now, Miro, and I must say I am impressed." The Group Leader broke the silence that had existed between them since coming through the gate. "I believe it is time you had a Group of your own."

Unable to believe his ears, Miro's heart pounded at this long sought for recognition. For a moment, he remained silent, not trusting himself to speak. "I'm honoured, comrade, Petr." He cleared his throat. "But I thought, after the graveyard incident...and how wrong I was regarding Kolybin's death, that... Not to mention the incident with the judge those few years back," he stammered.

Petr waved the younger man's misgivings aside. "Water under the bridge. We made far more serious mistakes during the war, than you have ever done."

A little girl rode her tricycle down the path towards them. Petr gave her a funny little wave, prompting the child to stand up and show how fast she could pedal.

"You like children, Miro?" Petr asked casually, watching the child disappear down the path.

Startled by his leader's recondite persona, Miro managed a nod.

"You are quite right not to tell me more. The least known about you and Henna." Petr referred to Krysty by her old code name. "I wish more people were as security conscious as you," Petr sighed. "Which convinces me more than ever you are the right man for what National Council has in mind." He indicated they should leave the path for a seat in the pavilion out of the rain.

Relieved by Petr's obvious sincerity of forgiveness and his promise of promotion, Miro was more than anxious to please. "You know I'll do my utmost to help."

They sat down on the bench. Petre shook the rain off his umbrella before folding it. "My Group leave tomorrow night. I shall refrain from saying to where." He leaned on the umbrella standing between his knees. "Pavel's Group will leave the following night." He went on. "Vaclaw's Group will remain here to create as much havoc as possible. Your new Group will comprise of what remains of the three Groups in the City, plus the boy, and the man, code named Bear, from your own Section. Leave Jan here in charge of what is left of your original Section to support Vaclaw." Petr handed Miro a small envelope. "In there you'll find Jan's instructions, also your own."

Thrusting the envelope into his pocket Miro waited patiently while his leader scratched at the grass with the point of his umbrella. "I know you are the right man for the job, Miro, don't let me down. I shan't go into details here, it's all in there." Petr referred to the envelope with a nod. However, what I can tell you is this. Of all the groups, yours has the most important task. Group South, will attack all the garrisons in their area. Group West, all trains and road convoys heading north. Your new group, Kiemer Dam...near Gravst."

Petr lifted his head to the sky, testing the weather. "Destroy it, Miro, Tetek depends upon it. He needs a diversion. He cannot hope to contain, far less defeat the number of Government troops ranged against him."

Stunned by the enormity of the task assigned to him, Miro stared across the park. The little girl had returned on her cycle, her parents hurrying after her out of the rain, their laughter reaching him across the stretch of wet grass. "What about explosives?" he asked huskily. "I've blown up a few railway lines during and since the end of the war, but know nothing of the amount of explosives required for a target like this." He had wanted so much to prove he could operate his own group, handle any assignment given to him, but this! Kiemer Dam! He buried his eyes in the grass at his feet at the enormity of the task.

"Group East will supply the explosives as well as those with that knowledge. Your main concern as I see it," Petr brushed aside Miro's question as if unaware of its existence, "is to help supply the manpower, and to get your Group back to their daily jobs before their absence arouses suspicion." Petr swiped a blade of grass from off his shoe with the point of his umbrella. "I should say there will be quite a number of absentees during this little crisis," he sighed. "During the occupation this problem was a lot less difficult, in those days employers and employees were on the same side. But now?" Petre rose. "Make sure you do the job well, Miro. Blow that dam to kingdom come, then someday we might all live in peace again" He gave Miro a brief salute and walked away.

Chapter 12

Stefan stood on the bridge of the warship, straight backed, legs wide apart, hands clasped behind his back. He chanced a wink at a fellow cadet, who looked away to hide a grin. Suddenly, the entire ship reverberated under the recoil of the battleship's guns. Puffs of smoke hung in the air where their barrage had hit the mountains some distance away. He felt a thrill of pride that he was part of all this. This, what his father, the president, had striven so hard to bring to fruition.

Empty shell casings littered the deck below as the guns continued to bark. Stefan felt the deck vibrate beneath his feet, saw his friend scurry from the bridge with the first of the messages. It would be his turn next. He cast a proud eye down the line of ships pounding the black mountains that swept down to the sea. Soon under the protective barrage of their guns, soldiers would disembark in their landing craft for the shore. Then the final offensive would have begun. Perhaps it would soon be over, and he could be with Indra again.

He too, was looking forward to the day they could all live in peace.

An hour after Stefan had stood on the deck of the battleship, General Silvo Jakofcic, two hundred kilometres to the west, closed the farmhouse door of his makeshift field headquarters, shutting out the continual noise of soldiers coming and going, doing he did not altogether know what.

Word had just reached him of the naval bombardment, and the subsequent successful landing of his troops. He sat down in the small scullery to read again the first communiqué.

'Under a heavy barrage of covering fire, we have established a bridgehead. We are now commencing to probe the surrounding mountains before continuing our advance. At this time of 1400 hours, we have encountered no opposition.' It was signed Colonel Ziotkowski.

Silvo folded the flimsy paper, stuffing it into his tunic pocket. Ziotkowski he knew to be an accomplished officer. He would not have chosen him otherwise. But....the big general felt in his pocket for a cheroot. No resistance? Ziotkowski, had been allowed to get his men off the beach without a single shot fired?

Having at last found a cheroot, Silvo rose, walked to the narrow scullery window seeing nothing of the hum of activity outside, for his mind was on all of the possible equations which would account for the present situation. Somewhere at the back of his mind, a voice was telling him to be careful. He took a handkerchief from his pocket and dabbed at the sweat on his brow. And once more went over the possibilities open to Tetek.

Ziotkowski was attacking through the mountains from the east. Similarly, Scurk from the west. He himself in the south with the intention of trapping the PFF leader between them. He lit his cheroot. So what would the devious man do, he mulled? If true to form, the most improbable.

Silvo drew deeply on his cheroot. Normally he would have expected his adversary to retreat higher into the mountains. Then if things got too hot, scurry across the frontier, regroup to return when things cooled down a little. But now that this door to the frontier was closed to him, what was his alternative? Attack south, where he was waiting for him? Which would mean Tetek having to leave the protection of his mountains to face the superior number and armament of Government forces in open terrain?

The solicitous General flicked ash on to the stone floor. For some unknown reason he felt uneasy. Was that the improbability? Was this why Tetek had not opposed the landings? Was he already mustering his entire force to break through at one specific point here in the south? If so, at which point? Silvo shivered. It made sense. He could not defend a two hundred kilometre front! He inhaled, trapping the tobacco smoke in his mouth. If only those heavy guns had reached him in time as promised. The ball of smoke he blew up at the ceiling dissipating in the cold afternoon air.

Politics and politicians, he swore. Kolybin had ordered those same artillery parts months before he had died. The key components were to be manufactured here in his own country, for security reasons...so the late President had said. Most likely the real reason was to boost employment. Politics again. And why was he, the Commanding Officer in the field, never privy to those decisions? More politics! And when this was all over, it would all revert back to politics!

The General returned to his seat. Originally those same guns were to have been ready for the Pienera trap. God! It was lucky for them

Tetek had not decided then to breakout south. But would he, this time?

Miro lowered his newspaper and glanced out of the railway compartment window. Beside him, the boy whom they had decided to code name, 'Yearling' sat as morose as ever.

Miro failed to understand why Petr had insisted that the boy be included in this of all missions, after the youngster's poor showing at the graveyard.

His understanding of the boy was that the he had joined the PFF. in some sort of fanciful belief of avenging his father's death; not knowing that man had killed himself while planting a bomb that had gone off prematurely. He hoped Group East who was responsible for blowing up *their* target was more efficient, and did not include any of Yearling's relatives.

Miro went back to hiding behind his newspaper. If the train was on time they'd reach their destination in less than an hour.

He was glad he'd decided to travel by train instead of by road with most of his new Group. Since the start of the offensive, roadblocks had tripled, making it virtually impossible to get through by car, without going through the rigors of a search at every stop. However, as this side of the country was well away from the main Government offensive, it had proved less stringent.

Seven of his group of fifteen were on the train, three posing as soldiers returning home to convalesce, their bandages and crutches making ideal hiding places to conceal smaller arms. Two sailors, were similarly affected. 'Bear' as a would be labourer in search of work at the dam, dressed in his own working clothes. He himself in the roll of an office clerk, attired in suit and tie, briefcase at his knee, Yearling, his 'assistant' by his side. The remainder of his Group, Miro hoped, would now be making their way independently to the rendezvous.

"The newspapers say, this latest offensive should see the last of those awful Communists who are ruining the country," an elderly lady, sitting opposite Miro, declared with a satisfied look on her face, handing her paper to her friend.

"And a good riddance, too. I thought we had seen the last of killing when we got rid of the Nazis, without fighting amongst ourselves," her friend added bitterly.

"Then they should have given the Communists the right to vote!"

Both women stared open mouthed at Yearling's outburst.

Miro let his paper drop into his lap and smiled apologetically across the carriage to the women. "I must ask you to excuse the boy, ladies. Perhaps he has learned too much of politics at school." Behind the fallen newspaper, Miro squeezed the boy's arm hard, wishing he could take him aside and knock the living daylights out of him. His only relief was that Yearling had not said 'us' Communists. Did this young upstart not realise he was putting the entire operation at risk, besides the possibility of having them all arrested?

The elderly ladies turned their wrath on Miro. "Too much traitorous talk, I should say," the one directly opposite Miro bit back angrily. "As his brother you should be ashamed of him...and yourself, talking like that."

"He's not..." Miro gripped the boy's arm tighter behind the newspaper, before he could say more.

"Such opinions could get your brother into serious trouble." A well dressed man interceded, from a corner seat.

"Now see what you have done Andre!" Miro cried in mock horror. "I spend four years in a Nazi prisoner of war camp, and you have these good people thinking I am not a patriot!"

"Oh! You poor man!" One of the elderly ladies gasped, aghast. "Please forgive me for what I have said."

Miro brushed the apology aside with a wave of his hand. "Let us say no more if you please. And you young man..." Miro turned angrily on his 'brother' "keep your opinions to yourself. At least until we get off the train."

The train was over an hour late on reaching its destination. Slowly shuffling towards the ticket barrier amongst the crowd, seething, Miro turned to Yearling. "What do you think you were playing at back there?"

Knocked aside by passengers hurrying by, Yearling quickly pushed back to Miro, his mouth working angrily. "Those women back there with their fur coats and fancy hats! What do you think my mother and sister had to eat all of last week?" he spat at his senior, tears of rage welling up in his eyes. "You had them believing I was a stupid little schoolboy!"

"I know," Miro clenched his teeth. "When all the time you were nothing more than a stupid little shit."

Miro stopped himself. This was neither the time nor place for such a confrontation. Others of the group drew closer, forming a moving screen around them as they drew closer to the barrier. He put his hand on the boy's shoulder, and whispered in his ear. "Right now boy, I don't give a monkey's turd. We have work to do. So, either you are part of this Group, or you take the next train home to your mother. Cry on her shoulder if you want to, but not on mine." At Miro's scathing tirade, Yearling drew closer to Bear, fear, as well as anger. showing on his face.

As Miro chastised the boy, his three 'soldiers' had reached the barrier, an armed sentry studying them as they passed through. He had no fears for them. The travel documents they carried were genuine, having been passed along the network of Comrades in the Admin, and Caserne. The sentry took a last look and stepped back, no doubt satisfied by the fact the soldiers insignia were of the local regiment.

Now it was the 'sailors' turn. The sentry moved to the ticket collector's side. "Show me your pass, sailor!" He thrust out his hand, his action clearly inflammatory. Miro stifled a curse. It never failed, this inter-service rancour.

"Give us a break, soldier, we only have a twenty four hour pass. Hardly time to stow our hammocks before we weigh anchor," the first sailor retorted.

"Yea. Next you'll be wanting to know what's in our kit."

The soldier's eyes narrowed. He would teach these arrogant sons of bitches who was in charge here. "Perhaps it's not too bad an idea. Empty them out!"

Behind Miro, the queue had come to an abrupt halt. "They're only sailors on leave, soldier," the old ticket collector pleaded. "And I don't have much time to punch tickets before the four ten is due."

Unaffected by the old man's plea, and clearing enjoying his moment of power, the soldier's submachine gun came up, waving it at the nearest duffel bag. "Open it," he command.

The first sailor shrugged. "You've got us to rights, soldier. You knew all along we had something to hide."

The soldier's face gleamed in triumph, and swiveled his gun to cover both men, convinced he had done his job well.

"We're deserters," Miro's sailor confessed, jerking a thumb at his friend. "He's hiding a battleship in his kit, and I've got a submarine in mine."

Those within earshot let out a roar of laughter, Bear amongst them.

"What's so funny, big man?" The soldier wanted to know, turning his embarrassment on the gargantuan.

Apprehensive of Bear's reaction, Miro's grin froze.

"I thought it was funny, soldier," Bear responded. "After all, aren't we all on the same side?"

A murmur of agreement arose from the queue which had begun to surge forward, their patience at an end now that the show was over. Reluctantly, but with a last defiant gesture of his gun, the soldier moved aside to let them pass.

Once through the barrier, walking as calmly as they could towards the exit, Janek, the first 'sailor' spoke to Miro out of the side of his mouth. "You made a mistake there, Miro. You should have had us all dressed as soldiers," he winked.

Outside the station, the Group merged easily with the afternoon shoppers. Miro passed Bear and Yearling waiting at a bus stop, while further along the street a 'soldier and a 'sailor' boarded a tram.

Risking a quick look at his tiny map, Miro decided to walk a few blocks more before imitating his comrades. The first drops of rain splattered the pavement.

A half hour later, the Group Leader strode out on the country road and was passed by a truck full of building material, which confirmed he was heading in the right direction to the dam. Thankfully, the rain had stopped.

Miro switched his briefcase from one hand to the other. His forearm ached from the self-inflicted wound sustained from 'falling against a piece of heavy machinery' in the factory, done for the express purpose of establishing an alibi for his forth coming absence.

He chuckled. He had played his part right by protesting at the nurse's suggestion that he take the next few days off, on the grounds he could ill afford the loss of wages. The concerned nurse had eventually persuaded him that it was better to lose a few days, rather than several.

His thoughts on his wife, Miro strode on. Usually, it was the practice of police and security to investigate all those who had reported sick from work, during and immediately following PFF.

activity. This time would be no exception. Indeed if everything went according to plan, the authorities would be even more meticulous in their scrutiny.

Miro was aware that security would call at his house which with any luck would not be for the next day or two, to interview his wife and neighbours to establish if or not he had remained at home during his absence from work. He knew he could not get away with it indefinitely. Sooner or later. when they checked his past records, they would discover that most of his absences coincided with PFF. activity.

Miro stared up the deserted road, now feeling conspicuous in his smart suit. He had wanted so badly to command a Group of his own. Yet, was it entirely fair to his wife what he was doing? Would her sacrifice, and his, make any difference to the cause? Or, would it only be the rich and powerful as usual who would win out in the end? But, was this not the precise reason for which they all fought, to ensure this would not happen? He reached a row of rundown cottages, which except for one old woman feeding her hens in her overgrown front garden, appeared to be deserted. Wishing her a good day, and hoping the rain would not come to much, he hurried on.

The new Group Leader felt good, his step lightened. At last, he was in command of his own Group. A Group which had made it this far undetected. Funny! He felt no more tension now, than when on any other dozen or so missions he'd carried out. After all, the greater responsibility of blowing up the dam lay with Group East.

A kilometre further on, the war had ended for a burnt out tank lying in a ditch. The Iron Cross markings barely visible, as it rusted away to oblivion. Or to that great scrap yard in the sky, where all good tanks were sure to go, he thought with a hint of sarcasm, as he reached the rendezvous.

A derelict two-storied house stood opposite the mortally wounded tank. Miro pushed open the gate and stepped gingerly through broken bricks and slates that littered the cement path, broken glass cracking beneath his feet on the way to the open doorway.

He heard the sound of a bolt of a gun. Bear stepped out of the shadows of the door, his weapon leveled at him.

"Good to see you so alert, Bear," Miro greeted him cheerfully, in the hope the big man would take it as a compliment. Instead, Bear merely grunted and disappeared back inside the house.

Miro scanned around the big roofless room Bear had led him to, happy to see that all fifteen of his Group were there, including those who had made their way there independently. The 'soldiers' and 'sailors' had already changed. Others sat on bricks, or munched food where they stood, or leaned lugubriously against the wall, each awaiting his arrival.

Although most of the men were from his own Group there were a few from other Groups in the Capital, who had made themselves known by the arranged password. Miro also hoped they knew their jobs.

Formalities over, Miro dug in his coat pocket for his own food, aware of Yearling across the room jealously watching those fortunate enough to have enough food left after their train journey. Bear saw the boy watching and offered him a piece of bread. His eyes gleaming, Yearling took what was offered, chewing at it greedily, while another handed him a slice of cheese. Heartened by this show of comradeship, Miro pretended not to notice.

A man brought a sack over to him containing his change of clothes, which the local Group had left the previous week for them.

"I'm glad to see you all have made it." Miro munched on his roll. "Anyone have any trouble?" His eyes swept the room. "Good. We are already an hour late. The truck should have been here by now. I hope to God they have not left without us." He rose threading his way through the room littered with fallen debris to the windowsill.

For a minute or two, Miro stood there scanning the deserted road. Despite what he had said, in his heart, he hoped they'd missed the truck, and Group East would have do the job for them. Then, as if to shatter his innermost wish, the truck suddenly appeared through the slanting rain. "Well here it comes, boys! Better get yourself ready!" He clenched his fists on the sill, forcing himself to sound cheerful.

Ten minutes later, they were all on board a high-sided vehicle, continually passed by empty construction trucks heading in the opposite direction.

A little later, the truck gave a sudden jerk and they bounced off the main highway on to a narrow dirt road, overhanging branches showering them with leaves and broken twigs as they squeezed past.

Fifteen minutes later, the tailgate dropped and they spilled out to stretch their legs.

The little dumpy driver pushed to Miro's side. "Group East should be at the dam by now. They waited for you but decided it would be safer to go on." He drew a finger under his nose flicking mucus into the bushes. "Unload and follow me. We don't have much time. The path can be tricky in bad light." The driver's attitude prosaically reminiscent of leading a gang of labourers on to a building site.

The load and weapons supplied by Group East having been shared out amongst them, Miro and his men followed the little driver in to the thick dark woods, where, on the narrow path which they were forced to follow, dry leaves stuck to their feet, undergrowth soaking their clothes as they brushed passed: ever in the distance, the sound of rushing water. Finally, after some time, they emerged out of the woods and onto a rocky shelf, sighting the waterfall they had heard a little earlier.

Involuntarily Miro shivered. In the half-light the place was eerie, foreboding, such a place, which as a child one had nightmares. He stepped away from the edge, grasping the scant vegetation growing out of the rock face to steady himself, their passage silent against the rush of angry water below.

"Not long now, comrade," the little guide threw over his shoulder. Miro muttered something in reply, happy that the rocky ledge was now behind them.

The path took them upwards, cutting back on itself above the river. Miro's guide walking directly in front of him gave out a long low whistle and almost immediately two men stepped out of the shadows.

"Do you want to trade passwords?" The little guide turned to smirk at Miro.

Ignoring the obvious sarcasm, Miro brushed passed him. "Not a night for cowards," he said self-consciously.

One of the men took a step forward, and thrust out his hand. "Not with work to be done." The man smiled to cover his embarrassment. "The rest of us are up there," he said, pointing up the hill.

Miro nodded. He and his Group followed their new guide into a clearing higher up the hillside, where the rest of Group East awaited their arrival.

"Glad you got here safely," one said, approaching the newcomers.

"I'm Miro, leader of Group Central." Miro identified himself, carefully hiding his feeling of pride as he said it.

"Chez. Leader of group East, comrade. I thought something had happened to you. You should have been here an hour ago. We waited up the road, but decided to come on here."

"Damned train was late," Miro said bitterly.

For a moment, Miro thought Chez was going to ask him a question, then with a shrug the Group leader turned to guide him to the edge of the clearing. "That's our target down there." He pointed below, to where the dam site lay some distance beneath the spur of rock on which they stood. An ugly man made scar in the beauty of the surrounding hills. The quiet flowing river, now almost invisible except for the occasional white speck of foam, reflected in a brief glint of moonlight.

"All the construction workers have gone for the day, only those two old night watchmen and one or two guards are left," Chez explained, pointing in the direction of the dam where the shadowy figures of two men stood leaning on the catwalk rail.

"We best get started if we are to catch our train home tonight," Miro said, in the same nervous tone he reserved for his dentist.

It seemed bizarre to comprehend anything beyond the blowing up of the dam at this juncture. Half his Group, himself included, were to catch the last Saturday night train back to the Capital from their same station. The remainder, plus Group East, to travel by truck to another station, in the hope that by doing so, all those under his command would be back in Zaltz by tomorrow at the latest, in order to report for work on Monday.

It had always been times like this, before the start of an operation, that the worry of being found out upon your return to work became an irrelevance. It was not until the job was actually behind you, that you began to grapple with the situation.

Miro had always thought of the unreal world in which he lived...forced his wife to live...No, that was not strictly true. Krysty was probably a better Communist than he, braver too, since it was she who had to do all the waiting and worrying.

How many times he wondered had he returned to work on a Monday morning, and casually listened to his work mates discussing what they had done over the weekend: went to a football match

(How he still missed Fiebo), Did a spot of fishing had a lazy weekend with the wife and kids. And often thought what would have been their reaction had he told them of how he had filled in his weekend. Such as, 'Oh I was blowing up a dam, actually. Killed a few people. Nothing much."

Miro returned to the present, pointing to right of the river. "My Group will take this side." Behind him Chez's Group were busily assembling their machine gun.

Cautiously the two leaders started down the slope closely followed by their respective groups. "Our machine gun will cover us if we run into trouble." Chez grasped a branch to steady himself. "Where do you want us while you're setting the charges?"

"We're not setting the charges, you are!" Miro exclaimed, surprised by the question.

Chez drew to an abrupt halt, and the man behind slid into him. The leader steadied himself. "But you've got the explosives! That is what Petr told me!"

Miro stared back, unable to believe what he was hearing. "Petr told me the same. He said you would bring the food, weapons and explosives, as it would be impossible for us to get them through the roadblocks." Miro's voice rose sharply. "Petr also understands I know nothing about explosives on this scale!"

Chez stared back at his opposite number, the corner of his mouth twitching, while trying to digest what Miro had said. "I wondered why you were not carrying anything."

It hit both men simultaneously.

"Quick back up the hill!" Chez shouted, all attempt at silence forgotten. One man hesitated, unsure what was happening and Chez grabbed him, swinging him round. The rest already scrambling and slithering back the way they had come on the slippery slope.

A burst of fire a little to the right of the trees above, stitched a swath across the path of the leading men. One yelled and went down. Another rolled back into the line of panicking men.

"What the hell's happening?" someone cried out.

Miro heard Group East's gun open up as he reached the clearing. "This way!" he shouted scrambling on to a path, Bear and the boy close behind him.

It seemed to Miro there was fire coming from every direction. He felt himself panic, unable to think which way to go, shakily recognizing this as the path that lead back to the truck. But even should they fight their way through, the truck would most likely be surrounded.

Yearling passed him, a wild frightened look in his wide staring eyes. "Steady boy," Miro gasped, as somewhere ahead a shadowy figure sprang out of the undergrowth onto the path, spraying the youngster with fire. The scream still on his lips, Yearling jacknifed in the air, his head smashing into a tree at the side of the path with a sickening crack.

Miro plunged into the trees to his right, too frightened for his own life to feel any sorrow for the boy.

An angry roar arose. Through the trees Bear had hurled himself at Yearling's killer, the big man's knife clear in the moonlight, slashing at the soldier's head.

Miro kept on running. The firing had still not receded. He let one of the three men from Group East draw level. "Do you know the way out of here?" Spittle ran down his chin as he gulped the question.

"That way!" the man gasped, pointing.

A solitary shot rang out. His companion fell. Miro hit the ground, rolling over on to his stomach. Another shot came out of the darkness. "Are you both all right?" Miro whispered to the other two, hoping he was not alone.

The sound of firing from behind grew louder, plainly others were also making their escape in this direction. Miro raised his head. A bullet smashed into a tree inches away. He rolled to his left, his experience from the war instantly returning. He threw a stone to his left, simultaneously rolling to his right, and firing at the flash. He heard a moan and leapt to his feet, running to where he'd seen the flash. A soldier sprang out from behind a tree, Miro fired his sub machine gun from the hip. The man went down. Another shot from his left missed him by inches, and he swiveled round, hitting this man with a second burst.

More trees ahead, Miro kept on running, swerving to his right, not wanting to expose himself by running through the fire break, as a dark line of soldiers rose from its farther side. He slid to a halt, searching for another way out.

It was then the bullet hit him and he staggered forward, cursing Petr and the trap he had set for them.

Stefan held the door of the telephone box tight against the efforts of his fellow cadets to open it. "Come on lads, be fair, let me make my call!" he shouted through the glass door good-humouredly.

Stefan's friend pressed his face against the glass. "Oh what it is to be in love!" he mouthed, pretending to swoon.

Stefan stuck his tongue out at him. "That you will never know, you little toad."

"Language! Language!" his friend scolded him.

Tired with the fun, the crowd of young cadets moved down the avenue, Stefan's friend offering him a final salute before turning to join them.

Stefan lifted the receiver, his grin fading. With any luck, he might get through to Indra before she went off duty.

A few minutes later, the boy's grin reappeared. Literally jumping up and down with joy, he hurried to catch up with his shipmates. She was coming here! Indra was going to meet him here! He slowed down, the prospect of getting drunk, now not so appealing.

Indra had given him directions on how to get to the nearby town of Sylna, which he knew was a lovely little place nestling in the valley of the same name. He remembered having visited it with his father just after the end of the war when Myra had gone back home to England, when, he had selfishly hoped, she would forget his father and not return.

His father had talked to him of many things while they fished together on that visit. Now, it was one of the few happy memories left to him. Thrusting the memory behind him he repeated his instructions over and over to himself least he bungle this golden opportunity of having Indra all to himself once more.

Stefan stared intently out of the bus window. He was nearing Sylna, this he knew by the recent corkscrew descent into the valley, and the meandering river across the meadow where he and his father had fished those few years ago.

A house flashed into view, then was gone. Next, a row of houses peculiar to the valley, with their sharply sloping blue pantalion roofs, whitewashed walls and teak verandas. He moved his head a little to see between two passengers sitting in front of him, and knew he was almost there when the tall steeple of the church a little way ahead leaped into view.

Indra saw him first as he got down off the bus. "Stefen!" she cried jumping up and down, and waving to attract his attention amongst the bus queue. At last, the boy saw her and jostled through the crowd to meet her.

"I can't believe you are here, Indra!" Stefan cried happily, taking her in his arms and smothering her with kisses.

"Nor I, you Stefan."

Self-consciously Stefan disentangled himself. "How long have you got?" he inquired anxiously.

She took him by the hand. "Two days," and in turn anxiously awaited his reply.

"Same here. Originally I had seventy two hours." He turned up his nose, "but that was yesterday."

Indra led him away from the bus station, into the cobbled square around the corner.

"I see I have arrived on market day," the boy remarked, surprised by the hustle and bustle all around him.

"Every day is market day in Sylna," Indra laughed, pulling him towards a fruit stall, where she bought some apples, while Stefan looked around him, unable to recall his father ever having brought him here. Though, he did recall the perpetual presence of bodyguards in the background. So, no matter what they did or where they went, they were never truly alone.

Indra held up a paper bag. "Grandmother likes apples," she shouted in his ear, above the noise.

Stefan nodded. "How does she know we are coming?" he shouted back.

Indra drew him aside away from people jostling passed. "I sent her a telegram. It will be all right. Grandmother loves me to visit."

"With a stranger?"

She took his hand. "Especially with a stranger."

Without warning, Stefan let go of her hand, and within seconds, was lost amongst the crowd. Puzzled, Indra stood waiting, her face lighting up when he re-emerged clutching a bunch of flowers.

"Oh, Stefan, you should not have done!" she gasped in delight, taking the flowers from him.

"I didn't. They're for your grandmother."

Indra made a playful swipe at him with her bag of apples.

"I have something much better for you," he grinned in her ear.

"Whatever could that be, kind sir?" Indra feigned embarrassment.

"Later dear child. Later." Sefan threw his head in the air, condescendingly.

Indra's grandmother's house was one in a row of whitewashed cottages. When the old woman saw them, she hurried up the short garden path, waving as she came.

"Indra my dear!" she beamed, hugging her favourite grand daughter, tightly.

"Grandmother!"

Then as if suddenly aware of Stefan's presence the old woman detached herself from the girl. "This must be Stefan, your young man?" she said, her sparkling eyes running over the boy, capturing every detail.

"Pleased to make your acquaintance, ma'am." Stefan introduced himself with a slight bow of his head.

"Very mannerly, not to mention formal!" the old woman chuckled, nudging her granddaughter with an elbow.

Blushing, Indra rushed to her young man's aid. "Yes grandmother. Do you approve?"

"Of his looks?" The old woman chuckled again. "Of course. Every bit as handsome as his father." She spun round smartly for one of her age, and waved impatiently for them to follow her into the house.

"Did she know my father?" Stefan whispered in Indra's ear.

"Didn't everyone?"

Stefan had taken an instant liking to the old woman. After the meal, in order to ingratiate himself, he'd volunteered to help wash up. At first, his host had declined, until he had relieved her of the washing cloth, and had sat her down firmly, but gently in her favourite chair by the fireside. By the time Indra and he had completed the chore, the old woman was fast asleep.

"She *is* nice," Stefan confided as they walked hand in hand down the cobbled street.

"I am glad you like her. I know she likes you." Indra tucked her arm under his.

In contrast to the earlier tumult Stefan had witnessed upon his arrival, the streets were now almost deserted. They passed a row of houses, and the boy glimpsing a meadow beyond, pulled Indra closer. "Let's go for a walk."

Indra wrinkled her brows. "I thought that was what we were doing?"

"You know what I mean. A real walk."

Before she had time to protest, Stefan had led her through a short lane, and across the meadow to a grassy slope of a hill beyond, where they lay staring up at the darkening sky.

"The fighting seems a million miles away from here," the boy said absently, his eyes slowly scanning the peaceful scene.

"Will it ever end?" Indra asked sadly, her head resting in his lap.

From what he had witnessed from the ship the day the troops had disembarked, when they had met with no resistance from the shore, Stefan answered that it would, shortly, for the word was, that General Jakofcic had Tetek bottled up tight.

"You really think so Stefan?" she asked hopefully, for her generation had known nothing other than war.

The boy did not answer at first but instead plucked absently at the grass. "Yes Indra I really do. This time there is no place for Tetek to hide."

Indra looked up into his face. "Let's forget the fighting. At least for one night," she pleaded. "Besides, you better show me you love me here. Although grandmother may have taken a liking to you, she is still a bit old fashioned you know. And I do have to share a room and a bed with her."

"I wish I did," Stefan said sorrowfully.

Indra sprang away from him laughing, unable to resist the joke. "What! You fancy my grandmother?" And felt herself being pulled back down, as Stefan moaned in mock despair.

"It is a beautiful day. You two young things better get yourselves out and make the best of it," the old woman urged, clearing away the breakfast dishes.

"What about you grandmother, would you not care to come along with us? To the market perhaps?" the girl asked cheerfully.

"And if I were to say, yes, young Indra, it would break your heart." The old woman winked across the table at Stefan. "Besides, I have prepared a picnic basket for you both."

Once more walking towards the meadow, Stefan declared admiringly, "Your grandmother is quite a character."

"Yes I know."

"She must have gone through a lot in her life."

They turned down a narrow cobbled street. Stefan lifted his face to the weak Autumn sun: winter would not be far behind. "How long has she lived alone?"

"Grandfather died before the war. Uncle Ivan...her only son, was killed fighting with the Partisans. It seems so long ago to us. Perhaps that's because we are still young," she decided with a nod of her head.

Stefan lay on his side, chin cupped in his hand, idly watching Indra sitting on the grass combing her hair. There was never a day, an hour went by, when they were not together that he did not find himself thinking of her. It would only take something as tiny as a word or a gesture to start him thinking of her. Even on Watch, she'd unexpectedly creep into his thoughts. Or, he would catch a glimpse of her in his mind's eye.

Indra caught him looking at her, and mischievously held a finger under her chin. "Do you like what you see, kind sir?"

Suddenly the sound of revving engines drowned out Sefan's ready quip, Indra's look of perplexity matching his own. In an instant they were on their feet , running hand in hand to the edge of the woods, breathlessly drawing to a halt at the sight of a line of military trucks grinding their way through the narrow streets of the little town.

"Ours," Stefan said softly, drawing the girl closer. "The last push north, I'd say."

When the last truck had disappeared, they started back, angry and not a little disturbed that the war should have reached them here in this serene little valley, intruding into what little time they had left to share.

Stefan picked up the almost empty wine bottle from the grass. Pouring what was left into a glass, he solemnly handed it to the girl.

Indra studied the bottom of her glass, as if the glass itself held all her unhappiness. "This is our last night together."

"Why so sad?" Stefan's voice was artificially cheerful. "Did we not have a wonderful time?"

"Of course!" She attempted to smile, afraid to think she may have spoiled their remaining time together.

"Well Indra, if this is the best you can do, perhaps I should spend the rest of my time in the local graveyard just to cheer myself up."

The boy lifted his jacket off the grass and threw it nonchalantly over his shoulder in pretence of being offended.

"I'm sorry Stefan, but those trucks," she said dolefully, staring at the ground.

"Those trucks are the end of a civil war, Indra, not the beginning." He crossed to her, hugging her to him. "Now, how about a smile?" He tickled her under the chin until she was laughing as much at her own depression, as by what he was doing.

"That's much better. Now perhaps I can give you that present I promised you yesterday in the market." With the air of a magician, Stefan put his hand behind his back, bringing it round again palm upwards.

Indra's eyes shone with disbelief. "Stefan, it's beautiful! But are you sure?"

"I am, if you are. Providing, I never see you so sad again. Not now. Not ever. Not until the end of time," he added with a flourish, to hide his embarrassment.

Drawing the dewy eyed girl to him, he slipped the jeweled ring over her finger, transforming the young girl's last few minutes of unhappiness into a paroxysm of joy.

Back at the cottage, unable to contain her excitement Indra showed off the token of her betrothal to her grandparent. The old woman with tears in her eyes kissed and hugged them both. Then, sitting in her favourite chair, the two lovers at her knee, they drank each other's health.

Stefan knew he would carry the memory of this evening for the rest of his life. The peaceful picturesque little town where he'd made love, and had asked a girl to share the rest of his life with him. The cobbled streets, friendly folk, a fairy land, light years away from the ravages of war.

Stefan lay awake that night thinking of the joy in Indra's eyes. Her sheer exuberance as she and the old woman planned out what had to be done for the forthcoming wedding.

At least, the old woman had spared them the lecture, of how they were both too young, and had hardly known one another for very long, besides the usual adult reasons of why they should wait. "But what about your mother?" he had asked Indra when they were alone. "Perhaps she will want us to wait. Or worse, even disapprove?"

"What! Object to my marrying the son of our country's greatest hero!" Indra had exclaimed, rushing on to include the long list of people she was just dying to invite.

The son of Paule Kolybin, he thought, staring up at the ceiling. The son of a father he'd hardly known. As plain Stefan Kolybin...Naval Cadet, what did *he* have to offer? Little as it may be, it did not appear to worry Indra. He closed his eyes, letting himself relax. Dear Indra, what the sight of a little silver ring had done, he sighed.

Gathering the bedclothes under his chin, he fancied hearing the stairs creak, followed a few seconds later by his attic door slowly opening.

"It's the future Mrs Kolybin come to pay you a call" Indra called out to him in a stage whisper, running to his bed.

"What, a call girl?" Stefan joked, pulling aside the bedclothes to let her in beside him.

Indra pinched him in the ribs, snuggling close to him.

"Won't the old lady be suspicious? At least disapprove, when she wakes up and finds you are not there," he whispered, kissing her nose. "We are not married yet, you know."

"If she wakes up," Indra giggled.

"What do you mean 'if'?" Stefan slid down beside her.

Indra's giggle was muffled by the bedclothes. "Well, sometimes grandmother finds it hard to fall asleep. This time, I thought, as a nurse I'd give her a little help."

Stefan put his mouth to her cheek to stifle his own laughter. "I never knew I had such a devious fiancé. Lord help me if you ever get jealous, nurse Indra Staron."

Chapter 13

Mark scraped the last of his lukewarm food out of his dixie. Three days had passed and still no sign Tetek. Given the man's reputation for doing the unexpected, it was not surprising that they all had the jitters. He cleaned the utensil with a handful of moss. The biting cold of the mountains had him thinking back to his 'leave' and the warmth of the beach and how much hotter it could have been had whoever 'they' were caught up with them.

He had not heard from Myra since then. Perhaps, she had returned home.

"It's freezing my family jewels off Sir. If you will pardon the expression." Shivering, Niew Grbesa moved over the uneven ground to Mark's side.

"I thought you had lost those a long time ago, Sergeant." Grbesa grinned.

"I did. The ones I have now are brass."

"Company Sergeant Grbesa, should you not be on guard duty?" The voice that came out of the dark, was harsh, authoritarian.

Grbesa snapped to attention. "No Sir, I have just come off duty."

The young captain who had asked the question walked into their circle of moonlight. Mark knew better than to intervene.

This was the young officer assigned to his old 'A' Company. The Company Grbesa had successfully held together in his humble capacity of CSM. Had the stubborn sergeant accepted a commission he'd not have to stand there pretending to be an 'eejit' in front of this pompous piece of shit, as this one surely was. Serves the wee man right, Mark thought.

"Now that you have, sergeant, don't you think you should catch some sleep?" The tall thin captain suggested, towering over the heavier built smaller man.

"I was conversing with the Major, Sir." Niew's tone was firm but polite. "I was asking the Major, Sir.... Why in his opinion, he thought we had not made contact with the enemy?. *Sir*" The squat sergeant drew himself even more stiffly to attention on the last word.

Mark read the younger man's expression. An expression that clearly stated a non commissioned officer did not ask such questions of their C.O. "It is a good question, CSM" Mark pretended to consider. "Perhaps, our esteemed foe is awaiting us at the place known as 'The Gap'"

Mark turned to explain to his captain. "That is the name of the defile where Tetek knocked seven bells out of us, not to mention shit." The startled officer recoiled at Mark's choice of description. Mark further added to the man's discomfiture, by continuing in the same tone, "And we would all still be there... presumably quite dead if the CSM here, had not found us a way out."

Annoyed by Mark's gibe, and obvious ease with his CSM Captain Drboski cast an eye over his senior officer. "You are not one of *us* , Sir?"

Mark knew what the upstart meant. He could never be mistaken for a native, not with his accent and command of the language . "I sure as hell am not one of *them*, Captain," and heard a slight chortle from Grbesa. "If however, you mean am I a mercenary? Then the answer is yes."

"I offer no offence sir," the captain apologised, however reluctantly.

"None taken Captain."

Captain Drboski took a step or two away, his eyes on the dark shapes of the distant mountains, tapping the side of his leg with a thorn stem he'd substituted for a swagger stick.   "Do you believe Tetek is still waiting for us up there Major?"

Mark's shrug was indistinguishable in the dark. "It's as good a place as any."

The captain drummed a tattoo on his leg with his makeshift stick. "Then we shall beat him...assuredly. For one thing he lacks our resources." The tone decisive, the demeanour self-assured.

"Depends on what you mean by resources , Captain." Mark winked at Grbesa. "Resourceful men can make do with a lot less than conscripted ones."

Drboski's lip curled. "Do I understand you to mean, that men fighting for a cause can be more effective than those fighting for wages, Major?"

Mark gave the man a twisted grin. "If I did captain, then it makes me hors-de-combat, would you not say?"

How the verbal battle may have concluded neither man was to know, for at that point a corporal rushed forward to hand Mark a slip of paper. Returning the soldier's salute,Mark studied the message before addressing his fellow officer. "It would appear your theory is to be tested, captain."

"Really Sir!" Drboski stepped forward eagerly.

Mark nodded. "But not by us, captain. A., C. and E. Company are designated a new position back down the mountain. It would appear, General Jakofcic has need of us there, in the event of his arch enemy attempting to break out south into the flatlands below." Mark gave an artificial sigh. "How very sad Captain, just when you were all set to give Tetek a good thrashing" Mark savoured his sergeant's grin as he turned on his heel.

"You were correct Sir!" Second Lieutenant Wysocki was in the room before Jakofcic realised it.

The General looked up quickly from the table he was using as a desk.

"Very well, Lieutenant, control yourself if you please."

"Sorry Sir." Wysocki tried to quickly regain his composure, as he thrust the slip of paper at his General.

Masking his own rising excitement, Jakofcic took the slip.

"Arrange to have my staff here in twenty minutes, Lieutenant"

Calmly Silvo laid the communiqué aside, and allowed himself a smile as the young officer ran from the room to carry out his orders.

It was already dark outside. From the window of the farmhouse, all Silvo could see was the dimmed headlights of trucks rolling passed. Deep in thought, he lifted his eyes to the starless sky. Tetek had attacked at precisely where he had expected him to, at the point where his own left flank joined with Scurk's right.

Silvo returned to his desk. It made sense. First, this was the weakest point of communication between two commands. Secondly, it was furthest from Colonel Ziotkowski's advance through the mountains from the east, and from where he had landed on the coast. How glad he was that he had the foresight to order a third of Ziotkowski's force to be moved here. He would need this additional strength more than ever, now that he'd been forced by Molnar himself to dispatch troops to counteract PFF activities in towns throughout the country, and above all, to ensure the safety of the construction of the new dam near the town of Gravst.

The tall General lit a cheroot, unable to help but feel a certain amount of apprehension. Had he got it right? What else could the

Communist leader do but attempt to mop them up from the flank? He would not try to drive a wedge between Scurk and himself, merely to drive on to the flatlands, and have the whole of the Government forces chase after him from flank and rear. Nor would he leave himself cut off from the protection of his precious mountains . No, Silvo decided, he had it correct this time. And if so, by the time Tetek did attempt to break through their flanks, his own heavy artillery would have arrived.

Now a little more at ease, Silvo sat back to finish his cheroot.

It was hard to make out where he was in the dark but Miro struggled on. With each step, the searing pain became more difficult to bear. There was the sound of a truck behind him and he staggered into the undergrowth, the full beam of its lights lighting up the delict house by the side of the road. The one they had sheltered in earlier.

Silently offering up a prayer of thanks to a God, he firmly believed did not exist, and too tired and weak to go on, Miro stumbled over the broken door lying in the pathway, groping and feeling along the walls until he came to the same roofless room they had left a few short hours ago with so much optimism, cursing as his leg hit a stack of bricks. It was the last straw, wearily Miro sagged down into a corner.

At times the pain from his wound would die away, lulling him into believing it had passed, until it hit him again with almost unbearable severity. To say he was frightened was an understatement. Never once throughout the occupation, or since, had he ever been wounded. And through the pain, he cursed Petr again.

Miro sat hunched against the damp wall. Above him, loose electric wiring waved in the biting wind. All night he had walked and run, dodging on and off the road as military vehicle after vehicle had roared by, never quite knowing whether he was headed in the right direction or not, and whether he was the only one to have survived.

He coughed, and the movement sent an excruciating pain down his back from the wound somewhere below the shoulder blade. Had the bullet pierced his lung? Probably not, as he could still breathe pretty freely, and had not coughed up any blood. Anyhow, he was too tired to care anymore.

Miro's head sank on to his chest, still unable to comprehend the enormity of Petr's betrayal. He was exhausted but his brain continued to swirl with a kaleidoscope of reasons, where everything and nothing made sense. Had it been Petr who had set the trap for Tetek at Pienera? After all, it had been *his* suggestion that Tetek attack that particular town. Did his Group Leader know more about Kolybin's death than he pretended? Had he, Miro, got too close to the truth? And was this the reason the Scot's mercenary had escaped at the beach? It was all too much. All he wanted now was to close his eyes.

The wounded man thought he had slept for hours, but it was still dark when he awoke. Using his one good hand, he levered himself to a standing position and staggered into the corridor to relieve himself, debating whether or not to start walking, if for no better reason than to keep warm. At least now, he knew where he was. Should he look for the sack that contained his suit?

Although sick from the pain in his back, Miro's body craved nourishment. He had no food, there having been no opportunity to distribute any as arranged before the trap.

Today was Sunday. He cursed again and sat down, intending to rest for just a little while longer. It had been his intention to have had his Group back in the Capital by this time, and had not paid any attention to alternative times of trains. Had any of his Group survived? Could he make it to the railway station at Gravst? If so, would any of the Government troops be waiting for him? Now increasingly angry with himself that his brain would not stop asking these questions of him.

Now he was thinking of his command...short as it may have been...of Bear, Yearling and others of his Group. Those too of Group East, men he had never got to know.

Miro sank against the wall, the pain of his wound throbbing in time to the pain in his head. Only the thought of seeing Kyrsty again and making Petr pay for his treachery kept him from giving up. He closed his eyes again. Just a little rest he told himself.

It was the sound of a motor engine that awoke Miro. By the time he had struggled to his feet and crossed cautiously to the window, a truck had halted at the corner of the road, troops rapidly alighting from the tailgate.

Miro backed away from the window. His feet caught on loose rubble, and he almost fell as he turned to run awkwardly for the back door, and through the tall unkempt grass of the back garden, heedless of the trail he was leaving behind.

Miro had almost reached the foot of the garden when his foot caught in the wire of a broken fence. He bent down trying to twist it free, the sound of running feet in the corridor of the house close behind him. Panicking, he tore savagely at the wire wishing he still had his sub machine gun, and in desperation pulled his shoe off, untangling the wire and throwing himself over the broken fence into the tall grass on the other side.

The shout from the garden told Miro that his swathe through the grass had been discovered. Struggling to his feet, he headed for an outhouse to his right, certain that the building would shield him from any line of fire. He heard a shout, but kept on running. If only he could reach the woods ahead?

Miro was lost. Since entering those woods miles back in order to shake off his pursuers, he had run in every direction known to man. Now he had no idea where he was. Whether, he was closer to the dam, or to the town of Gravst, he did not know.

A cowshed stood in a field a little distance ahead. He made for it, and eventually succeeded in getting through the wire fence surrounding it, despite the use of only one hand and slid down against one of its walls.

For a little while, Miro sat there hunched. Shivering, he squinted up at the weak morning sun. He was tired, hungry and, above all, scared. How bad his wound was, he did not know, and battled with thought of having to struggle out of the jerkin in order to see what state his clothing was in. Should it be that bad, it would lessen his chances of reaching the station without raising suspicion. Now he wished he had taken the time last night to find the sack with his suit and briefcase.

He had been right, his jerkin was bloodstained. He tried to rise and, as he took the first few steps to reach the water trough, found that his body had stiffened.

The water in the trough was a foul slimy green. Miro took out his handkerchief and dipped into the water, cleaning his bloodstained jerkin as best he could and drawing the torn material together where the bullet had hit just below the shoulder.

As the sweat dried on his shirt, he gave another little shiver and quickly put his jerkin back on. Once he found out exactly where he was, he'd head for the railway station. Perhaps, in his present condition, he'd pass for a down and out, and if he'd didn't get there before long, a very sick one at that.

At last, Miro recognised the road he was on. It was the one on which he and his Group had taken on their way to the rendezvous. Was it only yesterday he had strutted along this same road full of pride at commanding his own Group? His Group! His own command! His ultimate ambition realised, blown away in a matter of minutes not by his own incompetence, but by the very man who had awarded him that honour.

Miro had almost reached the bend in the road when he saw the line of soldiers up ahead. Instinctively he turned sharply round, gasping as the pain hit him again, and started back the way he had come, throwing an occasional glance over his shoulder in the hope he had not been seen.

To his right a line of trees bordered the road, if he went through those, he might be able to cut across the field and come out on the road again behind the soldiers. It was worth a try.

A little later Miro thought he had succeeded. He had almost crossed the entire breadth of the field and with the soldiers now some distance behind, strode confidently on his way, only to find a second line the same distance ahead. This time there was no escape. To halt or turn round would merely add to the soldiers suspicions. Miro slowed, and felt in his pocket for his pistol, at the same time wishing again for his Thompson.

It was the chatter of voices from a small house standing alone to his right, its open door spilling out a crowd of black clad children and adults that gave Miro the chance. Hurrying to catch up, he quickly mixed in with them as they neared the line of soldiers at the barricade.

A small boy stopped to pull up his stocking and looked up as Miro drew level. Miro winked at him and pulled a face, as he walked past. Catching up, the child walked beside him, staring up into his face, and for a moment the man thought he was about to speak and ask some awkward unanswerable question. Miro pulled another face, making a coin suddenly appear out of his ear. The child laughed, his eyes wide in amazement. A few steps ahead the adults looked around to see what was going on, and he gave them his warmest smile.

Now they were almost at the khaki coloured line. Miro's hand curled around the pistol in his pocket. Please Lord, if there is to be any shooting don't let these good folk get in the way.

With a whoop, the child ran at the soldiers, spraying them with fire from his imaginary gun. Miro ran after him, apologising for his 'son's behaviour' as he took hold of him and guided him through the soldiers ranks.

Mystified the child looked up at him, and was about to shout, protest he was not his father, when Miro winked at him again. "Good game eh! We fooled them. Okay?" The child stared at him, his face suddenly lighting up. He'd never had so much fun with an adult on the Sabbath before. He walked on with Miro, the boy's mother anxiously running to catch up.

Except for the omnipresence of soldiers, in direct contrast to the previous day, the town was completely deserted. The surrounding streets to the railway station entrance barricaded and completely sealed off. The few intending travellers stopped and searched.

With sinking heart and disappointment at having come this far, Miro turned away.

The pain in his back was worse, his shirt sticky with blood. He'd have to get the bullet out and soon. Behind him, nailed boots sounded on the cobbles. He dodged down a side street; the nailed boots still followed.

Across the way, lights shone out of a dingy cafe. Miro crossed the street and pushed open the door. The sound of the nailed boots receding in the distance.

He chose a table in the corner where he could keep an eye on both door and window. And when his order of soup arrived inquired of the young waitress the time of the next train to the capital, to be informed he had just missed one. The next one, she had said, brushing crumbs from the table would not be for another two hours. At least, it would be dark by then, he thought turning down his jerkin's collar, and was thankful for the heat of the room.

The soup was thick and hot, and as he supped Miro furtively surveyed the room, suspicious of anyone who unwittingly gave him a second glance. And, as the hot soup took affect, he felt a new life pour into him. Now, he must think over his present situation.

Miro had just settled down to enjoy the main course when a sudden spasm of pain hit him. His fork hit the plate with a clatter. Across the room, conversations died as patrons glared at him with expressions of annoyance and disdain. Angrily, Miro looked away. What would Krysty think of him if she could see him now and the reaction of these people?

His watch told him it was just under an hour before his train's departure. He had put off as much time as possible over the meal, even having gone to the extent of ordering a second cup of coffee. He felt warm and safe here, but he could not sit much longer, at least not without arousing some suspicion. Playing out his part as a tramp, he paid the bill with the smallest denomination of coins he could find, and stood up to leave as the first of the soldiers crossed the road towards the cafe. It was too late now to leave by the front door, and if he were to try by the back door, it was sure to arouse suspicion. Yet he had no alternative but to try.

Miro had almost reached the counter when the pain in his back hit him with unexpected intensity. His foot hit a chair leg and he staggered forward. Someone sniggered. In the corner a couple turned their heads away in disgust at this drunken bum.

"The toilet is this way."

Miro looked up into the face of his waitress, who had rolled up her eyes at this hopeless drunk for the benefit of her clientele, and taking him roughly by the arm lead him around the counter into the kitchen. "The toilet is out the back!" she said loud enough for the chef to hear. The man turned, wiping his hands on a far from clean apron, eyeing with disdain this tramp who had invaded his domain.

The girl pushed Miro through the open door. "Will you be all right, comrade?" she whispered.

Startled at finding such an unexpected source of help, Miro could only mumble his thanks. Now he had a second chance to make the train. But he would have to get away from here soon. For if the waitress had worked out what he was, it might not take long for the rest of her clientele to do likewise, more so when he did not make a reappearance from the toilet.

Icy wind blew rain into his face. Miro shivered and pulled up his coat collar and walked hurriedly to the end of the dirty alleyway, and once there was about to turn left when he saw a little way ahead the barricade blocking the street which led to the railway station. Dejectedly, he turned away.

The pain in his back had eased a little. Miro hurried on, walking in a direction he thought ran roughly parallel to that of the station, and had almost reached midway on a street of detached houses, when he heard the sound of a truck a little distance behind. Stealing a quick look behind, he saw that that the truck was full of soldiers. He had nowhere to hide.

As a solitary shabby figure in a smart street, they were sure to stop and question him. Miro's heart thumped. Suddenly the pain was back. He grabbed the wooden fence and levered himself along, until his hand found a gate. Hypnotically he drew back the bolt and stumbled up the neat garden path. The sound of the truck grew closer. He took a step or two on to the lawn and knelt down and pretended to be gathering dead leaves.

The truck was almost at the gate. Would it stop? Miro continued with his gardening, afraid to look behind. He heard it change gear. Should he look round? That is what an innocent person would do. The noise rose, and hung there for what appeared to be an eternity before moving on. And when it did, Miro let out a long sigh of relief and shot a quick glance up at the window of the house, fully expecting someone to be watching him from there. But the window was empty.

Miro walked back to the gate, discreetly scanning the houses opposite and wondering how many pairs of eyes were watching him from behind the secrecy of their curtains? How many hands at this very minute were reaching for the telephone? The wounded man pushed open the gate. The truck had disappeared.

Reaching the junction of the street, Miro leaned against a high red brick wall to recover his breath, and take stock of his surroundings. He heard a train whistle, levered himself off the wall and walked across the street.

Iron railings guarded the marshalling yards below, beyond which a line of coal wagons stood in one of the sidings. Miro searched for a way down, certain it would lead him to the rear of the station. He had twenty minutes left.

Five nerve racking minutes later Miro found a missing railing and squeezed his way through, careful to keep the row of coal wagons between him and the sheds as he made his way down.

The first of the platforms was some distance away, but to his relief, as yet unguarded. Cautiously he walked on, the train standing at the centre platform hissing its impatience to be gone. Miro walked between the rails toward the train, never having realised before just how high the platform was. Would he be able to climb up in the state he was in? And if so, could he do so without being seen by the miscellany of passengers, soldiers, engine driver or fireman?

Miro left the rails for the darkness of a shed wall. A few steps more and he would be in the full glare of the station lights. So far, neither driver or fireman appeared to be on board. If he hurried, approached the train full on, he'd be hidden from the soldiers manning the ticket barrier.

Taking his courage in both hands, Miro left the safety of the wall and crept towards the hissing train. As the engine let off another cloud of steam, Miro seized the opportunity to hoist himself on to the platform amid the camouflage of hissing vapor, and his elation at not being discovered helped to mask the pain of the effort as he hobbled to the nearest compartment. He had been lucky.

As yet, the first compartment was empty. Miro slid back a door and threw himself down in the corner, quickly covering his face with an old newspaper he'd found lying on the seat, and pretended to have fallen asleep.

After a few minutes, the carriage door slid back. Miro tensed in expectation of his paper shield being torn away and looking up the muzzle of a gun. Instead, came the excited chatter of womens voices, and the bemused expressions on the faces of two elderly ladies as they inspected him from the opposite seat, as his paper slid down from an unexpected jolt from the engine.

Stifling an imaginary yawn, Miro smiled at them. "I must have fallen asleep," he apologised with a sheepish grin. "Worked late last night up at the dam. Hence my appearance," he explained plucking at his dirty jerkin. "Not even time to change for Mass this morning."

The women were delighted by Miro's explanation. "We must confess we missed it too. We wanted so much to visit our dear cousin in the Capital," one admitted shyly.

"Well ladies, you have confessed to me, so perhaps the good Father will forgive you." Miro gave each a broad smile.

Although sick with pain, conversing with these two decent ladies was giving him a cover against prying eyes.

Suddenly, there was a commotion from the rear of the train and soldiers rushed passed. The curious women leaping to their feet and rapidly winding down the window, as Miro rose awkwardly to stand behind them knowing that it would appear suspicious had he not done so. One of the women put her head out of the window offering a running commentary to her fellow passengers. "There are soldiers everywhere! Some are running towards the end of the train!" Behind her, the man felt sick. It could only mean one thing.

Without warning, an explosion filled the air, the reverberations magnified in the confines of the station, the blast hitting the coach. The women screamed and fell back into their seats. Miro stepped to the window stifling his surprise at the oscillating bulk of Bear running for the protection of a large wooden barrow piled high with luggage standing some distance away in the dark recesses of a goods platform.

Shots rang out. Bear threw himself behind the barrow, bobbing up to rake the chasing soldiers with a burst from his machine pistol. Suddenly the gun jammed, and in that brief moment the giant was catapulted backwards as if struck by an unseen hand.

His own safety momentarily forgotten, Miro grasped the window frame, straining to see what had happened to Bear through the running figures converging on the big man's barricade.

A boot lashed out at something on the ground. A rifle rose, snapping down butt first. Another swung his weapon like a club. Then there were others hacking and chopping at the inert figure on the cold station floor.

Now, there seemed to be soldiers everywhere, some climbing aboard the train. Miro turned a way from the window, sickened by what had happened to Bear, and calmly prepared himself for a similar fate.

At the sight of one of the women weeping hysterically, Miro slipped down and slid an arm around her. Another explosion.... more firing....running footsteps in the corridor drawing rapidly closer.....the sound of doors being pulled open. Miro pulled the sobbing woman closer, and felt for his pistol with his free hand. The door slid back and a soldier stood there, weapon levelled, taking in the scene of two weeping women, one in the arms of her husband. Satisfied that neither of these women or the man could have anything to do with PFF the soldier closed the door with a jerk.

Then, at last the impatient, hissing engine had its wish and they were on their way.

Because of yesterday's delay, the journey from the Capital to Gravst had taken three hours: with any luck, Miro hoped to be back in two. The would-be-husband slipped back to his seat, leaving the two sobbing women to sit and hug one another, and wish they had not chosen this day to visit their cousin.

The pain was worse. Miro hoped by the time he reached his destination he would have enough strength left to phone Krysty and tell her not to worry. Initially, the plan had been to get off at the station preceding Zaltz, but now he remembered his waitress telling him this train only stopped twice, once in mid journey, the next in the capital itself. Somehow he was glad he did not have to face the prospect of a long detour home, as was yesterday's plan. Miro put his head back and let the weariness flow through him...if he could only sleep.

Miro *had* slept, brought back to wakefulness by the sound of a whistle as the train curbed its speed to enter the station. He yawned and through bleary eyes caught sight of a billboard passing slowly by in the darkness.

Two pairs of tear stained eyes stared across at him. Miro smiled back encouragingly, knowing he may still have use for these two old dears.

The train drew to a halt with a jolt, and Miro rose stiffly, biting his lip at the pain. He took the women's overnight bags and followed them down the corridor on to the platform.

"Thank you," one said, making to relieve Miro of his burden. Miro looked up at the line of soldiers standing by the ticket barrier. "Let me carry them to the barrier for you," he suggested, keeping hold of the bags.

She smiled wanly at him. "How kind of you."

They headed for the barrier, Miro quietly confident he might make it through in such innocent company. And should he be asked about not having a ticket, would simply tell them he had dropped it out of the open window when the firing had started back at Gravst.

Almost too late, he saw the soldiers by the barrier searching the row of male passengers that stood there, hands above their heads. Miro's heart skipped a beat, the pain intensifying. Even if his ruse regarding his lost ticket was to succeed, they were still certain to find his pistol when they searched him.

He was almost at the point when it would be too late to turn back. He had to do something, and quickly. A train stood silently at the next platform. Miro seized his chance. Letting go of the overnight bags, amid startled cries from the women, Miro jumped on to the track behind the stationary train, almost passing out at the pain from the jolt, and scrambled across the lines to the marshalling yards.

Miro heard the cries of alarm behind him but was too afraid to look back. A shot rang out, and he felt the sting of the ricochet on his leg. He kept on going. Another shot hit a steel coupling a little way to his left. Gasping and wheezing, the wounded man knew he could not go much further. So near and yet so far from home.

Miro reached the coal yards, a soldier ran round the corner of a coal wagon. Miro shot him before he could recover from his surprise. Staggering on, he heard the cries of alarm all around him. He fell and, with the outmost willpower, hauled himself to his feet.

Miro judged that to hide in, or under, one of the many wagons standing in the siding would be worse than useless. He'd not remain hidden for long. He ducked between two wagons, ducking back again as two soldiers rounded the corner.

Leaning against a wagon, the wounded man gulped in great lungfulls of air, then slowly and carefully retraced his steps. Everywhere soldiers. He heard them close behind, and cocked his pistol, he could go no further. There was no where to run.

Miro edged along to the end of a row of wagons and was about to make a final dash across the open space, when he saw the night-watchman. He did not want to fire, at an old unarmed man. The old man looked up, saw Miro and instead of raising an alarm, signalled to him that he should turn away to his right.

Beyond caring whether or not it was a trap, Miro did as he was advised. Hearing, as he ran, the old man calling out the opposite instructions to the pursuing soldiers.

Somehow Miro found the strength to go on. He had found his second miracle of the day in the shape of an old man. *Thank you comrade*, he sobbed, and got himself over a fence and into a dimly street. Now, with any luck, he could find that emergency doctor's house Petr had told him about unless, of course, Petr had betrayed him as well.

At the same time as Miro headed back to the Capital, Juri Trybala was taking leave of his wife and child.

Max ran to his father as he reached the door. The long forgotten yacht now replaced by a monkey on a stick. The analogy of the new toy to that of his own life, not lost on Juri.

Karina followed the child to the door, her face flushed with tears. "Why, Juri? Why now?" she asked, drawing the child gently to her.

Juri fondled the boy's hair. "The General needs me," he lied. "It's the last big push. Hopefully it will soon be all over."

"Then why go?" Karina demanded despairingly. "Now, when it's almost all over as you say?"

Caught between both parents, the child looked up, whimpering, infected by their fear and tension. Juri knelt down, the words he spoke to his son, intended for his wife. "I'm going away to fight, Max, so your daddy will be able to say, he has done his duty to his country. No one will be able to point the finger and say *he* stayed at home."

Max stared blankly into his father's face, too young to comprehend what had been said to him, only that his father was going away. His father drew him close, hugging him tight.

"No one who knows anything about you, could say that of you Juri. Why, with the fighting almost over, does General Jakofcic need you? Especially after all you have done. Remember, it was because of him that you came by that bad leg."

Juri rose, his resolve rapidly dissolving at their distress. He hated himself more than ever, more so about blaming the General for calling him to the front. The man had only agreed after he had argued that he owed him this chance to prove himself a whole man again. He would never forget the look on his General's face, and he knew their working relationship would never be the same again.

Leaning across the child, he kissed his wife on the cheek. "I'll not be in any danger, not with this leg." He shook it, hoping to lighten the situation. "The General wants a quick end to this offensive, so he's not likely to wait for me hobbling my way around the front."

Karina gave a weak choking laugh, wiping back her tears with a shaking hand.

Juri kissed her again. "I'll be back before you have realised I've gone."

Juri kneeled down, and kissed his son, holding him at arms length, etching every detail of the child's tiny face in his mind. Then he rose and, without looking back, was gone.

Perhaps it was because he still had his family on his mind that Juri failed to see the man emerge from the shadows of a nearby doorway as he turned the key in the car door. When he did, it was to find another gunman standing behind him.

"No fuss now, Sergeant," the gunman hissed. "Let's go for a ride as we did before."

Once more, Juri found himself blindfolded and pushed to the floor in the back of his own car, his instincts telling him he was being driven to the same place as before. He was right. The smell of the hut was the same.

They pushed him into a chair, tying his hands behind his back. He felt sick, and at the same time angry, not from fear, but from the sense of failure. He had been so close to getting away to the front.

"We have some work for you to do, Juri Trybala." This time the voice was different.

Juri had known they'd contact him sooner or later. Logically, the time was right now that the great offensive had begun. He waited. It had to be something important they wanted him to find out. His spirits rose. If so, they'd have to let him go. Then he'd take his chance and keep on going till he reached the front.

He was due to report at the Caserne that evening to carry dispatches and maps to the General. He hoped he'd not be too late to catch the convoy. Juri stiffened. Ch.... his kit bag was in the boot of his car! Were they to find it, they'd know for certain where he was headed!

Juri was still working out an excuse should they ask him, when the blow struck, smashing his face into the table. Someone behind him dragged his head back, and he took the next punch full in the face.

"Enough!" A strange new voice commanded sharply. "Now Trybala, we have no time to spare."

Juri heard the rustle of paper. "We want details! As Jakofcic's Staff Sergeant, we believe you can provide us with the answers."

Juri licked blood from his lips. His stomach heaved. If they believed he held the answers to their questions, there would be no need to let him go. Perhaps, he would not catch that last convoy after all.

"Tell us what we want to know." The new voice was patronisingly soft. "We have no wish to kill you, or even cause you unnecessary pain." The voice grew closer. "First, tell us Jakofcic's exact positions, his exact strength. Secondly, when and where will this new heavy artillery reach him? Thirdly, the number of reinforcements preparing to leave this evening for the north, and which route will they travel."

Juri was startled. Chr.... he thought. They know everything. They must have sources deep within the Caserne itself. He shook his head. Someone hit him from behind, jerking his head forward.

"Come come, Trybala, do not be ashamed of divulging such information! It is not as though you are betraying your fellow countrymen in arms," the unseen man laughed. "No." The voice serious again. "It is just that we wish you to confirm the information we already possess...plus a little more."

Juri tasted blood in his mouth. He swallowed hard, steadying himself to answer. "How can you be certain which information is correct, yours or mine?"

"Simply because our source has always been completely reliable, therefore, all we wish you to do is confirm it for us. Simple enough? Not all who wear a Government uniform have the same loyalties," the man chuckled.

The timbre of the voice changed and rose angrily, the smell of garlic inches away from Juri's face. "Now I will ask you these same questions once again."

"Perhaps your reliable source also knows how many sacks of potatoes we send to the front?" Juri smirked, in an attempt to bolster his own flagging spirits. If he had to die, at least he would not die a coward. He would not let them know how scared he really was.

Unlike his previous capture, this time they made no attempt to save his looks when they started to hit him again. Juri drifted in an out of consciousness, and from afar, heard the silky voice of his new interrogator asking the same questions over and over again. Eventually, the blows stopped and he crashed to the floor.

How long he lay there he did not know, hours, minutes seconds? From the inner recesses of his brain, the sound of a car drawing up; someone running up the steps; a hushed voice saying, "Tonight. Tell Wysocki, he must confirm the exact information tonight."

Gunshots echoing around his head.... Shouts filling the room....
Men rushing passed where he lay on the floor. The discharge of a
pistol close by, as if someone had snapped a shot at him. More shots
in the distance.... A car starting, accelerating away..... More shots,
rapid this time. The sound of a car starting up and gradually fading
away into the night. Silence.

It had sounded like a raid, and if so, it would not be long until he
was rescued. Juri lay listening intently for any hint of a sound that
might tell him he had been discovered. Nothing. He called out. No
reply. He was sweating. Was this some sort of a game? A bluff?
Were his kidnappers still watching him? Duping him into believing
he was safe, before destroying his mistaken sense of security, and
start all over again.

The next ten minutes brought Juri no closer to a solution, except to
confirm that all was silent and had been, since the sound of the car
had driven off. It would not do, he could not lie here indefinitely.
And certainly if he made a move, it would confirm if his kidnappers
were watching him or not.

Juri struggled to a sitting position. His fall had broken the old
chair he had been sitting on, enabling him to get to his feet. He
shook at his bonds, his brain working as to the reason why his
captors had panicked. Had it been a raid? If so, someone was sure
to have found him by this time. Yet no one had entered the hut.

Taking a chance Juri called out. He tried again. No one answered.
He stepped back, hitting his head against a wall. With his hands tied
behind his back, he could only grope around. His head hit a beam
then what he thought must be a vertical stab of wood. Putting the
back of his head against it he slid down, sliding his blindfold
upwards. The hut was in darkness.

The blindfold gone, it did not take Juri long to free himself. And
as he had surmised, he was alone. Nor, despite the shooting, were
there any bodies to stumble over in the darkness. Juri ran to the
door. His car was still there, and hopefully the keys were still in the
ignition.

A half hour later, nearing the capital, Juri was no closer to
formulating an opinion as to why he had been captured. Had they
kidnapped him for the reasons they had given, however forcefully?
He put up a hand to his bleeding face. Had he been indeed lucky to
have escaped? Or was it some sort of charade? A plot? He had

heard the name Wysocki whispered. It had meant nothing to him at the time, but now he remembered where he had heard it. Wysocki was the nephew of that boring old tennis club hag Lomova had been blackmailed into helping on to the General's staff? It made sense. Tonight! Tell Wysocki we must have the exact information tonight! Or had he imagined hearing this?

Juri stole a quick glance at his watch, accelerating at the same time. He could just about make that last convoy. He pressed down on the pedal, cursing himself for breaking his promise never to drive so fast again, after his killing of that unfortunate girl.

Juri eased his speed a little, his thoughts returning to his dilemma. Was it intended that he should hear the name Wysocki? Or did his captors believe he was still unconscious? If it was all a fake, why had they chosen that particular name? It had to be true. They said they already had the information they needed from a reliable source...a source wearing a uniform!

The hairs on the back of Juri's neck rose. He gripped the wheel tighter, shivering at the realisation that it had made no difference how he would look after they had beat him, for when they had got what they wanted, they had simply meant to kill him.

Juri reached the entrance to the barracks and, slithering to a halt, shoved his pass under the nose of a startled guard. Then, driving as quickly as he dared for the staff building, was out of the car grabbing his kit bag and running inside for the wireless shack.

"Transmission to Sector 8, Sparks!" he called out, drawing quickly to a halt.

The wireless operator swivelled round in his chair to face him, his expression changing from one of annoyance at this interruption to his break, to one of surprise.

"Too slow on getting your pants on this time, Sergeant?" he smirked, pointing at Juri's face.

Juri rubbed his jaw, humouring the man. "Yes! Yes! Something like that. Now, how about that transmission?"

"Sorry sergeant, there's a complete blackout 'till 2200 hours, unless for emergencies," he trailed off, lazily drawing a mug of coffee towards him.

"This *is* an emergency!" Juri yelled.

The operator sat bolt upright and let go of his cup as if it were red hot. "Then take it through channels, Sergeant," he bit back.

Cursing, Juri threw up his hands in despair and ran awkwardly down the corridor, his kit bag bouncing off his back, his wounded leg throbbing in time to the pain in his head.

"Staff Sergeant Trybala!" The officer's voice rang out, the sound reverberating off the walls and the inside of Juri's head.

Juri slid to a halt on the waxed floor. "Sir!" he called out drawing to attention.

"You are late reporting, Staff Sergeant!" The words spat out at him. "And what the devil has happened to your face?"

"An accident sir. Permission to speak sir?" Juri drew himself more stiffly to attention.

"Permission granted, Staff Sergeant. Make it quick. We are already ten minutes behind schedule."

Juri tried to conceal his impatience. "I have an important message for General Jakofcic. And I have just been informed there is to be no communication with Sector 8 for a further four hours, unless it is an emergency. Begging your pardon, sir, but by that time it will be too late. This *is* an emergency!"

The officer stared down an aquiline nose at Juri. Clearly the man was agitated, but he was damned if he was going to be browbeaten into breaking orders for any staff wallah, even if he was C in C. staff. Probably the nonentity had forgotten to tell his C. O. he had missed out packing his pyjamas.

Revelling in the N.C.O.'s discomfiture, the officer held out the despatch case he'd been carrying, his voice clipped. "You have these despatches to take to General Jakofcic this evening, have you not, Sergeant?"

"Yes sir," Juri replied, puzzled by the question.

"If your communiqué is so important that it cannot wait until you see General Jakofcic this evening, you may write it out. Leave it with the officer on duty, who will then present it for authorisation to Major Casteri, who, if he believes it justifies breaking radio silence, will have it transmitted forthwith."

God save us all, Juri thought, by that time we could all have died of old age.

In his frustration he thought of confiding his fear and suspicions to the man. Saw the man's set of the jaw, the eyes boring into him, challenging him to disobey. He also thought of what the PFF gunman had said about not all who wore the uniform being loyal. Instead he said aloud, "thank you sir. I shall do so immediately."

Juri ran back up the corridor, kit bag in one hand, dispatch case in the other, ignoring the angry shout of the officer for him to stop running.

Back at the wireless shack once more, Juri scribbled out his warning to his General, sealing it inside an envelope marked, 'confidential' to be read only by Major Casteri. He had to take the chance.

When the operator put out a still lazy hand for the envelope, Juri grabbed it by the wrist. "I mean it, Sparks, it's a matter of life and death."

Something in Juri's eyes and the way he hissed his warning frightened the soldier.

"Yes sergeant. Rest assured it will be done."

Satisfied that he had done all he could to warn the General, Juri reached the parade ground and, joined the long line of soldiers shuffling on to the waiting trucks. While back at the wireless shack, an officer held out his hand for the envelope Juri had left.

"Thank you corporal, I will take care of this." Then he put it in his tunic pocket.

"What's up now, soldier?" The sudden change in the tone of the truck's engine had brought Juri back to wakefulness.

The driver changed down a gear. "I don't rightly know, Serg, I'm just following the truck in front."

Juri screwed up his eyes to read his watch in the weak light of the cabin's dashboard. "Almost 2200 hours." He stifled a yawned.

"In a hurry to do your bit, Serg?" The driver seemed amused by his passenger's constant impatience.

"No, Corporal, just anxious to get these to our esteemed leader," Juri said caustically, pointing to the dispatch case at his feet.

"Didn't think you staff wallahs would want to get too close to the fighting?" the driver replied seriously, bringing the truck to a sudden halt.

"Out! Everyone out and take cover!" A Second Lieutenant hurled at them, running passed the cabin window.

Juri and his driver ran for the undergrowth at the side of the narrow road, Juri's intended obscenity to the driver's remarks still hot on his tongue.

"Bloody PFF!" the driver swore. "They bloody well seem to know everything"

"Yes they do, soldier," Juri muttered softly, releasing the safety catch of his weapon, his mind on the traitor Wysocki, and hoping his message had got through to the General.

"All clear! Board! Everyone back on the trucks!" Shouts came down the line out of the darkness.

His head throbbing, angry at yet another delay in reaching their destination, Juri hobbled back to the truck.

It was close on one o'clock in the morning before Juri heard the distant sound of gunfire. He had long since given up analysing the reason for his capture. Now all he could do was to warn the General; that was of course if he had not already been alerted by his message, and let his senior take it from there, and blow the consequences.

Juri feared that in order to substantiate his story, Jakofcic might ask him the reason for his 'capture'. He could, of course, lie. But somehow he had the feeling this would only succeed in making matters worse, and when he did tell him the whole truth, the great man might let him off by transferring him to some remote garrison, which would mean he'd be out of Lomova's clutches, and hopefully back into the forgiving arms of his wife. Juri laughed at himself. It might well be his luck for the General to throw Lomova at him with all the fervour she had shown when throwing herself at him. Or that Karina, when she learned how unfaithful he had been, would not want him back and deservedly so. Poor sweet Karina. What his lust may have cost him: a wife and son. Juri visualised the little boy as last he had seen him standing there, his eyes wide with fear, his tiny mind unable to take in what was happening. It was all his fault. A half hour later the convoy drew to a halt in an open field. Travel weary soldiers began to alight.

In the darkness, not waiting to be counted in the ranks, Juri ran through ankle deep mud of a ploughed field for the outline of a building.

"Halt! Who goes there?" A figure snapped at him out of nowhere.

Juri drew quickly to a halt, searching the darkness. "Staff Sergeant Trybala, Staff to General Jokofcic," he replied stiffly.

"Advance and be recognised!" the voice barked out.

Juri took a step forward, hoping he was not already too late to reach his general. The outline of the sentry drawing closer as the voice in his head said, *'it must be done tonight.'*

"Password!" the sentry snapped, now only a few feet away.

"Ch...!" He had forgotten it. He panicked. Then, as if by a miracle, it came back to him. He hurried on. It was already past one in the morning. Again, Juri was challenged by a sentry and had to contend with the whole procedure once more.

At last, he was inside the farmhouse. Throwing his kit bag aside, and forgoing formality, snapped at a startled corporal, "General Jakofcic is he present? If so where can I find him? I must see him at once!"

Not awaiting an answer Juri left the confused and protesting soldier in his wake as he strode purposely down a hall way, where two armed sentries stood outside a door. Juri guessed this was the right room. He rounded on the protesting corporal who had followed him, brushing aside the soldier's explanation of how the General had only just returned from the front line and was conducting a staff meeting before retiring for a few well earned hours rest.

"Inform the General, Staff Sergeant Trybala must see him at once. It is of the greatest urgency."

The red faced corporal gestured helplessly. "The General has given strict orders not to be disturbed!" he pleaded. "You must know how he hates to be interrupted during a conference!"

If he was to get passed this apology for a soldier and two armed sentries, Juri thought he'd better compose himself. "None better than I, Corporal. Please do as I have ordered."

Juri clutched the dispatch case in his hands. Communications between here and the Capital would have reopened; therefore there was no point in asking about his message. Clearly nothing untoward had happened as yet. Or, was it as yet no one had found out that someone may be passing on vital information to the enemy from here, in Field H.Q.!

The door opened and the red faced corporal reappeared. "General Jakofcic, will see you now, Staff Sergeant," he stammered. Juri hurriedly brushed passed the man.

Including the General, there were four men in the room, two of whom he had met before, the third he did not recognise but guessed by his rank could possibly be Wysocki.

"Well Sergeant, what is it that is so urgent that it cannot wait?" Jakofcic rapped at him, throwing down his pencil on the map they had all been studying before this rude interruption.

Juri snapped to attention. "Your despatches, sir." He did not know what else to say, or, how to begin, now that the situation was presented to him.

Clearly annoyed, Silvo took the case plopping in down on his desk. "Is that all Sergeant?" he snapped. His glare declaring that this was an absurd excuse for interrupting.

Juri took a few steps back, suddenly isolated in the tiny kitchen. He swallowed. "I thought they might have been of the utmost importance, sir," he stammered, trying to give himself time to think; all his brave rehearsing on the way here having gone clear out of his head.

Silvo's eyes softened. Clearly the soldier was acting out of character. Something was not quite right here. And what the hell had happened to his face? "There is another reason for this interruption, Sergeant?" his tone now more in keeping with someone he'd long known and trusted.

Faced directly with the question and four pairs of eyes, Juri decided to go for broke. "I have reason to believe Sir, there may be an attempt this evening to pass on vital information to the enemy regarding the disposition of our forces. This, and the arrival of our reinforcements and our heavy artillery."

Juri was sweating. He plunged on, thwarting any attempt by the General to ask specific details, and before he himself lost the courage to go on.

He saw the four officers' stand open mouthed, and averted his eyes to the ceiling and began, as if reciting from a statement learned off by heart. "Earlier this evening I was apprehended by the PFF who wished me to confirm the afore mentioned information...attempting to improve my looks in the process." Juri lowered his eyes to point to his face, and was disappointed when no one appeared to appreciate his humour. "They also led me to believe that they already had this information and my kidnapping was merely to verify this."

Such flowery language, Juri rebuked himself. Get on with it. "I shall not waste the officers' time by detailing how I escaped, or the manner in which this information was to be passed on by a member of your own staff, General Jakofcic, only that it was to be done tonight." Juri took the courage to study his watch. "That is if it has not already been done."

"Hold on, Sergeant." Silvo restrained the speaker with a jerk of his hand, his eyes boring into his sergeant. "You are not making any sense. You say, the Reds already know my troop strength and dispositions? More importantly, when my heavy artillery will arrive?" *God*, he thought, *not my artillery*!

"Yes sir...at least they implied they already knew most of it. Once I had confirmed this, the traitor was to pass on this *exact* information to them tonight."

Jakofcic faced the other senior officers in the room, his action suggesting that they offer him some assistance.

"Do you know the name of this *traitor*?" one of them asked Juri, making the word sound like an obscenity.

"Yes sir," Juri replied firmly. "The name was that of Second Lieutenant Wysocki."

His heart hammered as he stared at the man he had so blatantly accused, awaiting his reaction.

In turn the accused man stared wide eyed back at Juri as if struck by a physical blow. "This is ridiculous!" he exploded, his face beetroot red, his bulging eyes darting from one officer to another. "You cannot possibly believe this nonsense, General!"

Juri watched Wysocki carefully, while slowly moving his hand to his holster. Now that he had made the accusation, he felt strangely composed, as if at last having atoned for all his past demeanors. The man was good. The outrage, the look of incredulity.

"Perhaps not so ridiculous Lieutenant, Sir," Juri began. "Not if a person was to ask why you were so eager to have yourself attached to General Jakofcic's staff, in the first place?" Juri saw the faintest hint of comprehension on his General's face.

"It is absurd!" Beside himself with rage, Wysocki turned to his chief, for vindication. "Sir. Might I ask the sergeant how he obtained this information from the PFF. Perhaps it is *he* who is the traitor! And what was done to his face is merely a disguise to...."

"Enough!" Jakofcic barked, giving the junior officer a look expressly saying that if his staff sergeant was a traitor, he would not be so foolish as to waltz in here and warn them of such a plot.

Silvo bunched his fists on his desk. Could his staff sergeant have got it wrong? Mistaken the name? Wysocki had been with him all evening, so no information could have reached the P.F,F. through him.

"Perhaps, if I may be allowed to make a suggestion, General?" One of the two officers intervened, addressing himself to Jakofcic. Silvo nodded. "Now that you have been warned of this... plot, and the two main suspects appear to be present, also as we have much important matters to discuss..." he made an apologetic gesture. "May I suggest you place both of these gentlemen under arrest until such time as you are in a better position to assess the situation more closely. Also, by keeping them under guard, neither will have the opportunity of informing the enemy, should this information prove correct."

"Ideal solution, Colonel."a fellow officer commended.

Jakofcic considered for a moment while Juri shifted his weight from one foot to the other, hoping against hope that he had not made a complete fool of himself. Finally, with a decisive nod of his head, accepting his colonel's logic, General Jakofcic called for his guards. The door opened, the guards entered.

"Disarm both Second Lieutenant Wysocki, and Staff Sergeant Trybala. Place both under close arrest until further orders," Jakofcic ordered, his voice firm, at the same time giving Juri a curiously sad, almost apologetic look.

Juri wanted to say something to his General, the better to explain his action, but the great man had already sat down at his desk, as if having already forgotten his staff sergeant and the recent incident.

"Well gentlemen, back to work. Now that my sergeant has brought the co-ordinates we may as well discuss them," he said, drawing the dispatch case to him and clicking the lock open. And with that, the entire room exploded in a ball of fire.

Chapter 14

Mark shivered. Each day it was growing that bit colder, soon the high peaks would be snow-covered, and that would put paid to their 'great offensive.' He buttoned up his combat jacket, quickening his stride through the dew stained grass to Sector H.Q. must be important to order a briefing at this time of the morning.

Shadows descending the hillock to Mark's right caught his attention. He altered direction. Sergeant Niew Grbesa moved ahead of the column to meet him.

Apprehensively Mark's eyes swept over what was left of the patrol. "What's happened, sergeant?"

It was all the exhausted soldier could do to salute his senior officer. "Place is alive with them, they're everywhere. I think there is something very big brewing Sir. We got caught with our pants down," Niew was saying wearily.

Mark studied the haggard face in the half light. He knew if this was true the Sergeant was not to blame. " Captain Droboski?" he asked, searching the approaching column for the young officer whom he visualised standing tapping his leg with his makeshift swagger stick that last night on the mountain. So self assured, so certain of an easy victory over Tetek's PFF So dead, he grimaced.

Niew nodded. "Got it with the first burst. Caught in the open. We were..."

Mark stopped the tired soldier from going on. He was already late for the briefing. "So 'A' Company is once again without a captain and a lieutenant...unless?"

"My answer is still no Sir." Niew hitched his submachine gun higher on his shoulder as if it weighed a ton.

"Understood, CSM."

Stretcher bearers struggled passed. "Better get what's left of your Company bedded down soldier. Give your report...."

The exploding shells bursting a few meters away from where both men stood, drowned out the remainder of Mark's orders. "Oh! Ch...!" Mark swore diving for the ground, Niew by his side.

"I thought they were up to something, Sir!" Niew snatched, covering his head with his hands as the ground around them heaved upwards.

Mark spat out wet grass. "Where the hell did *they* come from, Sergeant? Those guns must be well down their side of the mountain, and bloody heavy, to hit us at this range."

Mark rolled over on to his back. Everywhere soldiers were disappearing over the small hillocks to the rear, away from the exploding shells as fast as their legs would take them.

A soldier from 'A' Company lying helplessly on a stretcher was blown into the air. Men rushing to escape the carnage threw away their equipment, none halting in their headlong flight to help the wounded.

Mark sprang up, heading again for the Sector H.Q. "Come on Sergeant, let's get out of this!"

Together they rushed across the open ground, dodging shell holes and discarded equipment.

"Jesus!" The word was out before Mark could stop himself. Where H.Q. had stood, now only a smoking ruin remained.

Mark pulled himself together and ran towards it, Niew behind him. He ran faster, lost his footing and skidded round the corner of what was left of the remaining wall, throwing himself down unceremoniously amongst a group of men already huddled there.

Regaining his breath, Mark levered himself from his undignified position. His eyes swept the crouching men, one of who he recognised as the wireless operator.

"How many were in there, soldier?" he asked sharply, nodding at the smoking ruin of the H.Q.

The man, little more than a boy, ignored him, his dead eyes staring directly ahead. Grabbing him roughly by the shoulders, Mark repeated his question. The frightened youth stared back vacantly, his lips twitching, either in answer to Mark's question or in silent prayer.

Angrily, Niew thrust his submachine gun under the dazed man's chin. "The Major asked you a question, now answer him you shitty excuse for a soldier," he growled.

Muttering incoherently, the young man tried to jerk his head away from the gun. "All...most of the officers. I don't know, I can't say," he choked. Disgusted, Niew lowered his weapon.

Mark snapped a look around the corner of the wall where shells still rained down, killing and maiming the retreating men. Jumping to his feet, he pulled the dazed wireless operator roughly after him. "Pull yourself together, soldier, you're coming with us!"

Running and dodging, Mark found a secondary shelter half a mile from the ruined H.Q., a map room, no better than a makeshift dugout, where three men sat huddled around a small table lit by a solitary oil lamp, busily trying to make contact with the flanking Companies.

Mark threw himself and the young operator in to the dugout. "I'm Major Stewart!" he shouted above the screech of incoming shells. "Until I find out otherwise, I appear to be senior officer around here." He jabbed a look at each of the perplexed men in turn. "Now , can you tell me what's happening on either flank?"

"We are trying to raise them Sir, but..." A shell exploded close by, shaking dirt from the sod covered roof. The soldier clutched his helmet. "But there appears to be some interference."

"You can say that again, Sparks," Niew said caustically, clutching his own helmet. The witticism brought a smile to the man's lips.

"Can you reach General Jakofcic's H.Q. and inform him of the situation here? Advise him of my rank, and that I await further orders," Mark rapped out the instructions. "The corporal here," he jerked a thumb at the young operator, "will help you."

"Then, you don't know? Have not been informed?" The coerced young soldier said shakily.

"Know what, corporal?"

A cloud of dirt fell from the low roof from a shell burst. The youngster drew himself tighter together, flinging his hands over his helmet. The dust settled, he lifted his head, searching the roof with fear filled eyes, as if expecting it to cave in at any second.

"Know what, Corporal?" Mark asked angrily.

The youngster tore his eyes away from the roof. "That....was the reason for the briefing!" he cried at Mark, now almost hysterical with fear. "General Jakofcic, is dead...as are most of his staff!"

"Sweet Jesus!" Niew swore staring disbelievingly at his major.

"What happened!" Mark snapped, losing patience with this frightened young man.

"Don't know exactly. I didn't take the message. But I understand it came from a temporary H.Q."

Mark swung on the original denizens. "Get that message through, then let me know when you receive an answer." He flung himself up. "You'll find me around somewhere."

Outside, Mark made for the ridge behind which most of his future command had found temporary shelter. Everywhere, officers struggled unsuccessfully to bring about some semblance of order.

"All officers to me here, Lieutenant!" he hurled at an officer scurrying passed. "And at the double!"

He swung to Niew, his tone only marginally softer. "You better get back to your Company, Sergeant Grbesa. Take them to the rear."

It was not the order Niew had expected to hear, especially at a time like this; not from the former commander of one of the best Companies in the army. He hesitated, hearing the mercenary add as if to himself. "Rest them Sergeant, I'll be in need of all the help I can get later on."

Ten minutes later, Mark drew the remaining officers together in the lee of a ridge. There were ten altogether, and to the Scot's chagrin, all junior to him.

"Well, gentlemen, most of you know me, and until I'm relieved, your commanding officer." He spoke tersely. "The barrage has ceased for the moment, but I do not think for long. Tetek is not about to let us know he has heavy artillery, unless he is prepared to back it up with an offensive of his own. That offensive will not be long in coming."

Mark's eyes swept the coterie. "As you may know, our own officers were caught in that building over there." He jerked a thumb over his shoulder. "Fortunately, I was late on arriving." He went on, the men silent. "And as something similar has happened to General Jakofcic...." Heads jerked up as if he was crazed. Mark swore under his breath; obviously, they had not heard what had happened to their Commander-in-Chief. "Therefore, it may be some time before this mess is sorted out. So you are stuck with me till then. As soon as I learn what has happened to General Jakofcic, I will let you know."

Some stood staring at the ground shuffling their feet, others mumbling to one another at the consequence of losing an office of Jakofcic's calibre.

Recognising the urgency of instilling confidence in to these men if they were to stand any chance of repelling the impending attack; rank and file having the ability to smell despondency in their officers a mile away, Mark barked out a flood of orders. "First, Captains, of 'B' and 'C' Company...trenches to be dug, right flank...., there." he barked, jabbing a finger at the ridge behind him. "'D' and 'E', Company Commanders, ridge, left flank. 'A' Company will occupy the centre. We'll halt them here, out of the range of their heavy guns. Any questions?" he asked with equal obduracy, daring anyone to refute his orders. No one answered. "Dismissed. Deploy your men as quickly as possible, the enemy are not going to allow us the luxury of waiting until we are dug in," he snapped. His officers saluted, however reluctantly this upstart of a foreign mercenary, and hurried off into the grey morning mist.

Mark lit a cigarette. He'd lost all his peronal belongings, not that he'd had much, but he could do with his field glasses, and a change of socks, probably a pair of underpants and a toilet roll if he judged correctly what he thought was about to happen.

"You are doing a good job, Major."

Mark swung at the sound of the voice to where two officers stood above him on the ridge watching the hive of industry he had initiated. He heaved a sigh of relief at the sight of their insignia; both were Majors. Surely, one would hold seniority to him, considering his own so recent commission, and with it would go the responsibility of commanding this shambles.

"Am I glad to see you guys!" Mark greeted them, blowing out smoke.

"Why, Major? You appear to be doing very well without us." The second, waved a hand at the work going on all around.

"I'm only holding the fort, so to speak, until someone with more seniority comes along...like you two."

The first officer held up both hands in a token of surrender. "I'm strictly artillery, Major. Wouldn't be much help here, I'm afraid."

"Same for me. Tanks my game," the other apologised.

Mark could not contain his anger at the refusal of what he saw was clearly the duty of one of these officers to assume command. *You bastards*, he thought.... *Leave me to carry the can!* He made towards them, bunching his fists.

The artillery commander read the anger on the Scot's face, and made a buffer of his hands in front of him. "We'll back you up whatever you may decide to do. Tell me what you need from my guns, and you've got it."

"Same goes for me and my tanks, Major. Just lucky to be alive. Good thing, Damir and me were a bit too far back to get to that damned briefing on time this morning. Something like yourself, no doubt?"

Mark nodded, swallowing his anger. A little voice warned him that confrontation would resolve nothing. Besides, he did not have the time, or the patience to argue. Perhaps there was something in what they had said. At least he knew infantry, especially this infantry.

"All right," he said stiffly. "I don't believe we have that much time before they hit us. And I do mean hit us. So keep your tanks out of sight, major." He shifted to the gunnery officer. "And your guns silent 'till I give the word. So now that's settled...if you will excuse me?" Mark spun on his heel, leaving the two officers, who had been so quick to abdicate their office, to carry out his instructions.

Milan heard the ringing. He searched the crowded room for his secretary. Found him in a corner, talking to a goldfish in a tank. The ringing made one of the fish jump. The ringing grew louder. He woke up.

Milan put out his hand and felt around for the telephone. The sleeve of his pajama jacket crept up exposing his arm to the cold of the enormous bedroom in the Kasel. He hoped he would not have to get up, although he knew that in all probability it would be a forlorn hope.

His hand found the receiver and he picked it up, his private secretary's voice at the other end informing him he had just received an important communiqué from the front. Milan thanked him and put down the phone, thinking how quick the man had been on reaching the phone from the goldfish tank, until remembering that this had been in his dream.

Elizbieta lay on her side in the bed opposite, a bare shoulder with a strip of pink ribbon of her night-gown visible above the bedclothes. Milan closed his eyes and yawned. How this life suited his wife, he smiled to himself. Although, he had to admit she was an excellent hostess, always in the right place at the right time.

Milan swung his legs and sat on the edge of the bed shivering. "May the good Saints preserve me!" His voice was strangely loud in the gigantic room. "Five o'clock!" He had not got to bed until two!

Wrapping himself in his dressing gown, Milan shuffled across the bare polished floor in his slippers. He opened the door and stepped back in surprise at the sight of his Private Secretary, standing there fully dressed.

"I apologise, Mister President, considering the late hour of your retiral, but I believe this is of the gravest concern to you."

Milan took the sheet of paper and stepped into the anteroom, closing the bedroom door behind him. He was not unduly alarmed, to Toso everything was of the gravest concern. "What is it, Toso? Is the war over? Have they captured that Pimpernel, Tetek?" he chuckled, his smile broadening even further at the man's grim demeanour. "Drat! I've forgotten my spectacles." Milan's expression changed to one of annoyance. "You read it man, considering that you are already familiar with its contents."

"As you wish, Mister President." Toso unfolded the single sheet of paper he had taken from his president and began to read.

"I regret to inform you that at approximately 0230 hours this morning, General Jakofcic, and several members of his staff were killed when a device exploded within the confines of his Headquarters. I shall forward additional information, as and when it comes to hand. Until then, I await your instructions. Signed, Colonel J. Tomoslo, acting Commanding Officer." Toso finished.

Milan groped for a chair, the chill of the anteroom as nothing to the ice-cold hand clutching his chest. "Arrange to have all Cabinet Ministers meet me as quickly as possible at Admin, Toso. Then, get me Senator Cibula on the line. The Opposition Leader has a right to know what has happened."

Dazed, Milan drummed his fingers on a small side table, in the now empty room. "With Jakofcic gone....Sturk !" Milan spoke out loud, drawing a deep breath. "The command is rightly his," he conceded, rising to stare unseeing at a portrait of one of his predecessors. "But God help us, he is no match for Tetek."

It was not the cold that made the tall president shiver, but the prospect of what Tetek would do while the pedantic old General thought out his next move. *Then God help us all*, he thought, and shivered again.

Tetek pressed the tobacco firmly down into the bowl of his pipe with his thumb. The cave was cold and getting colder; another winter was on the way. He struck a match, sucking on the stem as he put the flame to the bowl. He was getting too old for all of this, this had to be the finish, he could no longer face one wet cave after another.

The old General pulled his sheepskin coat more closely about him, and held out his hands to the small oil stove, sucking on the unlit pipe.

A cold draught had him turn, as the tarpaulin covering the entrance was thrown back, a figure ghost-like against the grey half-light of the morning, bundled into the cave.

"It's done, Comrade General!" The intruder's voice was shrill in the confines of the tiny cave.

Tetek raised an eyebrow.

Annoyed by his senior's lack of enthusiasm to the greatest of glad tidings since the first day of Christianity; not that he believed in such a fallacy, the man shouted again. "It's done, Comrade! . Jakofcic's dead!"

Drawing the pipe slowly from his mouth, the PFF leader examined it closely. "Damn! That's twice this stupid thing's failed to light, at this rate I'll soon be out of matches."

The huddled figure grew closer, convinced that either his esteemed leader had gone mad or deaf, or both. "Comrade. General!" He began again, prepared to shout louder if necessary.

"I know, I know, Comrade. No need to shout, I'm not deaf. Though I will be with that voice of yours screaming through my head." Tetek waved his unlit pipe impatiently at the man. "Has this news of Jakofcic been confirmed? Or is it just one more idle rumour?"

"No comrade, General, it is true!" the man hastened to assure him. "Jakofcic's H.Q. went sky high!" He emphasised the motion with an upwards swoop of his arms. "Sometime this morning, I understand. Forward Company witnessed it."

Tetek nodded his belief. "Very good comrade soldier." The harbinger waited. "I've dismissed you comrade." Tetek stared hard at the man.

"Yes Sir." The bundle made a reluctant way back to the exit, aggrieved that he would not be privy to the great man's plan.

When the man had gone, Tetek held out his hands to the stove. "So Group Capital's planning had at last come to fruition." He for one had not believed they could succeed in killing so close a guarded personage as Jakofcic. He would have to send them his congratulations....as well as an apology.

Now for my second surprise. Gleefully, Tetek rubbed his hands together. Once more he struck a match, this time succeeded in lighting his pipe. "One success after another," he grunted with amusement. "Perhaps at this rate, I just might not have to spend another winter in these mountains after all."

Apprehensive of the attack he was certain must follow the heavy bombardment, Mark Stewart unwittingly faced Tetek's second surprise at 0700 hours of that same Monday morning. Lying on the ridge he scanned the patchwork landscape through borrowed field glasses.

Fields of differing shades of green, some enclosed by low stonewalls, here and there dissected by hedgerow-lined lanes, lay beneath him. Smoke from whitewashed farmhouses curled lazily up into the pale blue sky. A landscape deceptive in its appearance of uniformity, hiding countless hollows and depressions all the way back to the mountains, now clearly visible in the full flush of the morning light.

Puffs of smoke on his left flank informed Mark, Tetek had turned his heavy guns on Sector 3. He swung his glasses to the right, focusing on the mountains away to the east, where he and his Companies had only recently been withdrawn. Sunlight filtered through the high peaks where Colonel Ziotkowski continued his snail like advance since disembarking from the ships almost two weeks ago.

Suddenly the silence was shattered by the first of the incoming shells. Instinctively, Mark ducked his head. The shells fell short, confirming that his front line was now out of range.

He stood up. Grbesa, leading his 'A' Company up the ridge saw him, and peeled off in his direction, while his men continued to take up their new positions.

"Have you any orders, Major?" the tired soldier asked, saluting. Mark responded by handing him the glasses. Niew swept the landscape, and handed back the glasses. "Their infantry are there all right, Major. How many I would not like to say." Niew hitched his weapon higher on his shoulder.

Mark took another look, freezing at what he saw. Like an army of ants the whole landscape seemed to move, line after line of previously concealed infantry advancing towards them, preceded by a solid line of tanks.

"When's the next bus home?" Mark breathed, his legs shaking. His mother had been right, one war should have been enough. Well, now it was too late. All for the sake of money. A lot of good that would do him with a bullet up the arse.

"I beg your pardon, Sir?"

Mark ignored his CSM How could he explain why he had come to this accursed country, not that the wee man did not already know? Money?

"Runner to me!" Mark yelled, throwing his glasses back to Niew.

A breathless corporal hurried to Mark's side and Mark thrust a torn sheet of paper at him. "Take this to the wireless shack immediately, Corporal." He swung again to his sergeant. "Well? What do you see?"

"It's no side-show, sir, this is the real thing. With your permission, major, I best get back to my men." Grbesa thrust the glasses back.

"Where did the tanks come from, Sergeant?" Mark asked, as Niew made to move off. "You saw nothing of them on patrol?" It was a question he need not have asked.

There was the same desperation in the mercenary's voice as Niew had heard at the roadblock back at Pienera. "Where those tanks came from, is irrelevant now, Major" Niew replied attempting to keep his own voice calm. "It's where they are going that should concern you." The squat soldier took a step closer to his Major. "However, it is my guess those tanks were there all the time." Uncomprehending, Mark listened to Niew's deduction. "We were not looking for *tanks*! And had we done so, it would most likely have been in all the wrong places. They were not in the mountains, but here in the flatlands. Most probably buried, or at least concealed on the lower slopes of the mountain. We just did not believe, Tetek had any tanks in the first place. We missed them because we were not looking for them!"

Shell bursts from the advancing tanks were now landing close to the ridge. Mark focused a glazed stare on Niew's right shoulder in the realisation what the sergeant had said was true. "I sent word to Scurk informing him this was no diversion, but the main thrust," he said almost in a whisper. "I only hope he believes me, and sends reinforcements as soon as possible. If not..." Mark shifted his gaze beyond the sergeant. "Then the ba's burst," he said under his breath.

As Niew Grbesa scurried off to rejoin his Company, Mark spoke hurriedly to the corporal carrying his field telephone. "Order, Major.... Hell !" he swore. "I don't know his bloody name!"

"Who Sir?" the corporal asked, wrinkling his brows.

A tank shell exploded on the ridge top, blowing a machine gun crew into the air, another hitting a mortar section close by.

"Give the Gunnery officer these co-ordinates," he yelled at the man above the noise of the exploding shells. "Tell him to commence firing. When you've done that, get on to the Tank Commander, inform him he has to withdraw to 0019! Got it Corporal? When you've done that, all company commanders to follow our tanks and dig in, with the exception of all gun crews."
The corporal looked stunned and it showed.

"I know soldier, we've only just dug in here, but I did not expect to be facing the *whole* of Tetek's bloody army, complete with T-34's. And those tanks are much bigger than ours!" Mark explained sharply.

A breathless runner from the wireless shack handed Mark a message. "Congratulations *Colonel*," the man grinned.

Mark took the chit, swearing out loud, as he read. "Believe attack in your area only a diversion. Main thrust will come my Sector. Hold your position. Promoting you acting Colonel, in the field. Congratulations and good luck. Scurk."

"Any reply, Sir?" the man asked in a tone usually associated with that of a telegram boy.

Mark threw him a withering look. "Bugger off, Private." The soldier grinned and hurriedly departed.

If this is a diversion, Mark thought, then I'd hate to face the real thing. Already, his line was crumbling. Where the hell was his artillery? As if in answer to his question, the first of their own shells exploded close to the leading tank. "Up twenty," he heard himself say. And, as if the spotter had had the same thought, the next shell found its mark, tank and soldiers crouching behind it lost in a haze of smoke and fire.

Mark counted the enemy tanks Tetek was not supposed to possess, they outnumbered his own by three to one. And unless he was mistaken, would continue to advance until they were under the lee of the ridge, where they would find safety from his own heavy guns.

The same private found him again, and scrambled to his side. Mark eyed him warily. "Don't tell me, I've been made General!"

The soldier looked at him, a smile crossing his face. "No Sir," he chuckled. Then seriously, "I got your orders through, Sir," he confirmed.

Advancing enemy tanks continued to shell the ridge, their infantry crouched in comparative safety behind them. His own artillery found more targets: tanks burst into flames: infantry were hurled into the air. Gradually fire from the ridge top abated as his orders to retreat were obeyed.

Mark slid down beside his runner. "Tell the wireless shack to get going."

Shells landed in the hollow behind the ridge catching stretcher-bearers in the open. He swiped dirt off his pad, and scribbled a note ripping it from his pad. "Get them to send this first. Then get the hell out of it yourself, soldier."

The first of the enemy tanks started up the ridge, anti-tank guns blasting them as they exposed their soft underbellies to the slope. Like some prehistoric monster mortally wounded one fell back, as another came on, its machine gun raking the crest. More tanks on fire, with others taking their place. Mortar teams lobbing bombs into the midst of enemy soldiers scrambling up the slope. It was now time to leave.

Mark ran. He ran through a gap in a stone wall, then veered to his right, putting a hedgerow between himself and the line of enemy fire. A machine gun stitched a swathe of fire through the grass a little to his left, helping him on his way.

Smoke from burning haystacks helped conceal their withdrawal. He ran past two stretcher-bearers carrying a wounded man. What would they have thought had they known it was their commanding officer running passed them like the clappers?

240

A few metres on, he caught up with Grbesa. The soldier recognised him as he drew level. "Take my advice Major Stewart , and quit acting the hero. You have a command to take care of," he rasped. "Your place is at H.Q. directing operations, not running around where no one can find you."

Stung by the rebuke, Mark blushed. His consternation all the more apparent that it had come from a N.C.O., and to compound his embarrassment, what the man had said was perfectly true, but be damned if he was going to admit it though. And as they ran over a wooden bridge, Mark spat out the corner of his mouth. "Someone's got to stay behind to prevent them ramming a tank gun up your arse," he rejoined. "And it's *Colonel* to you Sergeant."

"Well a *Colonel* should know better. And as far as my arse is concerned, it's only obeying its *Colonel's* orders!" Niew gasped back caustically.

Mark looked away to hide his grin. Then picking up his pace left the gasping sergeant behind.

Officers ran about Mark's farmhouse headquarters like headless chickens. There was so much organising to be done, which he did not believe he could do successfully before the next enemy attack. He was not, he decided, cut out to be a Napoleon. *If only his mammy could see him now*, he thought...*a colonel!* It could only have happened here. But for how long if he made a mess of it?

Gradually, thanks to some staff officers who clearly knew their duty, some semblance of order was established. In truth, Mark would dearly have loved to have been at 'the front' to see for himself at first hand what he was up against, but after his running rebuke from his former company CSM he had decided to remain in constant contact with his officers.

Mark's present line of defence was a low range of hillocks not much higher than the ridge where he'd made his first inglorious stand. However, as before, the enemy had to attack across open ground. He studied the map spread out on the kitchen table. In the background the ever present sound of the enemy tanks opening up on their positions, to be instantly answered by their own artillery.

Half an hour ago, Sector Commanders on either flank had informed him that, as his Sector had been pushed back, they too would have to retreat, in order to deny the enemy establishing a salient.

Mark poured over the map. On his left a shallow meandering river ran between him and Sector 3. A small valley protected his right. If his map reading was correct, a cross-roads lay some twenty kilometres to his rear. Should Tetek – and he was sure it was Tetek he was up against – reach the cross-roads, that General would have nothing more to do than swing right, on a road that would let him mop up the Government forces from the flank.

"Tetek, you are brilliant! You have drawn most of our forces away to the West where Jakofcic and Scurk thought your main attack would come from. Now here I am facing your full might with what forces are left to me." The sudden silence in the room, telling him he had spoken out loud.

By midday, Mark realised he could not hold the line much longer. Through a broken window in the farmhouse, he watched the wounded being carried back, intermingled with tired troops plodding wearily back to their former battle positions after a short rest. Still Tetek attacked.

Mark had already worked out his third defensive position, a village nestling between a low range of hills...the last before the cross-roads. For he knew to retreat from there would leave the road open for Tetek to mount his flanking attack on the entire Government forces.

The mercenary sank despondently into a seat. How had all this come about? A few short days ago, the entire Nation believed the war was almost over, the PFF beaten and Tetek forced into surrender or capture. Now the exact opposite appeared to be the case. Would this same Nation blame *him* for the failure? For fail he surely must.

"Sir! Sir!" The voice brought him back. "A message from General Scurk, Sir!"

Vacantly, Mark stared up at the man. "Read it to me soldier. It can only be more bad news."

"On the contrary sir, the general is sending you reinforcements. Tanks. Also the heavy artillery he had been expecting for himself, to be redirected to you." The wireless operator's eyes gleamed with hope and excitement.

Mark drew a deep breath. Why did the news nor excite him or fill him with renewed hope? It was because there was no way he could hold out with what little resources he had left. Even if he had, how could he against a man of Tetek's genius?

Yet, how was Tetek able to sustain his attacks? As with each Government retreat, his supply line must grow steadily longer. Mark stared hard at the map as if hoping the answer would suddenly jump out at him. He moved his pencil aside. The name leaped out at him.

"Corporal.! Get me Company Sergeant Major Niew Grbesa, from 'A' Company, at the double," he shouted excitedly, as if had finally found an answer to an unfathomable puzzle.

It took the soldier fully twenty minutes to locate and bring the indomitable sergeant to Mark. The brevet colonel scarcely able to contain his excitement as Niew entered the room.

"Sergeant!" he began, his voice unintentionally loud. "I believe I know how to halt...no I will rephrase that...at least contain Tetek, until Scurk's tanks arrive...and his heavy guns..."

"Not that fallacy, Major...Colonel!" Niew corrected himself with a frown.

"What fallacy, Sergeant?" Mark asked, refusing to let his newly acquired optimism be dashed.

"The one about the heavy guns, Sir. I've heard about those for weeks...months, but I've yet to lay eyes on them."

Mark nodded impatiently. "Okay! Okay! Lets forget about them for the moment. More importantly, I brought you here to discuss Tetek's lines of supply. You've patrolled those mountains more than most?" Mark jabbed his pencil in the direction of the mountains. "How do *you* think Tetek could have hidden the amount of equipment he's throwing at us, without you ever having found at least some of it up there?" Mark cut the sergeant off before he could form a reply. "And don't tell me it was hidden down here. There is no place or places big enough for all that amount of weaponry."

Shrugging his shoulders, Niew calmly took a cup of coffee from a corporal. "So why bother to ask me, Colonel, when you are just bursting to tell me the answer yourself?"

Mark stood up. Putting a foot on his chair he leaned on it grinning. "Okay! So I'm a genius. Do you remember that defile a few months back? The one we got caught in?" Mark asked, growing serious.

"The one called the Gap, Colonel?" Niew asked, showing no excitement as he sipped his coffee.

"Exactly, Sergeant. That is how Tetek is getting his supplies down here. They are coming through that very same defile!"

Taking his foot off the chair, Mark took a few paces towards the window, swinging round dramatically to face his CSM "We...*you* precisely, could stop him."

Niew put down the steaming cup. "I knew it had to be something like that. I did not think you ordered me here to sample your choice of coffee, Colonel. But why me?"

Mark's eyes gleamed. "Because, Sergeant, you are the only one who can get up there and stop him. You know where the chimney is. It was you who found it. Once up there you could halt anything coming through that defile!"

Niew stared blankly at his commanding officer. "I'd need a strong enough force. Yet one not too large as to be detected before we got there...or we'd be sunk. Heavily armed of course."

"Of course," Mark agreed, nodding enthusiastically. "Mortars, machine guns...anything you require, CSM"

"How about a miracle, Colonel?" Niew replied, tongue in cheek.

"Might take a bit longer to arrange," Mark grinned. "Then you'll do it?"

"Have I a choice? Or is it strictly voluntary?"

Mark looked gravely at the CSM "About as much choice as I had to volunteer to command this lot, Niew," he said softly.

Niew's expression softened. It was one of the rare occasions that he'd felt compassion for a man who merely fought in his country for money. Or perhaps it was because that same man had also called him by his Christian name for the very first time.

It was as far as he could take the trucks without the risk of being seen. Niew hurried the men into the woods. There were four hours of daylight left, and he had to be well into the mountains by nightfall.

Stewart had given him what remained of 'A' Company, the mercenary having used his newly acquired rank to 'commandeer' mortar teams and enough men from Sector 3, to bring his total force to fifty.

"A hard climb, Captain?" the officer asked.

Wiping sweat from his brow the older man nodded.

The officer found his position uncomfortable. That trumped up mercenary, Stewart had informed him in no uncertain terms that, as Grbesa knew the terrain better than anyone, he was to rely totally on the CSM In short, this uncouth N.C.O. was in charge, in all but name.

"How far to this defile you call the Gap, Sergeant Major?" he asked, in a tone that left Niew in no doubt as to his feelings at having to rely on an enlisted man for all his information.

"We shall not reach it tonight, Sir," Niew answered respectfully. The last thing he wanted was a clash of personalities over rank. "Very good, CSM carry on."

"Yes sir." Niew turned his attention away from the departing officer to the road beneath. With any luck, Scurk's tanks should be passing down there by this time tomorrow to reinforce Stewart, by which time they also should have reached the Gap. He hoped.

Chapter15

Approximately one hundred kilometres west from where CSM Grbesa looked down upon the brown road, the man code named Pavel, patiently waited in the seclusion of a small wood.

Having swept the meadow land bordering the road, he let the field glasses hang by their straps and moved back to the line of heavy artillery deeper in the woods.

Pavel was proud of his men and what they had achieved. It had been nice of the Government forces to assemble the guns for them. He clicked his teeth in amusement.

Thanks to Miro's thoroughness at having discovered the importation of the gun parts in the first place, they'd known where to look for them. Then, when they were finally assembled and heading for the front, they had simply ambushed the entire convoy.

Pavel clicked his teeth again. Vaclaw would have to reassess his view of Miro when he heard all about this. Vaclaw, the poor sod, had been left behind to cause as much trouble as he could in the Capital, but nothing like the trouble he hoped to cause here, Pavel laughed.

An old artillery man himself, Pavel's main concern was that they had not had the opportunity to test the guns, as having done so would have given away their position to any passing patrols. The first chance would be when they sighted the tanks.

Pavel waved reassuringly to the nearest man, though he was secretly apprehensive of the prospective shortcomings of some of the gunners and their loaders. Well it was too late now, he conceded. The test now was to ensure that the tanks did not reinforce Government forces opposing Tetek's main attack in the east. He swept the road again, confident they could stop the tanks getting through.

His men were in high spirits. And why not? A few days ago they had regarded their resistance as a last defiant stand against a Government and a Nation determined to crush them into oblivion and their right to vote as they pleased. Now they had just learned, Tetek had almost achieved the unthinkable. Not only had he contained the mighty Government offensive but had actually turned it and, by all accounts, was counter attacking himself. And, if all was to be believed, now had *them* on the run!

Pavel walked to the edge of the woods, scanning the meadow before him. Government forces, he hoped, would be scouring all roads north leading to the front, in the belief that was where they'd be heading with the captured guns. Instead, he had pushed south, but this was as far as he dared come.

Raising his glasses, Pavel took in the rustic scene of a farmer working with his horse and cart in the field a half kilometre away, on the opposite side of the road from the woods. The farmer was one of his men, and another dozen or so more lay hidden just beyond the crest. Pavel hoped the sight of such a normal domestic scene might prevent any patrol from searching the woods. This, and the fact, patrols might not stop to search every patch of woods, so far in their rear.

Pavel switched to the meadow on his own side of the road, sweeping to a clump of bushes on a slight rise to his left, where his observer lay hidden. Although Pavel knew his guns could out range those of the tanks, his dilemma was in deciding whether he should take a chance on hitting the rear tank, thus preventing the column from retreating back out of range. But taking into account, they had not fired the guns, and the unknown quality of his gunnery crews, he may have to settle on trying to hit the tanks whenever they came in sight, which would also mean the tanks would be capable of hitting his own artillery.

Pavel picked his way back through the dead scrub to his guns. A man with a patch over his eye, stacking ammunition stopped him. "What happens if infantry convoys come first comrade, do we stop them?"

Pavel chewed on his unlit cigar. "No comrade, General Tetek's orders are to halt the tanks at all cost" he cocked an ear. "Something's coming up the road."

The field telephone rang. A soldier held the receiver to his ear. "Two despatch riders coming this way comrade, also a truck about a kilometre back. According to our spotter, it looks like a patrol," he said, addressing Pavel.

"Quick! Everyone down!" Pavel shouted, waving a hand.

Two minutes later, two outriders appeared. Pavel held his breath. Would they pass? One threw the farmer a friendly wave as he drew near. Then almost immediately the sound of their engines changed and, much to Pavel's dismay, both pulled up at the edge of the woods.

The man with the patch who lay a few feet away from Pavel looked at him anxiously, awaiting his orders. Pavel scraped at the dead leaves with a finger. Should these two search the woods and discover the guns, then it was all over. He had not enough men to hold off infantry. Even if the despatch riders did not come across them or their guns, they still might see the trucks and their own motor bikes disguised as a Government convoy, which they had used to get them here. Pavel waited.

The first rider had dismounted and was walking in their direction. Suddenly he changed direction, and was hidden from their view behind a tree. The man with the eye patch grinned at Pavel. "Sure makes me want to go as well, comrade," he whispered grinning.

The sound of a patrol truck drawing up diverted their attention from the man behind the tree.

"Now they are all at it!" the same man whispered to Pavel as the soldiers alighted from the truck. "They think this is a bloody toilet."

"As long as they think this is all it is," Pavel whispered back, intently watching the soldiers running into the woods. It would only need one searching for a little more privacy to come closer.

It seemed ages to Pavel before the toilet users had gone. He rose, drawing a hand across his brow. "Those guys are the forward patrol of a convoy, it may well be an infantry one, so keep your heads well down 'till they pass."

However, Pavel was wrong. No further infantry conveys were to pass that day.

Another hour and it would be dark. Pavel put down his mess tin. Had he got it wrong? Were they in fact on the wrong road? He scratched at his arm in perplexity. No tanks, no infantry?

"Comrade! Our spotter says a convoy is headed this way. Two dispatch riders out in front as usual." The operator's voice was nondescript. Pavel nodded. "Here we go again."

The noise of the motor bikes drew rapidly closer. Once again, they halted at their woods.

Pavel watched as one made off to relieve himself, while the other took more than a usual interest in the woods. This dispatch rider walked slowly towards them, carefully watching where he was stepping, his head turning all the while.

A sudden shout from his companion who had completed his toilet made him stop and turn.

"That's right, soldier," Pavel whispered, "you tell him there's been hundreds of patrols passed here today, so why should he want to bother searching here now?"

Despite his companion urging him to be on their way, the inquisitive soldier remaining unconvinced, resumed his search.

Tapping the man nearest him on the shoulder to follow him, Pavel crawled behind a tree and pulled his knife, motioning to the man to do the same, now certain the inquisitive outrider was determined to search further into the woods.

They would have to be quick, and silent. The truck patrolling in front of the convoy would be here soon. Pavel touched his companion on the shoulder and pointed to the inquisitive soldier's companion. The man nodded, and together they rose, and had crossed the intervening space before either soldier could bring their machine pistol to bear.

Pavel almost missed his aim at the look in the inquisitive soldier's eyes. It was a man he had fought alongside with in the mountains against the Nazis, and was strangely disturbed to hear his real name spoken on the dying man's lips as he drove home the blade.

For a moment, as he lowered the dead man to the ground, a kaleidoscope of incidents flashed through Pavel's brain, of good and bad times shared together. Never in his wildest dreams ever having thought that some day he would have to kill this man. Pavel dragged his eyes away from the dead man's face. To have fought the Nazis to be free, only now to be destroying one another. Pavel cursed all politics and their so called righteous politicians.

"What now, Pavel?" his comrade was asking, having despatched the second rider.

Pavel tore himself back to the present. "Leave them here. Help me get those two bikes away from the side of the road."

"Comrade Pavel!" One of his men came running. "The troop convoy is on its way. Our spotter says the tanks are not far behind!"

Pavel nodded, pushing the motor bike into the undergrowth. "Let's hope the first truck guarding the convoy keeps on going after their dispatch riders," Pavel gasped. "Hopefully, by the time they realise they are not in front of them, we will have dealt with those damned tanks!"

Pavel was right. The trucks, assuming their outriders were still ahead, kept on going.

A few minutes later, the rumbling grew louder. Pavel bit hard on his cigar and swung the glasses towards the tanks. "0119 when I give the order to fire, comrade," he said calmly and bit harder into his cigar.

The man beside him put the field telephone to his ear, nervously awaiting the command.

"Now!" Pavel shouted with a demonstrative downward thrust of his hand.

The guns opened up. At least the guns worked, Pavel thought, although the first salvo had overshot the mark. The tanks came on.

Pavel called an adjustment to his field operator. He clenched his teeth on his unlit cigar, worried by the time it had taken his inexperienced gunners to reload.

The next salvo landed closer to the target, earth erupted skywards, and a tank slued sideways.

Three more rounds, four at the most, before the tanks found their range. Already they were deploying to right and left of the woods. Pavel shouted out more alterations to range and direction. A few more tanks were hit.

A few seconds later the first of the enemy shells fell short of the woods. Pavel ran to his gunners, encouraging them to load faster. A shell ripped through branches overhead. He shouted further instructions. The men worked the guns furiously in answer to his altered instructions, hitting and destroying the oncoming tanks as they drew closer.

A tank on their left flank smashed through the undergrowth hitting a gun battery. Pavel spat out his chewed up cigar, shouting out an order to the gunner nearest him. He fired, overshooting its mark. Pavel was beside himself with impatience as he waited for the gun to fire again. At last it opened up, setting the tank ablaze. He let out a long low whistle of relief. The tanks were getting just that bit too close.

Pavel knew he could not depress his heavy guns sufficiently should the tanks draw closer; therefore, he had to halt them within the next few hundred metres.

Now that shells were bursting all around them he was afraid the inexperienced gunners might give way. He ran down the line, exhorting a greater effort, determined that having captured these Government guns, they should not fail in their objective.

"Load! Reload!" he bellowed, helping to pass the shells from the nearest gun.

Nearby, a shell hit a gun crew. Ammunition exploded, tearing into neighbouring crews. Men ran screaming for the rear of the woods, the battle blown from their minds by their all consuming pain.

Pavel ran for the next gun, tripping over a branch in his haste. A tree crashed down on the gun he had been heading for, forcing him to run back to the gun he had left, where he found the loader already dead.

Cursing a government whose corruption had caused so much misery in his native land, Pavel rammed a shell in to the breach, his gunner sending the missile into the leading tank. Slapping him encouragingly on the back, they changed places, Pavel's experiencing telling by the number of targets hit.

The enemy tanks were now coming on at them from both flanks. Pavel shouted orders to the gunners. More tanks were hit, but the enemy too, had found their range. A few metres away, a gun crew lay a tangled mess of flesh and bone amongst their twisted gun. He snapped a quick look through his glasses, there were only seven tanks remaining. They had done their duty.

Above the whine of shells, Pavel made out the chatter of his own machine gun from the farmhouse. Time to leave. There were only two guns left.

"Right you men, time to get yourselves out of here!" he shouted to what was left of the crews. At his command, men sprang away from their charges, helping wounded comrades to the trucks that waited behind the woods.

Pavel adjusted the sights of his gun. "Time to go, comrade," he panted to his elderly loader.

Saying nothing, the man passed Pavel another shell. Pavel reloaded, repeating the order. This time the man looked up at him. "How far do you think I'd get comrade?" He tapped his hollow leg, the sound tinny.

Pavel nodded his understanding. "Then let's find out if we can finish them, before they can finish us, comrade," he snorted, jumping out of the way of the ejected shell case.

"Sure comrade. Can you think of anything better to do to pass the time on such a piss wet awful day?"

Mark had been wrong to have relied upon reinforcements reaching him by nightfall. All day they had succeeded in keeping Tetek at bay, but now regrettably he must order a further retreat.

Mark turned to his aide. "Advise all company commanders to commence withdrawal by sections," he ordered.

As his aide hurried off to carry out his orders, Mark sank down on a wooden bench by the side of the unlit fire. He was tired. He lacked the necessary experience to command so many men. Give him a gun and point him at the enemy that was about the limit of his ability. His entire experience had been on taking orders, not giving them. His real rank was about equal to that of Second Lieutenant, if not lower. Only in this particular theatre of war could he ever have transpired to anything as elevated as colonel.

A sergeant, with more questions, hovered over him, which he did his best to answer. When the soldier had gone, Mark slumped his head on his chest.

It was all really up to Niew now, he thought. Should Tetek still be at liberty to get his supplies through the Gap, there was very little he could do to oppose him. He'd always scorned staff wallahs, but since taking command he'd have to reappraise his thinking. It was they who kept him informed, indeed were responsible for maintaining his own continual line of supply.

Mark stared vacantly into the empty hearth. He was no Napoleon as he had so rightly assessed. His short, but involuntary, command had amounted to nothing more than a continual series of retreats, and how to train his men to walk backwards.

Wearily, the Scot got to his feet, telling himself that given the circumstances, he had very few alternatives. He was facing Tetek's entire force, even though an old woman like General Scurk did not see it. He was sending him heavy artillery and Tanks? He'd believe that when he saw them, Mark thought with disdain. He *was* facing Tetek's entire force; of this, he was certain. As certain as he was that

Third Lanark would not win the Scottish Cup this season...or the next for that matter.

The jaded soldier crossed to the maps spread out on the kitchen table. His next defence would be the little village north of the crossroads. Here, he must make his last stand. Perhaps he should have been named Custer, he thought wryly. To retreat from this position would leave Tetek free to swing west and role up the entire Government line from the flank.

A sergeant placed a cup of coffee on the table as Mark drew his finger down the map. About fifty kilometres south of the village stood the picturesque town of Sylna in the valley of the same name. Mark sipped the hot coffee, visualising the little town as he had last remembered it, a little over a year ago.

It had a lovely little Baroque church, he remembered. What was the name of that girl again? He smiled at the recollection of sunny days, peaceful walks in the meadows and long passionate nights, before the rumble of trucks jerked him back to reality.

Carrying a heavy basket in each hand, the old woman dragged herself laboriously up the narrow cobbled street. Mark watched. Stopping at a door, the exhausted women gave the soldier a despairing shake of her head, and he felt like a scolded child. She shook her head again, as if to say 'could he not go and play his game in someone else's street?'

An old man suddenly appeared from another doorway, giving the newly appointed commanding officer a long sad look that said he'd seen all this before, and, as before, it would achieve nothing.

"Sergeant!" Mark called out, angered and strangely disturbed by the action of the old couple. The soldier trotted over to him. "I believe my orders were to clear this village?" Mark's eyes blazed.

The sergeant looked to where the old couple stood, then back at his commanding officer. "Yes Sir. But some...especially the old ones, keep on coming back," he hastened to explain.

"Prevent their return, Sergeant, if you please. Or perhaps 'B' Company is unable to restrain an old man with a pipe, and a decrepit old woman wielding a shopping basket?" he relied caustically.

"No Sir.... I mean yes Sir. I'll see to it right away, sir" the mortified sergeant gurgled.

Watching the man depart, Mark drew a hand across his brow, ashamed by this unwarranted slur on the sergeant, and a body of men, who had shown the utmost resilience in keeping a superior force at bay. He must be cracking up to have spoken to a Master Sergeant the way he had. Not good for morale at all old boy, he said to himself in upper class English. Not good at all.

Further self incriminations were driven from Mark's mind by the first exploding shells and he started to run down the narrow cobbled street knocking over a flower pot on a window sill in his haste to reach the corner, where he saw that the enemy tanks by making the best of available cover were already bombarding the outskirts of the village. He flashed a look to his left flank where he'd positioned his artillery on a small escarpment. It would be up to them to halt the speeding armour.

Nearby, a shell dropped through a grey slated roof, blowing windows and doors out and into the street. Mark hoped the two stubborn ancients would now have the sense to get their old legs moving.

The tanks drew closer, with crouching infantry behind them. Mark ducked down behind a discarded cart, praying that the tanks would swing to the right, and gambling on their not wanting to cross the open space of the village football field. A shell blew one of the white goal posts into the air. "Penalty" a soldier shouted.
Smiling at the humour, Mark thought of when, or if, he was ever likely to see Hampden Park again.

The houses on the cobbled street where he'd seen the old couple were ablaze. Just then his own artillery opened up, supported by the infantry, firing at the short lines of enemy soldiers darting and weaving ever closer to the village edge. Still the tanks came on. Soon they would be firing point blank at the first row of houses and the men stationed there.

Suddenly an enemy tank was ablaze, then another, and another, until the approaches to the football field were engulfed in smoke and burning armour.

Mystified, Mark searched quickly around for this unexpected source of deliverance. He knew it could not be his own tanks, as he had sent them south, in the firm belief he could not hold this present position for any great length of time. Also, he had pinned his last attempt on defending his Sector closer to the cross-roads. The unmistakable grind of track on stone, told him instinctively that tank reinforcements had arrived.

With the arrival of the first of the long hoped for reinforcements, Mark, now back in his makeshift H.Q., sat once more pouring over his maps, and gambling on being just about able to hold Tetek until Scurk attacked from the west, and Ziotkowski, once out of the mountains from the east. It was here the new tank commander found him.

"Quite a welcome sound your tanks made, commander," Mark greeted the newcomer warmly. "We could not have beaten off that last attack without you." He had never been so glad to see anyone in his life, well almost anyone, except maybe that lassie from Govan.

Mark's happiness and optimism was destined not to last.

"Thank you sir. If only there were more of us."

"Why? How many do you have, Commander?" Mark asked, feeling his optimism short-lived and silently praying for no more setbacks.

"Five sir, since the ambush."

"You were ambushed on your way from the south?" Mark asked incredulously. "By whom, Commander?

The soldier studied his feet, while his new C.O. stared up at him from his makeshift desk. " I believe by the new twelve heavy guns the PFF captured from us a few days back."

Mark tried to control the weakness he felt in the pit of his stomach. "Not those newly acquired heavies we bragged about?" Then as if to himself. "Not those Scurk was sending me? Not captured?"

The young tank commander drew his eyes away from his feet. "If it is any consolation, Sir, we destroyed all of them, but we lost nine tanks in the process."

Mark did not reply. Instead, he asked, "how many infantry are on the way?"

"None as yet Sir. We had only a small escort. They should be – or what is left of them – should be here shortly. We left them to clear up, and help with the wounded. Personally, I thought you'd be grateful for any help. So I pushed on." There was an unmistakable note of resentment in the young officer's voice as he answered.

The mercenary colonel was in no mood to be appreciative. For a minuscule stretch of time, he had visualised holding Tetek, and in doing so hoped to prevent a major catastrophe. Now here he was back to running away from the man. "Very well, Commander," he sighed. "Get your tanks to this co-ordinate," He pinned a finger on the map on the table, "where you will find *my* entire tank force....all nine of them. Wait there for further orders."

"If you please Sir!"

The Scot looked up.

Plainly disconcerted, the officer stood stiffly at attention. Mark's silence further contributed to his discomfiture. "In our haste to reinforce you Sir, neither my men or I have eaten all night Sir. Is it possible to do so before leaving for our new positions?"

Mark glared up at him. "No it is *not*, commander! I am expecting an attack at anytime. Which if I am in the least fortunate to repulse, will mean an immediate withdrawal before the enemy can regroup and counterattack! By which time, I hope I shall be in my new position, ably supported by my loyal tanks! Do I make myself clear!"

Mark had not meant to regale an officer in front of enlisted men and felt a twinge of remorse as the wireless operator dropped his pad, and the mess orderly, on his way with a steaming mug of soup for the berated tank commander, did a rapid about turn.

Obviously, he should be grateful for any tanks having got through at all. "Once you are in position, you may then rest and eat. If there is time, that is," he concluded, a little kinder.

"Yes Sir. Thank you Sir." Spinning smartly on his heel, the aggrieved young officer headed quickly for the door.

Niew Grbesa helped the soldier over the narrow ledge, then lay back gasping on the hard rock. Sweat ran into his eyes and he snapped a quick look at his watch. It was almost noon. It had taken them longer than he had expected.

The captain threw himself down by his side. "How far to this Gap of yours, CSM?" The officer's voice so hoarse Niew thought he was about to choke.

"I reckon it will take us another two hours at least."

Fighting for breath, the officer levered himself to his feet. "Then we best not sit on our arses, soldier."

Niew rose, muttering what he thought of all officers and their mothers, and signalled the men to follow him, his order more visual than verbal.

They travelled for close on an hour, ascending and descending ridge after ridge, at times Niew fearing he had lost his bearings. At last, he gave the exhausted men the order to rest.

"Not lost are we, CSM?" the captain asked sarcastically, standing over the weary soldier.

"Nope. Should not be too long now. So may I suggest you sit your polished arse down a spell Sir, and rest it. Also, I should not speak too loudly, we're quite close."

Niew's rancour in front of the men caught the officer by surprise. He searched desperately for a suitable retort, then rapidly changed his mind at the squat little man's malevolent glare.

Niew's company and the two enemy soldiers ran into one another without realising it. Unable to believe his eyes at the struggling line of soldiers so high up the mountainside, now only a few metres away from where he stood, the PFF soldier, who, was nothing more than a boy, fumbled with the bolt of his rifle, while his equally young companion died under the knife of a quick acting CSM. His bolt now free, the boy swung it on the nearest soldier, at the same time as the captain launched himself at him, both men disappearing behind an outcrop of rock.

Two quick strides took Niew to the outcrop as an arm appeared grasping at the rock, and he caught a brief of glimpse of his senior officer before he again slid out of sight. The sergeant swung round. On the far side of the rock, the scared face of the boy soldier raised his rifle to fire, his high pitched shriek echoing around the mountainside as a private's bayonet caught him in the back.

"Quick let's get out of here. Let's hope there's no one else about to hear that scream," Niew said firmly.

"What about the captain, Serg?" The lanky soldier asked, extracting the bayonet from the boy's back.

"He's dead, soldier, and so will we be, if we don't get the hell out of here."

"The Reds must be getting bloody hard up, Serg, those two were only boys," a soldier muttered, sympathetically.

"Two boys with guns, Private, and had they fired them, you might not now be feeling quite so magnanimous." Niew pointed to the corpses. "Throw them in amongst the rocks and cover them as best you can." Adding at the look of disbelief from the soldiers, "Yes, the captain too. What else do you expect me to do, hold a funeral ceremony and fire a volley into the air for good measure? Come on, get your arses moving," he threw at them impatiently.

Niew's men scrambled, slid and groped their way over the next few ridges, desperate to put distance between themselves and the dead men: the CSM ever retracing his steps to help with the heavier load of the mortar teams

After awhile his forward scout came back. "Over there!" he pointed triumphantly. "The Gap. It's over there!"

Niew grinned into the eager face. "Well done soldier. So let's put an end once and for all to Comrade Tetek's little game," he winked.

Niew signalled to two men to head for the ridge overlooking the chimney, while the remainder of them waited. A few minutes later one appeared framed against the skyline, a PFF beret on his head.

Niew gave the command. "Come on let's go."

Now with the ridge top in their possession, it was safe for them to make their way down through the chimney. For a few fearful moments, Niew wondered whether the aperture might prove to be too narrow for some of the heavier equipment, but with a little luck and a lot of pushing and shoving from the company, they succeeded in safely maneuvering it all to the bottom.

Once at the foot, bent double, Niew ran for the edge of the defile, where he threw himself flat to look down at the army of ants, busily transporting every conceivable type of equipment imperative to waging war.

A soldier slid down beside him. "Not many soldiers down there, CSM," he commented in a voice tinged with relief.

Niew ran an eye over the hive of industry below, where women staggered under the loads they carried, or helped push handcarts bogged down in ankle deep mud. Here and there children coaxed laden mules along with a tickle of their sticks, and old men drove swaying creaking carts all intent on getting their charges through the defile. He looked away saddened and yet proud of what he had witnessed.

A few short years ago, it had been these same people who had stood against the Nazi tyranny. These were still his people, his countrymen. Divided they may be by theology, but as yet each were striving for the same end to make their country a better place. Here, the similarity ended. Those people, those P.F.F, had no more right to enforce their ideology on anyone by force of arms, any more than had their former Nazi oppressors.

"You're wrong, Corporal, they are *all* soldiers down there," he said sadly, and crawled away from the ridge edge.

Ten minutes later, Niew had his men in position. Taking a sergeant aside, he detailed his plan to him in the event of his having to take command. "This is the widest part of the defile, Sergeant, close on two kilometres I'd say." He pointed to the hills opposite. "I don't think Tetek has any heavies that could reach us from there."

Niew pointed to each end of the defile in turn. "I've placed mortars above both entrances at the narrowest points. We'll let their supplies in, but not out. I've also positioned machine guns at both ends on the lower ridge, to prevent us from being outflanked when they realise what has happened to their supplies. Those on the ridge above, will support us with additional fire, should we require it. Any questions?"

"No, Sergeant Major." The man shrugged complacently. "I don't foresee any problems. We should have the job done and be off this mountain by evening."

Niew hid a smile at his sergeant's quiet optimism. "Somehow I don't think so. Not unless you have a dirty great gun hidden somewhere to block that passage...and I don't mean what you use to scare the women with either!"

Holding his field glasses with one hand, Niew swept the extremity of the defile, to where a caravan of mules wound a slow laborious way over the boulder strewn floor. For a moment, he lingered fractionally on a mule with a mind of its own, that had trotted out of line, and was being promptly brought to heel by a young girl wearing a blue scarf. She was pretty, he thought. she should be courting her young man in some peaceful village, instead of up here. He blew out his cheeks, sweeping back to the narrow bottleneck at the near end of the defile, in time to see the sudden appearance of three half-track trucks.

"Fire!" Niew shouted, dropping his arm, and letting out an oath as the first mortar landed short. The second, however, having found some ammunition boxes, blew mules and their unfortunate drivers into the air, the remaining salvos helping to send the half tracks scurrying back the way they had come, like two frightened animals cut off from their lair. The mortars following them until they were out of range behind an outcrop of rock. All the while, bombs pounded into the defile, amid screams of terrified animals and humans.

Niew ran the length of the ridge. Their own machine gun was now under fire as the enemy fought their way up from the defile floor. He barked an order. A platoon ran to the gun crew's aid, pouring fire on the ascending men until there was no one left. Niew raised his hand and the firing ceased.

When the smoke had cleared, only dead and dying lay on the valley floor. Niew searched for, but there was no sign of the pretty girl with the blue scarf.

Mark rode between the line of soldiers marching on either side of the country road. Craning his neck, he caught a glimpse of the burning village behind. He swung back to his driver. "Drive to the opposite side of the woods, Corporal."

The driver edged through the gate, gunning the jeep over the churned up field towards the woods. Mark sank deeper into his seat. For men who had experienced nothing other than retreat for the entirety of his command, they had shown a remarkable spirit.

He pulled a cigarette from the packet, offering one to the driver, who shook his head.

Mark thought, poor sods, they believe this is the last stand, and that there is no other place left to run to without handing Tetek the cross roads on a plate. Well, they would soon find out.

The mercenary sighed. He had never wanted this command to begin with. Sure, he'd always thought it would be nice to be a colonel. But didn't every private? And back in W.W.II that was like wishing for a date with Lana Turner. But now? Responsible for the lives of these men! No thank you! All he wanted was to survive; get home to where he should have been months ago had they let him. They could say what they liked, it was not his fault that this was happening.

Mark returned the salutes of the waiting captains, and ducked inside the bell tent to take up his position behind the small card table, that was to serve as his desk. His headquarters were getting considerably smaller, as was his command and his own ability.

"Well gentlemen, no need to tell you what we are up against."

Listen to yourself Stewart, he thought to himself. You sound just like one of those stupid antiquarians of that last lot you were in. The ones you despised so much. Aloud he went on. "I want a demolition squad to blow up the bridges between here and Route 9, in the event of our losing the cross roads, but not until then, and only then," he emphasised. He saw his officers vainly try to hide a smile at his determination, and felt a twinge of guilt at what he *did* have in mind. "With any luck, General Scurk will have reinforcements here any time now." He lowered his voice a half note. "There is no more I need discuss with you gentlemen; you have already proved your proficiency."

When the last of the officers had left, Mark sat back in the uncomfortable wooden chair. God! What a con artist! He should be working in the Glesca Barras. His little speech had put new life into them. If only he possessed that resilience. Then again, it was not his country he was fighting for. Perhaps had the Commies been over the hill from Milngavie, he'd have seen things differently as well.

Twenty six kilometres away, Tetek sat in the very same house in the village, as his adversary had done before him. It was beginning to get quite a habit. The thought amused him.

Successfully lighting his habitually stubborn pipe, Tetek stared out of the window. The next few hours were crucial. As in a chess game, so much depended on an opponent's next move. Or in this case, various opponents next moves.

Tetek inhaled, enjoying the texture of the tobacco. At first, he'd wished to have his heavy guns remain on the foothills behind him as a deterrent to the enemy sections on his flanks. Also, should Ziotkowski come down off the mountains before he'd reached the cross roads, he wanted those guns to prevent him attacking his rear. Now, however, he did not have the time at his disposal. Scurk, despite a penchant for excessive caution, would by this time have ordered reinforcements from the east. He had already sent tanks, but thanks to the Capital's PFF, these had been halted, ironically by the Goverment's own guns.

"Excuse me Comrade General." A sergeant interrupted his thoughts, saluting him. "I have just received a communiqué from the Gap"

"Read it Sergeant," Tetek ordered brusquely.

The soldier unfolded the sheet of paper, while Tetek focused his attention on a bird sitting on a branch of a tree outside the shattered window.

Supplies halted by Government troops on nearby hillside. Strength unknown," the soldier read. "Reinforcements urgently required." The soldier looked at his commanding officer apprehensively.

"Thank you, sergeant. Apprise Captain Yvere of the situation. Have him attend to it immediately."

The sergeant hurried passed the window, frightening away the bird on the tree. Tetek looked up into the leaden sky, his thoughts on the Gap. He could not let himself be denuded of supplies, nor could he let down all those working so prodigiously to bring those same supplies through the Gap. People of all métier whose sole desire was to see an end to this war, and be back by their own fireside once more. He though of his own neice driving those stubborn mules through the Gap, and hoped she was safe, and wearing the blue scarf he had given her, to help keep her warm.

Chapter 16

The first salvo from Tetek's heavy guns came around midday, shattering the woods and surrounding area . Mark leaped from his canvas H.Q., shocked by the sheer intensity of fire. Trees split and crashed down amongst the trenches of the infantry; ammunition, thought to be safely out of range, exploded. He ran to the edge of the woods, the searing heat from burning trees forcing him back.

Within minutes, the first soldiers coughing and spluttering stumbled out of the dense smoke. Wounded fell by the roadside, gasping for air.

Somehow Mark mustered his officers around him. "Demolition squads to the bridges," he began, striving to keep his voice steady. An officer gave a rapid salute and run off to carry out his order. "Gentlemen, we shall withdraw immediately to co-ordinate 116."

Heads snapped up. Faces stared at him in disbelief.

"With respect Sir, that will place us twelve kilometres, south of the cross roads! Is it not your intention to deny those same roads to the enemy...Sir?" It was a big man who spoke, voicing all their fears, and hoping he had mistaken the co-ordinates.

Mark had seen him many times in the past, leading his men in the thick of battle. He sensed trouble, as if he did not have enough as it was. "No Captain, this is no longer feasible, now that Tetek has brought up his heavies from the foothills. The best we can hope to achieve is to extricate ourselves as best we can, in the hope we might live to fight another day."

The big captain's look was incredulous. "Should that not be...live to run another day, Colonel?"

Smothering his anger, Mark stared at him contemptuously. "No Captain," he answered flatly, daring the man to challenge him again.

"If we give up the cross roads, it will open up our own army's flank, and Tetek will roll them up! Cut them to pieces!" another officer cried desperately.

No neophyte to this type of situation, Mark stood his ground. "So, you would have your men die here? Cut to pieces without firing a shot?" Mark pointed an angry finger in the direction of the burning woods. "How long would you be prepared to let brave men die needlessly? Until your pride allowed you to admit you were wrong? At least this way, we have a chance."

"A chance, Colonel?" The big man asked sarcastically, bunching his fists and taking a menacing step forward. "We did not have a chance against the Nazis...at least, not until we tried. Understand, we are fighting for our country. We just cannot pack up and go home when we are beaten. We *are home*, captain!"

Mark blanched at the insinuation, and the fact that he, Mark Stewart, wanted to get the hell out of this alive, and the only way he knew how, was to retreat as quickly and as far away from Tetek as possible. He scanned the inimical men standing around him. The last thing he wanted was to let them smell his fear, although his dearest desire was to get his spikes on and run like the clappers. Three retreats and a mutiny in three days, was quite a career, he thought, better not try for assassination as well.

Shells clumped down on the road bordering the woods, testimony to Tetek advancing unopposed. He had no more time to waste in discussion.

"We have a chance if we withdraw *now*. Take up our new positions south of the cross roads." His voice was harshly cold, thrusting all other thoughts from his mind. "Time is on our side. Tetek will be forced to deploy men to watch our flank, while he wheels west, thereby weakening his own force. Also, as I have ordered the bridges west of here to be blown, this will prevent him from attacking our own men in the flank. All this will give Scurk and Ziotwoski time to come at him from west and north."

He was convincing them, he saw it in their eyes. He pushed home his argument. "Besides, with each passing hour, we are receiving more reinforcements from the Capital and the south. A detachment that repulsed an attack on the Kiemer Dam at Gravst, arrived an hour ago." Mark halted fractionally to draw breath. "Sergeant Major Grbesa, from 'A' Company, has reported having halted all supplies coming through the Gap from reaching Tetek. Therefore, if we move *now*, we can salvage something. Maybe turn this whole thing around."

Mark seized the initiative, staring aggressively at the big captain who still remained unconvinced, and sternly barked out his commands. "Infantry will withdraw by sections. Tanks and artillery to cover them. Supplies, medical, etc., will follow the usual line. That is all." Mark swung on his heel, signifying the briefing and confrontation was at an end.

A little distance away, the entire tree line was ablaze. Machine gun crews were fighting a running retreating action with an enemy ever close behind.

"Corporal!" Mark shouted to a soldier outside. His men desperately needed some sort of encouragement, a success however small to boost their flagging spirits. The soldier brushed back the flap ducking into the tent. Straightening up, he saluted. "Sir."

"Field telephone, Corporal, if you please. Whistle up a third of our tank strength." Mark leaned forward on his makeshift desk, pointing a finger on the map. "To advance to here. Hold the position until otherwise instructed."

"Yes Sir!" the soldier beamed. It would be the first tank engagement since the retreat from the ridge, and about time too, having let the poor bloody infantry do all the dirty work.

Later, standing outside his tent, Mark watched his tanks trundled forward, supported by the infantry, open up on the enemy soldiers emerging from the burning woods. Even above the din, Mark fancied hearing the wild cheering of charging men. Thrusting the glasses to his eyes, he focused the lens fully on the insubordinate captain in the vanguard of the infantry. "If that's what you wanted big man, then the best of luck to you," he said, tight-lipped at the gargantuan leading his men into the smoke. "But now it is time to save my tanks. I have to keep something up my sleeve besides my arm."

Secure in the lee of the hills ten kilometres south of the cross roads, Mark heaved a gigantic sigh of relief. It had been a miraculous withdrawal, all thanks to the adroitness of his officers. He sat back in the jeep, searching his tunic pocket for his cigarettes, and surveying the array of arms lined up at the foot of the hill. Foremost in line, the tanks, wraith-like in the dying light, flanked on either side by the remnants of his artillery. The last of the trucks, that had transported the wounded through the valley en route to the Capital, had long since gone. Now, there was nothing left to do but wait.

Mark swung himself down off the jeep, his foot caught and he almost stumbled. He was tired...no exhausted. He could never have opposed Tetek much longer. But here, at last, was sanctuary. Tetek was sure to leave him isolated here, while he swung right to deal with the rest of the Government army.

He felt a little ashamed by the way he was duping his officers into thinking his intention for withdrawing this far, was to support Scurk and Ziotwoski, when in fact it was to keep himself well out of Tetek's reach. Had they known back at those damned woods that he had intended to run away, he never would have got them to leave. Even had it meant all their lives...his included.

"I'm turning in now Corporal," he yawned at his aide. "Don't wake me unless it's something important."... such as my demob papers, he thought.

"Very good, Sir." The soldier saluted and went back to his writing.

Mark slept well; too well. It was the corporal's vigorous shaking that awakened him.

"Colonel! Colonel!"

Mark's unfocussed bleary eyes stared up into those of his agitated aide, endeavouring to make some sense out of the inconsiderate non-com. "What's the matter, soldier?" He yawned unceremoniously into the man's face.

"Tetek, Sir! He's advancing!"

Mark sat up stretching himself. "I did expect this Corporal. He did not come down out of the mountains not to attack our main force."

"I know, Sir, but you don't quite understand, Colonel!" the man cried agitatedly, taking a hurried step back. "Tetek is advancing on *us*! Tetek is coming *here*!"

Mark sat bolt upright. "Here!" He almost shouted the word. Then remembering his rank, fought to control himself, and grabbing his tunic flung himself out of his tent.

Already there were signs of activity. Fumes filled the air as tanks swung into position. The long gun barrels of the artillery poked their noses skyward. Infantry went to ground. Officers ran towards him, intent on carrying out his orders. After all, was this not why he had brought them here?"

Mark felt a sickening feeling in the pit of his stomach. Tetek had not swung right to outflank the army, instead he was coming here! Pushing south! Driving straight for the nation's Capital! And to compound matters, he, Colonel Bawheid of the First Imbecilian Nutters, had ordered all bridges blown between the cross roads and all points west, preventing Scurk coming to his aid! Tetek had out thought him again.

Mark's officers arrived, the gargantuan amongst them. He had no brilliant strategies left. By blowing the bridges on either flank, he had expected Tetek, either to hold the position he had won, until he had re-established his supplies through the Gap, or gradually withdraw back to the cover and safety of his beloved mountains. Never, had he expected him to try and break through into the flatlands, whereby inviting the entire Government forces to cut off his supplies, as well as attack him from the rear. Tetek must be gambling everything on a swift push on to Zaltz itself and, with only Mark's small force in the way to halt him, it was not much of a gamble.

Mark took his remaining courage in both hands. "We stand here gentlemen," he addressed the coterie of officers, endeavouring to sound resolute. "Until relieved, or until I say differently."

"Very good Sir!" his officers echoed.

For the first time the big captain smiled at him. "I knew you had something in mind Sir."

Wanly, Mark smiled back a silent answer. Oh if only you knew what I had in mind soldier, he thought grimly, such as running away.

Tetek came at him. Punching and probing, from early morning to almost mid day. His artillery the first to slacken, shortly followed by his tanks firepower. Mark heaved a sigh of relief, Grbesa must still be at work. Tetek's supplies were dwindling, but so was his own manpower. No more reinforcements had reached him from the Capital. Now was the time. "Officers to me!" he shouted to the wireless operator.

A few minutes later, a dozen eagerly smiling officers arrived on his doorstep.

"Now is the time gentlemen," he started. The men grinned. "Tetek is running low on munitions. We shall make our withdrawal now." Grinning faces changed to sheer incredulity.

Mark understood that they had expected him to say that he was going to counter attack, now that Tetek's firepower had slackened.

He had a plan, but it was a plan he could in no way discuss with these men. If Tetek broke through...the Capital....the nation was at his mercy. "Gentlemen," he began hoarsely. "These next few hours are crucial to this army...indeed to this nation. Therefore, I reserve the right to command as I see it. You *will* obey my orders, however improbable or distasteful they may appear to be. Do I make myself clear?"

Mark's voice had grown more confident, more resilient as he had gone on, until he stood before them as their commanding officer, and all it exemplified.

No one spoke. All were too shaken, horrified by the complete contradiction to what they themselves had expected to hear, to what they themselves would have done. But then again, this man was not one of them. This man fought for money. This man was a mercenary.

Disconsolate, they moved off, their step mirroring their feelings. They would obey this man, even should it mean an inglorious retreat all the way to Zaltz, for they were soldiers, and a soldier's first duty was to obey.

The maid scurried down the hall, pretending not to have seen Milan enter. He opened the high double doors leading into the drawing room, where Elizbieta stood in front of the unlit fire, her face a deathly white as she turned to face him. Milan felt a deep sorrow for her, too soon her world had come to an end.

"Is it true, Milan?" she asked huskily.

He could have asked, to which of the dozen or so questions did she refer to, considering the House was in a greater state of panic than it had been following Paule Kolybin's assassination.

Now was the time for endless recriminations. Senators, with rousing speeches, all set to take to the streets to defend their city, while others were already hard at work, preparing a reconciliatory document for Tetek's triumphal entry; the remainder, less decisive. But at least on one subject they were all unanimous, that he, Milan Molnar, should go. Never before had he seen so many so quick to distance themselves from him.

Elizbieta answered her own question. "Have they asked you to resign?"

Milan sat down in his favourite chair by the fireside. At least he'd be free of this iceberg of a place. "Yes, it is true, my dear," he answered sadly.

"But why?" His wife threw her hands in the air. "How can they do this, after all you have done for this country, since Paule died?

Milan stared opaquely into the empty fireplace. "Politicians are seldom remembered for their successes, only their failures."

"They cannot hold *you* responsible for that...that Tetek person breaking through!" his wife stammered, seething with anger. "Unless." A modicum of hope broke into her voice. "What the radio and papers say about Tetek being close to the Capital is exaggerated?" She took a step forward, her eyes pleading, begging her husband to tell her it was so.

"This time, what the papers say *is* true, my dear."

Milan's calm demeanour rekindled Elizbieta's anger. She sat down heavily in a chair across from her husband. "Even so, it is the Generals who have let *you* down. It is they who should resign, not you!"

"If only I had one loyal supporter like you in the House, dear wife." Milan gave her a thin smile.

Long had he ridden on the Kolybin success. And when his old friend had become irrational, he, Molnar, had personally modified his plans for the 'Great Offensive'. Had it worked out otherwise, he would just assuredly have taken the credit. Now that the plan had failed, he must as readily accept the blame.

"I suppose I must prepare the staff to vacate the Kasel. You were right, Milan, about not bringing all our belongings." Wearily, Elizbieta struggled out of her chair as if all life had suddenly drained from her. She drifted to the window, her steps slow, unsteady. "Poor little people," she said sadly, drawing her hand idly down the drapes. "They seem to be running about so afraid." She turned away. "When will we go home Milan?"

How could he spare her? Tell her the truth? A few short days ago, the world had been her oyster, with nothing more to worry about than to ensure that the correct soufflés were served. Or overseeing the perfection of the meal, with the best Torta as sweet, at their soirees. How she had always remembered to flatter, observe protocol, when demanded. The numerous little things, that made so many diplomatic evenings a success. All this had come and gone in the briefest space of time. "We shan't be going home, Elizbieta, my dearest."

The woman stepped back from the curtain, her look uncomprehending. Had it all been too much for poor Milan? Had he lost his reasoning? Not going home? What was he saying?

"With the Communists in power, I do not believe, the President and his lady, will be treated as honoured guests. Would you not say?"

Ashen faced, Elizbieta clutched the back of a chair, scarcely able to ask. "What will happen.to us?"

"They say Austria is very lovely at this time of year."

Swaying, tears in her eyes, Elizbieta grasped the chair tighter. "You mean we must leave our country?" Dazed, she shook her head. "Our home? Our friends?"

"Yes, my dear. This is the price you must pay for marrying a failure."

Miro lay on his stomach, looking through the bars. He was in jail. Yet, why had he a cell with a carpet and a blue carpet with red flowers at the edges? He moved his head awkwardly. A table stood in the corner of the white painted room. A clock chimed on the wall.

"It is good to see you awake, comrade," a voice said above him. A figure of a woman dressed in white hovered over him. Miro let out his breath in a long sigh of relief. The woman pulled up a chair by his bedside and helped him on to his side, away from the iron headrest.

"Where am I?" he asked, passing a hand across his eyes.

"The doctor's," she answered softly. "Do you remember?" Miro shook his head. "You arrived at the door on Sunday night." She helped him, like a mother coaxing her child to say its first word. "You had been wounded in the back. Now do you remember?"

This time Miro nodded. "Yes. Now I do." He looked at her intently. "How long have I…?"

"This is the longest you have remained conscious," she said in answer to his unfinished question.

Miro twisted to a more comfortable position. "What day is it?" Told, Wednesday, he moaned out loud. "My wife...she will think I am dead." He pulled himself up, reaching out for the nurse's arm. "I must contact her...let her know I am still alive," his voice urgent. "Wednesday," he said despairingly, and fell back onto the pillow.

"When you have eaten something and become a little stronger, you may phone her. I do not think the good doctor will object," she assured him, tucking the bedclothes around him.

"Is there anyone else here besides myself ? From the mission I mean." His voice sounded strange to him as if listening to another person.

The nurse cocked her head to one side. "You should know better than to ask such questions, comrade." She smiled down at him, softening her gentle but firm rebuke.

"I know," Miro apologised, feeling his strength failing, "but I have my reasons. Things did not go well on our mission, you will understand."

The nurse sat back down, brushing back a strand of hair from Miro's eyes. "Do not worry, everything will turn out just fine."

Miro failed to see the gleam that came into his nurse's eyes as he lay back on the pillow.

"Great things have happened since you had your little nap, comrade."

"Such as?" he asked, too tired to open his eyes.

"Comrade Tetek has burst out of the mountains. The capitalist radio even admits to his ingenuity. He has those greedy pretentious mongrels on the run. Would you believe it? Our cause is not yet lost!"

Miro snapped his eyes open, all tiredness gone, scarcely able, or willing to believe what this woman had told him. Perhaps it was not true, only a matter of therapy.

She seemed to read his mind. "No comrade, I swear what I have said is the truth."

She seemed to be genuinely pleased, Miro thought, sitting there beaming down at him. "Perhaps, I could just manage a little something to eat after all. Then contact my wife," he blushed.

"Yes, I think that can be arranged, comrade." The nurse smiled back, and rose to do as he had asked.

Miro's hand shook as he held the phone to his ear. It rang, his wife's voice at the other end, asking who it was. "Hello, Krystyna," he began shakily, not using her pet name of Krysty. "It is your cousin, Damir. I was wondering if I may call on you, perhaps tonight if it is convenient?" He heard the sharp intake of breath. The brief pause, before his wife spoke again.

"Of course, Damir. It will be nice to see you again. Are you well?" she asked, following their well rehearsed procedure.

"Quite well thank you. I'll ring off now, as I should like to catch the seven o'clock bus. I'll see you soon, cousin."

The old doctor took the receiver from him. "Do you not think you had better wait until you are stronger comrade?" He put the phone gently back on it's cradle. "You have lost a lot of blood. The wound could open again at anytime."

Miro ran his eyes over the worried man's face. "As your patient you are concerned by my condition, and wish me to stay. But as PFF you would much prefer, the sooner I leave the better."

The doctor stuck his hands into the pockets of his white coat. "Something like that, comrade. Since comrade Tetek's advance, the good citizens of our capital see communist traitors on every corner. I must be very careful, you understand. And you must also, comrade. There are secret police everywhere."

Miro nodded.

The nurse came into the room and helped him into his coat, now cleaned and patched. She handed him a package. "Have your wife change the bandages comrade. These are a fresh supply."

Miro thanked her.

The doctor followed him to the door. "I cannot give you a medical certificate, as I am not your registered doctor." He reached passed Miro to open the door.

"I understand Doctor. However, I already have one which extends to Monday next."

"The cut in your forearm?" the doctor ventured.

"Yes an accident at work." He stepped outside and turned to face them. "Thank you, Doctor. Thank you both."

"Be careful!" the nurse called after him, as he started down the garden path and into the night.

The bus journey across town had been a nightmare, and he was sure his wound had opened. His leg still throbbed, but was as nothing compared to the pain in his back. Therefore, to see his own home was the most welcome sight he'd ever seen in his life.

His wife came down the front steps to meet him, taking a hurried look up and down the darkened street before helping inside.

Krysty changed his bandages, insisting he sup the hot soup she had made for him. All the while fussing, filling him in with news, briefing him.....So far, there had been no one from the police inquiring about his absence from work. Doubtless, his prearranged 'accident' had stood him in good stead......Was not Tetek's success simply brilliant? The pressure on Krysty's verbal dam dissolved in a flood of words, now that her husband was safe. He nodding as he supped.

On the bus home, he had listened to people's whispered conversations, all of them apprehensive, but not quite panicking as yet. To them, the PFF General, was still too far away. In any case, did the Government not have too many troops for him?"

Krysty was worried about his wound, and had urged him to go to bed. He had shaken his head, saying he had one or two things to do.

There had been no answer when he had phoned Pavel and Vaclaw at their prearranged number. Miro put down the phone and took the hot mug of coffee from his wife. "I want you to phone this number, Krysty. Should anyone answer, do not speak, simply put down the receiver. Do you understand?"

Krysty had never seen that look on her husband's face before, it frightened her. Choking back a sob, she simply did as she was asked.

It was Petr's number she rang. She looked at her husband and put the phone down.

"Was someone there?" Miro asked, feeling the thumping of his heart.

"Yes," she answered solemnly, wanting to ask what it was all about, and believing she had a right to know, considering how many times she had shared the dangers with this man.

"Was it a man's voice?"

Krysty nodded. "It sounded like Petr."

Miro took his wife in his arms, and felt her tremble. "I must ask you to do one more thing for me Krysty. I know I should not involve you in this, but I cannot do this thing alone."

She saw the pain in his face. She wanted to tell him to rest...to wait until morning.

"Please, love. This I must do."

She hugged him tight, reaching up to kiss him, then, gently broke away to pick up the phone once more.

It was almost midnight when Miro left his home. A barking dog ran at him from across the street, its master breaking out of the shadows after it, shouting his noisy canine to heel, and offering Miro a hurried apology, as he set off down the street in hot pursuit.

Miro watched man and dog disappear into the night, suddenly envious of their normal mundane lives, and aware of being addressed by his own name of Gerd, instead of his code name for the first time in days. He turned his head, the pain returning.

Krysty stood at the window, the wave she gave him only a slight movement of her hand. Her expression, the same as it always was when he left on a 'mission', except this time, he thought, he saw something else, and wished he could have told her everything that had happened, but he knew that it was for the best that he did not.

Miro took the last tram across the city, alighting near the bombed out square, close to the location of the cellar.

His wound had opened, the blood hot and sticky on his back. He drew in a long breath shuffling round the puddles and rubble of the square, when suddenly the headlights of a military jeep penetrated the darkness, its twin beams cutting across the skeletal buildings, almost catching him where he'd drawn to a halt. He heard the soldiers talking, and for a moment thought he'd been discovered, then, with a screech of tyres, the jeep was gone.

The cellar was cold and dark. Miro groped his way down the broken stone steps, waiting until he was well below ground level before switching on his torch, and following its pencil beam of light to the far corner of the room, where he squatted down against the wall.

He knew Petr would come. The Group Leader could not resist discovering who it was that had simply said 'the cellar' on the phone. Miro put out the torch and waited. Petr would come.

Two hours. Had he been wrong? Was Petr not going to come after all? Miro dug into his pocket for his hip flask. Unscrewing the top, he put the flask to his lips, and let the fiery liquid run down his throat, his wound throbbing in time to his heartbeat.

He heard a noise and retreated further into his corner. The noise came again, then was gone. A rat maybe, but not the one he was waiting for. Then another sound, louder this time, followed by a finger of light. Miro steeled himself, afraid to breathe.

A torch beam swivelled from side to side, as the shadowy figure descended the stairs. At the foot, it turned towards the wall, and when it turned again, Miro saw the lit oil lamp in its hand.

"I knew you would come, Petr." Miro rose to his feet the gun in his hand.

The sudden voice and movement sent Petr stepping hastily back with a sharp intake of breath. *"You"* he choked, setting the lamp down on the rough table with a thud.

"What does it feel like to be taken by surprise, Petr?" Miro asked, steadying himself against the cold hard wall.

"My, Miro, you did give me a fright!" Petr put a hand to his brow, attempting to laugh.

"I suppose I did, considering you thought me dead."

"Why Miro? Why should I assume such a thing?"

Petr's supercilious tone angered Miro. "Because you betrayed me, my Group and Group East. Perhaps also Pavel? Vaclaw?"

Petr rested a hip on the edge of the table and threw his head back in laughter, the sound eerie and unreal in the cold dark confines of the cellar. "Come on Miro, you do not really believe that?"

"It all fits, Petr. Tell me who knew, or should I say ...suggested, that Tetek attack Pienera? How it just so happened, that Government troops were on hand to surround him?"

"There was a leak," Petr shrugged, the laughter still on his lips.

"And you were the sieve, you bastard!" Miro shouted. "Don't tell me, you did not warn the Government forces that we intended to attack the dam?"

Miro felt his strength ebb, and would dearly have loved a sip from his flask, but dared not risk taking his eyes from his quarry. "You led both Groups into believing the other was responsible for the dam's demolition, thus ensuring that neither leader would be suspicious at not having explosives," Miro seethed. "How does it feel to be responsible for the lives of so many good men, *comrade?*"

To Miro's surprise, Petr shook his head in amusement. "You poor, stupid fool!" He thrust himself away from the table. "You really believe I am a Government spy? A traitor to the Cause?" Petr moved away to the further most end of the table. Miro watched him intently.

"Tetek needed all the diversions he could get to take the pressure away from him. Hence the need for our bombings throughout the country. But we needed a big diversion, one, that would take a few *hundred* troops away from the front, where Tetek was planning to mount his main offensive.

"We knew the Government, for political reasons, would never allow the dam to be destroyed. As you know, so much depends on

American goodwill...and dollars," Petr sneered. "So it was proposed, we alert the Government forces to our proposed destruction of the dam; consequently, your mission." Petr finished his explanation with a dismissive gesture.

"So we were expendable. It mattered nothing that we were all to be slaughtered? Did you expect no one to learn of this, unless, of course, you expected all of us to die?"

Petr calmly took out a cigarette packet from his top pocket. "We had hoped you would have made a better fight of it, comrade. However, you were late, and Government forces were ahead of you. They were there waiting for *you*. However, scattering as you did, served its purpose. Government forces were tied down chasing you lot all over the place." Petr lit a cigarette, casually blowing smoke up into the cold dark ceiling.

Miro was beside himself with rage at the cold offhanded way this man had of speaking about their death warrants. "Bear!" he exploded, the gun shaking in his hand. "Yearling! They died trusting you...not to mention how many more? Do you think you will be safe when the survivors find out that it was you who had betrayed them?"

Petr drew on his cigarette. "What will happen to *me?* Should this fill me with fear?" he mocked. "I, who have fought in those very same mountains for the very same cause? Who did I betray? Bear? That great Centaur, a senseless oaf, who almost destroyed us all that night at the graveyard? Yearling? A boy whose wish was to emulate his father, a father who blew *himself* to pieces, as well as some good men with him, and who's son *wet* himself every time someone said boo!" Petr slowly rounded the table. "Group East, with their equal number of morons? It was a simple matter of arithmetic, comrade."

"And what of me Petr? What was my circa vita for liquidation?" Miro asked, leaning against the wall, and hoping its coldness would help dull the red hot searing pain.

"Ambition, Miro." Petr pursed his lips. "You are as dangerous as I am in a way. You thought you had stumbled on to something that would impress us all regarding our late President. It did not matter to you that you had broken procedure, and in doing so, jeopardised the lives of *my* agents. No one does that to me and gets away with it," Petr said steely. "You were so ambitious....so cocksure of yourself, as you were that day by the canal. And besides, did you really believe I could ever forget your mission with the judge, and the damage it did to our cause? Yet despite this, you still saw yourself at the head of your own Group, together with those ambitious fantasies of yours, that even had you sitting beside *me* on National Council!"

Miro saw his wife as he had last seen her framed in the window. The life they had chosen to lead, simply and totally for the Party, and their unshakeable belief in the cause. All blown away by deceit and by someone whom they believed shared in those self same ideals.

Their decision not to have children, for fear of being caught. All those years wasted, risks taken, all for nothing.

Miro's anger reached boiling point, willing Petr to make a move, a gesture even, that would give him all the excuse he needed to pull the trigger, pump shell after shell into his traitorous body.

Though he had watched Petr's every move since his entering the cellar, he still did not see the gun when Petr fired it at him. He only felt the power of the blow, followed by the red hot searing pain in his stomach, and Petr standing over him ready to fire again. Somehow his own gun went off, and Petr went down, a look of incomprehension on his face. Then everything black.

The possibility of completing that infinite journey back home, relegated to the back of his mind, Miro crawled up the cellar steps. Somehow, someway, he was determined to see Krysty for one last time, to tell her how sorry he was for the life he had inflicted upon her.

It was dark...very dark when he reached the top step of the cellar and clawed his way over the cold black mud, and around the never ending concrete pillar that hid the entrance.

In the distance a tram clanked passed the square. *It was morning,* he thought. Yet why was it so dark? He fumbled for his hip flask, and stared up at the sky. Suddenly his view was blocked out by an even darker shape, and a small voice asking him if he was drunk, and was he trying to go home?

Miro smiled and pressed the flask to his cheek. *Yes, in a way*, he thought...*in a way.*

Chapter 17

General Tetek sat by the roadside surveying the maps on his knee, now and again lifting his head to acknowledge the cheering men as they rode passed. He was about to take his greatest gamble, and should he lose? He bit deeply into his unlit pipe, wishing he shared his men's optimism.

Scurk would soon be on his flank. Neither, could he expect Ziotkowski to remain in the mountains much longer, not when he heard he had broken out into the flatlands. Therefore, he must leave his heavier guns here to protect his rear.

Now came the gamble. He must chase this mercenary commander incessantly, and without mercy.... Harass him all the way through the valley, so that he had no time to regroup, turn and trap *him*.

Tetek knew the further he moved away from his mountain base, the longer and weaker became his line of supply. He tapped angrily at a spot on his map. He had to send more men...men he could ill afford to loose, back to deal with the Government forces blocking the Gap.

He was well aware that he was pinning everything on public reaction. A swift breakthrough to the Capital would have those same peace loving inhabitants rushing like frightened rabbits to the Senate, where they would no doubt implore their beloved Senators to negotiate a peaceful settlement with the man they so dearly wanted to hang, before he decided to hang some of them! The PFF leader took the pipe from his mouth, strangely pleased by the thought.

It did not take a genius to know the closer he got to Zaltx, the more the populace would irrefutably deny ever having anything other than an inherent sympathy for his movement, however well hidden it may have been. However, should he fail? Tetek emptied his pipe on the ground. Then those very same 'sympathisers', would not be slow in demanding of their Senate that he pay the price.

The old General sighed, and waved to his men again. If only they knew, he thought, and sighed again.

Even the rain failed to dampen Indra's high spirits. Bursting into the kitchen, she wished her Grandmother a cheerful good morning, inquiring, in the same breath, as to Stefan's whereabouts, as she set about laying the breakfast table.

"You should know better than I, Indra." The old woman cracked another egg into the pan. "But, seeing as you already miss him so much, I best tell you, he left early this morning...saying something about the sea being his only mistress."

"Oh no!" Indra howled, the visions of last night flashing through her mind. The promises made, the thrill of the future together. "He could not....!"

The kitchen door creaked slowly open, and Stefan backed into the room carrying an armful of logs.

"Oh grandmother!" Indra admonished, stamping a foot, not knowing whether to laugh or cry with relief.

"Indra thought you had changed your mind Stefan...almost had a fit!" The old woman turned an egg in the pan, cackling at her own humour.

Happy now that Stefan was here, Indra winked at her beau, asking covertly of her grandmother, "Did you sleep well , grandmother?"

"Very well, thank you, Indra, and without that bedtime drink you prescribed," she replied, a twinkle in her eye.

Indra almost dropped the sugar bowl and flashed an eye across the table at Stefan who had suddenly found something interesting on the ceiling.

Blushing, Stefan kept his eyes on Indra, preparing the table. She was beautiful he thought, and she was his, for the rest of his life. This was someone who loved him for what he was, not for being the son of a hero.

Aware that Stefan was watching her, the girl made a face. He made one back. Wasn't life wonderful? She drew her eyes away from the boy to the window. "Is that thunder I hear, grandmother?"

"No." Stefan answered, carelessly, "It's the guns."

"They sound closer than they were yesterday," Indra replied a little anxious, though determined not to let anything spoil the day.

"We are safe enough, the Reds are beaten. I should think the sounds you hear are their parting shots so to speak."

"The radio says, that man Tetek, has severely shaken our defences, Stefan," the old woman volunteered, while expertly whipping away a cloth from under the hot plate of food she had set before him. "But they expect to drive him back before long. However, the Senate has asked poor President Molnar to resign."

Indra lowered herself into a chair opposite her fiancé, the earlier glow of happiness receding despite her self promise. "Why, if they believe the PFF are beaten? I don't quite understand." She wrinkled her brows.

"It's the price of politics, Indra," Stefan ventured to explain. "Tetek's successes, however limited they may have been, will have angered some important people in the capital, so someone will have to take the blame. Who better than the man in charge? The President?"

"But the PFF are not close to Zaltx." Indra thought again of the sound of the guns. "They are not close to here, are they Stefan? We will turn them back.... Won't we?" Suddenly afraid, she reached out to grasp his hand.

Stefan squeezed it reassuringly. "No. I don't think they are that close, Indra. I expect we will counter attack if we have not already done so. I still believe this is their last shot."

Gently, Stefan took his hand away to lift his knife and fork. "I saw a convoy of trucks heading up the valley when I was out fetching logs, I think they are reinforcements from the capital."

What her grandmother had said about the radio broadcast had made Indra uneasy. The Reds were not being so easily beaten as they had been led to believe, or what Stefan would have her believe. She was sure it would mean the fighting would continue, and Stefan would still be in it until it ended. "Where will they send you Stefan, when you report back?" she asked softly, pouring out a cup of coffee for both of them.

The boy shrugged. "Beats me. Could be anywhere."

She put down the pot, absently stirring her coffee, her eyes on the bottom of her cup.

Sensing her uneasiness, Stefan asked, light-heartedly, "What's the answer?"

"...What?"

He stroked her hand, nodding at the cup. "I thought you were going to tell my fortune."

Indras forced a smile. "In a coffee cup?"

"Good trick if you can do it," he laughed.

So young and so much in love, the old woman thought to herself, and so afraid for one another. She half turned from the sink, still scrubbing at the frying pan to ask, "What bus are you two love birds catching?" Her voice cursory, as if it was the end of an ordinary weekend visit by a granddaughter and her young man to a grandparent, and there could never be such an absurdity in the world, as men killing one another.

"The one at midday," Indra answered, her eyes still on Stefan, and wishing somehow, however hopeless it may be, that they would not have to leave, that they could relive these last few days. "Then we split up for our trains."

"I've made you both sandwiches, you know what railway food is like." The woman edged round the girl's chair. "Tell that mother of yours child, I am looking forward to seeing her." She swung round to open a cupboard door, and reached inside. "It is months since she has been here. Am I so awkward a person to get on with?"

Indra shook her head in validation, as she spread butter on a slice of bread.

"So give her this strawberry jam. I know she likes it. Do not forget it as you did the last time you were here," she warned, setting down the jar in front of the girl.

Grandmother pointed a finger at her granddaughter, her next words drowned out by a babble of voices from outside. "What was that?" The old woman swung round, crossing to the kitchen window that looked into the street . A street, normally so quiet, now filled with a crowd of people shouting and gesticulating as they hurried in the direction of the market square.

Indra got up and hurried behind her grandmother.

"What does it mean?" The old woman held a hand to her throat as she asked.

Indra looked out. She would liked to have told the old body not to worry, it might mean nothing at all, but knew she would not be so easily fooled. "Stay in the house, grandmother, Stefan and I will got and see what it is all about."

Leaving the old woman standing at the window, the young couple left the house and hurried up the garden path to the gate. Only a few people halted to offer a hazy explanation to the youngsters questions as they hurried passed.

Indra turned to her grandmother at the window, gesturing to her, that she and Stefan were leaving to find out what was happening. The old woman nodded back her understanding.

"What do you think it's all about Stefan!" Indra shouted in his ear as they were swept along by the human tide.

"I don't quite know!" he shouted back above the din, grasping her hand. "But I think something awful has happened. Of this I'm certain!"

"Down this way!" Indra pulled at Stefan's hand, dragging him away from the jolting mass, first down one cobbled street then another, until they emerged in the town's main thoroughfare a little beyond the square, where both drew up, unable to believe their eyes at the sight of truckloads of despondent soldiers heading back up the valley.

Stefan pointed to a gap between the houses to the meadow land beyond, where a column of tanks were churning up the short Autumn grass, behind which more trucks, jeeps and half tracks vied for space to reach the narrow winding road out of the valley.

Indra looked everywhere and nowhere at once, her heart thumping, unable to believe this was the same idyllic valley, that she and Stefan had enjoyed these past two days. "What's happening Stefan!" she cried, clutching his hand tighter and close to panic.

Stefan needed time to think, and to make some sort of sense out what he was witnessing, and why their supposedly invincible army was in full retreat.

Stefan led his frightened sweetheart to a line of stationary trucks. "What's going on soldier?" Stefan shouted to a private, who sat dejectedly in the back of the last truck.

Lacklustre eyes slowly sought out the voice. "Get your arse out of here, sailor, Tetek and his crowd will not take too kindly to anyone in uniform, unless they answer to comrade."

Perhaps it was the soldier's soporific tone that sent cold shivers down Indra's spine. Or, the inculcate sense of foreboding that had her clutching Stefan's hand tighter, pulling him away. "Stefan!" she exclaimed. "Oh no, Stefan! This cannot be happening! Not now! Not to us!" All her plans...dreams, drowned, swept aside.

They hurried back towards their home, passing the disconsolate sight of an army in full retreat, unable to fathom how this catastrophe could ever have materialised. The sound of guns ever closer.

"You must get out of here at once, Stefan." Indra drew herself closer to the boy as if cold, her voice shaking.

Stefan put his arm around her protectively. He shook his head. "I won't leave you here, Indra."

"You *must!* You heard what that soldier said back there. Were they to catch you in uniform, and find out you are the son of Paule Kolybin..." She shuddered leaving the rest unsaid.

Stefan did not want to think more about it. "We must see to your grandmother," he said, as a means of drawing the frightened girl away from the subject.

A jeep flew passed, and for a moment he thought he recognised the Scot's mercenary, whom he had seen at the Kasel the day of his father's funeral. Then it was gone.

They were almost back at the square. Trucks continued to roll passed, throwing up jets of water from black puddle holes. A car with a pitiful bundle of belongings tied to the roof tried to merge with the military flow and found itself unmercifully knocked aside by a truck. While, a little way on, a van with a loudspeaker on top blared out the penalties incurred against any civilians who might delay the orderly withdrawal of the army to a new defensive position, by attempting to leave the valley on any road used by the military.

"That settles it." Stefan feigned a sigh. "I will have to stay here with you after all."

"You're not a civilian, Stefan Kolybin, there would be no difficulty in your leaving!" Indra was beside herself with fear for the man she loved. Had he not listened to what she had said about what they would do to him him, the son of the man who had been most hated by the PFF?

"No!" That was said firmly by the boy.

"But your oath Stefan! You have a duty to your country!" She was using every possible argument to persuade this obstinate fiancé of hers, her future husband to leave.

Stefan felt a pang of guilt. . But what about Indra? He was not quite sure how safe she would be. Perhaps they should attempt to leave together; after all, she was a nurse. Then there was the old lady. The guns were much closer now. He drew her to him. Perhaps there was still time to get out under the cover of darkness.

Despite the seriousness of the situation, the old woman smiled to herself at the way these two young ones were trying to gently break the news of the disaster to her. Did they not realise how many wars this old body had lived through? Another one would make little difference to her now. She concentrated on unpicking the dropped stitch in her knitting.

"So there will be no midday bus?" she asked, in a tone implying she did not know what the world was coming to. "But you two young things had better make yourself scarce," she suggested, with a calmness that had both those same young things shaking their heads in admiration and disbelief. The midday bus! That was for another day, in another time, in another world.

Tetek's advance guard overran the Government rearguard just before dusk, and did not halt until they were through the valley, and had consolidated the heights beyond.

Tetek received the communiqué at 2100 hours. He had done it. His gamble had succeeded. The mercenary had fled, leaving behind a trail of weapons and supplies, including a few prisoners...a very few prisoners.

As a means of hiding his jubilation from his staff, the PFF General took out his pipe, and knocked out dotal from the bowl, his action intended to suggest that nothing out of the ordinary had taken place, asking, "Where is the Government front line now?"

"The last report Comrade General, was that they were about ten kilometres beyond the valley and still in retreat! I think it will be close as to who reaches the capital first, General, them or us, the speed at which they are retreating." The aide's laughter was echoed by those gathered around their leader.

Tetek gave a brief smile at the man's humour. "Very good comrade. Have our main force enter the valley." He rose from his camp stool by the roadside, drawing his greatcoat more closely about his shoulders. "It is getting cold, comrades, but unless I am very much mistaken, things will already be a great deal hotter in Zaltx." He treated his staff to a second of his very rare smiles.

The lieutenant saluted. "Tetek's main force has now entered the valley, Colonel Stewart."

It was now dark. The road, although lined with stationary trucks and tanks, was completely silent. Mark's heart thumped with excitement. Colonel Stewart, he whispered to himself. If it were only plain Sergeant, or Private Stewart, or if he had not come here in the first place. He felt the same sensation in the pit of his stomach that he usually had before 'something big' only, this time he was responsible for the whole affair, not just part of it. He was solely responsible for what was about to take place. This time he had no one to blame for it going wrong.

A few metres away from where Mark stood by the roadside, a captain studied his map for the hundredth time, his look cadaverous under the pencil glow off his torch. Suddenly, he looked up. Mark averted his eyes, he had no alternative, he rationalised but to do what he had planned, for should he fail, Tetek would chase him non stop to the very gates of the Kasel.

A red light penetrated the wind blown rain of the night, flickering on and off from the direction of the valley. Mark cleared his throat. "Wind up engines! Lets get going!"

Instantly, the silent road sprang to life with the noise of revving engines. Tank Commanders shouted orders, infantry ran to trucks, all pent up tensions dissipating in a surge of adrenaline.

An hour later, the Government armour, which the PFF Commander did not believe existed, ground to a halt along the heights where they had taken his advance guard by surprise. While below them, the long straggling line of Tetek's main force slowly wound through the narrow valley.

Standing beside the mercenary, an ashen faced captain drew his tongue over dry lips, wanting to, but afraid to ask his Colonel, if what he was about to do was morally correct. No other way? Finally he shrugged his shoulders in resignation, the movement almost imperceptible in the darkness. He looked up at the starless sky, vindicating himself by deducing, that it was not his responsibility for what was about to happen. At least, *he* had a reasonable chance of seeing this thing through, thanks to this mercenary. Something he had not thought possible all the way back from that first bloody ridge. And in every war there must be casualties...even civilian, he reasoned.

"Fire!" Mark shouted, and the first salvo thundered into the valley. The firepower from the tanks and what artillery remained to him shaking a surprised PFF,the salvos hitting the enemy tanks and trucks on the narrow winding valley road.

In the meadows below, terrified citizens ran from homes unintentionally hit by shells. Shops, houses, as well as martial equipment were ablaze. Still the bombardment continued.

Inside the hostelry at the northern end of the town, Tetek strode up and down the littered floor, his disposition in stark contrast to that of a short time before. "Where did this mercenary's armour come from? I was informed he had little or none left at all. Why was I not advised of this?" Tetek's face twitched angrily as he harangued his cringing staff.

The furious General kicked out at a chair. So this mercenary was not as lily-livered as he had imagined him to be. When he thought he had him running for the Capital with his tail between his legs, he had abruptly turned and came at him. But where had his tanks come from? The fox must have kept them in reserve, not committing them till now.

One of his staff, with a little more courage than the others, hurried to appease his raging General. "I understand he held his entire tank force in reserve, sir."

"*He had his tank force held in reserve,*" Tetek mimicked. "Why did my vanguard lose the heights? Did they not hear a hundred tanks approaching? Were they all deaf?" Tetek stormed, halting to thrust out a finger at the same unfortunate soldier. "Tell me you dolt!"

"I don't believe the enemy have a hundred tanks, Sir," the soldier started shakily.

Tetek threw his hands in the air in a gesture of disbelief. "But I do believe," the soldier went on, "we were driven from the heights by infantry hiding in the woods in the valley, together with enemy reinforcements on our eastern flank, who combined to attack our forward units from the rear."

The infuriated General fought to control himself. "Was not the town and valley cleared of enemy during our advance?"

"Yes comrade, General, but you gave specific orders, nothing was to forestall our passage, as you did not wish to be trapped in the valley."

Tetek nodded, and his staff sighed with relief, only to be jerked out of their false security by their commanding office raging at the top of his voice, "But I was trapped! Was I not?"

While the guns continued to destroy Tetek's P.F.F, Indra hurriedly ushered her grandmother and her elderly neighbour under the stairs of the house.

"Just like old times, Vera!" the old woman cried with excitement, settling herself into her small wooden seat.

"Indeed!" Old Vera's eyes gleamed like a cat in the darkness; the prospect of such excitement a welcome break to her mundane life. So, what if something did happen to her? At least she had had a good life, and a long one at that. "See! I brought my knitting!" Triumphantly, the old woman held up her needles.

Indra fussed ornately over the old couple. "We will see what is going on outside. I'll put the lights out. Now! Stay where you are, both of you," she added firmly. Muttering under her breath that she would be damned if she would let a bunch of terrorist ruin her life, not when she had everything to live for.

"Listen to the child!" Vera laughed, winding up her ball of wool, and calling out to Indra to be careful as she closed the door on them.

After putting the lights out, Stefan led Indra into the garden. The entire valley, it seemed, was on fire. The ancient church ablaze, as was the town hall and every surrounding house on the far side of town. Miraculously their street had escaped unscathed.

"Oh Stefan!" Indra said sadly, resting her head on the boy's shoulder. "Why?"

It was inconceivable that it was their guns that was doing the damage to this lovely little town. By whose orders Indra did not know or care to know, all she knew as she sprang for the gate, was that people innocent people were dying out there.

Stefan grabbed her by the arm, swinging her round. "What are you doing, girl?" he snapped at her.

Indra tried to struggle free. "Are you forgetting I'm a nurse? People out there need my help!" she railed.

"And are *you* forgetting there are also enemy soldiers out there?" he flung back angrily.

"You told me Tetek was in retreat!" she shrieked, as if blaming him for this catastrophe.

"Yes! But there will be many of his men still in the valley. A retreating army is also a desperate one. They will shoot at anything that gets in their way. They have nothing to lose!" Stefan shouted back, rapidly running out of patience with this stubborn fiancé of his. "Remember it's our guns that's doing the damage!"

As if in support of his statement, the first of the shells exploded in the street, pieces of bitumen, mingled with red hot shrapnel flying in all directions.

Letting out a cry, Indra thrust her hands over her ears as another salvo landed close by. Unceremoniously, Stefan grabbed her, throwing her to the ground amongst the wet bushes of the garden, burying her head in his arms, protecting her with his body. Another salvo tore the white garden fence away. There was the sound of breaking glass. Tiles hurtled into the soft earth with the velocity of bullets. He buried the terrified girl beneath him, her tears wet on his cheek, his own eyes closed, silently praying for the bombardment to move on.

How long it lasted Stefan did not know, but at long last he found the courage to lift his head to look around. The street had ceased to exist. Where neat white washed houses once stood, nothing now remained except smoking ruins. He twisted on his back. "Oh no!" he cried unable to stop himself.

Thrusting himself to his feet, he ran up the short garden path to the burning house, which for a few days had been his home, Indra's hysterical cry at his back. The heat from the blazing house forced him back along the path.

"Grandmother! Vera!" Indra screamed hysterically, attempting to run passed him. The boy made a quick grab for her, spinning her round. "It's no use!" he howled, pulling her awa,; the searing heat sucking the breath out of his body. "Quick! Back, before the roof caves in!"

Indra struggled in his grasp, lashing out at him with her fists in one final desperate attempt to free herself. He, heedless of the blows, half dragging, half carrying her away from the blazing house. Red-hot sparks falling like star shells all around them.

Stumbling over the broken fence, spluttering and coughing as the heat reached their lungs, Stefan threw the girl down on a minute patch of grass, all that remained of a neighbours front lawn, an oasis in a world gone mad it seemed, where at last her anger and energy spent, she fell sobbing into his arms.

By two in the morning, Tetek concluded, all was lost. His gamble had failed; beaten by a vacuous mercenary. Now he had to get his men back to the mountains before his line of retreat was completely cut by Scurk and Ziotkowski. Though, thankfully, the mercenary's blowing up of the bridges back at the cross roads had bought him some time. He cleared his throat, and gave his wireless operator the order, "Prepare to withdraw from the valley....Heavy guns back to the cross roads to cover our retreat.... All companies back to the mountains as quickly as possible.' The old General thrust his pipe back into his pocket. "And let us hope to hell the Gap is not still blocked."

Tetek cast an eye round the ruined tavern. It had been good to have lived in something civilised, even for a little while, now it was back to living like an animal in a cave once more.

Outside, the PFF Commander looked down through the valley. The difference between victory and defeat had been so close. He levered himself on to the waiting jeep, contemplating on what he must do now. There was no way back, of this he was sure.

Retreating further into his greatcoat, hands deep in his pockets he thought of what the next generation might achieve. Perhaps capitalism might defeat itself?

The burning town was behind them now, the cross roads not so far away. They passed their rear lines where the heavy guns still pointed silently into the night sky. Tetek leaned forward to speak to his driver as a half track sped towards them. It was the last the old General knew, until he lay bleeding on the hard metalled road, his thoughts, that at last Scurk had reached his flank, but more importantly, that he would no longer have to spend another winter living like an animal in those cold accursed mountains.

Indra immersed herself in the work she knew best. What had happened to her grandmother and her old neighbour now a red hot burning anger. She squeezed her eyes closed, blocking out the vision of the blazing house, praying that both the old people would have died instantly, mercifully in that inferno.

Stefan had been right to stop her. Poor Stefan, she must tell him how sorry she was, as she remembered again the intense heat, and how he had dragged her away, his hair singed, his oversized overalls that had hid his uniform, peppered with scorch marks from sparks that had sizzled in the wind blown rain.

She thrust out of her mind what could have been. How, earlier that day her grandmother had put an arm around her, and had guided her to the kitchen dresser, pointing proudly to the rows of Dresden china, now hers she had said, her wedding present. How the old lady had waved her protests aside, saying she seldom used them. Now they would never be used, destroyed, as was everything else her grandmother had struggled through two world wars to preserve. Destroyed, gone as much as the old lady herself.

The shape of two men, carrying a makeshift stretcher, emerged out of the smoke. Spotting an empty space amongst the dead and dying lying in the open meadow, they gently laid down their burden, and turned again towards the burning town.

The remnants of a coat partially covered the shape lying there, wet mud in an open wound. Indra found a cloth and bent to clean the wound, offer some reassurance.. unable to fathom why the poor wretch did not scream , writhe in unspeakable agony. Then through the darkness she saw the face, or what was left of it, the eye less sockets, the bone where the flesh should have been, the seared flesh. Now she realised why the figure had not moved, screamed out, cursed whoever was responsible for this atrocity to humanity.

Indra drew the coat carefully over the macabre face as if not wishing to inflict further pain on an innocent body that had already borne too much. The girl's lips moved in a silent prayer of thanks that the poor soul was beyond suffering. Hoping too, that whoever was responsible for the destruction of this once lovely valley and all its kind gentle people would pay the ultimate price. Perhaps then, and only then, would her anger die.

Sometime later, Stefan found Indra, she was moving on from a soldier to an old man, who had both arms badly burned. Stepping carefully between a row of stretchers, he'd almost reached her side when a doctor shouted to her that she was needed. She looked up, barely recognising him in his blood soaked overalls, and he wanting to take her in his arms, comfort her, but there was no time. She waved briefly, the gesture, weak, tired, before she moved to the doctor's side.

His mind still on the girl he loved, Stefan made his way back to where a soldier waited for him to lift his end of the stretcher. It was best she was kept busy he thought, and have no time to dwell on what had happened to the old woman and her neighbour. Stefan shook his head, contemplating on the irony of two old people having survived the Nazis, only to be killed by their own guns. Similarly how many more?

Mark rode in the jeep down the narrow valley road, passed burnt out trucks and black smoldering tanks, where soldiers toiled at moving the dead and dying. Streets ceased to exist in mountains of rubble. The fine old church, a ruin, as was the seventeenth century town hall. He, Mark Stewart, had done this. Not that scenes like these were anything new to him, simply an extension of the last war.

He passed a detail of soldiers weighed down by the bloody sagging sacks they carried between them. They looked up, none attempting to salute or acknowledge his rank. For a few moments, he had to wait until the road was cleared, and as the jeep drew level again, one directed a muttered obscenity at him, and Mark had a strange uneasy feeling that this was only the beginning.

Chapter 18

In one corner of the meadow, Scurk's reinforcements had set up field kitchens and medical tents, their dim lights filtering weakly through the black smoke from the burning town. A film of soot and ash covered rows of wounded lying intermingled with broken vehicles of war.

Wearily, Stefan let down his end of the stretcher, the casualties seemingly endless. Somewhere a woman screamed in pain; a child cried out; a man swore, cursing all of humanity. He turned in preparation of repeating the journey, and his eye caught the woods beyond, an oasis of peace, where he and Indra had made love, so very long ago.

"Stefan!" Indra's voice jerked him out of his reverie. He stood for a moment, catching and losing sight of the girl through the swirling smoke. She waved.

"Indra!" He quickly found a way through the rows of stretchers to her side. "Are you all right?" he asked urgently, engulfing her in his arms.

Indra mumbled something, and hid her face in his chest.

"Come on, let's get some food down you, then you'll feel better." He put an arm around her, drawing her with him towards a field kitchen.

A team carrying someone on a stretcher passed them. Indra shook herself free, interrupting what he was saying. "Wait a minute Stefan," she pleaded, breaking into a run.

Reluctantly Stefan followed her to where they had laid down the stretcher, annoyed that she should feel the necessity to attend every casualty she saw.

Indra knelt down beside the stetcher and held the wounded man's hand in hers. The soldier's eyes flickered open and he stared up blankly into her face.

"Do you remember me?" she asked softly, giving him a tiny comforting smile. "It was the night..." Then aware of Stefan behind her, started again. "You held the president in your arms. I was the nurse you pushed away."

Though she was out of focus, Dryak heard the girl. It did not take a nurse to tell him he was badly hit. He wanted to sleep and make the best of the morphine while it lasted.

The girl was speaking again, something about Kolybin's son. He opened his eyes. A young man in bloodstained overalls stood beside her. For a moment, his senses cleared, and he was able to understand her telling him, that this was Paule Kolybin's son. Then he was drifting into unconsciousness again.

Indra bent over the dying man and brushed back the blood matted hair from his forehead. "There is something not quite right about this, Stefan. When this man held your father in his arms, he told me he was a doctor. Doctors hold the rank of Captain in our army. This man is a lieutenant...and by his insignia, a field officer, not staff."

Stefan bent closer, confirming what the girl had said with a nod.

Dryak opened his eyes. Somewhere, something was telling him, this may be his last chance to help Molnar.

He had not found out until a few days ago, that it was Stewart who commanded this sector, so, when reinforcements were desperately needed to prevent Tetek from breaking through the valley, he had volunteered, as at the time it had seemed the only way of getting close enough to kill the mercenary. But then he had found himself in a cleft stick, Stewart may not have been a Jakofcic, but he was the only one in a position to halt the Commie leader. Therefore, to do the job, he had to choose the right time.

Now, of course, it was all academic, he had failed, as had he and his brother back at the beach house. Doubtless, Stewart must have held the PFF responsible for the attempt on his life and not Molnar, for, had he done so, he would surely have blackmailed the President into letting him return home. It had been – still was essential – that he stop the Scot's mercenary, for as long as he was alive, Molnar would never be completely safe.

He coughed, and the girl helped him into a more comfortable position. He must think. The morphine was wearing off, the pain returning. "I must tell you why Kol..." He coughed again. Indra wiped the blood speckles from his lips. "I am not a doctor." Chest heaving, he stared passed Indra to Stefan. "I and my brother Rajko were two of your father's security guards."

Dryak lapsed into silence, trying to form in his pain racked mind some sort of a story that both these young people might believe, and not treat as the mad raving of a hallucinogenic. "Mark Stewart killed your father, boy," he started, and heard the gasps of astonishment from very far away. "I found out Stewart was in debt. When he found out he was to be allowed to remain in this country with a few other mercenaries for only a short time, he probably decided he was in no financial position to let this happen."

"But why should Stewart want to kill my father?" Stefan dropped down beside the girl, his tone incredulous, and not at all certain as to whether or not the soldier was compos mentis. "What had he to gain? He has always fought with the Government against the PFF!"

"Money." Dryak coughed. His body lurched in pain. He bit his lip. He must hold on. "Your father was becoming too popular with the people,.. too successful...talk of making him president for life. So someone paid Stewart to have him assassinated. Perhaps even someone within his own Party."

"Molnar!" Stefan gasped. "He had the most to gain by my father's death!"

Dryak's heart sank. This was the last thing he wanted. Why did he not just close his eyes, forget it all? He had done his duty to his President and country, no one had done more. Yet, he had to try one last time. Gathering his remaining strength, he whispered, "Molnar was your father's best friend...had been all through the war, and since. No, Stewart killed your father. "His voice trailed off. Stefan looked searchingly at Indra. "Your father," Dryak started again, "was investigating allegations, that some time in the past, Stewart was responsible for the massacre of women and children...The Miera Incident, he called it. Faced with a civilian jail for debt, or a military one for war crimes, to Stewart your father's death presented a means of nullifying both.. at least for a while."

A spasm of searing hot pain shot through Dryak's body. He gripped the sides of the stretcher, biting back a scream until it passed, willing himself to go on. "It has worked out all right for him too. Your father's death saw an escalation of the fighting, it even made the mercenary, a Colonel. He fought for money...hopes to make more...become the hero who stopped Tetek." Dryak waved weakly at the meadow. "Not his people, you see." He saw the boy glance around him at the carnage, and knew he had done enough to convince him. That had Stewart already been responsible for killing innocent civilians, it would not have been beyond him to have done this same thing again. Now exhausted, Dryak lay back.

"Then we must tell President Molnar!" Stefan seethed, jerking himself to his feet, bunching his fists. Should there be any consolation to his father's death, it was in knowing that it was a foreigner who had done the deed, and not one of his own people. Stefan looked unseeing around him, suddenly unsure of himself. Was this man telling the truth? Did he in fact know what he was saying?

"No!" Dryak spluttered, putting all his strength into gripping the boy's sleeve. This was not as he had planned. He closed his eyes again, letting his hand fall. "This is the last thing you must do. Do not involve President Molnar. At least, not until you have spoken to my brother. When he has all the details, *he* will present it to the President as a fait accompli. Meanwhile...tell no one..." Dryak spat up blood. Indra leaned forward to wipe it off his chin. "Trust no one."

Dryak felt himself drifting down a white tunnel where everything was warm and peaceful. His eyelids too heavy to open, he beckoned the boy closer. "Tell Rajko Dryak, that his brother wants you both to help him punish Colonel Mark Stewart."

He was almost at the end of the tunnel now. He felt the boy's cheek close to his lips as he whispered where to find his brother. Then he was falling...falling, and there was no more pain.

Molnar had never seen his wife so ecstatic. Only one short week ago, her world, including his own had come to an end. Now, she could not be happier. For him too, things had changed. Molnar sat down on the couch while his wife busied herself rearranging a cancelled dinner party for the American Ambassador and his wife.

He had come straight from the House, where events were altogether different. Milan allowed himself a satisfied smile at the thought of how so many Senators, who had been so quick to demand his resignation, were now tripping over themselves in their haste to apologise, or endeavoured to convince him that he may have misunderstood their intentions.

"Mister President." His private secretary caught his attention. "Your first appointment is at one o'clock, Sir."

"Thank you Valdir. Just give me a couple of minutes."

Milan waited behind his desk for his office door to open. There was a knock, Valdir preceded the woman into the room. "Mistress Lomova Jakofcic, Mister President," he announced, holding the door open.

Milan rose as Lomova, dressed in widows' weeds, entered the room. "My dear, may I offer you my most sincere condolences on the unfortunate demise of your husband," he offered, taking hold of her limp hand between his own.

Lomova gave a wan smile, and sat down in the proffered seat, a white lace handkerchief appearing from nowhere to brush an imaginary tear from her eye.

"Your husband was a great patriot, without whose genius this war against the P.F.F could never have been won," Milan went on. "And I can assure you, you will find this nation not unappreciative. I know a financial reward is no substitute for the loss of a dear one, but I am sure the General would wish you to live in a manner befitting the wife of a national hero."

Lomova moved her lips in appreciation, secretly amused by her President's magniloquence. He could afford to be magnanimous. With Tetek dead, the war was as good as over. "I thank you, Mister President. I am certain Silvo, as a soldier, knew the risks that had to be taken. It is just a little hard to bear." The handkerchief came out again, "that he and others had to die by the hand of a traitor." Lomova's silky voice trailed off.

She would never believe the rumour that her husband's assassin was her own beloved Juri. Nor could she imagine, how Juri's wife must feel, not only to lose her husband, but also to have him branded a traitor. Strangely, she could almost feel a certain sympathy towards the woman she had always resented.

"I know, my dear," Milan was saying sympathetically, rising to indicate that the audience was at an end.

"It was good of you to take the time to see me, Mister President." Lomova offered her hand as she got to her feet.

Milan took the outstretched hand, mumbling something appropriate and, with a few words of comfort and assurances, escorted her to the door.

Outside, Lomova climbed into the back seat of her black limousine. The young driver swung down the drive. "Where to milady?" he inquired, affecting an upper crust accent, and glancing in the rear mirror at Lomova crossing her legs.

"Where do you think, Alex?" she asked, sitting back, laughing. "Where else but home, my dear?"

Karina Trybala buttoned up her son's coat. He looked so like his father, she thought, and reminder herself of her promise not to cry in front of the child again. Young Max stared up into his mother's face, and held up his latest toy. She *was* going to cry. She hugged him to her, so he would not see her tears. "We are going to live with Aunt Sanda in Vienna." She broke away, holding the child at arms length, and hoping he would not ask again about his father. "You like Aunt Sanda, don't you Max?"

The child nodded. "Will daddy be there? Can I show him my new horse?"

Karina stroked the child's hair. "After we leave Aunt Sanda we will be going on a big boat on the big water to England. Perhaps daddy will meet us there, Max?" she suggested, her eyes glistening.

The woman took a last look round the empty house. It felt as if she was leaving part of her and Juri behind; so many memories, things left unsaid, so little time together. Juri had been a good husband and father, now nowhere would be home without him. But she could not stay here, not with what they were saying about him. Also, she had Max to think about, children could be so cruel to one another.

How she had survived the investigation, the endless interrogations before they were convinced she was not involved, she would never know. Only the thought of Juri's innocence, and her child's future had kept her going. Now she was free to leave, almost forced to, in a way.

Her sister Sanda had agreed to let her live with her, until hopefully an immigration document could be obtained for her and Max to join her elder sister in Britain. By which time she hoped it would be easier to make little Max understand about his father, but never believe what people said about his involvement in a PFF assassination plot. Why would her husband attempt to kill the man whose life he had saved almost at the cost of his own?

At the sound of the taxi, Karina opened the door. The driver did not help her with her luggage.

Milan Molnar's second visitor that same day was Rajko Dryak; not as tall as his elder brother, or as extrovert, but to Milan every bit as astute.

The visit reminded him of their last meeting, the day Paule 'died' for a second time. Rajko and his brother, acting as security guards, had been detailed to carry a chest, which was normally used for holding official Government papers, into the Admin Building.

By the time they had got it down to the cellar undetected, rigor mortis had set in on the dead president. And, having found the chest too small to carry Paule's body in, this man standing before him now had suggested breaking the dead man's legs. Fortunately, this had not proved necessary.

He could barely watch as they unceremoniously crammed Paule into the chest, his unclosed eyes still staring at him accusingly. That was the day, he realised more than ever, the breed of men with whom he had become involved.

Milan waited for Rajko Dryak to speak again.

"So, as I see it Mister President, you have no other choice than to let me deal with Stewart."

"Is it really necessary to kill him? After all, we do have him to thank for halting Tetek. Could we not just put the unfortunate man on a ship and send him home? It is what we promised him in the beginning."

"I am afraid not Sir. You must understand, now that my late brother, God rest his soul, has succeeded in convincing young Stefan Kolybin, that Stewart killed his father, the boy wants nothing less than justice." Dryak splayed out his hands. "I have persuaded him…and the girl...his female companion," Dryak briefly explained, at Molnar's wrinkled brow, "to say nothing of this to anyone for now...even you Mister President. But for how long before he...they...insist something must be done, I cannot say."

Milan left his desk to stand at the window. For a few seconds he stood there looking down through the quadrangle at the rows of young women busily sitting typing at their desks on the floors below. While behind him his visitor continued. "Then there is the matter of Stewart himself. Now that the war is as good as over, he will expect Paule Kolybin, to rise from the grave like Christ himself. And if I remember correctly from my brother, was not this the original plan?

Milan's stare left the quadrangle to the sky above. Good Lord! He'd almost forgotten how it had all began. Perhaps, after all was said and done, he should not blame himself entirely for the whole sad miserable affair.

"You cannot jeopardise your own position, Mister President. Should Stewart come to trial he may choose not remain silent to save his own neck. Therefore, in order to keep the whole conspiracy secret, it is either Stewart or the two young ones."

God! Will it never end? First the father, then the son. "Where is Colonel Stewart now?" he asked in a tired voice.

"Scurk has him, in what you might call, house arrest, held secretly in the military hospital on the coast."

"Not in that mad house! The man deserves better."

Milan drew a finger down the window pane. But Stewart *was* a problem. First the newspapers had hailed him a hero for stopping Tetek from reaching the capital and saving the nation. A sentiment eagerly echoed by those too far away from the carnage of war, to worry about the plight or sacrifice of those near it. But, then as pictures of Sylna began to hit the headlines, those who had been quick in their praise of Stewart, had become as equally quick in their condemnation of the man. Now the mercenary's ignominy was nothing short of an embarrassment, something to be rid of as quickly and as unobtrusively as possible, regardless of what he may have done to save *them.*

"General Scurk, means to have Stewart court- martialled."

Milan swung round. Rajko saw the look and quickly went on to explain. "Scurk is taking the line, that there was no necessity to devastate Sylna, when he had already reached Tetek's flank, and Zioitkowski was on his rear, cutting off any hope of retreat."

"And had he?" Molnar asked quietly.

Rajko shrugged. "Not quite. But he has to say this in order to save his own reputation."

"So the court martial will be nothing less than a formality ...a..sham."

Rajko took out his cigarette case. He held it out to Milan, who shook his head. "May I?" he asked. Milan waved assent. Rajko struck a match. "It would serve everyone's interest, should the court martial not take place." He inhaled.

` Milan returned to his desk.

Rajko blew twin jets of smoke up at the ceiling. "The newspapers blame Stewart for Sylna, branding him a monster who cares nothing for human life. A man who fights and kills for money, nothing more, nothing less. Now they have resurrected what happened at the road block back at Pienera when Stewart was in command, to substantiate their case." He flicked cigarette ash in to an ash tray by his chair. "Somehow..." Dryak dragged out the words for affect. "They have also got hold of the story of the Miera Incident."

Milan stifled his surprise. He was caught in a web of his own making, or to be more precise, that of Paule and the Dryak brothers, with the unfortunate Scot's mercenary as the fly. And heard himself ask, "What do you suggest?"

"It need not concern you, Mister President. All I require from you is that I have your permission to proceed."

Milan focused on his ink pad, hating this man and everyone involved in this sordid affair. Hating himself even more, for though President, he was helpless to do anything about it.

Rajko crushed out his cigarette in the ash tray. "Therefore, if that is all you require of me Sir, I shall not take up any more of your most valuable time."

Long after Rajko Dryak had left, Milan Molnar sat hunched behind his desk. He had never wanted it to come to this. Whether he liked it or not, he was party to murder and dirty political intrigue, from which he'd never be free, as long as there were fanatically depraved people such as Rajko Dryak alive. "Oh Paule, old friend, had you never conceived such a folly, how different all this would be today," he sighed, and closed his eyes.

Mark stood on the balcony of his room. Below him, white robed men shuffled across the lawn in 'un-exerted' exercise, while others, sat dozing on benches in the luke warm afternoon sunshine. A man in a wheelchair propelled himself towards the gate to pass the time of day with the security guard. Mark stubbed out his cigarette and returned to lie on his bed, his hands behind his head where he lay watching the progress of a spider crossing the ceiling.

How long before he knew what was in store for him? Denied access to radio and newspapers, he had no idea what was happening in the outside world. This place gave him the creeps. Not all were patients in this so called military hospital, and of those, who, like himself were not, were probably political. Now, he was beginning to realise the regime he had fought for, was not all it had seemed, not all lily white.

But, where the hell was Kolybin? Surely, he would have come out of hiding by this time to receive the victor's plaudits. Have him released from this asylum. And why had he this uneasy feeling in his stomach, which no amount of hospital attention, was ever likely to cure?

He thought again of Sylna, of all the lives lost. General's Scurk's triumphant arrival. His own arrest. CH ....he thought, if he had not seized the opportunity to do what he thought was right to do, Tetek would now be sitting in the Kasel, and where would that tortoise Scurk be now?

There was a knock at the door. Mark shouted to whoever it was to come in, sitting up in surprise at the unexpected appearance of Company Sergeant Major Niew Grbesa.

Marks sprang off the bed. "Sergeant!" he exclaimed in delight at not only seeing the soldier but that he was alive. "So you survived! No one told me what had happened to those I detailed to the Gap."

Now that he was here, Niew did not know what to say, only somehow he felt it was his duty to the man that he should do so.

He'd passed through Sylna a few days after his colonel's counter attack on Tetek, by which time they'd cleared the place of bodies. But if the scale of destruction had been anything to go by, the casualties, both military and civilian, must have been enormous. The town, as he had remembered it, ceased to exist.

How the man could have brought himself to give the order to direct fire upon the town he could not imagine. Over and over again, he had reconciled himself with the thought that it would have been easier for a foreigner to have done so, rather than of their own. Yet, knowing how the mercenary had reacted at the roadblock back at Pienera, he had realised the man could have had no alternative.

"Oh, I'm not so easy to get rid off as that Major ....sorry I mean Colonel" Niew corrected himself, thrusting a bottle of whisky at the Scot.

Grunting approval at the label, Mark set it down on a side table. "How did you sneak this passed the guard, CSM?" he asked grinning, but failing to see the shrug or the frown that replaced Niew's smile.

How could you tell your commanding officer, the price of your visit was a detailed account of their entire conversation? "In the eyes of some soldiers you are nothing short of a hero," he lied.

Mark returned with two glasses of whisky, handing the uncracked one to his guest. "Here's to you CSM" he said raising his glass.

"And to you Sir."

Mark took a sip, asking enthusiastically. "Well! Tell me Grbesa, how was it up there? I knew if anyone could hold that ridge it was you."

Niew swilled the rough spirit round his mouth. "We lost our captain on the way up," he began. Mark sat back to listen.

"At first it was easy having taken them by surprise." Niew let the fiery liquid slide down his throat. "It was mainly women, children and old men, running the supplies through the defile. We blasted hell out of them Sir." A twinge of remorse in the tough soldier's voice. His look implying as he stared directly at Mark, that as a foreigner he could never understand. "Things did get a little hotter...and colder later that night. We hadn't accounted for the number of soldiers they had up there." The soldier swirled his glass around. "Some of our younger ones almost cracked that first night, listening for the slightest sound. They got nine of us." Niew looked into his glass. I heard a sound on my left, and crawled to it. A PFF had got behind Private Shaliv."

"Shaliv? A good soldier," Mark acknowledged with a nod, remembering the man from his own 'A' Company.

"Was..." Niew corrected. "I didn't reach him in time."

Mark nodded his understanding. "I suppose Tetek was finished by that time," he suggested, reaching out to refill his guest's glass. He gave out a long sigh. "What's happening in the Capital?" he asked, changing the subject.

Niew opened his eyes, his expression suggesting he had difficulty in understanding the strange question. "What do you mean, Sir?"

Mark repeated the question, hoping Niew would offer some clue as to the whereabouts of Paule Kolybin.

"The Senate say the war is as good as over. We took plenty of prisoners. What are left have made for the mountains. Everywhere President Molnar is the man of the hour."

So what had happened to Kolybin? Was this victory too inadequate for his glorious resurrection? Had he decided to play dead after all? Mark had a flash of him somewhere in England with his pretty, and perhaps all the while, knowing wife.

Niew studied his glass suspiciously, debating whether or not to try some more. "What about you, Sir? What will happen to you?" He was beginning to have difficulty with his words, and the Scot's replies. Perhaps it was his accent...no, the man spoke his language fairly well now.

Mark crossed to the window where he stood silent for a moment looking out across the bay. He turned, leaning on the rail to face Niew. "I understand there is to be some sort of a court martial."

"Some sort would be the right word Sir." Niew hiccupped, putting his hand over his mouth in apology.

Mark laughed. "I hope you have been driven here, Sergeant?"

"No" Niew said seriously, "I came of my own free will."

Mark threw his head back, in laughter, Niew followed when he realised what he had said.

An hour later, a far from sober CSM Niew Grbesa, of the Fourth Regiment, gave a far from true detailed report of his conversation with his former commanding officer, at the same time wishing the mercenary well, and almost audibly, if not erratically, damning his captors.

Mark saw no one for a full week following Niew Grbesa's visit. Then late one afternoon there was a knock on his door. A man stood there dressed in a smart dark suit. Mark studied the face, certain of having seen him before.

"May I come in? I am Karl Burda," Rajko Dryak, said crisply. "Your appointed defence lawyer."

Mark stood aside. Uninvited, Rajko seated himself. Mark closed the door, and leaned against it. "I've seen you before, you know," he mulled.

Rajko's heart missed a beat. Should Stewart recognise him as the man who had chased him into the woods that day back at the beach house, he would be in a difficult situation.

"Now I know!" Mark snapped his fingers. "You're the officer who drew the guards off in order to give me a clean run at assassinating Kolybin." The mysterious fourth man, Mark said to himself.

Dryak covered his relief by opening the briefcase he'd placed on the small table before him. "You have a good memory Colonel, considering the situation at the time," he said meaningfully.

Mark grunted his appreciation. "Yet?"....he wagged a finger, "I'm sure I've seen you somewhere since then. But for the life of me, I don't know where."

For the life of you is right, Rajko thought caustically.

"Well I believe we should leave that little puzzle aside for now," Rajko returned, taking a few sheets of paper from his case. "President Molnar has requested that I act in your defence." He spread out some papers on the little table, "this way he hopes to keep our little secret...mm..secret."

Mark opened his mouth to ask about Kolybin, but his visitor went on. "As you may know, General Scurk has brought serious charges against you regarding your actions at Sylna."

Having been left on his own in this place day after day, Mark had ample time to reassess what he had done. He had found it more difficult to conciliate his conscience over his actions *prior* to reaching the valley, than during, or after it.

His main priority had always been self preservation, and, knowing he was no match for the Commie general, had attached more importance on keeping out of his way, rather than on fighting him. Perhaps, had he wanted to fight Tetek with the same resolve as had his men, it may have prevented what had occurred later in the valley. It was this fact, and this fact alone, which still kept him from sleeping as easily as he might, more than what had happened in the valley itself.

"What led you to give the order to fire upon the town, Colonel?" Dryak's voice floated into his thoughts from across the room.

Mark sat down opposite his visitor. The remaining chair in the room was hard, and he shifted his weight to make himself more comfortable. "My first reaction was to hold Tetek to a stalemate if I could, with me holding the heights south of the valley, and he the north, whereby I might force him into retreating before Scurk appeared on his flank and Ziotwoski his rear. Unfortunately, I was wrong. Tetek pushed through the valley, perhaps believing as he had me on the run I would not order an about face and attack *him*, which I did, catching him in Sylna and in the valley itself."

Rajko nodded, making some notes in a notepad.

"Tetek is as much to blame for the destruction of the town as I. Had he not chosen to attack, but had instead, retreated or stood his ground...." Mark trailed off leaving the rest unsaid.

"Unfortunately, Colonel, Tetek is not alive and you are, for if it were so, he, as the vanquished would be on trial, not you."

"So they need a scapegoat? Is that it?" Mark said bitterly.

Putting down his pen, Rajko sat back in his chair steepling his fingers. "President Molnar deeply regrets what has transpired and understands what you have achieved militarily." Rajko's voice rose an octave or two in desperation. "But you must realise public opinion is very much against what you have done. So many innocent people have died... unnecessarily."

"Of course, they are all military geniuses!" Mark spat out sarcastically. "I'd still be on a hiding to nothing if Tetek had marched right through to the capital. Then what would you have heard those same geniuses shout? Why didn't that bloody mercenary stop him? That is what we paid him to do! And had I answered, I can, but it will mean destroying a town... killing innocent people. Well? So be it. What are you waiting for? Better them than us." Mark mimicked.

Rajko said nothing, but sat staring through his steepled fingers at his pen on the table. "There is a slim chance of a solution," he started slowly, as though he had not heard what Mark had said.

"What, leave me a revolver? The gentleman's way out?" Mark sniggered.

"No. I believe the President would rather see you on your way home. It would avoid embarrassment all round." Rajko halted awaiting Mark's reaction.

Mark's heart skipped a beat at the first glimmer of hope he had in days. "I don't see how?"

Rajko rose abruptly. "I think I shall have this finalised in a few days. Then I shall return. Until then, keep your hopes up."

He had reached the door when Mark had finally time to ask. "What happened to President Kolybin and his master plan? Surely I have a right to know?"

A hand on the door handle, Rajko said simply. "Paule Kolybin died of a heart attack some time ago. Since then President Molnar has been operating the original plan." He stroked his nose, "with some modifications," he smiled wryly.

"So there was no resurrection?" Mark sighed softly.

"No." Rajko opened the door. "It was always a President's folly, don't you think?"

A week crawled by. Mark heard nothing from the outside world. He'd a slight bruise on his face as a result of an altercation with one of the 'male nurses' having at last lost his patience with the whole damned thing.

Then on the evening of the eighth day, Rajko Dryak returned. The guards led Mark to the ground floor, where Rajko and two more guards stood waiting.

Rajko stepped forward. "Colonel Mark Stewart, you are now being taken to the Caserne in the nation's capital, where you will be court martialled three days from now."

A guard stepped smartly forward to handcuff the Scot.

"That will not be necessary, Sergeant," Rajko intervened.

Mark was marched to the waiting truck and helped into the back, where it immediately took off.

"Cigarette, Colonel?" One of the guards offered, holding out a packet.

Mark shook his head, his eyes on the surrounding coast line flashing passed. Suspicious, he attempted to asses his position. It would be so easy, convenient too, to kill him. 'Died while attempting to escape.' Yet there had been ample opportunity back at the 'hospital.' A quick hypodermic whilst asleep, something extra in his food...such as flavour! He thought wryly of the horrible concoctions that passed as food. No wonder so many people died in hospital.

His hand stroked the comb in his top pocket, the back honed to razor sharpness by rubbing it on the hard concrete of his veranda floor, his only means of defence, his sole weapon, manufactured despite the guards ceaseless scrupulosity.

They left the main road, following what was little more than a dirt track down to the sea. Mark's heart beat faster. The truck braked to a halt.

Rajko rounded the side as Mark was helped down. "Well Colonel, we've done it after all." He smiled broadly, showing a row of white even teeth.

"Done what?" Mark asked, a little perturbed by the man's demeanour, and backing unobtrusively against the truck.

"President Molnar thinks it wise if you were somehow to escape."

Mark swallowed hard. He had been right they meant to kill him...make it look as if he had tried to escape. "Won't that be a little risky for him?" he croaked, clearing his throat to add, "politically speaking I mean."

Rajko continued to smile. "Not really, servicemen are pledged to secrecy, and loyalty to their president, as you are no doubt aware, Colonel."

Mark scratched at his tunic pocket, his hand hovering near his sharpened comb. Determined, if he was to die, a few would be in stitches for the next few days and not from laughter. He might even bow out with one or two Glasgow kisses, and thought sadly, of how close he had been to making it home.

A soldier stepped smartly round from the front of the truck. "All is ready Sir." He saluted Rajko.

"Very good, Lieutenant." Rajko turned to his prisoner. "There is a naval launch waiting in the cove, it will take you out to a cargo ship bound for the port of Marseilles. All expenses have been met. Doubtless, you will have no difficulty in making your way home to England from there. You will, however, have need of this." He held out his hand and Mark caught the slight glint of the gold motif in the moonlight as he took his passport from the man.

"They will fire a Verry Light when you are safely on board, and on your way out to sea. Goodbye, Colonel Stewart." He motioned Mark to follow the soldiers.

When Mark turned, Rajko Dryak had disappeared behind the truck. Shrugging, he followed the soldiers, the reassuring feel of his passport in his hand. Surely if they had meant to kill him, they would have done it on the truck, with any noise made, drowned out by the engine. Or were they meaning to do it at sea.?

Mark threw the thought aside. Soon he'd be home. It would be good to see his folks again. Also get himself that pub he had set his heart on.

Mark stood by the porthole in the launch's small unlit cabin, absently watching white horses dancing on the water. It was good to be alive, to be finally away from all the horrors of war…of civil war, and the unfathomable intrigues of politics.

A launch, smaller than their own suddenly appeared from behind the headland, white foam streaming from bows almost out of the water with the speed with which it streaked towards them, followed by unmistakable sound of gunfire raking their vessel.

Instinctively, Mark threw himself away from the sidelight. He shook his head unable to suppress a wry grin that despite the irony of making it this far, he was going to fail at the last moment.

Molnar had sent the launch. This he had to do, if not so much for the mercenary, at least to prove to himself, he was not cast in the same opprobrious mould as Dryak or his coterie. No one knew who had sent the launch, this much insidiousness he *had* learned. The crews' orders; to save Stewart, put him on a ship for home.

Mark's launch was returning fire. He chanced a quick look out. The enemy launch was drawing alongside. Men stood on its deck blasting away and upwards at the larger vessel. Then one minute it was there, the next gone, engulfed in a sheet of blinding light.

Mark steadied himself against the bulwark unable to believe what the sea had swallowed up in so short a space of time. He squinted to his right, the epicentre of where the launch had been, marked solely by a white centrifugal foam, before it too quickly reverted once again to the dark foreboding sea.

Mark heard the sound of feet on the ladder above, doubtless crew coming to reassure him everything was all right. He heaved a sigh of relief. He had made it after all. Whoever had sent the launch to stop him had failed. Suddenly the light went on, the hatch opened and the face of a young man stared down at him.

Mark gasped in surprise. "Stefan Kolybin, is it not?" he asked with a smile, a foot on the ladder.

"Yes," replied the grim faced boy, "and this is for my father."
And with that, the gun exploded in Mark's face.

Waiting by the truck, Rajko Dryak watched the launch's Verry Light soar skyward, briefly lighting up the night sky. The boy had done his job well…or should he say, did *his* job well. The Verry Light plunged into the sea, returning everything to night, and Rajko Dryak, code named Vaclaw, climbed back into the truck.

© W.G. Graham 2015

Printed in Great Britain
by Amazon

21334223R00181